Looking for Other Worlds

NEW WORLD STUDIES
Marlene L. Daut, Editor

Looking for Other Worlds

BLACK FEMINISM AND HAITIAN FICTION

Régine Michelle Jean-Charles

University of Virginia Press

Charlottesville and London

University of Virginia Press
© 2022 by the Rector and Visitors of the University of Virginia
All rights reserved
Printed in the United States of America on acid-free paper

First published 2022

9 8 7 6 5 4 3 2 1

Library of Congress Cataloging-in-Publication Data
Names: Jean-Charles, Régine Michelle, author.
Title: Looking for other worlds : Black feminism and Haitian fiction / Régine
    Michelle Jean-Charles.
Description: Charlottesville : University of Virginia Press, 2022. | Series: New World
    studies | Includes bibliographical references and index.
Identifiers: LCCN 2022015978 (print) | LCCN 2022015979 (ebook) |
    ISBN 9780813948447 (hardcover ; acid-free paper) | ISBN 9780813948454
    (paperback ; acid-free paper) | ISBN 9780813948461 (ebook)
Subjects: LCSH: Haitian fiction—Women authors—History and criticism. | Haitian
    fiction—20th century—History and criticism. | Feminism and literature—Haiti. |
    LCGFT: Literary criticism.
Classification: LCC PQ3944 .J43 2022 (print) | LCC PQ3944 (ebook) | DDC
    843/.920992870899697294—dc23/eng/20220525
LC record available at https://lccn.loc.gov/2022015978
LC ebook record available at https://lccn.loc.gov/2022015979

Cover art: Beny (Blessed), Tessa Mars. (© 2021; used by permission of the artist)

For my students and mentees, especially those who are looking for other worlds. May you find them, may you imagine them, may you create them, may you build them.

Écrire, pour moi, c'est prendre des engagements. C'est aussi prendre des positions. C'est pourquoi quand j'écris, je prends des positions. Je cherche d'autres univers . . .

(To write, for me, is to make commitments. It also means taking positions. That's why when I write, I take positions. I look for other worlds . . .)

—Kettly Mars

Black feminism has never only been about Black women, it's never been this. It's been about a more just world. And a planet that said if you listen to the insights of the least of these, which is us, that we can do something transformative.

—Farah Jasmine Griffin

Contents

Acknowledgments

THIS BOOK is first and foremost a product of God's grace. It began, as I am sure many books do, with a writing group conversation. I was working on a different project when I told Nadève Ménard, Chantalle Verna, and Darline Alexis I wanted to write about Yanick Lahens, Kettly Mars, and Évelyne Trouillot. They responded simply with, "Why don't you?" And so, I did. I am incredibly grateful for their wisdom, sisterhood, and love. Similarly, my prayer circle sisters Maria Lawrence, Kia Martin, and Jody Rose have been an unwavering source of support and encouragement. After I became pregnant with my fourth child and thought I might never publish another book, Kia said: "You're going to write more books, sister."

The research conducted for this book was made possible through grants and leave time from Boston College. At O'Neill Library, Larry Busenbark and Amy Howard were especially helpful in locating materials. Many of my African and African Diaspora Studies colleagues, Amey-Victoria Adkins-Jones, Allison Curseen, Kyrah Daniels, Jonathan Howard, Rhonda Frederick, Shawn McGuffey, Richard Paul, and Martin Summers, read early chapter drafts and offered precious feedback. Andrea Javel and Juliet Fry also assisted with proofreading, translation, and so much enthusiasm for the project.

I am blessed to belong to many communities of brilliant and generous scholars that include friends, mentors, and coconspirators, all of whom I thank for their support, insights, and inspiration: Nadège Clitandre, Orly Clergé, Soyica Diggs Colbert, Darnel Degand, Marlene Daut, Lorgia Garcia-Peña, Kaiama Glover, Farah Jasmine Griffin, Alexis Gumbs, Daphne Brooks, Régine Joseph, Annette Joseph-Gabriel, Jessica Marie Johnson, Stéphanie Larrieux, Claudine Michel, Vanessa Perez-Rosario,

Robert Reid-Pharr, Dixa Ramirez, Micheline Rice-Maximin, Alyssa Sepinwall, Salamishah Tillet, and Gina Athéna Ulysse.

This book is dedicated to all of my current and former students who teach me so much, especially Lynda Musilwa, Laura Vargas Zuleta, Grace Assogba, Sherina Elibert, Taleah Pierre-Louis, Nurun Nahar, Latifat Odetunde, Janasia Little, Bilguissa Barry, and Berlindyne Elie.

I am infinitely grateful for all of the academics, artists, authors, and activists whose work is included on these pages and who endlessly inspire me: Carolle Charles, Edwidge Danticat, Gessica Généus, Rutshelle Guillaume, Nathalie Jolivert, Yanick Lahens, Sabine Lamour, Danièle Magloire, Kettly Mars, Tessa Mars, Mafalda Mondestin, Nadine Mondestin, Fania Noel, Lilliane Pierre-Paul, Régine Romain, Pascale Solages, and Évelyne Trouillot.

Thank you to the faithful team at University of Virginia Press (with Marlene at the helm!), especially Eric Brandt, Helen Chandler, and Morgan Myers for shepherding this project through to the end. I also owe a debt of gratitude to the anonymous reviewers who helped to make this project more ambitious and precise.

My family has my infinite gratitude: parents, sisters, brothers, cousins, aunts, uncles, nieces, nephews in the Jean-Charles, Asare, Joseph, Acacia, Wells, Murray, and Weekes families. Thank you to my wonderful, beautiful, smart, special children Bediako Dessalines, Kwaku Toussaint, Farah-Adwoa Heureuse, and Afia Anacaona, each of whom helped me to write this book and made a unique contribution: Dessalines's thoughtful word suggestions, Toussaint's attentive encouragement, Farah's exuberant affirmation, and Anacaona's quiet companionship in my pandemic office. Most of all, thank you to *my* perfect husband, my beloved, Ohene Kwaku Asare, who always made sure I had the space to write and think and is unrelenting in his love, passion, prayers, partnership, and support.

Looking for Other Worlds

Introduction

The Art of Haitian Feminism

Dès le XVIIIe siècle, la littérature de Haïti est une littérature de l'urgence, urgence de dire et rêver d'habiter . . .

(Since the eighteenth century, Haitian literature has been a literature of urgency, urgency to speak and to dream of living.)

—Yanick Lahens

Nous vivons dans un monde où les inégalités criardes et constantes, entre les individus et entre les peuples, semblent pourtant passer inaperçues aux yeux de beaucoup. Parfois, l'écriture arrive à rendre les injustices insoutenables, impossibles à ignorer. Le pouvoir de l'écriture confère ainsi à l'écrivain une certaine responsabilité.

(We live in a world where the glaring and constant inequalities, between individuals and between people, seem to go unnoticed in the eyes of many. Sometimes writing can make injustices unbearable, impossible to ignore. The power of writing thus gives the writer a certain responsibility.)

—Évelyne Trouillot

FEMINIST INTELLECTUAL, activist, and fiction writer Paulette Poujol Oriol (1926–2011) is a formidable figure of twentieth-century Haitian literature who deserves more scholarly attention than she has yet received.[1] A trail-blazing feminist, prolific essayist, and inspired creative writer, Poujol Oriol worked first in theater, then as a feminist organizer and fiction writer. As an educator and a writer whose prodigious body of work spans the twentieth century, she explored a number of social issues, each time approaching the ideas intersectionally, writing about how class, race, and gender operate multiplicatively and inform the lived experience of diverse Haitian women. A devoted champion of the arts and an accomplished artist herself, Poujol Oriol was the founder of Piccolo Teatro and for many years the director of *École nationale des arts,* impressively influencing the theatre scene in Haiti. Paulette Poujol Oriol is also one of the few Haitian authors to receive, in 1988, *Le Monde*'s coveted prize for the best short story written in French in that year, as well as Haiti's prestigious literary prize, Le Prix Henri Deschamps.

In her activity with La Ligue féminine d'action sociale (Haiti's first official women's organization founded in 1934), Poujol Oriol advanced gender justice from her exuberantly feminist perspective. Describing the origins of this organization, she explained in a 2011 interview with historian Chantalle Verna that these women "started to go to the public hospitals to see how the women were treated, not only for medical treatment but also to see if [the female patients] were being treated like human beings. They started visiting the prisons, and the asylums," unabashedly highlighting their advocacy for more ethical and humane treatment of all Haitian women, but especially the most marginalized.[2] Many of the concerns addressed by the *Ligue* align with the questions that I attend to in this study—organizing, the needs of the elderly, women's human rights, moral and intellectual life—were central to their platform. That Poujol Oriol explores these themes in her fiction underscores the productive alliance between her activism and her art. An examination of her oeuvre reveals that ethical reflection shaped her creative project; she was compelled by feminist principles. As was written in the foremost Haitian newspaper, *Le Nouvelliste,* at the time of her death, Poujol Oriol was undeniably "une des grandes figures du mouvement féministe haïtien" (one of the great figures of the Haitian feminist movement), who left an indelible imprint on generations to follow.[3]

Looking for Other Worlds: Black Feminism and Haitian Fiction begins with Paulette Poujol Oriol because as a feminist intellectual she prefigures the contemporary authors featured in this study, Yanick Lahens, Kettly Mars, and Évelyne Trouillot. For them as for Poujol Oriol, literature creates a space for ethical reflection, and their novels can be read as part of a tradition of feminist writing in which ethics and aesthetics intertwine. Their approach, like hers, is undergirded by Black feminist principles such as the relational dynamic between the individual and the collective, a dialectical relationship between oppression and activism, the linking of experience and ideas, and the centrality of social justice, among others.[4]

Situating Lahens, Mars, and Trouillot in the literary lineage of Poujol Oriol, I argue in what follows that there is a Black feminist ethic animating contemporary Haitian fiction and that this ethic can also serve as a framework for reading the broader world of African diasporic texts.

Looking for Other Worlds explores what ethics as a fundamental concept can mean for how we study Haitian literature. My use of the term *ethics* proceeds from a simple definition faithful to the word's etymology. *Ethics* derives from the Greek *ethos,* meaning custom, habit, character, or disposition. Ethics denote a set of principles that guide and inform actions. When Black feminist scholars refer to "an ethic," we are invoking a way of being in the world that acts as both theory and praxis. The idea of "ethical imagination" connects these actions to thoughts and expressive culture. Through close readings of selected novels, I delineate how the ethical imagination of Lahens, Mars, and Trouillot coheres around Black feminist thought.

I purposefully use "Black feminism" rather than "Haitian feminism" in order to establish the work of these writers within a feminist project that is transnational and global. Haitian feminism has a distinct tradition that has been championed by figures like Paulette Poujol Oriol and activists like Myriam Merlet. What strikes me, and what I foreground here, is that Haitian feminism is indeed an example of how a multidimensional Blackness circulates in the Caribbean as well as a manifestation of Black feminism as a global project.

In point of fact, Caribbean feminists have *always* been active in Black feminist theorizing, even when they have not been fully recognized as such. Scholars like Carole Boyce Davies, Joan Anim-Addo, Kaiama Glover, and Alexis Pauline Gumbs have often brought to light Caribbean women's contributions to Black feminism, especially given the foundational role of theorists like Audre Lorde, June Jordan, and Barbara Christian. As Glover astutely points out, too often, Caribbean feminists are not included in the canon of Black feminism "*as* Caribbean women."[5] This is especially the case for Lorde, born in New York City to Grenadian immigrants and who Michelle Wright correctly describes as: "a global feminist par excellence who made explicit and frequent connections between Black women from the United States and the Caribbean and the working classes, gender relations, labor relations, colonialism."[6] Agreeing that thinkers like Lorde and Jordan are embraced as Black feminists but not regarded as examples of Caribbean feminism existing within Black feminism, Alexis Gumbs repudiates that tendency by drawing on her own experiential knowledge and sensibilities as a feminist of Caribbean descent whose entry into US-based Black feminism occurs *because* of the Caribbean strands. For Gumbs, exposure to Lorde and Jordan as *both* Black *and* Caribbean feminists not only resonated with her personally but also helped to spark her feminist consciousness.[7]

At the same time, Boyce Davies rightfully points out that "Black feminism is sometimes reduced to one generalized category which hides all kinds of differences and subsumes all sorts of submerged identities."[8] This recognition has given rise to a healthy ambivalence toward a totalizing Black feminist standpoint. We can understand the resistance to an all-encompassing, monolithic Black feminism as a call to affirm the specific within the universal. As Joan Anim-Addo correctly asserts, "the voices of Black women represent a key part of the literary whole within the [Caribbean] region. In a socio-political context premised upon hierarchical racial divisions riddled with issues of oppression, dominance and resistance . . . Black women's writing is a vital sign. . . . the umbrella term 'Caribbean literature' however, is, by intention, antithetical to the pointing up of social divisions."[9]

In *Looking for Other Worlds* I frame that primary intellectual problem identified by Anim-Addo and others as a way to expose how a dialectic of recognition and lack of recognition is a doggedly present tension in our thinking, scholarship, citational practices, and intellectual work. To this end, Tonya Haynes insightfully notes that "Caribbean feminism has been forced to confront plurality, privilege and the multiple axes of oppression which Caribbean women face. These continued negotiations, tensions and contestations that fill the interstices between two equally contested concepts with multiple meanings: Caribbean and feminism; are not resolved (nor do they need to be) by a move to the plural feminisms."[10] Haynes's point resonates with me because she is unequivocal in her stance that a mere addition of the plural form is insufficient to accommodate the tensions in Caribbean feminism. I initiate this conversation holding Black feminism and Haitian feminism together because, like Gumbs, my own entry into these fields has always been coupled based on my positionality as a Black feminist of Haitian descent.

Or, to riff off of Gina Athena Ulysse's limitlessly generative concept of *rasanblaj*, by bringing Black feminism and Haitian feminism together, *m'ap fè yon rasanblaj* (I am creating a gathering)—I am purposefully placing these traditions alongside one another with the overarching goal to facilitate a conversation between Black feminists from different geographical contexts and to acknowledge multiple feminist genealogies.[11] By referring to this approach as a form of *rasanblaj,* I acknowledge that, as Ulysse and M. Jacqui Alexander do (and enact) through their conversation, "when people from different areas, different reaches, different geographies, different disciplines, different practices are all calling for the same thing, some Spirit of re-assembly is already at work."[12] The reassembly unfolding in

Looking for Other Worlds examines how Haitian feminists, Caribbean feminists, and Black feminists commune in a Spirit of reassembly.

Still, it is worth noting that Haitian feminists have not figured prominently in discussions of Caribbean and global Black feminism. Probing the various webs of affiliation woven around feminism for Black women in the diaspora, M. Jacqui Alexander challenges us to pose bolder questions about the genealogies of "Pan-African feminism" to which we lay claim. It is both revelatory and relevant that she asks, "shall we continue to read Edwidge Danticat while Haiti remains, like the Pacific, on the rim of consciousness, or enters our consciousness only in relation to continued U.S. dominance?"[13] I take Alexander's provocative point to mean that the popularity of Danticat, a Haitian American author, has not led to sustained and meaningful engagement with thinking and theorizing Haiti. I would add to this that the inability to see Haitian feminism as a manifestation of Black feminism stems from a similar lack of knowledge and an unwillingness to engage Haiti beyond the most common signifiers.

Of course—and as Évelyne Trouillot has pointed out in an essay on the power of translation—how Black feminist thought circulates is also related to languages of publication.[14] One of my primary aims is to elaborate and expand traditional notions of Black feminism by not only including Haitian feminist authors writing in French and Kreyòl but also by placing them in productive dialogue with US-based, African diasporic, transnational global, and postcolonial feminists. By beginning with Paulette Poujol Oriol, situating my study within a longstanding Haitian feminist project, and referring to Haitian feminist scholars, artists, and activists throughout, I invite others invested in seeing Black feminisms through a global optic to do the same. That is, I invite you to do what Alexander alludes to above and allow Haitian feminism to penetrate our global Black feminist consciousness in sustained, meaningful ways.

Describing her own feminist consciousness, the consummate champion of women's rights Myriam Merlet (1956–2010) explained her activist work as such: "I look at things through the eyes of women, very conscious of the roles, limitations, and stereotypes imposed on us. The idea is to give women the opportunity to grow so that we may end up *more complete human beings* who can really change things. Individuals should have the opportunity to be complete human beings, women as well as men, youth as well as old people, the lame as well as the healthy."[15] Merlet's attention to looking through the eyes of women within their social environment performs Black feminist work by observing and critiquing how intersectionality compounds oppressions in myriad ways and contexts.

Looking at things through the eyes of women is a concept that I return to throughout this book, and my use of the gerundive "looking" intentionally signifies Barbara Christian's explanation of "theorizing" as "active and dynamic."[16] As bell hooks declares with precise simplicity, "there is power in looking."[17] The power of the look and what looking suggests about power interest me because looking is a form of encounter. I am also drawn to the concept of *looking for other worlds* for how it functions as an ethic, inviting us to pose ethical questions as we look at the world around us in search of both others and the other.

Again, it is in the spirit of what Ulysse cleverly conceptualizes as *rasanblaj* (gathering, assembly, and reassembly) that I gather numerous Afro-diasporic, postcolonial, and transnational global feminists for this conversation about Black feminisms, literary ethics, and Haitian fiction.[18] Contemporary Haitian and Haitian-American feminists such as Ulysse, Darline Alexis, and Sabine Lamour, are especially important to my project because they, like Poujol Oriol, embrace and identify as Black feminists in both their scholarship and activism.

My inquiry establishes Trouillot, Mars, and Lahens as Black feminist authors who interrogate the interlocking, mutually constitutive relationships between race, class, gender, sexuality, religion, and other locations of identity precisely because they are committed to raising ethical questions through an intersectional lens. The ethical questions they raise are diverse and rarely simple; they delve into issues like the dynamics of social class, the complexity of family relationships, and the feelings and emotions associated with sex and sexuality. What does it mean to write a novel about a sexual predator that includes the voices of his victims? What happens when there are competing narratives about the meaning of belonging within a single family? How can people care for a landscape that seems to unfailingly betray them? What kind of weight should we give to the account of a deceased narrator? The novels in my corpus wrestle with these kinds of troublesome questions, and in so doing allow for new revelations about literary ethics. *Looking for Other Worlds* deploys Black feminism as a lens with significant value for current studies of Haitian literature as well as African diasporic expressive culture in general.

This project sits at the crossroads of two related premises: first, that twenty-first-century Haitian literature should be read in relation to ethics and, second, that Black feminism is a lens through which we can read the work of these three contemporary writers. Placing Haitian studies in conversation with Black feminist theory and literary ethics, I investigate what it looks like to think and write ethically, as these authors do in their fiction. The idea of thinking ethically serves as a guiding framework made up of four related components: it refers to how novels "think" (the internal logic of the text), how characters think, how readers think as a result of these encounters, and what each of these components reveals about the worlds the authors create.

Postcolonial theorist Gayatri Spivak identifies ethics as "continual questioning from below," a definition that resonates with me for its focus on inquiring rather than concluding as well as its recognition of the power differentials involved in ethics.[19] The questions, challenges, and problems that I confront in what follows demonstrate the need for a theoretical-analytical framework that equips us to explore the ethical complexity of these novels. Because "ethics is not just a problem of knowledge, but a call [in]to relationship," I contemplate how this fiction imagines, invokes, and influences relationships among authors, readers, characters, and texts.[20] This relational dynamic typifies a Black feminist ethic, which is a terrain made up of spiritual, familial, environmental, erotic, sexual, and social bonds.

My methodology acknowledges Black feminism as a *global project* with an *ethical imperative*—a Black feminist ethic. Attention to ethics also recognizes how "Black feminist theory has become newly and emphatically preoccupied with care."[21] Following scholars like Christina Sharpe, I am committed to developing a theoretical framework and a reading praxis that, in her words, "insists and performs that thinking needs care."[22] I am compelled by how these novels continually demonstrate an ethic according to which everything has value and requires care. Applying an ethic of care means engaging a practice of deep reading inviting us as readers and scholars to pay attention to the messages embedded in the narratives for the characters and for ourselves as well as the embodied principles of Black feminist thought.[23] An ethic of care, as I "insist and perform" it in this study is a process of uncovering, searching, and questioning that is always intersectional.

But what is a "Black feminist ethic"? First, I define it as a way of looking at the world that meditates on how the lens of intersectionality influences quotidian life and lived experience. It does not end, as the title of my book emphasizes, at seeing the world as it is; rather, a Black feminist ethic embraces the process of looking for other worlds and eventually leads to the work of building them. The ethical paradigm that I elaborate is above all a Black feminist project that asks us to examine the world differently, and eventually recreate it. In a 2006 interview with *Le Nouvelliste*, Évelyne Trouillot responds to a question about *L'œil-totem's* message with the following: "J'hésite à utiliser le mot message, il me fait trop penser aux dogmes. Je préfère dire aux lecteurs de mettre de temps en temps certaines certitudes de côté et de *regarder autrement la réalité*" (I hesitate to use the word message; it makes me think too much of dogma. I prefer to say to readers that from time to time they should put aside some certitudes and look at reality differently).[24] To me a Black feminist ethic is a way of looking at reality differently that embraces a dynamic and evolving point of view, privileges both/and, is activist and action-oriented, sees the natural and supernatural worlds as fully integrated, locates individual selves in relation to community, links experience and ideas, and is built on an intersectional understanding of identity.

Second, taking the view that Black feminism is ultimately a theory of personhood, I also apply a Black feminist ethic as a mode of interpretation that illuminates how aesthetic and formal choices demarcate the moral imagination, and urge us to examine difficult questions through the prism of intersectionality. A guiding principle here is that Black feminism has global reverberations, iterations, and implications, and therefore the term "a Black feminist ethic" establishes the ethical potential and import of narratives that center Black women's multitudinous lived experience. What can these specific experiences and narratives about Haitian women tell us about the universal experience of humanity? A Black feminist ethic reflects the different challenges that Black women face, while also accounting for our joys, and suggesting alternative possibilities that nonetheless imagine the world otherwise.[25]

By pairing Black feminism and literary ethics in the context of Haitian Studies, my goal is to situate the ethical imagination as a space of reflection and possibility that is nonetheless rooted in its specific historical and cultural context. The Black feminist ethic of care I use to read novels by Trouillot, Mars, and Lahens, reveals an imagination that confronts an array of issues, ranging from concerns facing the elderly, the problem of class division, the role of intimacy in sex, and environmental questions.

I posit that the "Black feminist ethic" emerging from these novels can be used as a method for reading fiction and a framework for personal and societal transformation that arises from the texts themselves. There is, then, a transformative aspect that a Black feminist ethic should lead to—looking for other worlds carries with it the mandate to reimagine in order to build and transform. Just as Black feminists like Poujol Oriol have always questioned the theory/praxis split and emphasized the importance of activism, a Black feminist ethic is a perspective in which knowledge and reflection lead unequivocally to action.

Françoise Lionnet elucidates how feminist criticism can offer a corrective that expands our worldviews and capacity for comparative analysis: "Such an approach aims not at conflict resolution but rather at *reframing* issues in such a way that dialogue can remain open and productive, allowing critics to map new articulations of cultural expressions."[26] The goal of "reframing" rather than conflict resolution suggests that, although not every problem raised within the moral imagination will be resolved, there is something to be earned (and learned) from raising and reflecting on ethical questions. Similarly, the same impulse of reframing inspires and motivates Gina Athena Ulysse, whose clarion call for "new narratives" can be interpreted as a need for *reframing* the existing narratives. "Looking for other worlds" means acknowledging that the world as it is needs to change, as well as imagining a new world. A Black feminist ethic committed to reframing rather than resolving allows us to map new articulations of cultural expression for fiction throughout the African diaspora.

Ethics is deeply dialogic: it invites questions that trigger further questions and inspire multiple answers rather than simply proposing a single solution. Black feminists have long championed the both/and frame as a way of looking at the world. This perspective is essential in contesting the way moral dilemmas are so often reduced to the question of "right" versus "wrong." With this perspective in mind, my view of what constitutes ethics relies not on taxonomies but on questioning. Mae Gwendolyn Henderson identifies this practice as discursive diversity or "simultaneity of discourse," positing it as a theory that undergirds Black women writers' commitment to multivocality and plurality in their texts. Building on Henderson, I treat the simultaneity of discourse as a defining characteristic of a Black feminist ethic.[27] A Black feminist ethic establishes a value system in which the binary of right and wrong requires reframing, reconsideration, and reevaluation. Because it is relational and dynamic as well as guided by what literary theorist Hortense Spillers refers to as "neither/nor" and "both/and," there are no facile conclusions about what and or who is right or wrong.[28] More often than not, the ethical problems that the three authors illuminate leave us resolutely in the gray—in the in-between space—rather than simply (and simplistically) with the framework of right or wrong, good, or evil. The reader's own moral imagination and ethical engagement with the text matters greatly in this dynamic. Literary ethics relies on this relational rapport.

In the following chapter I reflect on the three conceptual areas that are foundational to this book—Haitian women's studies, Black feminist theory, and literary ethics. As I show, the interanimation of these areas is central to my elaboration of a Black feminist ethic that emerges in Haitian fiction. Black feminist writers of both critical and imaginative texts regularly affirm how the specific experience of Black women points to a universal project. So, while this is a book about Black Haitian women, the questions herein can and should also be applied in a broader context.

Guided by this global vision, part of what I want to understand is what kinds of possibilities emerge when we anchor our study of Haitian literature in the contemporary and when we read Haitian novels through a Black feminist lens. How does doing so complicate our view of Haitian womanhood specifically, and more generally how does gender function in the Haitian context? At the center of this book is what the Canadian Black feminist scholar Katherine McKittrick aptly refers to as *Black women's geographies*—their knowledge, negotiations, and experiences. In each chapter I also refer to and analyze visual, popular, and sonic texts by Haitian women in order to reinscribe my concern with the current moment, "the ordinary and everyday," as Michel-Rolph Trouillot calls it, and to see how Black feminism lives in Haiti beyond academic inquiry.[29]

The ways in which Mars, Trouillot, and Lahens regularly frame their own writing is consistent with the embrace of both specificity and universality that marks Black feminism. In a 2015 interview with the scholar Alessandra Benedicty-Kokken, Kettly Mars explains: "I would say that my work with gender is informed by a Haitian sensibility first . . . But my ambition as a writer is to reach the universality of the human condition through the prism of my experience and sensitivity as a Black woman living in the very complex society of a Caribbean country."[30] Mars's perspective is a vivid expression of what it means to "look for other worlds." The texts I analyze further illuminate this approach, providing insights, inviting questions, and offering possibilities that connect us to our own ethical imaginations.

1   Haitian Women's Studies, Black Feminism, and Literary Ethics

Il était temps de remettre à l'honneur les récits produits par les Haïtien.ne.s, de positionner et valoriser les recherches haïtiennes sur la question du genre . . .

(It was time to return the spotlight to the stories produced by Haitians [of all genders], to foreground and promote Haitian research on gender.)

—*Déjouer le silence*

REFLECTING ON the role of feminism in Haitian society, Évelyne Trouillot identifies it as a pressing moral responsibility for all:

Dans un pays comme le nôtre, où les inégalités sociales et sexuelles sont tellement évidentes, je crois que tout citoyen responsable, toute citoyenne soucieuse de l'avenir de la société, devrait remettre en question les bases sociales qui nous ont conduits à ce bourbier et se battre pour arriver à l'égalité des hommes et des femmes de toutes les catégories sociales.[1]

(In a country like ours, where social and sexual inequalities are so obvious, I believe that any responsible citizen, any citizen concerned about the future of society, should question the social bases that have led us to this quagmire and to fight to achieve equality between men and women of all social categories.)

Attuned to how the multiplicity of identity shapes the lived experience of women in the first Black republic, Haitian feminist scholars, authors, artists, and activists similarly espouse the view that feminism connects to responsibility. The groundbreaking study *Déjouer le silence: contrediscours sur les femmes haïtiennes* spotlights how the field of Haitian women's studies has evolved over the years. As an interdisciplinary gender studies project, *Déjouer le silence* both pays tribute to Haitian feminist thinkers and presents a counterdiscourse for theorizing gender.

Published in 2018, *Déjouer le silence* situates Haitian women's activism, scholarship, and writing as an identifiable tradition that dates back at least one hundred years. Like their Black feminist counterparts elsewhere

in the Americas, the editors—Sabine Lamour, Denyse Côté, and Darline Alexis—were invested in connecting their present-day analyses to an
archive of women's contributions from the past. Taking silence as a telling
point of departure, they insist in the introduction that "Il était temps de
remettre à l'honneur les récits produits par les Haïtien.ne.s, de positionner
et valoriser les recherches haïtiennes sur la question du genre" (It was time
to return the spotlight to the stories produced by Haitians [of all genders],
to foreground and promote Haitian research on gender).[2]

The authors identify a general lack of engagement with Haitian feminist critical thought across disciplines, going so far as to say that scholarly
work about Haitian women by Haitian women has been *silenced* in academic communities abroad. They deploy the trope of silence in order to
immediately refute it, making the title—*Déjouer le silence*—more than a
rhetorical gesture. The title acknowledges that although the significance
of this tradition has been overlooked by some, contemporary scholars
actively fill the voids, bridge the gaps, redress the silences, and—in the
lexicon of the collection—deny the silence altogether. In its commitment
to identifying and exploring "les contre-récits produits sur les femmes
haïtiennes" (counternarratives produced about Haitian women), *Déjouer
le silence* not only critiques the extant narratives about Haitian women
but also posits counterdiscourses that interrogate and reimagine analyses
of gender.[3]

The publication of *Déjouer le silence* emerged from an international
colloquium that took place at Quisqueya University in 2016, born out
of local organizing by scholars based in Port-au-Prince. The colloquium
called for "renewal." Building on tradition, its conveners and the con-
tributors to *Déjouer le silence* present a productive pathway for establishing Haitian women's studies. When they explain that "il s'agissait de
réfléchir à partir de paradigmes *ancrés dans la réalité haïtienne* et de lever
le voile sur *la richesse des traditions intellectuelles* qui ont façonné cette
société" (it was a matter of reflecting on paradigms anchored in Haitian
reality and of lifting the veil to reveal the richness of the intellectual traditions that shaped this society), these scholars signal the importance of
theorizing rooted in experiential knowledge.[4] Their initiative evinces a
twenty-first-century Black feminist commitment to identify and uphold
the intellectual histories of Black women.

Referring to "the richness of intellectual traditions that have shaped
society" the authors critically engage an established tradition that is neither silent nor absent. In the collection, the choice to deny the silence by
positing a counterdiscourse shifts our attention from void to abundance.[5]

Continuing in the vein of Gina Athena Ulysse's call for new narratives, *Déjouer le silence* highlights numerous narratives that have long been in circulation. Furthermore, by explicitly linking their scholarship to the birth of the Haitian women's movement, the editors anchor their study in a century-long tradition. Haitian women's studies as presented in *Déjouer le silence* affirms and examines the subjugated knowledge of Haitian women, drawing from and building upon an established intellectual tradition. The essays in *Déjouer le silence* move against the grain of silence while doing the Black feminist work of recovery and critique.[6] Taken together, the counternarratives that comprise *Déjouer le silence* remind us that, as Patricia Hill Collins notes regarding the distinguishing features of Black feminist thought, "no homogeneous Black woman's standpoint exists."[7]

This same perspective manifests in Paulette Poujol Oriol's essay on women and Haitian literature, in which she effusively celebrates the panoply of available texts. In her essay's opening paragraphs, Poujol Oriol indulges in a naming practice that identifies a community of women writers both in Haiti and abroad. The essay, "La femme haïtienne dans la littérature haïtienne: Problèmes de l'écrivain," begins by citing what she passionately describes as, in effect, an embarrassment of riches: "Pour parler de la 'Femme Haïtienne' dans la littérature, dans un passé encore récent ou de nos jours, nous n'aurions eu que l'embarras du choix" (To discuss the "Haitian Woman" in literature, in the recent past or nowadays, we have much to choose from).[8] Generously listing the names of Haitian women whose creative production includes novels, poetry, short stories, and theater, Poujol Oriol orients her essay toward plenitude rather than lack, a gesture that is characteristically feminist. Refusing the separation of interior/exterior, she includes writers in both Haiti and the diaspora who shape the literary landscape.

As Poujol Oriol and the authors of *Déjouer le silence* indicate, over the past century numerous feminist intellectuals have contributed to the development of Haitian Women's Studies. Most notably, Madeleine Bouchereau-Sylvain (1905–1970) published *Haiti et ses femmes: Une étude d'évolution culturelle* in 1957. The study begins in the precolonial period with an explanation of gender roles among the Tainos and traverses several time periods. Bouchereau-Sylvain charts the evolution of feminism in Haiti, describing its creation as a gradual and globally minded process. She argues that up until 1934, "le féminisme était inconnu en Haïti. Les femmes bien qu'y jouant un rôle considérable n'avaient jamais pensé à se grouper en vue d'une action commune pour la revendication de leurs droits. Pourtant, petit à petit, elles prenaient conscience du nouveau rôle de la femme dans le monde" (feminism was unknown in Haiti. Although playing a considerable role in it, the women had never thought of grouping together for a common action to claim their rights. However, little by little, they became aware of the new role of women in the world).[9] Bouchereau-Sylvain refers to the explicit naming of a feminist consciousness and notes that it was by *looking to other worlds* and witnessing a global conversation about women's empowerment that Haitian women began to participate. In addition to her work as a pioneering lawyer and sociologist, Bouchereau-Sylvain was instrumental in the founding of Haiti's first women's organization, which she describes in her study. Prior to writing *Haiti et ses femmes*—which she envisioned would be the definitive record of Haitian women's contributions to history—Bouchereau-Sylvain wrote essays, pamphlets, and letters defending Haitian women's rights. An activist and an author, she paved the way for many similarly formed Haitian feminist intellectuals that would follow in her wake.

In literary studies, two works by French-speaking Caribbean women pioneered analyzing women-authored texts in their own geographic and linguistic contexts. Published in 1979, Maryse Condé's *La parole des femmes: Essai sur des romancières des Antilles* identified what VèVè Clark calls "a separate tradition developed for over five decades [that] was not recognized as such."[10] Condé opens her foundational study with the point of provocation that "tout ce qui touche à la femme noire est objet de controverse" (everything that touches the Black woman is the object of controversy).[11] Declaring that "la littérature haïtienne est la plus achevée des Caraïbes" (Haitian literature is the most accomplished in the Caribbean), Condé notes that for Haitian women, the "souci majeur [est] Haïti dans son ensemble" (major concern is Haiti as a whole).[12] She posits that, differently from their sister authors in Guadeloupe and Martinique, Haitian women eagerly espouse the vaunted practice of *engagement* in which "le souci premier est la situation socio-politique du pays" (the first concern is the sociopolitical situation of the country).[13]

Condé's *La parole des femmes* can be read as a precursor to Madeline Gardiner's *Visages de femmes, portraits d'écrivains,* one of the earliest scholarly interventions exclusively devoted to fiction by Haitian women. Gardiner published her study in 1981, at the same time that an explosion of Black feminist writing was occurring globally, especially in the United States and on the African continent. *Visages de femmes* surveys Haitian women novelists' approaches to "le problème de la femme haïtienne, femme du peuple, ouvrière, femme du monde, demi-mondaine, provinciale aux prises avec les préjugés, les interdits, en butte à toutes sortes d'injustices, de part sa condition féminine" (the problem of the Haitian woman, woman of the people, worker, woman of the world, somewhat worldly, a local woman struggling with prejudices, prohibitions, exposed to all kinds of injustices due to her feminine condition).[14] By associating Haitian women with these distinct signifiers, Gardiner evocatively highlights the multiplicity of identity and recognizes the injustices that Haitian women are subject to.

Although not explicitly a feminist text, *Visages de femmes* raises points that interest me for its allusions to the ethical imagination. First, Gardiner writes that the authors in her corpus "se sont efforcées de nous ouvrir les yeux sur la grande misère du peuple haïtien" (have tried to open our eyes to the great misery of Haitian people), acknowledging the need for a class-based analysis.[15] Second, her argument that "la vraie valeur de ces écrits réside dans l'études des mœurs" (the true value of these writings lies in the study of morals) stresses the importance of ethics in these early works.[16] While Gardiner's use of "morals" here has a more traditional connotation, it clears space for thinking about how an ethic of care emerged in the twentieth century. Within the ethical imagination, the idea of a social responsibility of the writer vis-à-vis the community she writes about is paramount.

Similarly, two decades later in *Regards littéraires haïtiens: Cristallisations de la fiction-monde,* Yolaine Parisot insists that "l'incorporation du politique au féminin . . . joue un rôle critique essential" (the incorporation of a politics of the feminine plays an essential critical role).[17] While the notion of *politique du féminin* can be understood as "gender politics," it also implies the political role of writing. The ethic that the logic of *engagement* encourages is the author's moral obligation to intervene in social and political issues. A Black feminist ethic unravels *engagement* as formula because it recognizes that creative production can intervene in social and political issues from multiple perspectives. It also rests on the fact that "one of the earliest lessons we have learned from feminism is that the personal is political: the insight that some of the most infinitesimal details of our lives are shaped by ideological and political forces much larger than our individual selves," a lesson well understood in Black feminism, as M. Jacqui Alexander has indicated above.[18]

Despite the undeniable significance of *engagement* in the history of Haitian literature, it is a term to be complicated and retooled. That contemporary Haitian authors are increasingly wary of *engagement* as an organizing principle for framing their works should also give us pause. Explaining this dynamic, Darline Alexis asserts:

En Haïti, si de plus en plus d'auteurs rejettent l'étiquette 'engagé' longtemps accolée à leurs œuvres et à leur personne parce qu'elle est jugée réductrice, ils acceptant néanmoins volontiers de reconnaître que leur *art s'inspire de la réalité sociale observée*. La création est possible parce qu'il y a une parole à porter et des réflexions à susciter sur la société et sur le monde. En ce sens, leur production est donc politique.

(In Haiti, if more and more authors have rejected the label of engaged writing which has been attached to their works and to their person for so long because the idea is considered reductive, they nonetheless voluntarily recognize that their art is inspired by an observed social reality. Creation is possible because there is a need to say something and [there are] reflections to elicit regarding society and the world. In that respect, their production is therefore political.)[19]

The tension Alexis identifies recognizes contemporary authors keen to distance themselves from the term *engagement* as a rigid taxonomy but without minimizing the social relevance of their work. Francophone authors have wrestled with similar tensions for decades, pitting the classic formula *l'art pour l'art* against *engagement*. Black feminist epistemologies of the both/and help us to negotiate this debate by questioning the exclusivity of various modes of inquiry. In my view, ambivalence around the use of *engagement* as the primary lens through which to analyze Haitian literature stems from a marked concern for form as well as for ethics. Indeed, each of the authors I examine in this study demonstrates an acute sense of responsibility to the reader and to the world. Expressing a similar view, when asked by Annette Joseph-Gabriel if writing as a Haitian woman is an act of revolution or resistance, Évelyne Trouillot responds:

Pour la femme, c'est encore plus symptomatique, car les obstacles sont plus nombreux pour celle qui veut écrire de manière systématique. Le poids du quotidien, les pressions sociales sont plus grandes pour la femme que pour l'homme dans le choix de certaines activités. Donc, je dirai que *c'est un privilège pour lequel il faut parfois se battre*.

(For women, it is even more symptomatic, because the obstacles are more numerous for she who wants to write in a systematic way. The weight of everyday life, the social pressures, are greater for women than for men in the choice of certain activities. So, I would say that it is a privilege for which we sometimes have to fight.)[20]

Trouillot's response does not capitulate to framing writing as an unequivocal act of resistance or revolution. Rather, she reflects personally on the conditions around writing. What I read in her answer is an ethical pause—that is, by creating distance from the question about resistance in the Haitian context, Trouillot can envision other possibilities. By characterizing writing as a private, personal act and as a privilege, Trouillot reinforces the notion that Haitian fiction can have political significance and reverberations in the world but need not be framed exclusively by the discourse of *engagement* and its attendant tropes like resistance and revolution. Similarly, Yanick Lahens highlights specificity and interiority as a way to challenge political writing by acknowledging that she "reconnaît l'apport indéniable des femmes écrivains qui n'hésitent pas à affirmer, à regarder le présent en face non pour communiquer un message politique mais pour présenter la spécificité de leur vie quotidienne avec toutes les contradictions dont elle est faite" (recognizes the undeniable contribution of women writers who do not hesitate to assert, to look at the present directly, not to communicate a political message but to present the specificity of their daily life with all the contradictions of which it is made).[21] When viewed alongside Darline Alexis's point of caution, these remarks by Trouillot and Lahens remind us that the interiority of writing does not exclude its social and political significance.[22]

As one of the hallmarks of Black feminist literature, interiority highlights how the inner lives of Black women reveal social realities and delineate a politic.[23] I see interiority as a form of looking; it represents looking inward toward the self as well as outward at the world. In this same sense, my focus on looking also aligns with the "womanist ethical task of uncovering Black women's stories and highlighting their experience as an important source for their moral framework."[24] A Black feminist ethic does not deny the social and political role of writing even as it resists the rigidity of taxonomies demanding that Haitian literature serve as a political tool. Throughout this book, I propose that attending to ethics in fiction is one path we can take to complicate the idea of *engagement* and that looking is central to the ethical imagination. I am convinced that the ethical dimensions of Black feminist fiction help us attend to what Hortense Spillers refers to as the intramural, a complex network of historical, cultural, and literary inter-imbrications that help us to analyze Black life.[25] It is the ethics of these entanglements that concerns me here.

Beginning with Cléante Desgraves Valcin, who published her novel *Cruelle destinée* in 1929, Haitian women authors have placed female protagonists at the center of their fiction in order to highlight the multiple challenges faced by women. Valcin, who was born Cléante Desgraves in

1891 to an African American mother and Haitian father, has been cred-
ited with publishing the first woman–authored novel in Haiti. Valcin's
heritage is noteworthy especially in terms of her affiliation with African
American women. As historian Grace Sanders observes: "elite Haitian
women's collective sympathies with African American women played a
significant role in early articulations of women's activism in Haiti."[26] Set
during the US Marine occupation (1915–34), *Cruelle destinée* is an early
example of how race, class, and gender operate multiplicatively in the
lives of Haitian women.[27]

Valcin was also one of the founders of the journal *La Voix des femmes*,
the first feminist newspaper in Haiti created in 1935 by *La Ligue féminine
d'action sociale*. As Myriam Chancy has noted, *La Voix des femmes* also
"has the distinction of being the first feminist women's publication in
the Caribbean," attesting once again to Haitian women's contributions
to feminist thought in the region.[28] Their stated mission was to advance
the "improvement of Haitian women's economic, intellectual, social and
political conditions."[29] The women of the *Ligue* were activists and intellectuals zealously participating in Haitian political and cultural life.

In her charting of a Haitian feminist genealogy for *Déjouer le silence,*
the activist Danièle Magloire locates the genesis of the movement alongside resistance to the Occupation. When these activist women developed
a platform that was condemned as too subversive due to its focus on
"droits sociaux (éducation, santé, sécurité sociale) et sur la citoyenneté
des femmes (droits civils et politiques)" (social rights [education, health,
social security] and on women's citizenship [civil and political rights]),
they were outlawed by the government.[30] Shortly thereafter, the *Ligue*
was reconstituted in a different configuration that nebulously proposed
"amélioration physique, économique, et sociale de la femme haïtienne"
(physical, economic, and social improvement of Haitian women) so as
not to arouse the concern of a political system deeply invested in the
patriarchal order.[31] As Kaiama Glover observes, "very much of a kind
with the bourgeois, intellectual leftist groups active during the period,
the *Ligue* was made up of primarily upper-class women who, entirely
conscious of their own privilege, sought to create a site of community
unconstrained by color or class."[32]

Like many members of the *Ligue,* Valcin's feminism was a formative
aspect of her life. Noting Valcin's investment in feminism and suffrage,
Thomas Spear's digital literary archive *Ile-en-île* offers this biographical
sketch by Nadève Ménard:

Cléante Valcin est co-fondatrice en 1935 du journal féministe *Voix des femmes,* l'organe de la Ligue féminine d'action sociale. Elle rédige plusieurs portraits de femmes dans l'ouvrage *Femmes Haïtiennes,* publié en 1953 par La Ligue Féminine d'action sociale. En juin 1955, elle représente le gouvernement haïtien à la 10ème assemblée générale des femmes et préside la délégation à Puerto Rico . . . Dans un entretien avec Georges Lescouflair à la fin des années 1930, Valcin affirme 'je suis féministe et je vais jusqu'au suffrage des femmes.'[33]

(Cléante Valcin was co-founder in 1935 of the feminist newspaper *Voix des femmes,* an organ of the *La Ligue féminine d'action sociale.* She wrote several portraits of women in the work *Femmes Haïtiennes,* published in 1953 by *La Ligue Féminine d'action sociale.* In June 1955, she represented the Haitian government at the 10th general assembly of women and chaired the delegation to Puerto Rico . . . In an interview . . . in the late 1930s, Valcin said, "I am a feminist and I [take that belief] as far as suffrage for women.")

Valcin's use of "feminist" in the 1930s was hardly uncommon. The entwining of feminist activism and all forms of writing was par for the course for many of her peers, many of whom were also active members of the *Ligue.* Over the years Haitian intellectuals, including Jeanne Perez, Marie-Thérèse Colimon-Hall, and later Paulette Poujol Oriol, women steadily involved in the work of the *Ligue,* would similarly deploy their writing to take up feminist causes. The example of Valcin and Poujol Oriol, among others, upholds Myriam Chancy's clear-eyed pronouncement that "literature produced by Haitian women . . . is rooted in a long tradition of feminist organizing and theorizing of women's condition in the Haitian context."[34] As a tradition rooted in organizing, Haitian feminist literature models a method in which the theory and praxis split dissolves. Still, as privileged women, these early Haitian feminists were an example that, as Gina Athena Ulysse explains, "access to expression is classed."[35] Despite these women's sense of responsibility to the poor and underprivileged, their writing was a product of their lived experience ostensibly shaped by socioeconomic privilege.

While the *Ligue féminine* in many ways marks the genesis of institutional Haitian feminism, the story does not end there.[36] Tracing the evolution of Haitian feminism(s) into the 1980s, Danièle Magloire identifies a second wave after the fall of the Duvalier dictatorship (1957–86), calling it "ce second soufflé du féminisme haïtien" (this second breath of Haitian feminism) marked by "sa vigeur, sa continuité, l'évantail des problématiques soulevées et une présence au niveau international, notamment dans les Amériques" (its vigor, its continuity, the range of issues raised, and its international presence, particularly in the Americas).[37]

Magloire's essay on the different strands of Haitian feminism also exposes its repudiation by members of the Haitian intellectual and political elite. If the movement has remained active, it is "grâce au travail des féministes que les contributions sociales des femmes sortent de l'invisibilité" (thanks to the work of feminists that women's social contributions are emerging from forced invisibility).[38] What interests me most about Magloire's genealogy of Haitian feminism is how she characterizes it as local and global, concerned with social justice, and *guided by an ethic:* "Le féminisme haïtien n'est pas construit à partir des théories, mais s'est forgé dans l'adhésion à des valeurs: liberté, égalité, autonomie, inclusion, justice sociale, participation, souveraineté" (Haitian feminism is not built from theories, but forged in adherence to values: freedom, equality, autonomy, inclusion, social justice, participation, sovereignty).[39] Magloire names these values not to offer a formula but to describe something more in keeping with *an ethic* conveying feminist values.

The first iteration of Haitian feminism was not intersectional in the most robust sense of the word. In fact, the *Ligue féminine* has been rightly accused of elitism. Notwithstanding these criticisms, the *Ligue's* mark on the development of feminism in Haiti and the Caribbean is undeniable. As Chancy contends, "despite its elitism, the roots of Haitian feminism can be found in the Ligue's early efforts; it is to these roots that Haitian women who re-organized Haiti's feminist agenda in the late 1980s and 1990s returned, re-envisioned, and enlarged."[40] As twenty-first-century Black feminists in Haiti, Lahens, Trouillot, and Mars exemplify how this enlarging continues today.

Like Magloire, Yanick Lahens explicitly establishes a continuum between Haitian feminist activism and Haitian women's studies across disciplines in which literature plays an important role today: "La redécouverte de Marie Chauvet à partir de 1986 s'inscrit dans une nouvelle réactivation du mouvement féministe des années 1930 et une reconnaissance de figures féminines de l'histoire comme Sanité Belair, Victoria Montou; ou de la vie intellectuelle, comme les trois sœurs Sylvain ; de la vie politique comme Yvonne Hakime-Rimpel, ou littéraire comme Cleante Valcin, Annie Desroy, Nadine Magloire" (The rediscovery of Marie Chauvet in 1986 is part of a new reactivation of the feminist movement of the 1930s and a recognition of female figures in history such as Sanité Belair, Victoria Montou; or intellectual life, like the three Sylvain sisters; of political life like Yvonne Hakime-Rimpel, or literature like Cleante Valcin,

Annie Desroy, Nadine Magloire).[41] Lahens notes that in the twenty-first century activists and scholars are returning to earlier Haitian women as intellectual producers, thinkers, and creators.

Indeed, as my interlocutors in this book repeatedly corroborate, Black feminism "foregrounds Black women as intellectual producers, as creative agents, as political subjects, and as 'freedom dreamers' even as the content and contours of those dreams vary."[42] The brief history of Haitian women's intellectual production provided above demonstrates that literature has long been the province of Haitian feminists. Moreover, the theoretical framework of Haitian feminism as I deploy it throughout the book is necessarily both local and global, insular and diasporic. *M'ap fè yon rasanblaj* (I am creating a gathering) in which the scholarship of prominent feminist intellectuals in Haiti like Sabine Lamour, Darline Alexis, and Danièle Magloire and in the diaspora like Myriam Chancy, Carolle Charles, and Gina Athena Ulysse are of equal importance. Each of these thinkers has developed theories that accommodate the complexity and multiplicity of Haitian women's lived experiences, attesting to the fact that, as Ulysse puts it, "in spite of the simple narratives that tend to reduce us to singular notions, we are and have always been plural."[43]

The rich literary tradition of Haitian women's writing dates back to before the Revolution and includes poetry, novels, short stories, and songs. To date, very few monographs focusing exclusively on multiple Haitian women writers exist. Among these, Madeline Gardiner's *Visages de femmes, portraits d'écrivains* (1981) and Myriam Chancy's *Framing Silence: Revolutionary* (1997) are the most noteworthy.[44] This book is closest to the latter, especially given Chancy's use of feminist theoretical frameworks. However, the major difference between *Framing Silence* and what I propose here is that Chancy analyzes texts by women authors in the diaspora as well as in Haiti, both living and dead. By situating my study in the contemporary with a focus on writers currently living in Haiti, I aim to make a contribution that is focused on the present as well as the future. For English-speaking audiences, relatively few studies examine the works of contemporary women writers currently residing in Haiti. While several monographs include one or two novels written by the authors that I focus on, none have argued, as I do, for a Black feminist approach to reading these works together.

The themes of resistance and revolution in Haitian women's writing have been identified as central tenets of the tradition by literary scholars like Myriam Chancy, Marie-Denise Shelton, and Régine Latortue. Shelton states emphatically in 1997, "what needs to be explored is whether one can speak of a feminine writing in Haiti and whether women writers are bound by common concerns, perceptions, and practices. . . . Is there a territory of the feminine in which their project acquires its full meaning?" Chancy posits that "much of Haitian women's literature should be read as a literature of revolution," and she cleverly plots the ways in which Haitian women writers both invoke and revise the Haitian canon.[45]

My study picks up where Chancy's pioneering *Framing Silence* left off in the late twentieth century to ask what kind of works are being produced in the twenty-first century. More than two decades after its publication, Chancy's critical engagement with Haitian women's fiction remains pathbreaking in its commitment to analyzing the linkages between Haitian and Third World feminisms in particular. A predecessor to my book, *Framing Silence* was the first book-length study written in English to focus exclusively on women-authored Haitian novels. From Chancy's vantage point, "as a Third World movement, Haitian feminism counters rather than follows Western models of French and North American mainstream feminism, at the same time that it finds parallels with the enunciation of feminist politics by Third World women in the West, most notable by their African-American counterparts."[46] She argues that Haitian feminism should be seen as a distinct iteration of "Third World feminism" that diverges from the mostly African American school of Black feminism. Weaving together postcolonial theory, feminist theory, and French critical thought, Chancy delineates a path for theorizing Haitian literature beyond the local milieu. Highlighting as a pattern in women's writing "the covert and overt feminist discourse [that] reflects the necessity of creating a new, yet unobtrusive woman's space in the everyday life of the nation-state," Chancy offers a framework for Haitian literary criticism with women at the center.[47]

While the necessity she describes is true of the period that Chancy covers, the Black feminist ethic that contemporary writers take up is now is more concerned with how these authors freely look at and imagine a different world. What distinguishes Lahens, Trouillot, and Mars from the generation that Chancy describes is how tenaciously they espouse the legacy of the previous generation and how they both draw from and challenge established traditions. Chancy identifies "a pattern in Haitian feminism, which progresses from speech activation to dialogue integration, to the paradoxical creation of an imperceptible woman's space, to the enforced implementation of women's writing beyond a closed sphere of woman's interactions as revolutionary consciousness is developed and honed."[48] My study builds on and extends Chancy's argument by asking what happens when feminist consciousness is already developed and honed. That is to say, what kind of texts are uniquely possible in the twenty-first century written by authors who have been inspired by a tradition that includes feminist foremothers like Poujol Oriol, Valcin, Chauvet, and Sylvain-Bouchereau?

Differently from Chancy, who draws extensively from French and postcolonial theoretical models, feminist sociologist Carolle Charles's conceptualization of Haitian womanhood, for which she uses the phrase *machann ak machandiz,* exemplifies an approach that turns to local concepts as a point of departure for theorizing. According to Charles, machann ak machandiz "reflects a paradox, which, . . . in many ways characterizes gender relations in Haitian society. I have always argued that Haitian women have been in a subordinate position in all fields of gendered, racialized, and classist relations of power within Haitian society, yet at the same time they have been able to act as agents defining and negotiating these same relations of power."[49]

I am compelled by Charles's theorization which emblematizes a Black feminist ethic attentive to dynamism and nuance and centers the experience of Haitian women as a point of departure for theorizing. Espousing the Black feminist both/and, a machann ak machandiz can be both victim and survivor, oppressed and liberated, silenced and vocal, empowered and dispossessed. Even more, the concept machann ak machandiz helps us to see a way out of these false binaries that reduce Haitian women's experience to simple extremities. Complexity is essential to a Black feminist ethic because it refuses to limit the possibilities of who and what women can be. As a frame for Haitian womanhood, machann ak machandiz effectively takes us beyond single stories of strength and resilience, refusing to limit theorizations of gender to binaries, encouraging us to complicate and deconstruct them. Charles entreats us to understand how much agency functions as a prerequisite for these Haitian women, especially when we take into account that, as Karen McCarthy Brown tells us about the machann figure, "the keen business sense that is part of the popular image of the machann is a key survival skill for poor Haitian women."[50] In the pages that follow I return to Charles's formulation of a machann ak machandiz, whom I see as thriving in many of the literary women I analyze in this book.

I have already noted that anthropologist and performance artist Gina Athena Ulysse's concept of *rasanblaj* is foundational to my analysis because it is an example of Black feminist theorizing indicating that "dynamic rather than fixed ideas seem more to our liking," as Barbara Christian observes.[51] Ulysse identifies *rasanblaj* as a keyword, method, practice, and catalyst. Ulysse explains that the word "invokes Audre Lorde's feminist erotic knowledge in its fullest dimensions from the personal as political to the sensual and spiritual."[52] *Rasanblaj* is useful for my purposes because it is a Haitian-derived theoretical framework that embraces a feminist stance as it evokes and invokes an ethical project. Furthermore, the work of assembly that *rasanblaj* espouses is what I attempt to enact by bringing together Black feminists in a way that is local, transnational, and global. As M. Jacqui Alexander notes, *rasanblaj* dovetails with "a transnational feminist methodology."[53] With its emphasis on individual agency within the collective, *rasanblaj* sheds light on the multiply configured relational dynamics that unfold in the subsequent chapters.

There are at least three ways in which I attempt to enact rasanblaj on these pages. First this is a rasanblaj of authors—not only Mars, Trouillot, and Lahens but earlier writers like Paulette Poujol Oriol and Marie Vieux-Chauvet who help me to understand what a tradition of feminist writing looks like in Haiti. Second, it is a rasanblaj of texts; the novels that I explore relate well to one another and together express the different themes of the book. Last, this rasanblaj is a gathering of thinkers from Haiti specifically, the Caribbean in general, and the diaspora, especially the United States. Focusing on multiple works of fiction by the three authors in each chapter and drawing my inspiration from Black feminists in Haitian, Caribbean, and African American contexts, I want this book to create its own form of rasanblaj. I gather these authors together for their proximity of geography, thought, and experience, as well as for how the "paradoxes, contradictions, intersections, and ingenuity" of their creative projects illuminate one another.[54]

By grouping Lahens, Mars, and Trouillot together, I am also calling for a rasanblaj of these proximate Haitian women authors who are often publicly in conversation with one another. That each of these women regularly invokes a tradition of Haitian women's writing also reveals a Black feminist sensibility to identify women-centered genealogies in Haitian literature. The Black feminist lens through which they appreciate their literary foremothers never isolates gender from the other parts of their identity. This attitude is what we see at work, when, for example, speaking of Marie Chauvet Yanick, Lahens opines: "undisputably, Marie Chauvet opened the way for the modern novel in Haiti, even if, unfortunately, she has remained completely misunderstood in her own country."[55]

Another Haitian interpretive framework that operates alongside my use of *rasanblaj* is what theorists of queer performance Mario Lamothe,

Dasha Chapman, and Erin Durban-Albrecht describe as *nou mache ansam* (we walk together). They describe this concept as "forging commonality not through gender, sexuality, or other identities but through walking together, through shared activity, experience, and support."[56] *Nou mache ansam* is a fitting descriptor for the works and authors I discuss because, though they may differ, they, in their status as Haiti-based feminist authors writing in the contemporary moment, do indeed walk together through shared activity and experience.

I began by identifying the centrality of Paulette Poujol Oriol to this book, and it is worth noting again that before gender identity in Haiti was theorized with terms like *déjouer le silence, rasanblaj,* or *machann ak machandiz,* Poujol Oriol advocated for innovative intersectional approaches to account for how class influences the power dynamics of gender and race. A look at her fiction and nonfiction texts, as well as her activism, reveals that she was constantly thinking about how gender, race, class, and sexuality overlap. For example, in an interview with Chantalle Verna, Poujol Oriol theorizes how class influences agency for women, explaining that less elite women have historically been more empowered in decision-making and economic self-determination because the patriarchal structure of marriage effectively stripped elite women of their rights: "[Men] had all the rights, to sell the house, to take the money, to spend it. . . in any way, give it away. The women had no rights in 1934, no rights at all. But the street women [the merchants] already had rights because they were already very active traders and most were not married. They were living with a companion but they were not married so they were free to [move about] in and out the way they liked [unlike] the 'society' woman, the 'cultured' women."[57] By homing in on the ways that class identity shapes the lived experience of gender, Poujol Oriol offered an analysis that looked differently at class privilege and acknowledged the power of patriarchy. Her insights into how power and privilege intersect and diverge in the context of gender prophetically theorize the multiplicity of identity when few were expressing it in this way.

The reliance by these writers and activists on local knowledge and figures—from the market woman and the use of Kreyòl terms to the suggestion of Vodou concepts—offers a vital point of departure from which to theorize Haitian women's studies. These thinkers unabashedly foreground the specificity of a Haitian standpoint without sacrificing or abandoning Black feminism as a critical framework. Even as Haitian feminists are rooted and established in their own local context, they have a transnational and global vision that looks outward and embraces the tenets of

Black feminist thought. Encompassed in their *looking for other worlds* is an awareness of and attention to Black women's solidarity and proactive alliances across the globe, as well as an acknowledgment of "the Caribbean as a space created within and through local and global formations."[58]

The Ethical Imperative of Black Feminist Criticism

For the purposes of this book, I hew closely to theories of Black feminism(s) as an animating force in my analyses of Haitian fiction. Black feminism is a dynamic and evolving political, social, ethical, and creative project. At the same time, my discussion presupposes that Black feminism is first and foremost an ethical stance. When I refer to a Black feminist ethic of care, it is rooted in a vision that aims to preserve human dignity for all and therefore recognizes a common humanity, whether it is for the elderly, people at the margins, or disadvantaged women and girls. An ethic of care issues a challenge to models of consumption or accumulation because it requires sharing, mutuality, sacrifice, and connection as opposed to competition, greed, hierarchies, and individualism. The relational ethic of care calls attention to what society tends to overlook. Putting Black women and girls at the center of our questioning from below is to re-align our visions of the world.[59]

A question that grows out of this framework is who or what is worthy of ethical concern. Patricia Hill Collins's ur-text of Black feminist theory, *Black Feminist Thought: Knowledge and Consciousness*, repeatedly highlights the international dimensions of Black feminism: "we must recognize that the U.S. Black feminists participate in a larger context of struggling for social justice that transcends U.S. borders."[60] Haitian feminism and Caribbean feminism have always been global, and, similarly, African American feminism has never been exclusively national. For example, by describing the need for "solidarity between Black women in the United States and Third World Women," Barbara Smith asserts that Black feminist theory and praxis have been global in scope since their beginnings.[61] For Collins, Black feminist thought is deeply concerned with ethics. Explaining this investment, she writes: "The rationale for such dialogues addresses the task of examining concrete experiences for the presence of an ethic of caring. Neither emotion nor ethics is subordinated to reason. Instead, emotion, ethics, and reason are used as interconnected, essential components in assessing knowledge claims. In an Afrocentric feminist epistemology, values lie at the heart of the knowledge-validation process such that inquiry always has an ethical aim."[62] Indeed, the interconnectedness of emotion and ethics emanates from the lives of the characters Mars, Trouillot, and Lahens create in their fictional worlds.

How does a Black feminist ethic differ from the area of feminist ethics, a subfield of philosophy? To answer this question, we can turn to the work of feminist ethicists. Carol Gilligan defines an ethics of care as "an ethic grounded in voice and relationships, in the importance of everyone having a voice, being listened to carefully (in their own right and in their own terms) and heard with respect. An ethics of care directs our attention to the need for responsiveness in relationships (paying attention, listening, responding) and to the costs of losing connection with oneself or others. Its logic is inductive, contextual, psychological, rather than deductive or mathematical."[63] Gilligan's definition helpfully designates voice and relationships as essential elements in care ethics. Other feminist philosophers have questioned this approach, resisting the idea of care and relationships based on how that framework suggests a biological view of gender that feminists should be skeptical of. Whereas feminist philosophers question whether care, justice, and relationality should be included in a feminist ethic, Black feminists locate these values as central to our ethical claims because, as Alice Walker explains in her use of the term womanist, we do not have the luxury to disassociate ourselves from male-identified peers and allies. These are not questions to be debated but rather are required for the elaboration of a viable ethical framework.[64] Perhaps, put most simply, where I diverge from "feminist ethics" is that I am proposing Black feminism as an ethic but I am not situating my work in the larger field of ethics.[65]

Whereas the opposition between justice and care is a feature of feminist ethics described above, a Black feminist ethic takes a both/and approach in which concepts like care, survival, intimacy, and justice can combine, overlap, and inform one another. My approach is distinct because with the term "Black feminist ethic" I actively invoke the ethical imperative of Black feminist thought, which distinguishes that ethic as oriented towards social justice. A Black feminist ethic is necessarily dialogic; it is in conversation with the work of Black feminist intellectuals, activists, scholars, and writers across generations and geographies, creating the conditions for moral agency.

Although this discussion of a Black feminist ethic presupposes that feminism is first and foremost an ethical stance, I do understand Black feminism overall as a political, social, ethical, and global creative project. *Looking for Other Worlds* examines works of fiction that account for structures of power while still valuing identity and subjectivity in multiple kinds of encounters.[66] The novels under consideration here are representative for how they approach ethical problems from a perspective that privileges the stories of vulnerable, multiply marginalized people. At the same time, each author creates characters who vary in perspective and experience, rather than offering a singular narrative of Haitian womanhood.

M. Jacqui Alexander explains in *Pedagogies of Crossing* that a feminist approach to ethics is "centrally concerned with the promise that oppositional knowledges and political mobilizations hold with the crafting of moral agency."[67] In other words, the positionality of people who experience multiple oppressions has ethical implications for how they make sense of the world and potentially contribute to transforming it. From paying attention to the moral experience of women, as well as the knowledge they have to offer, there emerge female-centered, feminist visions of the world. These world-making thoughts add meaning to topics such as aging, class division, sexual intimacy, and the environment.[68]

Another theoretical well in which ethics is evaluated intersectionally is the theology subfield of "womanist ethics." Womanism derives from Alice Walker's beautiful explanation that "womanist is to feminist as purple is to lavender" and homes in on the lived experience of Black women within feminism,[69] highlighting that Black women are "by nature more disposed toward care and mediation [and the Spirit] than her Western counterparts."[70] As Melanie Harris explains, "the primary goal of womanist ethics is to 'uncover' black women's experiences, lives, and stories as key resources for theological and religious reflection."[71] Famously conceptualized by Katie Cannon (leaning on Walker) in the theological context, "womanist ethics" refers to an interdisciplinary method that places the daily experiences of ordinary Black women at the center of ethical analysis in order to explore how race, gender, class, and sexuality combine in the staking of moral claims: "Naming themselves 'womanists' aligned the project of womanist theology and ethics with the lineage of Black women's literature and more specifically with the black woman writer Alice Walker."[72]

That the idea of a womanist ethic is inspired and animated by literature written by Black women resonates with me especially for how it accounts for religious and spiritual modes of knowing and being. In fact, the articulation of a womanist ethic necessitates that womanist ethicists "open their eyes and expand the boundaries of their thought to incorporate interreligious and interdisciplinary dialogue, as well as focus on the global links and common worldviews shared among women of African descent and their communities."[73] This means that the ethic is deeply global, dialogic, and attentive to the spirit and is what I see as my task too, as I embark on reading these novels by Haitian women. Cannon contends that "the Black woman's literary tradition is the best repository for understanding Black women's ethics."[74] Her position has meaning for me as I explore the literary tradition by Haitian women as a site for envisioning ethical consciousness. Still, while I am drawn to womanist ethics for how it foregrounds the lived experience of Black women as the basis of ethical inquiry, based on my own standpoint and scholarly formation, I lean toward Black feminism.

I deliberately use Black feminist rather than "Haitian feminist" or "Caribbean feminist" because I want to underscore global dimensions of Black feminism that have been there since its origins. For example, when the Combahee River Collective penned their definitive Black feminist manifesto, they argued for "Black feminism as the logical political movement to combat the manifold and simultaneous oppressions that all women of color face," referring to Black women not only in the United States but also throughout the world.[75] Likewise, Myriam Chancy depicts the work of Haiti's first feminist organization in a similar light: "the Ligue's main purpose was to act as a bridge between the global and the local."[76]

This book is therefore a conscious effort to both frame Haitian literature according to its Black feminist concerns and to participate in broadening the scope of Black feminist criticism, as scholars like M. Jacqui Alexander, Carole Boyce-Davies, and Alexis Gumbs, have done in the past. Their scholarship on Caribbean literature elaborates and expands Black feminist theorizing; for them and many others, their positionality as feminists who are Black and Caribbean informs their commitment to articulating, as Carole Boyce-Davies has, "that the experience of Black women lends itself to the notion of fluidity, multiple identities, repetition which must be multiply articulated."[77]

As Boyce-Davies asserts, an important part of complicating Black feminism is theorizing that involves "critical relationality," which means appreciating that "each feminist articulation is intersected by geography, sexuality, class, cultural identity, economics, history, social factors, race, ethnicity, age, ability, language."[78] More recently, scholars like Laurie Lambert have outlined the utility of Caribbean feminist criticism in relation to specific islands. As Lambert notes in *Comrade Sister* on literary representations of women in the Grenadian Revolution, "A Caribbean feminist literary criticism focuses attention on Caribbean women authors while also reading all texts (by writers across genders) intersectionally, accounting for gender and sexuality alongside race and class. As a critical tool, Caribbean feminist literary criticism can be used to illuminate texts and testimonies by authors of any gender or generation, while recognizing how different forms of oppression are particularly compounded in Caribbean women's experiences."[79]

Intersectionality affirms that the complicated identities of both the authors and the characters I include in this book cannot be discussed or explored in isolation from one another. Thinking alongside Caribbean(ist) scholars who attest to why and how Black feminist epistemologies have much to offer in literary analysis, I focus on contemporary Haitian literature as a rich site for excavating the intersections of race, class, gender, sexuality, religion, ability, and other markers of identity. In terms of the specificity of the Haitian context, the inclusion of religion as a location of identity that recurs throughout my study is especially critical because, as Yanick Lahens has noted, it "dévoile une dimension du vécu non prise en compte par l'intersectionnalité, mais un des lieux de pouvoir de la femme dans la culture populaire" (reveals a dimension of lived experience that intersectionality does not take into account, but one that is [an important] site of power for [Haitian] women).[80]

Religion plays a prominent role throughout this study, especially the Haitian traditional religion of Vodou. As Vanessa Valdés argues in *Oshun's Daughters,* Caribbean writers often "turn to diasporic religions as a source of inspiration for creating more full portraits of womanhood."[81] For my purposes, the ethical framework is especially significant for how it parallels the Vodou ethic that Claudine Michel meticulously outlines in *Aspects éducatifs et moraux dans le Vodou haïtien,* which I refer to throughout this study. As Michel explains, "La moralité pour ceux qui servent les loas représente donc un effort constant pour maintenir la cohésion sociale, l'harmonie, et l'équilibre. Ce qui est 'bien' et 'juste' dans le monde Vodou ne l'est jamais, mais en fonction d'un raisonnement abstrait, mais l'est en relation avec ce qui potentiellement peut réaliser l'unité du groupe" (For those who serve the spirits morality represents a constant effort to maintain social cohesion, harmony, and balance. What is "good" and "just" in the world of Vodou is never so as a result of abstract reasoning but as a result of that which can potentially realize group unity).[82] Overall, my exploration and elaboration of a Black feminist ethic in the Haitian context is indebted to Vodou philosophy that is imbued with intersectional significance and that simultaneously represents "une éthique et une foi" (an ethic and a faith).[83]

As a work of literary analysis, *Looking for Other Worlds* evaluates how ethics and aesthetics overlap in contemporary fiction. How does form help to convey ethical problems? What kind of techniques appear in ethically invested narratives? I am interested in a reading practice that values ethics and aesthetics together—as such my use of a Black feminist ethic operates thematically and formally. Often, the ethical complexity of these novels is expressed in narrative terms. Through narrative choice, literary devices, and plot structures, Lahens, Mars, and Trouillot make use of their textual space to raise questions about ethics both explicitly and implicitly. Their novels display a lively ethical imagination that is deeply invested in engaging readers, authors, and characters. For them ethics and aesthetics are indissolubly entwined; they approach form in a highly stylized way creating an ethical poetics. Paying close attention to narrative structure, linguistic details, and generic innovation, I observe how these formal elements shape discourses about gender, power, and ethics. Narration plays an especially important role in the selected novels, many of which are written in polyphonic registers and thus accommodate multiple perspectives that are then placed in relation to one another. The formal elements of these novels often hold the keys to unlocking the doors to the moral imagination. In an interview with *Africultures*, Yanick Lahens divulges what she calls her obsession with form: "J'ai essayé le roman pour pouvoir déployer davantage la narration . . . Je suis obsédée par le temps, la narration, et l'interrogation de l'agencement de la forme" (I tried the novel genre in order to use narration more . . . I am obsessed with time, narration, and the examination and arrangement of form).[84]

As a genre, the novel provides more textual space to experiment with form. As Farah Jasmine Griffin writes: "As a form, the novel can raise questions about the possibilities and goals of justice. It allows us to imagine what a society governed by an ethic of care, a society devoted to restoring and repairing those who have been harmed, giving them the space for transformation, might look like."[85] Each of the novels in my corpus and the issues they take up—aging, sexuality, the environment, and class—are linked to an ethical discourse rendered through poetics. The contemporary texts that I examine here not only invite the reader to contemplate the ethical implications of literary praxis (and thus include the reader in moral reflection) but they also feature protagonists who make difficult, ethically challenging decisions. My pairing of ethics and aesthetics is also informed by a desire to attend to the formal elements of these texts as well as their implications within and outside the novels. It is inspired by my own appreciation of how form and function come together, my recognition that politics and beauty are not mutually exclusive or, as Toni Morrison states about her own writing, "it has to be beautiful and political."[86]

My project endeavors to articulate an ethic that resonates across the work of three different authors, and by exploring their ethical imaginations, I aim to show its relevance in contemporary literature. The novels that I bring together in this study are remarkable for the mundane topics they pursue: an elderly woman serving the spirits and honoring her religion prior to death, a family dealing with mental illness and its repercussions in the family, an enslaved woman grappling with her future, a queer artist who returns home to find love. By insisting on the "ordinary and everyday," these authors ask us to engage social realities beyond the spectacular. Beginning with a Black feminist ethic of care as my point of entry is also an attempt to reveal a new narrative in which life, joy, and plenitude take center stage rather than lack, death, precariousness, and destruction. Ultimately, a focus on ethics calls attention to the multiple roles of literature as well as to the importance of encounters among the authors, characters, and readers.

Directions in Literary Ethics

Looking for Other Worlds draws from literary and narrative ethics, fields of research that possess their own history and method. While seeking to consider the possibilities that emerge when we pair literature and ethics, I wrestled with how frequently ethics is tied to morality. By contrast, my focus on "ethics" is distinct from "morality," and I find Terry Eagleton's definition particularly useful as a way to clarify the difference between ethics and morality. Eagleton explains that "an ethic is enabled and invigorated by the capacity for transformation . . . A morality on the other hand, operates within the bounds of a given set of conventions, within which social and political problems must be solved."[87] In other words—and in keeping with Black feminism—an ethic is dynamic, whereas morality is fixed. More precisely, when we note that morality "deals with what is good or bad, permissible or forbidden," the term suggests a binary worldview that is far removed from what interests me here.[88] As the theorist Chielozona Eze helpfully notes, "whereas morality might be personal, ethics is always about the quality of one's relationships with others . . . Ethics as relationship is intrinsically a recognition of the other."[89] This focus on ways of being or relating to others is *both* individual *and* communal, *both* specific *and* universal.

Ethical thought as it pertains to literature has been explored in numerous contexts. Following the ethical turn that occurred between the 1990s and early 2000s, scholars have developed diverse frameworks for thinking about how ethics relates to literature.[90] Within this expansive critical landscape, there have been inquiries as varied as those of Gayatri Spivak, who links literary ethics and reading while placing both in a global frame; Martha Nussbaum, who champions the ethical imperative of literature; and Simon Gikandi, who explores postcolonial literature in relation to an ongoing ethical project.[91] In a relevant essay that inquires about the role of ethics in the field of literary studies at the dawn of the new millennium, Dorothy Hale succinctly explains that the return to ethics "is not just the attempt to recuperate the agency of the individual reader or author for positive political action but also an attempt to theorize for our contemporary moment the positive social value of literature and literary study."[92] The utility of ethical inquiry is that it helps us to understand the manifold functions of literature in society while nonetheless maintaining space for the evaluation of form. As a literary scholar and cultural critic, I am committed to the relationship between ethics and aesthetics, the latter calling attention to how the three authors deploy language, structure, and narration in ways that are bound to their ethical concerns.

Ethics is inherently dialogic; it beckons questioning. On the one hand, the significance of ethical thought in fiction contemplates how characters and authors make moral decisions. But at the same time, the ethics of a text and the ethics of narrative raise questions about the work literature does in the world. My own ethically sensitive method focuses on four thematic areas: aging, class, sex, and the environment. I also pay close attention to ethics as relational because "contemporary ethical criticism is not simply concerned with our relationship to literature and to the good, but, more specifically, with our relationship to the other: it is the singular encounter between reader and text as other that is at stake in the ethics of literature."[93] A relational view of ethics also helps to emphasize the importance of thinking about Black feminism *internationally* or diasporically.

The relational nature of narrative ethics brings into greater relief the significance of how characters interact with one another and how readers interact with texts. As such I am interested in literary ethicist Adam Newton's argument that "ethics signifies recursive, contingent, and interactive dramas of encounter and recognition, the sort which prose fiction both crystallizes and recirculates in acts of interpretive engagement."[94] I want to highlight the importance of "encounter" as a generative term from which to theorize ethics. When we think about ethics as encounter, the dialogic dynamic comes into focus especially as it relates to my own critical frame of "looking for other worlds." The notion of "encounter" is far from singular because ethical engagements with fiction can be productively imagined *as a series of encounters:* between the reader and the text, between the author and the text, and between the characters and one another. The kinds of encounters that I pursue are not only contained within the text, they also live outside it. It is a perspective that "conceives of narrative as a site of and for intersubjective relations, in which interaction among subjects, whether fictional or real, matters."[95]

The view that these relations and encounters matter resonates with a Black feminist framework. Taken together these novels acquire meaning that is born out of how they wrestle with ethical questions and the processes through which they do so. An important part of my argument is that the authors make aesthetic choices in order to reflect ethical concerns, which suggests a mutually dependent relationship between aesthetics and ethics. In this vein, my goal is to illumine the "intricacy and interwoven character of ethical-aesthetic relations and how they manifest themselves in literary art."[96] The intersection of narrative and ethics takes into account how formal choices—narration, plot devices, language, and imagery—combine to articulate the moral imagination.

If, as Martha Nussbaum argues, "literary art can be ethical, and . . . responsible criticism of literary artworks can legitimately invoke ethical categories," then exploring the ethics of literature demands that we also consider the ethics of criticism.[97] How can scholars be more transparent about the kind of ethic we are bringing to our critical praxis whether we are reading, writing, theorizing, or analyzing? I find Black feminism to be instructive in this regard, because it is a critical framework that takes our individual positionality into account, encouraging us to ask ourselves, "for whom are we doing what we are doing when we do literary criticism?" (to use the words of Barbara Christian).[98] A Black feminist ethic is one in which the significance of literary criticism relates to a social responsibility for how these messages circulate in the world. The ethical logic delineated in a novel is therefore important not only within the pages of that text but also for what it suggests about the world. Again, how these authors and the characters they write look at the world and look for other worlds informs my critical approach. Chielozona Eze takes a similar view in the insightful study *Ethics and Human Rights in Anglophone African Women's Literature,* positing that feminist writers' commitment to exploring the human condition results in sustained engagement with ethics and that feminist writers are especially aware of the need to "raise questions of immediate ethical relevance."[99] Eze further contends that "the contemporary African woman writer . . . understands her feminism to be an ethical statement; it involves people relating to people as individuals and not merely as members of groups."[100] For these writers then, the creation of narrative itself is a relational and world-making gesture inextricably bound to the idea of ethics.

Beyond facile ideas about good and bad, the term "ethics" presupposes an understanding of human experience as inherently nuanced. To quote Spivak again, "ethics is questioning from below," meaning that it engages the active critical inquiry from the vantage point of the most marginalized. Pairing literature and ethics then becomes another way to acknowledge both the social and human dimensions of literature. As described by literary ethicists, this process involves "exploring the texture and quality of human behavior as richly and as sensitively as you can."[101] It also suggests a dynamic relationship between the reader and the author through which we can locate "ethical relationships between writing selves and reading others."[102] Paying attention to this relationship between the self and the other also urges us to ask questions about recognition (looking). Citing gender theorist Judith Butler, Eze insists that an ethically sensitive approach means continuously returning to the question *who are you?* and that this question must be posed "without any expectation of a full or final answer. This Other to whom I pose this question will not be captured by any answer that might arrive to satisfy the question. So, if there is a question, a desire for recognition, this will be a desire which is under an obligation to keep itself alive as desire, and not to resolve itself through satisfaction."[103] It is in this spirit that I also engage the notion of ethics as questions, relations, and recognition. A central argument in this book is that a Black feminist ethic shows us what it looks like to pose questions, observe relations, and invite recognition rooted in intersectionality and the multiplicity of identity. As an ethical approach, questioning, relating, and looking (recognition) will emerge as keywords throughout my study of these novels by Lahens, Mars, and Trouillot.

Building on this perspective, understanding the ethical imagination of these authors means asking questions in multiple registers, each time interrogating a different set of relations. There are, first, the questions we pose of the text itself—what is the value system within the universe of the novel? Second are the questions the author poses of the reader. What does our reaction to the novel reveal about us? What can we learn from our encounters with this textual world? Last, there are the ethical questions that the characters in the novels ask of themselves. How does the author challenge the reader's value systems through representations of particular issues? Is there an ethical grammar espoused in these writings? Further, how do ethical approaches to different topics manifest in fiction? Why is fiction a productive space to express the moral imagination? With these questions in mind, I propose a methodology informed by narrative ethics and rooted in Black feminism that proceeds in three directions: how are ethical problems present in the lives of characters, how do ethical questions manifest for the reader, and how do the ethical commitments of the author shape their texts?[104]

Yanick Lahens, Kettly Mars, and Évelyne Trouillot

Yanick Lahens (b. 1953), Évelyne Trouillot (b. 1954), and Kettly Mars (b. 1958) are three proximate authors who explicitly espouse feminist politics. The term "feminist" is not only one they embrace personally but one that they urge others to take on in service of human rights and equality for all. I am, of course, aware that there are a number of contemporary Haitian women writers whom I could have chosen to focus on, in both Haiti and the diaspora. Émmelie Prophète in particular, comes to mind as a feminist author who has written six novels and whose active role in literary life in Haiti today is undeniable. But whereas Prophète was born in the 1970s, each of the authors I study here was born in the 1950s, making them relatively of the same generation, a factor that helps to unite them conceptually. Being born in the 1950s means that each of these women came of age during the Duvalier dictatorship. For each of them, the regime in particular and the Haitian sociopolitical context in general figure prominently. In this section I will briefly situate and describe each author in chronological order before turning to their feminist politics and poetics.

Yanick Lahens was born in 1953 in Haiti, where she began her education prior to moving to France as a teenager. In France, she studied modern literature at the Sorbonne and wrote a thesis on Haitian author Fernand Hibbert. When she returned to Haiti as an adult, she began teaching literature classes at *École normale supérieure de l'État,* where she remained for many years. In addition to her work as a professor, Lahens has also worked for the Ministry of Culture, cohosted a program for Radio Inter, and served as an editor for the Haitian press Henri Deschamps. As one of the founders of the *L'Association des écrivains haïtiens* (Association of Haitian Writers), she regularly hosts programs for writers throughout the island and abroad. Lahens's contribution to the Haitian literary scene has also come through her work with *Institut français,* through which she has editorial responsibilities for the reputable journal *Conjonction.* Lahens's first literary publication, *Tante Résia et les dieux,* is a collection of short stories that appeared in 1994, four years after the publication of her landmark literary essay *L'exil: Entre l'ancrage et la fuite*. Lahens's renown is international; most recently she was elected to the Collège de France and received the Prix Fémina in 2014 for her novel *Bain de lune*. To date Yanick Lahens has authored five novels and five short story collections as well as two books of essays.

L'exil: Entre l'ancrage et la fuite (1990) is a work of literary criticism in which she explores the topic of exile from multiple perspectives. Among the salient points she advances in this study is a plea to flee from binary formulations of Haitian literature: "il nous apparaît possible et urgent à la veille du XXIe siècle de repenser la question de l'identité, de la nationalité et de l'origine de manière à quitter le cadre de l'alternative dedans/dehors" (it seems possible and urgent to us on the eve of the twenty-first century to rethink the question of identity, nationality and origin so as to abandon the framework of the inside/outside alternative).[105] As Lahens's first publication, this study establishes her as a literary critic, though she eventually moved to fiction as her primary genre of writing. While the study focuses almost exclusively on male writers and barely signals her investment in and indebtedness to Haitian women writers, she notably credits Marie Chauvet (along with Frankétienne) for introducing the "techniques du monologue intérieur en cassant la linéarité traditionnelle, en jouant des points de vue du narrateur et en donnant une dimensions psychologique intéressante, individualisé à leurs personnages, qui n'apparaîtront plus comme personnages-clichés" (inner monologue techniques [that] break the traditional linearity by playing with the narrator's points of view and by providing an interesting psychological dimension, individualized to their characters, who will no longer appear as cliché characters).[106] I will just note here that this same interiority and attention to the individuated selves of their characters is a feature of the fiction I examine in the chapters that follow. Today Yanick Lahens continues to participate in an ample range of literary and cultural activities in Haiti and abroad.

Évelyne Trouillot is the author of seven novels, five collections of short stories, four books of poetry, four children's books, and one play. She was born in Port-au-Prince in 1954 and educated there through secondary school. It is often noted that Trouillot was born into a family of intellectuals: her uncle Hénock Trouillot was an august historian; she and each of her siblings have flourished as celebrated writers and academics. In 1972 her family departed for the United States, where she completed her education. Trouillot obtained a bachelor's degree in French from Florida International University in 1985 before returning to Haiti in 1987, one year after the fall of the Duvalier dictatorship. Her first collection of short stories, *La Chambre Interdite,* was published in 1996, then followed by two more story collections in 1998 and 1999. Although her short stories were published first, Trouillot has always written poetry, short stories, and novels. Discussing her generic permutations she specifies, "Je pense que les textes viennent à l'écrivain . . . avec leur forme, leur genre et je ne peux pas choisir d'écrire à l'avance des romans ou des nouvelles. Je pense que le texte vient avec ses propres contours" (I think that texts come to the writer, at least me, with their form, their genre and I cannot choose in advance whether I write a novel or short stories. I think that each text comes with its own contours).[107] Though most of her works are in French, one of her children's books, *La fille à la guitare / Yon fi, yon gita, yon vwa,* appears in a bilingual edition, and her poetry collection *Plidetwal* was written and published in Kreyòl.

Trouillot has received numerous prizes for her writing, including the Prix Soroptimist de la romancière francophone for first novel *Rosalie l'infâme* after it was published in 2004; the Beaumarchais award from ETC Caribbean for her first play, *Le bleu de l'île;* and the coveted Barbancourt prize for *Le Rond-point.* She is currently a professor of French at the Université d'État d'Haïti. A passionate advocate for the rights of women and children, Trouillot regularly addresses these topics in her public writing and lectures. For example, in 2002 she authored "Restituer l'enfance: Enfance et état de droit en Haïti," in which she advocates for the rights of children, specifically with regards to education. More recently, in an essay published at the end of 2020, she tackles the subject of disparities in publication with suggestions for how Anglophone editors and translators can better accommodate the linguistic complexity of the African diaspora.[108]

Trouillot is also one of the cofounders, along with several members of her family, of the *Centre Culturel Anne-Marie Morisset,* whose mission is to promote the arts in the lives of young people.[109] Named after her mother, the center honors Morriset's commitment to education by offering cultural enrichment and resources to children. With her daughter literary scholar Nadève Ménard and her brother Lyonel Trouillot she also founded *Pré-texte,* an organization that sponsors reading and writing workshops in Haiti. Trouillot speaks widely internationally and has been featured in festivals like the Yari Yari Celebration of Women Writers that last took place in Accra, Ghana. For Trouillot, to be a contemporary writer carries with it a serious responsibility: "Aujourd'hui plus que jamais, écrire en Haïti c'est dire non à la laideur, non à la médiocrité et non à la paresse pour un peu plus de bonheur au bout du chemin" (Today more than ever, to write in Haiti is to say no to ugliness, no to mediocrity, and no to laziness for a bit more happiness at the end of the road).[110] Trouillot's sense of responsibility has always been forthright in her public writing. In particular, since 2018 as Haiti has undergone a series of political upheavals from the PetroCaribe protests to the assassination of Jovenel Moïse and the dramatic rise of kidnappings, she has regularly deployed the essay as a form to decry these accumulating injustices.[111]

Born in 1958, Kettly Mars is the youngest of the three authors whose work I examine. Indeed, Mars "incarne parfaitement le jeune auteur haïtien de cette génération ayant grandi dans les années soixante et commençant à publier dans les années quatre-vingt-dix" (perfectly incarnates the young Haitian author of this generation, having grown up in the sixties and started to publish in the nineties).[112] Because she was born one year *after* the beginning of the regime, her entire infancy, childhood, teenage years, and young adulthood were under the yoke of the dictatorship. The youngest in a household of five children, Mars grew up in a middle-class family with four older brothers. Her literary career was launched in 1997 when she began writing poetry after several years working in the private sector. Up until very recently, Mars lived in Port-au-Prince her entire life. She is the author of ten novels, four collections of short stories, and two books of poetry.

While in her thirties Mars began writing poetry, then moved on to the short story genre and eventually the novel. Describing her trajectory, Mars explained, "j'écris mes premiers vers, expression d'une musique intérieure qui cherche ses couleurs propres" (I write my first verses, an expression of an interior music looking for its own colors).[113] Beginning with poetry, Mars then transitioned to popular writing with her *Kool-Klub* series, which appeared in the form of *roman feuilleton*. Her first collection of poetry was published in 1997, and a book of short stories appeared in 1999. Mars's first novel, entitled *Kasalé,* was published in 2003. She has authored eight novels and won several literary prizes, including the 2015 Prix Ivoire for *Je suis vivant.* Despite this steady stream of fiction writing in the early 2000s, it was not until 2010 that Mars began to devote herself entirely to writing as her only profession. Of this transition she explained, "après le 12 janvier 2010, j'ai décidé de prendre le temps qui me manquait. De vivre pour et par ma passion d'écrire . . . De libérer mon souffle. Le béton c'est aussi fragile que du papier quand les plaques tectoniques se rompent sous nos pieds. Il y a urgence. Je décroche. Un saut dans le vide. Un acte de foi en la vie" (after January 12, 2010, I decided to take the time I was missing. To live for and by my passion for writing . . . To free my breath. Concrete is as fragile as paper when the tectonic plates break under our feet. There is urgency. I pick it up. A leap into the void. An act of faith in life).[114] Currently the president of PEN Haiti, Mars is actively engaged in promoting Haitian literature on a global scale. As Joëlle Vitiello has observed, today, "elle est devenue véritablement un auteur mondial" (she has truly become a global author).[115]

Each of these writers was born in the early years of the notorious Duvalier regime (1957–86). Both Lahens and Trouillot were toddlers when Dr. François Duvalier rose to power, and Mars was born one year after his election. They are undoubtedly marked by the traumatic legacy of *la terreur* as well as subsequent periods of unrest and military crackdown that have punctuated life in Haiti during the late twentieth and early twenty-first centuries. Duvalier was responsible for tens of thousands of murders, imprisonments, kidnappings, tortures, and disappearances. After his death in 1971, his son Jean-Claude continued this reign of terror with the help of the notorious private militia the Tonton Macoutes, who waged unmitigated violence throughout the Haitian population.

Feminist scholars like Carolle Charles have argued that the contours of Haitian womanhood transformed under Duvalier because women were routinely subjected to political violence in ways they had never been before. As Charles explains in her well-known essay about gender-based violence under Duvalier, state violence became gendered in heinous ways during this period, and the "particular relationship of gender to the authoritarian state under the dictatorial Duvalier regime has shaped the configuration of women's consciousness, demands and claims, and forms of organizing."[116] Building on Charles's work, Nadège Clitandre explains that "during the Duvalier regime . . . Haitian women writers tackled issues of history, nationality, gender and class from a female point of view to critique Haiti's political and social circumstances and expose the ways in which Haitian women have been oppressed and rendered invisible."[117] As feminists who came of age during the regime, Lahens, Trouillot, and Mars are undoubtedly similarly shaped by the specter of Duvalierism. It is well worth noting that each of them has written at least one novel inspired by the dictatorship and set in that period, although that focus will not figure strongly in this book.[118]

Yanick Lahens, Évelyne Trouillot, and Kettly Mars are prolific authors, and my choice of them for this study is in no small part due to that quality. Their publication records span a wide diversity of genres and languages. As locally rooted contemporary writers, their work appears regularly in Haitian venues and in publications such as *Le Nouvelliste,* and they are frequent guests on local programs and radio shows in Port-au-Prince and beyond. With an international audience, these women have a global reach that expands conversations about Haitian literature.

In an interview organized at the Morisset Cultural Center in Port-au-Prince, Mars explained her approach to writing in world-making terms that inspire my title for this study: "Écrire, pour moi, c'est prendre des engagements. C'est aussi prendre des positions. C'est pourquoi quand j'écris, je prends des positions. *Je cherche d'autres univers,* pousser aussi loin que possible mes audaces et arpenter des lieux inconnus" (To write, for me, is to make commitments. It also means taking positions. That's why when I write, I take positions. *I look for other universes,* pushing my daring as far as possible and exploring unknown places).[119] What Mars calls a search for universes—the idea of "looking for other worlds" that inspired the title of this book—is inspiring and instructive. Writing as a process of looking and seeing animates these authors' creative process and expression. World-making characterizes their fiction. That Mars sees writing as "taking a position" relates directly to the power of ethical questions in her work.

Évelyne Trouillot has also referred to the need to create new worlds in her writing. In an interview with Chantal Kénol published in *Écrits d'Haïti,* Trouillot explains that while her lived experience informs her positionality, as a writer she must be capable of imagining beyond that lived experience: "Je voulais entrer dans ces êtres là et je pense justement que c'est ça le défi de l'écrivain. S'oublier soi-même et entrer dans un autre univers" (I wanted to enter into these beings and I truly think that is the challenge of the writer. Forget yourself and enter into another universe).[120] Like Mars, Trouillot envisions writing in terms of universes; it is a world-making impulse. Reflecting on the reality of her intersecting identities, Trouillot wrestles with the impossible task of parsing who she is:

Je suis tout à la fois femme, écrivaine, haïtienne. C'est difficile de faire un tri et de privilégier un aspect sur un autre . . . Il y a des gens qui ont peur du mot féministe. Moi, ça ne me fait pas peur, parce que selon moi ceux qui pensent (femmes et hommes) et veulent des changements dans l'intérêt de tous ont une responsabilité par rapport au traitement que la société fait aux femmes.[121]

(I am a woman, a writer, and a Haitian all at once. It's hard to sort and prioritize one aspect over another . . . There are people who are afraid of the word feminist. I am not afraid of it, because in my opinion those who think [women and men] and want changes in the interest of all have a responsibility for society's treatment of women.)

Trouillot affirms that the various locations of identity are multiplicative and interimbricating. Her approach to feminism invokes its universal appeal—men and women alike stand to benefit from feminism.

Similarly, Yanick Lahens has openly reflected on how race, class, and gender operate for her as a Haitian writer. When asked if there is a Haitian-specific version of *écriture féminine,* she responded: "Et je suis femme, haïtienne, noire. Je ne peux pas m'empêcher d'écrire à partir de ma situation de femme aussi! Je n'ai jamais milité pour la cause féministe. Mais quand je lis Marie Chauvet, ou les contemporaines comme Évelyne Trouillot et Kettly Mars, je remarque qu'on écrit les choses différemment. Parce qu'on a des vécus différents de ceux des hommes" (And I am a woman, Haitian, Black. I cannot escape from writing with my own situation as a woman as a point of departure! I have never fought in the feminist movement, but when I read Marie Chauvet, or contemporary writers like Évelyne Trouillot or Kettly Mars, I notice that we write things differently. Because we have life experiences that differs from those of men).[122] Lahens's passionate response and her reference to past and present Haitian women authors mirrors the objectives of this project. By naming Chauvet, Mars, and Trouillot, she identifies herself as part of a longer tradition of Haitian feminist writing and locates herself within a cadre of contemporary feminist writers. In what follows I extend her point to pursue the "difference" that she notes, which, in my view, is their adherence to a Black feminist ethic that holds these authors together.

The rasanblaj of thirteen works of prose fiction that I analyze across the next five chapters are in productive conversation with each other, reinforcing the principle that intersectionality is a lens for examining multiple issues simultaneously.[123] Several of the books appear more than once in different chapters precisely because they show how the themes that I examine recur in different manifestations and iterations. An abiding concern for raising ethical questions about intersectionality weaves through each of these texts, allowing "the novel's function as an agent of the reader's ethical education," to create a relational dynamic that moves beyond the page.[124] Taken together these novels point to an engaging and dynamic Black feminist ethic that encourages reframing, questioning from below, and continuous dialogue. The ethical questions that Lahens, Mars, and Trouillot raise are diverse and rarely simple; they probe issues like the dynamics of social class, the complexity of family relationships, the tensions inherent in sex and sexuality. Many of the characters we meet in these novels make ethical decisions that contrast with an individual who balances their own interests in relation to the interests of others. These characters address and account for communal needs as well as their own and understand that all members in the community operate in dependency with one another.

The Black feminist ethic at work in this fiction also reframes how we see divisions between people—the margin and the center, estranged family members, sexual predators and those they prey upon. These divides are both real and perceived. A determined preoccupation with difference as a form of ethical engagement reaffirms that "ethics is the main arena in which claims of otherness are negotiated."[125] Black women's ideas about "the other" are central to any claim we can make about ethics because "otherness" is a position that we ascribe to as well as one that we must call into question. For this reason, the friendship between Sophonie and Antoinette in *Kasalé,* the contentious bond between the sisters in *La couleur de l'aube,* the close-knit dynamic between Lisette and the older women of *The Infamous Rosalie,* and the romantic relationship between Norah and Marylène in *Je suis vivant* figure prominently in my analyses. The relationships that these Black women characters have with one another place them in proximity with someone who might otherwise be seen as "other," and what we ultimately see is that, by approaching "the other," these Black women see themselves more clearly.

The centrality of women's relationships in these works of fiction affirms Mary Helen Washington's observation: "If there is a single distinguishing feature of the literature of Black women . . . it is this: their literature is about Black women; it takes the trouble to record the thoughts, words, feelings, and deeds of Black women . . . Women talk to other women in this tradition, and their friendships with other women—mothers, sisters, grandmothers, friends, lovers—are vital to their growth and well-being."[126] Alongside Black women's interiority a relational dynamic in which *women talk to other women* is essential to the elaboration and cultivation of a Black feminist ethic.

My fundamental argument here is that a Black feminist ethic acknowledges that moral life and social life are intertwined. Mars, Trouillot, and Lahens move beyond the idea of *engagement*/engaged literature to develop a relational ethics that puts marginalized voices at the center, whether those marginal voices belong to an enslaved girl, a lesbian, a mentally ill person, or an elderly woman. This centering of the margins, which is a defining characteristic of a Black feminist ethic, is carried out through narrative strategies, plot innovations, and thematic devices. In this regard, their work is also consistent with a longer tradition of Haitian women's writing, which, according to Yolaine Parisot, combines attention to the political context with an emphasis on the individual: "Si les romancières haïtiennes ne mettent pas, comme on l'a souvent dit, le réel sociopolitique à l'arrière-plan, elles accordent cependant davantage d'importance que leurs confrères à la question de l'individualité . . . elles analysent les conséquences ontologiques" (If Haitian novelists do not [place], as has often been said, the real sociopolitical in the background, they nevertheless give more importance than their colleagues to the question of individuality . . . they analyze the ontological consequences).[127]

With these novels, the authors also ask us as readers to pose ethical questions to which there are no easy answers. The decisions that the characters make are informed by multiple issues that are exposed to the reader but rarely resolved. In the quotations that begin this book's introduction, Trouillot and Lahens reflect on what it means to write in Haiti during the twenty-first century. Their comments locate writing as responsibility, as urgency, as critique. The ethical considerations of the novels are clearly informed by the contexts in which they emerge. With its history as the first independent Black republic in the Americas; its dynamics of political unrest in the form of slavery, revolution, dictatorship, foreign occupation and coups; its capacious diaspora whose members primarily reside in France, Canada, and the United States; its robust spiritual and cultural landscape routed through Vodou; and rich language associations of French, Kreyòl, and English, Haiti offers a particularly rich terrain for analyzing the key currents in postcolonial and francophone studies.

I want to emphasize here that my investment in uniting Black feminism and Haitian feminism is both academic and personal. First, I am committed to Black feminism as a global project whose reach extends far beyond the United States. Notwithstanding this position, I am also indebted to the development of Black feminist thought as an intellectual project with underpinnings in the United States. Transnational postcolonial feminists like M. Jacqui Alexander have mined the continuities and discontinuities between African American feminists and Black feminists abroad. While Alexander's point that "there is nothing that can replace the unborrowed truths that lie at the junction of the particularity of our experiences and our confrontation with history" does resonate with me, I do seek to understand and foreground how the international scope of Black feminism is a framework that includes Caribbean feminisms in general and Haitian feminism in particular.[128] When I speak of Black feminism, it is to designate a global multiethnic Blackness that includes Haitian women.

Second, Black feminism has always been a global movement invested in solidarity across national lines, cultures, and continents. To equate Black feminism only with African American feminists is to misunderstand its original project. In an interview about the beginnings of the Combahee River Collective, a group of radical Black feminists founded in the late 1970s, Barbara Smith explains that internationalism "is not a part of our politics that has necessarily been uplifted widely, but that's where we were coming from . . . We were Third World women. We considered ourselves to be Third World women. We saw ourselves in solidarity and in struggle with all third world people around the globe. And we also saw ourselves as being internally colonized within the United States. We identified as Third World people. And that kind of solidarity was not just true of the very new Black feminism that we were building."[129] Like Smith, I recognize that that the term *Black feminism* has in some ways been wrested from its "Third World" and Global South beginnings. Over the years, the development of feminist subfields such as transnational global feminisms, postcolonial feminisms, African feminisms, and Caribbean feminisms has further reified the notion that Black feminism is singularly rooted in the United States. My appreciation of "Black" as a capacious term that accommodates people of African descent throughout the diaspora also informs my commitment to Haitian feminism as Black feminism. This does not deny the specificity of Haitian feminism, especially when we acknowledge Black feminism's deep preoccupation with dissolving binaries like local and global, or specific and universal. With this backdrop in mind, I hew closely to the following definition of Black feminism succinctly captured by Angela Davis: "[It is] a theoretical and practical effort demonstrating that race, gender, and class are inseparable in the social worlds we inhabit."[130] As a strategy for reading inscriptions of race, gender, class, and sexuality in various modes of cultural expression, Black feminist theory makes room for the articulation of an ethic that is sensitive and attentive to those indivisible categories. Taking Davis's definition as a guide, we notice how Lahens, Mars, and Trouillot demonstrate the intertwining of these factors in the social worlds of their characters and how they simultaneously look for other worlds in which their characters move beyond this reality.

What would it mean to reorient our study of Haitian literature toward ethics rather than politics? And what happens when we do so with Black feminism undergirding that ethic? *Looking for Other Worlds* turns to the novel as a site of ethical engagement, and in so doing presents a framework for analyzing contemporary literature that brings together Black feminist theory, literary ethics, and Haitian studies. Reading contemporary Haitian fiction through a Black feminist lens deepens and enriches our understanding of what feminism can be, just as it enhances and expands our approaches to Haitian literature.

Viewed through the novels written by Lahens, Mars, and Trouillot, the "ethical imagination" of Haitian fiction provides insights into the imagination as a place of possibility. This sense of the imagination, this "looking for other worlds," frames my entire project. After all, as Omi'seke Tinsely reminds us, "the work of the imagination is, as other scholars have beautifully stated, a central practice of Black feminism—indeed it remains a Black feminist necessity."[131] When read together, Lahens, Mars, and Trouillot's representations of aging, sex, class, and the environment meditate on what it means to be human, also a central preoccupation of Black feminist ethics. These novels articulate an ethic in which all kinds of Black women are given space to just be and are inherently valued. Taking seriously the point that "Black feminist theory . . . demands an ethical engagement with past and present" means paying attention to how these authors represent the past, intervene in the present, and imagine the future in their world-making fiction.[132]

The Positive Affects of a Black Feminist Ethic

Looking for Other Worlds is inspired by my own special affinity for the three authors I have chosen, and so reading, analyzing, and theorizing *with care* is a practice that I commit to enacting in these chapters that follow. Those chapters will raise questions about literary ethics and Haitian studies in service of a Black feminist ethic that is global, careful, and deeply committed to what is possible and imaginable. I utterly agree with Katherine McKittrick that when Black feminist scholars "pursue the links between practices of domination and Black women's experiences in space, we see that Black women's geographies are lived, possible, and imaginable."[133]

Love is an investment, a positive and productive affect that can be brought to analyzing literature, and for me in this study it is also personal. It is informed by my own positionality as a first-generation Haitian American woman whose entry into Black feminist thought was always informed by Caribbean sensibilities. It is a love of literature, a love of Haiti, a love of Black feminism, a love of Haitian women and girls that both inspires and informs my inquiry. This love begins with my grandmothers Ursula Hérard Scharoun (1917–2017) and Anna Joseph Jean-Charles (1916–2007), two formidable women born at the beginning of the United States occupation of Haiti. They were remarkable women born in opposite regions of *Ayiti chérie*—one in the north (Gonaïves) and one in the south (Jacmel).

Both daughters and mothers of families with four children, these women worked for their entire adult lives. Each had a vigorous faith in God that led her to make unconventional and courageous decisions. My paternal grandmother, Anna Joseph Jean-Charles, was known for taking care of and educating many children on her street, rue Clerveaux, and in the neighborhood, just walking distance from the Cathedral of Gonaives and Jean-Jacques Dessalines Square. She was a force in her community who worked as a *madan sara*, ran her own business, and sent her children away one by one during the Duvalier dictatorship, believing that they would someday return.[134] Unfortunately, she died before her two youngest children—my father and my godmother—moved back to Port-au-Prince for good after many decades in the United States.

My maternal grandmother, Ursula Hérard Scharoun, was born into privilege in Jacmel but then moved to Cape Haïtien after marrying. A survivor of domestic violence, she eventually left a first and then a second husband, then emigrated from Haiti, leaving three of her children behind. She went first to Venezuela and then to the United States, where she remained in Massachusetts for the rest of her life until she died at one hundred years old. When she lived in Somerville, Massachusetts, she was known for gathering large groups of Haitians living abroad, for whom she would cook and entertain. Eventually she sent for each of her children in Haiti and paid for them to come to the United States. All of this she did living as a single, Black, immigrant woman.

My love for these women as well as my curiosity about their lives also motivates this study. Although they did not identify as feminists, both of my grandmothers lived by feminist principles. I intuitively understood that there was a place for feminism and love to cohabit and interrelate long before I read my first Black feminist text. That love blossomed when my own formal Black feminist education began for me as an undergraduate student when I read Barbara Christian, Audre Lorde, Marie Chauvet, Mary Helen Washington, Maryse Condé, Paule Marshall, and many others for the first time under the careful guidance and loving mentorship of Black feminist scholars. Love is far from out of place in a scholarly exploration of Black feminism. Like Jennifer Nash, I have found that

Black feminism is distinctive in its commitment to love as political practice. From Alice Walker's definition of womanism that places self-love at the center of Black feminist subjectivity to the Combahee River Collective's statement that its political work emerged from "a healthy love of ourselves, our sisters, and our community," Black feminists have long emphasized the importance *of love as a form of collectivity, a way of feeling, and a practice of ordering the self.* In other words, love operates as a principle of vulnerability and accountability, of solidarity and transformation, that has both organized and undergirded Black feminist practice.[135]

To Nash's conclusion that love is a form of collectivity, a way of feeling, and a practice of ordering the self, I would add that love is an ethic able to texture and guide our reading and writing practices. And yet love is rarely at the center of our critical analysis. It is an unpursued affect in a critical discourse that is more preoccupied with struggle, multiple oppressions, and violence. Anchored in a Black feminist love ethic, the care that I take with these novels radiates from my own positionality. Throughout this book I return continuously to care and love as critically relevant affects that should be a part of ethical relations. When we think of "the ethical relation as an embrace, as an act of love in which each learns from the other," we can see how care, proximity, and intimacy figure within it.[136] I want to reiterate that I take ethics in the broadest sense of how life ought to be lived and how we ought to live with one another, an expansive view that accommodates a range of perspectives and approaches as it beckons questioning and reframing.[137] These authors and their fictional characters are visibly preoccupied with what love, care, and respect for their fellow people look like in the context of a literary universe.

I began this book by naming the centrality of Paulette Poujol Oriol to my study because of the way Black feminism and ethical reflection radiates in her work. Now I turn to her novel *Le Passage/Vale of Tears,* which emblematizes how feminist writers make creative sense of ethically charged issues. *Vale of Tears* begins with a precocious little girl playing alone outside her stately home. While seven-year-old Coralie plays with her beautiful and beloved doll, her stepmother Aline shouts in the distance. Aware that Aline awaits her, "with a threatening lash in her hand," Coralie nonetheless refuses to end her precious playtime (13).[138] When the little girl finally makes her way back to the "big, white house with its round pillars," she is severely punished. After whipping Coralie for the offense of disobedience, Aline takes the doll and smashes its head against the banister, shattering it into tiny pieces. The stepmother's violation of her doll sends the little girl into a rage: "Coralie throws herself at Aline, pummeling her with awkward blows. She scratches, she bites, she is wild, a howling little beast carried off to the first floor by the servants" (14). Poujol Oriol's prose reveals a spirited little girl, but her stepmother's actions also portend problems that she will encounter in the future after years of outrageous neglect and abuse.

The scene that follows occurs more than sixty years later, in a physical setting that is the exact opposite of Coralie's opulent childhood home. The elderly Coralie awakens in a desolate shack on the last day of the year. Struggling to move her aging body, "she places her pointed elbows on her bony knees, Wisps of gray hair hang down alongside her hollow, ash-colored cheeks. She raises herself and slowly stands up . . . Her body rocks when she moves about, and she always seems on the verge of falling" (15). Coralie now faces a crisis: six months of rent are past due, and her landlord will evict her in one day. As a result, she decides to approach her sons for help. But, for reasons explained later in the novel, the likelihood of her sons actually helping her is far-fetched: "They are so ashamed of her—the reprobate the shameful one, the street vagabond, Cora the abject, the worthless, debased being she has become over the years, a pitiful creature, a beggar, one of those abandoned souls to whom people give money without daring to look them in the eye" (16). The profound contrast between the two scenes leads us to wonder—how did that little girl become this poor old woman? As Coralie sets out in search of the money that will prevent her from becoming homeless, *Vale of Tears* charts the dramatic sojourn of a woman who sinks tragically into a life of poverty, abjection, and humiliation.[139]

First published in French in 1996, then translated into English in 2005, *Vale of Tears* is ethically complex. Coralie's fall is complicated by the fact that much of what happens to her results from her own choices; her challenges propel the novel's ethical vision forward. She represents a flawed and controversial woman whose life raises questions about her personal character, as well as the society in which she lives. As a probing exploration of what it means to be a poor and disenfranchised woman in Haitian society, *Vale of Tears* grapples with moral questions. By juxtaposing the protagonist's past and present in each chapter, Poujol Oriol situates Coralie's present condition in relation to her past. She walks through the city of Port-au-Prince on a quest for help, while the narrative flashes back and forward in time, ambling toward her uncertain future. Along her journey, the novel's map of Port-au-Prince is also a map of her descent—what other characters refer to contemptuously as her moral decline. Is Coralie to blame for her fate? Given the limited choices available to her, how do we make sense of her plight?

The novel complicates what it means to be born into privilege and to grow old in Port-au-Prince. Throughout, one of the central messages is that belonging to the light-skinned elite does not necessarily mean having an easy and carefree life. Or, rather, that for women in particular the privilege of class is an unstable form of protection at best. Despite the luxurious life once afforded to her through class privilege, that Coralie has plummeted so desperately into a life of misery suggests the precarious nature of life for women, regardless of their class status. By charting the protagonist's winding path through the city, Poujol Oriol marks Port-au-Prince's geography in relation to gender, color, sexuality, and class. *Vale of Tears* makes clear that for a Haitian woman living life on the margins, gender and socioeconomic status are interlocking oppressions.

From a formal standpoint, *Vale of Tears* is written in what Thomas Spear befittingly describes as the "multilayered and multilingual French" that characterized Poujol Oriol's writing style.[140] The novel's narrative structure steers us down the treacherous path of Coralie's demise, asking us to contemplate how and why this doom befalls her. Each chapter includes a corresponding station, numbered from one to fourteen, like the Catholic stations of the cross. By framing the story in relation to this particular religious ritual, Poujol Oriol implicitly evokes her protagonist's suffering within a hierarchical and patriarchal frame. The format imitates the steps of Jesus Christ's arduous walk toward death and crucifixion as he carried the cross up a hill. Again, Poujol Oriol invites the reader to ask: which cross does Coralie carry? Can it be determined that she is a type of martyr? The stations are also situated in place: next to each one, Poujol Oriol notes a physical location in Port-au-Prince, with a date and a time marked.

Coralie's journey gains meaning as she meanders through Port-au-Prince. After the initial scene from her childhood, the novel brings us to the end—on the morning of the last day of her life, which is also the last day of the year (December 31, 1967), inauspiciously described as "the end of the month, the end of the year, the end of everything" (15). The journey (and the novel) concludes when Coralie is suddenly struck by a car as she walks up a steep hill. Her abrupt death in the novel's conclusion comes as no surprise to the reader who anticipates a tragic end to the painful story.

Throughout *Vale of Tears* Coralie poses numerous questions about herself, her life, and her surroundings. Her interiority reveals a commitment to interrogating herself as well as the world around her. She exhibits what Kevin Quashie calls "the agency of paying attention, asking questions, and considering."[141] Coralie's continual *questioning from below* informs all of her interactions with other people. When she returns to Haiti after being away in France for eight years, she finds a lawyer to assist her attempt to gain back her inheritance. His suggestion that he will only help her in return for sex triggers the following question for Coralie: "Did she owe it to her beauty and her appearance as a touching victim to attract men's praise the moment she found herself in need? Did she only have her body as currency? And only her favors as her fortune?" (99). In this moment Coralie weighs her options as a machan ak machandiz, understanding how her body is situated within a sexual economy. During another conversation with her stepmother, Aline, Coralie attempts again to claim what is rightly hers. Aline excoriates her stepdaughter for what she deems a scandal of ethics: "Your notorious misconduct, your unpleasant dealings with the post-war French government, the scandal about your morals, everything about you predicted that you would squander all of your money with your numerous lovers before Féfé [her son] would come of age" (117). Aline's reference to "the scandal about morals" shows that to her one of Coralie's greatest crimes is her sexual freedom, again reminding the reader of the limits placed on women in society and the chokehold of respectability.

Later, when Coralie reaches the eighth station on Champs de Mars, her grim future is set against a grandiose Haitian past, and she asks herself: "Coralie, what have you done with your life? Everybody can ask her this question. As you make your bed, so you must lie in it, and nobody cares about the downtrodden" (106). The implication is clear: Coralie has walked herself into this situation, and now that she belongs to "the downtrodden" she should only expect to be discarded by society because she is no longer of value.

Several times on her journey, Coralie encounters other people living in poverty. Coralie's predicament raises questions about how color and class combine in Haitian society: "She is nothing more than a beggar, a pauper. The only difference is that she is aware that her fair skin and blue eyes, washed out from so much crying, make her, without her even trying, a cheater, a social anomaly" (106). Assuming that their lives are different from hers, she takes pity on them. But the reader notices the similarity between Coralie's life and that of the people she pities. At one point on her sojourn, she overhears a conversation between two vendors that shifts her perspective. One confides to the other, "I was only fourteen years old when my own uncle raped me. He got me pregnant, and I had a baby. I was not even fifteen. Thank God, the baby died two months later . . . God saved me from having to care for him" (107). Listening carefully to the conversation between the two women, Coralie evaluates what they say through her particular moral lens: "'They are resigned to their fate' thinks Coralie.

'They're not seeing the end of the tunnel of miseries. Someone, somewhere, has committed them to life without asking their opinion. They are destined to die poor and naked just as they have lived'" (108). Her judgment is an evaluation that does not imagine other possibilities. Furthermore, her harsh view of these women mirrors the harsh view that others have of her. At the end of the chapter Coralie falls asleep, and, when she wakes up, the vendors are gone. They leave behind some candies for her as though *they* take pity on *her*. But they also steal her purse. Their act of kindness is coupled with theft, contradicting her ability to claim that they only wanted to help her. By using the story of Coralie to explore ethical questions, *Vale of Tears* emblematizes how race, class, color, and gender shape the lives of Haitian women in ways that are constantly in negotiation.

Such examples from the novel demonstrate that for every action that can be viewed through a narrow moral lens, there is a counteraction challenging the reader's ability to draw easy conclusions. Poujol Oriol's refusal to present clear right or wrong scenarios opens a space for ethical reflection. Through Coralie, Poujol Oriol imagines a character who is critical about the world around her, the injustices she witnesses, and those she experiences firsthand. By using the story of Coralie to explore moral truths, *Vale of Tears* emblematizes how the intersection of race, class, color, and gender shape the lives of Haitian women in ways that are constantly in negotiation.

This study unfolds in five subsequent chapters; the themes that I explore—aging, sexuality, class, and the environment—have been selected because they figure as tropes that the three authors continuously explore in their fiction and use to both communicate and contemplate ethical concerns. Throughout this entire project, I connect my readings of the novels and ethical issues that they raise to other social movements, art forms, and current debates. I have included as a point of departure in each chapter various forms of cultural production, both digital and visual, that reveal the stirring presence of these themes throughout Haitian life.

Chapter 2, "*Gran moun se moun:* Aging and Intersectionality," begins with a photograph of an elderly Haitian woman by Régine Romain from the photo essay "Haiti: Reaching Higher Ground." Considering this and other images of elderly Haitian women from folk and visual culture serves as a starting point to examine the cultural significance of the elders through my readings of the elderly protagonists in Kettly Mars's *Kasalé* (2003) and Évelyne Trouillot's *L'œil-totem* (2006) as well as *The Infamous Rosalie* (2003). Examining the cultural significance of these elders in the Haitian context, I argue that age and aging must operate as a location of identity alongside class, sexuality, and gender. Privileging the point of view of these older female characters illuminates their own perspectives, and my analyses put forward a preoccupation with the complexity of aging that contrasts the lived experience of aging women with the idea of how older women are perceived in society.

Along with literary and cultural studies and Black feminist methodologies, I draw from the field of age studies, looking at age as a category of analysis that functions *alongside* race, class, sexuality, and gender for how it can determine power relations and locations of marginality. At the same time, I depart from much of the work done by scholars of age studies in my view that the elderly Haitian protagonists are reminders of the importance of cultural specificity for understanding how age functions as a category of analysis.

The figure of the *poto-mitan* (central post or pillar) is also essential to my analyses in this chapter as I think through the possibilities and limitations it presents for Haitian womanhood. Here I enter into conversation with scholars such as Gina Athena Ulysse and Darline Alexis, whose thoughtful excavations of the poto-mitan trope help to frame my own readings of how it applies to aging women. Throughout this chapter I also engage an interpretive framework stunningly rendered in Kaiama Glover's consideration of self-regard and freedom in the context of Caribbean womanhood. Inspired by Glover, I investigate how these elderly women "disorder" the literal and textual worlds they inhabit in ways that are striking given their age. The ethical, spiritual, and material realms of aging for these protagonists are manifestly informed by connection and mobility, which reveal that aging as an idea is not static or contained, thus challenging the normative constructions of how the elderly are perceived.

Chapter 3, on the ethical-erotic, begins with popular Haitian singer Rutshelle Guillaume, whose songs speak to how sexual intimacy and relationships register sonically. I also end the chapter with visual art by Tessa Mars in order to ruminate on the possibilities for how the ethical-erotic registers in a visual frame.

This chapter proposes the ethical-erotic as a framework for reading representations of sex and sexual relationships using Kettly Mars's *Je suis vivant* (2000), Yanick Lahens's *Guillaume et Nathalie* (2013), and Évelyne Trouillot's *The Infamous Rosalie* (2003). My view acknowledges sex as a multidimensional and multiaffective act that generates a range of feelings associated with pleasure and desire. I explore how representations of sex in these novels deploy narrative techniques, the logics of intimacy, and descriptions of the physicality of sex to highlight the relationship between ethics and erotics. My conceptualization of the ethical-erotic emphasizes erotic agency and subjectivity, foregrounds intimacy, and pays attention to dialogue and discourse to elaborate sexual relationships. I draw on the scholarship of Caribbeanist and feminist scholars such as M. Jacqui Alexander, Omi'seke Natasha Tinsley, Mimi Sheller, and Lyndon Gill, all of whom focus on how "uses of the erotic" plays a critical role in representations of sex and sexuality. Gill's elegant formulation of the erotic as physical, sensual, and spiritual is especially instructive for me as I think through what else the erotic signals in these novels.

The phrase "uses of the erotic" was famously coined by Grenadian feminist poet and lesbian thinker Audre Lorde, who urged thinking "across difference" as I try to do throughout this book. By mobilizing the ethical-erotic as a critical frame, I offer a way to think about sex in Haitian literature beyond ubiquitous and disturbing tropes of violence. I track representations of sexual acts, encounters, and desires, paying close attention to the role of intimacy in these interactions, and illustrate how pleasure, practice, and play function as tropes of intimacy. For the characters in *Je suis vivant* and *Guillaume et Nathalie,* sexual activity becomes a way to express the fullness of their personhood as desiring, feeling, and thinking subjects. In *L'œil-totem,* sexual pleasure for an elderly woman is linked to artistic expression, and, in *The Infamous Rosalie,* intimacy is explicitly coupled with freedom. Central to my argument that these novels present sexual relations as inextricably bound to the concept of intimacy is the idea that erotic subjectivity is a useful lens for examining sex and ethics together. How does one represent sexual relations and sexual encounters according to an ethic of the erotic? I argue that by experimenting with narration these authors convincingly convey a sense of intimacy that extends to the reader's relationship to the narrator and the characters themselves creating an ethical-erotic heuristic.

Chapter 4, "Geographies of Class Location: Space and Class," takes as its point of departure Facebook post by Évelyne Trouillot which invites questioning from below about the 2018 anti-government protests in Port-au-Prince. This chapter identifies representations of class division as a way to raise ethical questions to and about a contemporary society. I argue that Trouillot's *Le Rond-point* (2015), Yanick Lahens's *La Couleur de l'aube/The Color of Dawn* (2008) and *Dans la maison du père* (2005) highlight the problems of class division through formal choices—narrative voice, plot devices, and interior monologues—that should be interpreted in relation to narrative ethics. Portrayals of class division in Haiti have a long history. By beginning with a brief discussion of how class division is addressed in novels by Marie Chauvet and Paulette Poujol Oriol, I situate the contemporary novels within a longer tradition of female-authored texts in which class tension abounds. My readings of these novels show that the use of form and genre inform the authors' approach to representing social inequalities and class division and is a self-conscious attempt to reflect class division as an ethical problem.

The novels studied in this chapter use aesthetic innovations that grapple with genre and visual representation. In this they reveal class division as a vexed moral imperative and emblematize the extent to which, in contemporary novels, social differences are present not only thematically but also aesthetically. Here we see how narrative techniques play an important role in reflecting those differences, making it such that study of narrative devices reflects and probes the construction of social class.

I propose that the key concepts of encounter, recognition, and questioning from below that I identified as elements in a Black feminist ethic help us to understand why class has such importance to these authors. As I argue in this chapter, representations of class division in contemporary Haitian novels have become a way to pose ethical questions about the responsibility that people of different classes have to one another. Borrowing from Rolland Murray the idea that class division functions as "form, ideology, and epistemology," I look to how these Haitian novels inspire the reader to envision a class ethic that holds all members of the society—though especially the elite—responsible for these divisions.

Chapter 5, "An Environmental Ethic: Land and Sea," begins by analyzing paintings by artist Mafalda Mondestin to make observations about how the natural environment is represented in visual culture. The chapter then attends to the longstanding importance of the environment in Haitian literature, using the lens of ecocriticism to investigate how the relationship between human activity and the environment becomes an ethical concern in the novels. What kinds of ethical questions emerge when we look at how these novels represent Haitian ecologies and topographies? What is the relationship between the characters of the novel and their natural environments? In what ways do these Haitian novels meditate on nature and culture together or against one another? How does fiction promote moral visions of the environment? My investigation of the environmental ethic here draws from theories of Caribbean and postcolonial ecocriticism, as well as ecofeminism.

Kasalé (2007), *Bain de lune* (2014), and *The Infamous Rosalie* (2003) explicitly engage the environment, allowing nature to function as much more than a mere backdrop and representing land and sea rhetorically, symbolically, and materially. Taken together, these novels lend themselves to ecocritical readings because of how they showcase the environment and the characters' relationships to it as well as how they propose a relationship to nature that is informed by history and rooted in the local. The environmental ethic that I see at work in these novels is manifestly informed by Vodou and attends to how different characters relate to the natural realm.

Inspired by scholars of Vodou like Claudine Michel, LeGrace Benson, and Charlene Désir who have deftly explained the ethical dimensions of the religion, I argue that a Vodou ethic of care surfaces in how the characters relate to nature in each novel. The premise that spirit is nature and nature is spirit informs and guides my readings of how the environment is present in these works.[142] Whether that relationship is contradictory, as we see in *The Infamous Rosalie,* completely balanced as we see in *Kasalé,* or contentious as we see in *Bain de lune,* familiarity with the land and an understanding of its inner workings become a form of ethical discourse. I illustrate how Mars, Trouillot, and Lahens elaborate an environmental ethic rooted in a relationship between characters and the physical environment. Their representations of land and sea highlight its importance through the intimate relationships that their characters have to it.

I am especially interested in how these authors renegotiate/reconfigure the relationships between nature and humans as a hierarchy in which humans are not in control and foreground nature's importance to people, whether because of religion as in *Kasalé,* because of genealogy/family ties across generations as in *Bain de Lune,* or because of resistance to slavery as in *The Infamous Rosalie.* By analyzing characters' relationships to the environment through an intersectional lens that also attends to spirituality, familial bonds, and slavery, my readings of these texts elaborate a Black feminist ethic in which nature is spirit and spirit is nature.

Finally, "Coda: A More Just and More Beautiful World," takes the current work of feminist activist organization Nègès Mawon as a point of departure for looking toward feminist futures in Haiti. I reflect on the journey that I have embarked on throughout this book and theorize the possibilities for a Black feminist ethic that are born from looking. What does it mean to look for other worlds, and what is at stake in a study of feminist ethics and literature in the twenty-first-century Haitian context?

"Haiti needs new narratives."[143] For the past several years Gina Athena Ulysse's declaration has been a clarion call for a generation of scholars working in a broad range of disciplines. Yet, too often we cite Ulysse's pithy phrase without reflecting on the nuance she intended to capture with it. In fact, our proclivity for repeating her plea flagrantly contradicts her stated intention in her book's conclusion, prudently titled "A Plea Is Not a Mantra." In the final paragraph of this "post-earthquake chronicle," Ulysse writes, "I took a definitive decision to stop taking an oppositional stance in favor of an affirming one. From this point on, I knew . . . I would stop insisting that Haiti needs new narratives . . . I would simply do it."[144] As a literary scholar, I turn to literature as a lush terrain in which new narratives are constantly being created. Looking for other worlds is nothing if not an affirmation of the unbounded creation of new narratives. Because one of the prevailing narratives of Haitian literary studies situates ethics as politically motivated and informed by identity, my invitation to focus on the role of ethics as encounter, care, questioning, recognition, and reframing can be viewed as a position that is, like Ulysse's, affirming rather than oppositional. Examining fiction by Haiti-based writers through a Black feminist ethic allows us to appreciate and evaluate how multiple narratives are constructed and how they circulate. Yanick Lahens, Kettly Mars, and Évelyne Trouillot demonstrate how exactly the world-making impulse that creating new narratives demands has long been the project of fiction writers in Haiti.[145]

Reorienting our study of Haitian fiction toward ethics rather than the often-deployed tropes of *engagement,* or even disaster, crisis and catastrophe (as we have seen in the last decade), begins the work of wresting Haitian literature from a master trope that has long been deployed and reified in the fiction of Haiti as "weird."[146] If the idea of an ethic that I am interested in embraces affirmation rather than opposition, it is because the fiction I read here does so as well. The novels that I examine in this corpus attest to an omnipresent *life,* as well as the intricacies of personhood: the intimacies of lived experience, the ordinary nature of daily life, the making of subjecthood for women in different circumstances, and the quiet interactions with the sacred and profane. By subjecting these novels to a critical examination, I respond to Carole Boyce Davies's provocation that "the search has to be continued for ways of seeing our worlds beyond the given," an impulse reflected in this book's title inspired by Kettly Mars's gorgeously expressed point about craft.[147] How these writers approach topics such as aging, sexuality, class division, and the environment displays an ethic that operates intersectionally and is concerned with intimacy and care. It is my hope that a Black feminist ethic—a way of being in the world that operates relationally and dynamically—can function not only as a method but also as a visionary and affirming narrative that celebrates life, abundance, and multiplicity. The novels assembled here in *Looking for Other Worlds* teach us that multiple ways of looking can lay the foundation for shifting paradigms and changing perspectives.[148]

2 *Gran moun se moun*

Aging and Intersectionality

La vieillesse c'est une chanson inachevée, c'est ce sentiment
d'urgence qui vous tient à la gorge alors que vos pas s'alourdissent
et que le temps canaille s'enfuit avec le vent.

(Old age is an unfinished song, it is this feeling of urgency that holds
you by the throat as your steps get heavier and that scoundrel time
flees with the wind.)

—Évelyne Trouillot, *L'œil Totem*

RÉGINE ROMAIN's stunning photographic essay "Ayiti: Reaching Higher Ground" includes an arresting image of an elderly Haitian woman.[1] The title of the photograph, *Mama Ginen,* invokes her African heritage through a reference to the ancestral homeland (Ginen/Guinée/Guinea) as well as to the Haitian religion, Vodou.[2] As a signifier of the afterlife and the African continent, Ginen is both ethereal and real. Mama Ginen's deep reddish-brown skin glows in the Haitian sun. Her face is impossibly smooth with no wrinkles. The expression she wears is stern, almost defiant. Her look is one of disagreement as she scowls at the photographer and the viewer. She looks displeased, nonplussed, and disapproving all at the same time. The look is not an invitation. Rather, it seems to tell the one who looks to look away or, at the very least, to explain herself for why she looks. Mama Ginen's look refuses to welcome the spectator's gaze (see fig. 1).

The concept of a look of refusal that I intentionally call forth here recalls Tina Campt's arguments about Blackness and visuality, in which she concentrates on what the photographic subject does and does not communicate.[3] As Campt has noted, photography "has created rich strategic terrain for practicing refusal within and among Black communities throughout the diaspora."[4]

I am so taken by the practice Campt suggests that moves from looking to listening. It asks that we absorb photographs in a way that takes into account the affective labor of images. That is, it compels us to ask

Figure 1. *Mama Ginen,* Port-au-Prince, Régine Romain. (© 2010; used by permission of the artist)

how exactly an image, like the photograph of Mama Ginen, move us? As a critical framework, listening clears space for what Campt calls "reading out of" rather than "reading into." It enables us to see photographic subjects through a lens that asks questions about what takes place before and after the moment the image is taken. By reading out of the image, we acknowledge that the photograph exists long before the viewer looks at it. This unsettles the centrality of the viewer who looks at the image and instead casts attention on the photographic subject and the photographer. Although Campt deploys this framework as a way of reading archival photographs, I find it useful when looking at contemporary photographs of Haitian women for how it asks the viewer to center the subject differently. When we *listen to the image* and take Mama Ginen's seniority into account, we see an elderly woman entitled to her look of refusal.

The practice of listening to an image asks that we look for what is hidden by contemplating what the image reveals rather than what it documents. As Campt points out, "if we think about it grammatically, photography is always about positioning yourself in a way that projects you into the future."[5] Consideration of the future fundamentally shifts our viewing practices because it projects the photograph into time. For this woman in Romain's image, it means that we imagine her future, rather than her past. To think of Mama Ginen's future is to contradict the primary way we see the elderly because, more often than not, it is their past—their role as the holders of history and keepers of memory—that we focus on. To peer into the future of our elders is to anticipate their approaching death. Because there is presumably much more past behind the elders than there is future ahead of them, our usual view of aging is one more beholden to the past than to the future.

Listening to the image of Mama Ginen, we also hear her disapproval and the tone of her stern demeanor. And we hear questions: How do we see her? How does she—an elderly Haitian woman—register under our gaze? How does *she* see us? What do we expect from images of Haitian womanhood and where, or how, does she fit into these? Why are we even looking? How dare we look at an elder without permission? Even more, how dare we look into her eyes, because to show true respect for the elders means we must avert our eyes.[6]

Cultural representations of the elderly invariably cite a tradition in which older people must be respected and honored. Take for example the Haitian proverb, "Fanm se kajou, plis li vye, plis li bon" (the woman is like the *acajou* tree, the older she is the better she is) that seems to celebrate feminine aging and calls our attention to the position of elderly women in society.[7] Deconstructing its meaning, I wonder: what does "better" refer to in the proverb?[8] Better in what sense? Is it a reference to her social standing or to her contribution to society? Is it a comment on her value to men or to the entire community? Is it simply that, as a woman's age increases, she grows in wisdom, knowledge, and virtue? Is it the accumulation of her memories that positions her as a living monument to history?

The sentiment behind the proverb is consistent with the venerated position of the elderly in cultural tradition. Having earned their position of honor, elders are considered undeniably knowledgeable and worthy of utmost respect. If we follow the logic of the proverb that "fanm se kajou," what should happen is that as women age, their importance rises in the family structure in particular and in society in general.[9] They are to be revered for their wisdom and respected for the wealth of experience they have accrued over many years. Closer in proximity to the ancestors because of their age, the elders are endowed with a spiritual maturity and sacred significance.

Both the photograph and the proverb situate elderly women in relation to time—one in the future and one in the past. In the case of the proverb, we imagine the future of the woman beyond what her past dictates; with the photograph we focus on her past as a determination of her future. But what about her present? It is with both the photograph and the proverb in mind that, looking at the novels *L'œil-totem* (2006) and *The Infamous Rosalie* (2004) by Évelyne Trouillot and *Kasalé* (2003) by Kettly Mars, I begin my discussion about the ethical questions stemming from how elderly Haitian women are represented and seen in the present.

This chapter is charting new territory: sustained attention to age and aging is not widespread in critical studies of Haitian literature.[10] To be clear, it is not that elderly protagonists are absent from the literature itself, only that literary criticism rarely focuses on aging and how it figures in the subject's ontology.[11] Of course, this tendency to disregard age is not specific to Haitian literary analysis: "unlike gender and race and other social constructs that affect our identities, age has often been overlooked as a subject of study," as other feminist scholars have pointed out.[12] But radical Black feminists like Audre Lorde were among the first to include age as a category of identity relevant to intersectionality. Lorde's essay "Age, Race, Class, and Sex: Women Redefining Difference" is a powerful example of how including age enhances Black feminist theorizing. Enumerating the ways that society refuses to embrace multiple subjectivities, preferring instead to lock people into binaries, Lorde writes, "Much of Western European history conditions us to see human differences in simplistic opposition to each other: dominant/subordinate, good/bad, up/down, superior/inferior . . . Within this society, that group is made up of Black and Third-World people, working-class people, older people, and women."[13] As Lorde makes clear, thinking about age as a category enables us to move beyond difference. Lorde also examines age as a category in relation to Black women's interiority when she asks what being seen as "old" does to how Black women see the world.

My readings of elderly protagonists attend to the dynamic that Lorde observes, namely that being part of a group usually defined as "other, deviant, inferior, or just plain wrong" requires cultivating a practice of observation—what she calls "watchfulness."[14] What does being old mean about how these women look at the world? Lorde's description of how members of oppressed groups must become "watchers" aligns well with my readings of our elderly protagonists who look at the world around them and watch how others perceive them.

As Lorde points out, aging is often processed through the lens of difference: "Certainly there are very real differences between us of race, age, and sex. But it is not those differences between us that are separating us. It is rather our refusal to recognize those differences, and to examine the distortions which result from our misnaming them and their effects upon human behavior and expectation."[15] This can aptly be said of Marie-Jeanne in *L'œil-totem,* Grandma Charlotte and Ma Augustine in *The Infamous Rosalie,* and Antoinette in *Kasalé.* The refusal of others to appreciate their differences results in human behavior and expectations that trouble relationships in the novels.

My readings of these novels demonstrate the complexity of aging that contrasts the lived experience of elderly women with the idea (*respekte gran moun*) of how they are perceived in society. These narratives also suggest that despite the prevailing idea that members of the older generation are to be honored, in practice as well as in cultural production, there is often a casual disregard for their individuated selves. It is as though the older the women become, the less they are seen for their fully developed personhood. I argue that the Black feminist ethic that emerges highlights aging as a location of identity alongside race, religion, class, and gender and asks that we look beyond the age of elderly women to see them for what they are other than old.[16]

Privileging the point of view of these elderly women allows us to appreciate their own perspectives on aging as well as to observe the challenges posed in familial relationships and social bonds as the women age.[17] Along with literary and cultural studies and Black feminist methodologies, throughout this chapter I draw from the field of age studies, which has been defined as "an area concerned with understanding how differences are produced by discursive formations, social practices, and material conditions."[18] I consider age as a category of analysis that functions *alongside* race, class, sexuality, and gender in determining power relations and locations of marginality. At the same time, I depart from much of the work done by scholars of age studies in my approach to these elderly Haitian protagonists, who are reminders of the importance of cultural specificity in interpretations of age as a category of analysis. Reading these novels with a Black feminist ethic reveals the utility of considering aging and intersectionality together because, for these Black women from the Global South, aging holds a trove of meanings that the local context illuminates.

There are two particular questions about aging that this chapter seeks to answer. First, how do these women experience their age through their bodies, their memories, and their social positions? Second, how do others within the community perceive them and the significance of their age? My analyses focus on the thoughts, feelings, and voices of elderly women in order to explore how traditional beliefs unfold across generations. How they look at themselves and how they look at others who look at them show that these women see and are aware that they are seen. Their interiority demonstrates the disconnect between how they see themselves and how others see them, as well as their acute perception of the latter. Just as Lorde points out in her essay mentioned above, the elderly women in these novels have cultivated "watchfulness." As older women, they are defiant and obstinate as well as calculating, sexual, and only rarely maternal in the conventional sense.[19]

Importantly, these women characters also exhibit signs of extreme weakness, contradicting the resilience trope that undergirds the figure of the poto-mitan, one of the dominant tropes of Haitian womanhood.[20] Both *Kasalé* and *L'œil-totem* disrupt socially regulated views of elderly women as the reliable maternal pillars of society. *The Infamous Rosalie* reinforces those claims, but in a way that makes them essential to the protagonist's development and links memory, history, and generational trauma. Ultimately these novels undermine the dominant construction of aging by offering alternative figurations of elderly identities.

In my view, this attitude of disruption and undermining is central to a Black feminist ethic because it asks us to imagine the lived experience of elderly women in a different frame and stages an encounter with elderly women that asks us to acknowledge their full humanity. As Kaiama Glover cautions in her riveting study, *A Regarded Self: Caribbean Womanhood and the Ethics of Disorderly Being,* "the codification of potentially constraining counter-discourses" risks limiting our readings of what women ought to be and do.[21] By acknowledging age as an important site of analysis or a location of identity that is consistent with how we understand the operations of sexuality, class, gender, and race, this chapter intervenes in the field of age studies from a perspective that is literary, Black, and Haitian. To date, scholarship in the area of age studies has rarely ventured into such terrain.[22] In *Figuring Age: Women, Bodies, Generations,* Katherine Woodward proposes that, "along with race and gender, age is [one of] the most salient markers of social difference."[23] What Woodward fails to acknowledge, however, is that these locations of identity function intersectionally: they are mutually constitutive and multiplicative. How *Kasalé, L'œil-totem,* and *The Infamous Rosalie* portray feminine aging introduces ethical questions for both the readers and the protagonists that revolve around class, gender, and spirituality. What does end-of-life care look like for women living in community, and how does it differ based on the setting? How does the value and respect for elderly people translate into the everyday? How are elderly people made visible as more than the bearers of wisdom and holders of tradition?

L'œil-totem's Marie-Jeanne and *Kasalé*'s Antoinette experience aging in diverse ways, three of which I focus on here: they process age mentally (interiority), materially through their bodies (embodiment), and socially in the community's view of them (watchfulness). As constitutive elements of the women's identities, the concepts of interiority, embodiment, and watchfulness enrich my analyses of these elderly protagonists. Also, the ethical, spiritual, and material realms in which they locate themselves are informed by the concepts of connection or intimacy, and movement or mobility. In the context of aging, these concepts reveal that aging is not static or contained but actually processual. This point may seem obvious when we recall that "age offers an interesting corrective as a way of approaching cultural analysis . . . because unlike gender, race, or even class, age is inherently transitional."[24] But still, when taken as central tropes for understanding feminine aging, mobility and connection challenge the normative ways of perceiving the elderly.

This contrast with usual views of the elderly is significant because "like Judith Butler's concept of gender, most age studies contend that women are more aged by culture than by their bodies, so that age may be understood as performance."[25] I agree that theories of performance are helpful for thinking through representations of aging, most especially if we want to challenge the prevailing idea that "aging is culturally understood as decline and not growth and change."[26] For the elderly protagonists I examine, growth and change are presented through the body: the physical movement of their bodies and how those bodies move from place to place show what it means to grow old from an embodied perspective and in relation to a place.

Attention to how Haitian women's bodies are marked by history, by trauma, and by different sociopolitical forces has been a major theme of Haitian women's writing. As the example of Coralie in Poujol-Oriol's novel *Vale of Tears* from the previous chapter demonstrates, the female body emerges as a site onto which these histories and tensions are mapped. Poujol-Oriol's careful descriptions of Coralie's body throughout *Vale of Tears* illuminate how it changes over the years throughout the novel.

While movement relates to how aging women exist in their own bodies, connection relates to how they exist with others, thus recalling the relational element of ethics that I highlighted in the previous chapter: "when we engage profoundly with one person, the responses come from both sides: this is responsibility and accountability . . . The object of ethical action is not an object of benevolence, for here responses flow from both sides."[27] Taking into consideration the ways in which "responses flow from both sides," I am interested in understanding how these elderly protagonists see themselves, how they are seen by others, and especially their awareness of the looking of others.

Representations of aging are often constructed around polarities used to define and describe the elderly, as can be seen through the lens of binary oppositions that (dis)regard aging in relation to youth: able-bodied/disabled, healthy/sick, desirable/undesirable, mobile/immobile. Such polarizations tend to be even more the case for women, for whom aging confers fewer social privileges than for men. While the proverb quoted earlier suggests that elderly women are valued, these three novels present a lived experience that does not align with this view. Poujol-Oriol offers an especially jarring portrayal of this alignment by juxtaposing the old and young versions of Coralie throughout *Vale of Tears*. The pretty, vibrant, and desirable young woman contrasts sharply with the disdained elderly woman she becomes.

It is important to recognize, however, that a Black feminist lens helps us to see through the binaries that define life for the elderly. Trouillot and Mars highlight the minds and bodies of elderly women, calling attention to their lived experience and emphasizing what positionality means for them. In doing so, they attend to "what *else* these women are other than old."[28] Focusing on mobility and connection facilitates an understanding of aging as growth and change rather than as decline. Overall, my focus is a gesture that refuses to cast older women in abject terms, a perspective that a Black feminist ethic facilitates by affirming relationality and care.

Connection involves myriad relations: it can be what bonds people together, it enlivens relationships, it invokes intimacy and care. For the elderly, connection is especially important because it can also prolong life. One of the main ways that these authors present connection is by pairing characters of different generations. But rather than highlight the difference between the older woman and her younger interlocutor, this pairing helps to dissolve the old/young binary as the reader notes the similarities between the two characters. In each novel, the relationship skips one generation so that we have a grandmother and a grandchild in *L'œil-totem*, two neighbors who are sixty years apart in age in *Kasalé*, and an adopted granddaughter, grandmother, and godmother in *The Infamous Rosalie*.

This juxtaposition communicates to the reader that the people in the generation immediately beneath the elderly person are unable to see them in the same light as the younger people in the third generation. Intimacy is created in these relationships through the body, through the sharing of stories, and through mutual understanding or recognition.

Because women so often move closer to the margins as they age, connection becomes increasingly important. For the protagonists in these novels, connection is not only exterior (how they relate to others) but interior (how they relate to themselves) and includes how they connect to a force greater than themselves, whether it is their faith, religious practice, or even in some cases superstition.

Mobility is another modality that informs the lives of the protagonists, drawing our attention to how these women move within the spheres they inhabit, pointing to agency and dynamism. Mobility as I interpret it is both the literal embodied movement of the protagonists and their various figurative movements. For example, how do they change positions in their mind or move from one memory to the other? What causes them to change course in their movements and decisions? When do they move and where do they go? In foregrounding the body, I mean to acknowledge how the bodies of older women are often disregarded or rendered invisible. Focusing on these women's bodies intentionally disrupts that tendency and opens space for thinking about feminist preoccupations, such as the body and desire from a different perspective. Through the mobility and connections that come to light in these women's interiority, embodiment, and watchfulness, Mars and Trouillot show the value of a Black feminist ethic for analyzing the multiple locations of Black women's identities.

"Je ne bougerai pas d'ici": Évelyne Trouillot's *L'œil totem*

As the example of Coralie in Poujol-Oriol's *Vale of Tears* demonstrates, encounters with difficult women—those Kaiama Glover provocatively dubs "disorderly women"—raise ethical questions for the reader as well as for other characters in the novel.[29] Citing Toni Morrison, Glover asks, "what choices are available to Black women outside of their own society's approval?"[30] Marie-Jeanne Thévenot Dorcil, the protagonist of Évelyne Trouillot's *L'œil-totem,* is one character whose life showcases what it looks like to grapple with limited choices. *L'œil-totem* tells the story of eighty-eight-year-old Marie-Jeanne, who refuses to leave her home despite her children's attempts to uproot her. Marie-Jeanne is a problem character who disorders the worlds of her family and neighbors and is determined to live beyond the confines of her family and society's approval. As a character who demands the right to be fully herself and do only what she wants, despite what those around her think, Marie-Jeanne's agency thwarts convention and poses problems for others. *L'œil-totem* presents a Black feminist critique primarily through the example of Marie-Jeanne's acute "sense of self-regard" evident in her extraordinary life and others' responses to her.

L'œil-totem begins with Marie-Jeanne's entrenched connection to the physical space she inhabits.

> Je ne bougerai pas d'ici. Au milieu de la nuit, les odeurs me réveillent pour me chasser de mon logis. C'est la prison la plus lourde à porter, cette persistance des senteurs de misères et de malheurs que je ne peux empêcher d'envahir ma demeure . . . Mais je suis encore prisonnière des odeurs qui me rappellent que mon permis de séjour a expiré depuis bien longtemps dans ce quartier qui ne se définit que par ce qu'il n'est plus . . .

> (I will not move from here. In the middle of the night, smells wake me up to chase me from my home. It is the heaviest prison to bear, this persistence of the scents of miseries and misfortunes that I cannot keep from invading my home . . . But I am still prisoner to the odors that remind me that my right to stay here expired a long time in this neighborhood that only defines itself by what it no longer is . . .) (13)

From the outset, Marie-Jeanne obstinately maintains her refusal to move. Her determination *not to move* stems from a willful attachment to the jar, what I read as the only agency available to her in her old age. Rooted in her sense of self-determination, her refusal disrupts her family's future plans for the home that is rightfully hers. Her immovability, her desire to remain planted, and her defiance of her children strike the reader as choices that pose problems for the novel's other characters. Marie-Jeanne's relationship to the space she inhabits stems from her belief that there is a treasure-filled jar hidden somewhere in her home. This legend of the jar and Marie-Jeanne's obsession with it inspire her to live on, and her intractable position is fundamentally about what she understands as her own right to agency.

As a willful heroine, Marie-Jeanne represents "the sociality of will" because she is "someone who does too much, too little, or in the wrong way."[31] For Marie-Jeanne's children, her community, and many others around her, what she does wrong is to refuse to allow others to dictate what must become of her life. From this perspective, it is helpful to read

Marie-Jeanne as an example of what Glover cogently articulates in *A Regarded Self*, describing women characters who "encourage us to imagine refusal itself as a legitimate critique and to not burden the refuser with an obligation to fix things or to refashion the world for all of us."[32] Everyone around Marie-Jeanne seems to desperately want her to fix herself according to what they deem appropriate for her. Her refusal to do so is all the more vexing to them because of her age.

Here I look at how Trouillot's unconventional character is remarkable for her militancy, her craft, and her sexuality. Well aware of how she is perceived by others, Marie-Jeanne is resolutely unperturbed by other people's expectations. Her determined self-possession can be read as a form of refusal invested in her own sense of what is right. She is a woman who exhibits a "refusal to cede primacy of their self."[33] Repeating "Je ne bougerai pas d'ici" multiple times, she reinforces her independent position and her intention to remain in her home no matter what. I also read this as a determination to center her own positionality. Her unwillingness to move from the house reflects an unwillingness to be removed from her sense of self.

As a quintessential *fanm vanyan*, Marie-Jeanne's name also recalls a famous (and unrelentingly defiant) protagonist of Haitian history: Marie-Jeanne Lamartinière. Lamartinière was one of the rarely discussed female soldiers during the Haitian Revolution.[34] She is one of the few women whose story is at least somewhat known albeit through a very narrow lens. As one source describes her,

Compagne inséparable de Lamartinière, elle ne manque pas en effet de se distinguer hautement à ses côtés dans cette Crête-à-Pierrot assiégée par une armée française de plus de 12.000 hommes. Vêtue d'un costume genre mamelouk, elle portait un fusil en bandoulière et un sabre d'abordage attaché à un ceinturon d'acier. Une sorte de bonnet emprisonnait son opulente chevelure dont les mèches rebelles débordaient de la coiffure. Sous la pluie des projectiles, Marie-Jeanne allait d'un bout à l'autre des remparts, tantôt distribuant des cartouches, tantôt aidant à charger les canons. Et lorsque l'action devenait plus vive, crânement elle se précipitait au premier rang des soldats et jouait de la carabine avec un entrain endiablé.

(An inseparable companion to Lamartinière, [her husband, Louis Dare Lamartinière] she did not fail to highly distinguish herself at his side in Crête-à-Pierrot siege by a French army of more than 12,000 men. Wearing a mamelouk uniform, she carried a rifle slung over her shoulder and a boarding saber attached to a steel belt. A kind of bonnet contained her opulent hair, whose rebellious locks overflowed from her hairstyle. In the rain of projectiles, Marie-Jeanne went from one end to the other of the ramparts, sometimes distributing ammunition, sometimes helping to load the cannons. And when the action intensified, she would brazenly rush to the front row of the soldiers and deploy the rifle with a frenzied excitement.)[35]

Trouillot's use of the name Marie-Jeanne reflects her fascination with history and desire to amplify the stories of historic Haitian women. As she has written, "If we accept history as we are told it, women appear to have played a very small part in the Haitian revolution," but the story of Marie-Jeanne makes a small dent in the historic landscape.[36] Haitian history has remembered the revolutionary-era Marie-Jeanne as a bold and courageous soldier determined to fight for complete autonomy from France. Motivated by a love for her husband and her people, the historic Marie-Jeanne sacrificed herself for the Haitian Revolution. By mentioning her appearance as well as her unswerving fearlessness, the historic accounts draw attention to her "femininity." Perhaps she too is an early example of Glover's "disorderly feminine."[37] Naming the novel's character—who is determined to be the author of her own destiny despite her children's best efforts—after a Revolutionary-era soldier invites us to evaluate her as an example of militancy, courage, and resistance. The link to the historic Marie-Jeanne becomes even more clear after we learn that Trouillot's protagonist was tortured and put in jail for refusing to betray her militant lover. I will return to a discussion of Marie-Jeanne's time in prison later in this chapter, but I mention it here to draw out the embedded reference to a version of Haitian history in which women are at the center. As a woman physically punished for refusing to betray her beloved, *L'œil-totem's* Marie-Jeanne displays how romantic love can also inspire an ethical stance of refusal.

The relationships in Marie-Jeanne's family reveal the patriarchal structure that she resists by her refusal to adhere to familial expectations. bell hooks has convincingly argued that Black feminism offers a model with a "vision of relationships where everyone's needs are respected, where everyone has rights, where no one need fear subordination or abuse, [running] counter to everything patriarchy upholds about the structure of relationships."[38] The disrespect of those needs and the disregard of those rights shore up the patriarchal order. Marie-Jeanne's interactions with family members demonstrate that her needs are not respected and the children are offended by her assertion of her rights. She refuses to yield or remain silent to allow her children to determine the outcome of her life, emblematizing what Glover calls "a woman character animated by a preservationist self-regard." [39] Her immovability frustrates and disrupts her children's sense of how an elderly woman should behave, and in that attitude, they disregard both their mother's present and their past ancestral heritage.

Even as it exposes the fraught dynamics that can ensnare women as they become elderly and must relate to family members differently, *L'œil-totem* ultimately serves as a tribute to the elderly that depicts the vicissitudes of old age in how they are perceived by both the aging subject and those around her. Trouillot's homage to older women begins in the novel's dedication honoring her own mother and grandmother, as well as "toutes ces figures de femmes, porteuses d'histoires, qui ont nourri mon enfance et posé sur moi *leur œil-totem*" (all of those women figures, the carriers of stories, who nourished my childhood and placed their lucky eye on me).

In an interview with *Le Nouvelliste,* Trouillot shares that the novel was born out of her own fascination with the elderly and a desire to explore the interior life of a much older person.[40] The title *L'œil-totem* has a double meaning because it represents the "lucky eye" named in the dedication and also refers to Marie-Jeanne's actual glass eye. The title acknowledges Marie-Jeanne as an elderly woman nourishing her grandchildren's generation with her lucky eye and as a woman whose participation in political resistance led to her being tortured and losing an eye as a result. I also read the "lucky eye" as a manifestation of the author's perspective; the novel is written from the vantage point of a writer looking to the elderly with curiosity and care. That Trouillot devotes so much of the story to Marie-Jeanne's rich inner life underlines her fascination with the elderly as she attempts to uncover "ce qui se cache derrière un sourire ridé, des pas qui traînent" (what hides beneath a wrinkled smile, dragging footsteps).[41]

Beneath Marie-Jeanne's wrinkled smile and dragging footsteps, the reader encounters a sexually liberated woman artist who is unconventional in the context of her generation, gender, and class. Keenly aware of what it means to be an aging woman in Haitian society and how others perceive her, Marie-Jeanne engages her interlocutors in her mind. She is viewed by her neighbors as strange and maybe even mentally unwell. Referring to the "carolus," the eighteenth-century form of currency that she believes is hidden in the jar, seen as an example of her eccentricity, the people in the neighborhood call her "Madame Karolis." Like her children, the neighbors do not understand why she remains in her home: "Ses habitants aujourd'hui n'expliquent ma présence qu'en se référant à mon excentricité. Je me répète à moi ce surnom qu'ils m'ont donné.

Madame Karolis, Madame Karolis" (The people who live here today can only explain my presence by referring to my eccentricity. I repeat to myself this nickname that they have given me. Madame Karolis, Madame Karolis) (13). While the moniker is based on their belief that she is odd and erratic, the neighbors still refuse to say it to her face, a fact that is not lost on Marie-Jeanne: "cela m'amuse qu'ils n'osent toujours pas me crier ouvertement ce surnom de folle" (it amuses me that they still will not dare to openly shout this nickname of crazy woman at me) (14). Here, as she does throughout the novel, Marie-Jeanne attests to her unfettered understanding of how others see her. As her inner thoughts reveal to us, her whole connection to the community pivots on how they see her in relation to how she sees herself.

If Marie-Jeanne learned from someone to espouse an ethic of self-regard, it was certainly from her Tante Clara Thévenot Anglade, a feminist who spoke unabashedly to her niece about pleasure and sex. Marie-Jeanne's affinity for Aunt Clara influences her determination to live her life as she pleases and not according to what those around her prefer. Marie-Jeanne describes how Tante Clara shared "histoires et légendes familiales qui remplissent nos esprits d'envolées d'images et d'idées dans lesquelles nous nous embrouillons avec délices" (stories and family legends that fill our minds with soaring images and ideas in which we entangle ourselves with delight) (21). An unconventional woman in her own right, Tante Clara was viewed negatively by the family for not abiding by the socially acceptable standards of respectability dictated to women of her generation. From a young age, Marie-Jeanne is intrigued by and drawn to this quirky aunt, whose way of being leaves an imprint on the girl: "Je devais avoir douze ans à l'époque, mais les paroles de Tante Clara Thévenot Anglade avaient déjà le pouvoir de fouetter ma sensibilité et de m'agripper par leur densité, même si leur sens profond m'échappait encore" (I must have been twelve years old at the time, but the words of Tante Clara Thévenot Anglade already had the power to stir up feelings in me and grip me because of their density, even if their deeper meaning still eluded me) (47).

Part of what made Tante Clara so memorable was her explicit public disavowal of gender norms. For example, unlike her Haitian women peers at the time, Tante Clara chose to remain child-free: "Je n'ai jamais voulu d'avoir d'enfants, disait-elle. Aucun sentiment maternel ne m'a suffisamment traversé pour que j'aie envie de me rendre aussi vulnérable face à quelqu'un et de voir en plus grossir mon ventre. Accusez-moi d'être inhumaine mais je ne trouve pas particulièrement esthétique le spectacle d'une femme enceinte" (I never wanted to have children, she used to say. No maternal sentiment had sufficiently crossed through me, for me to want to make myself so vulnerable to someone and to see my belly grow bigger. Accuse me of not being human, but I don't find the sight of a pregnant woman aesthetically pleasing) (47). She was also bald-faced in speaking to children about sex, love, and relationships, giving advice to her young nieces on topics from childbearing to falling in love: "Croyez-moi mes chères nièces, il ne faut jamais se donner corps et âme à quelqu'un. On se retrouve au bout du chemin avec les bras ballants et le cœur en écharpe" (Believe me my dear nieces, you mustn't give your body and soul to someone. One finds oneself, at the end of the road, with arms dangling and heart in a sling) (48). Tante Clara's advice for women to never give their bodies and souls away reflects a desire for self-protection and wholeness that must be guarded above all else. By establishing Tante Clara as a feminist force in Marie-Jeanne's life, Trouillot delineates her protagonist's development in terms of gender and power. To the student of Haitian feminism, the name Anglade recalls Miriam Neptune Anglade (1944–2010), the feminist intellectual whose work on Haitian women's contributions to the economy transformed the study of gender and development in the 1980s. Anglade's seminal study *L'autre moitié du développement: à propos du travail des femmes en Haïti* (1986) examines Haitian women's labor and their contributions to a society where they had been routinely overlooked.[42] Like the use of the name Marie-Jeanne, the reference to Anglade links Trouillot's protagonist to a longer tradition of Haitian women's history.

Marie-Jeanne can be accurately described as a feminist subject who is first and foremost "attentive to [her] individual needs and desires."[43] As Sara Ahmed notes, the "perception of feminist subjects as having too much will, or too much subjectivity, or just being too much, has profound effects on how we view ourselves as well as the worlds we come up against."[44] Among the different "worlds she comes up against," we find her family, her surrounding community, the US Marine-occupied state she lived in as a child, and the totalitarian regime she lived under in her adult life. Her determination to embody her own subjectivity and to be an agent of her own will becomes a problem that places her on the margins of her community and her family. This scenario confirms Glover's point that Caribbean women characters who choose to define their freedom for themselves and according to their own sense of self-regard rather than according to others' wishes challenge other characters in their textual worlds as well as the readers and scholars who analyze them.

Portrait of the Artist as an Elderly Woman

Repeatedly described as "Marie-Jeanne femme peintre, artiste et femme" (Marie-Jeanne the woman painter, an artist and a woman), *L'œil-totem*'s protagonist invites a meditation on what it means to be a woman artist in Haiti (69). The novel thus responds to Alice Walker's query in her impassioned collection, *In Search of Our Mothers' Gardens:* "What did it mean for a Black woman to be an artist in our grandmother's time?"[45] Évelyne Trouillot posits an answer to the question through Marie-Jeanne, whose anecdotes and reflections show what it was to be an artist and a Haitian woman in the early twentieth century. Art and creativity act as another sign of Marie-Jeanne's difference from those around her. That she is a woman artist disregarded and undervalued by those around her, including her family, is even more important given the significance of the woman artist as a Black feminist trope.

Marie-Jeanne's art emanates from her own lived experience. Describing her artwork in relation to the time she spent in prison, she said, "les tableaux . . . se divisent en deux périodes, avant et après, la prison pour moi" (my paintings are divided into two periods, before and after prison for me) (105). The traumatic event of imprisonment is explicitly linked to creative production; for the artist, trauma and politics color her oeuvre, both literally and figuratively. There is also a productive link between memory and her creative praxis as an artist: "Dans l'un des premiers tableaux que j'ai peints, j'ai saccagé ma mémoire pour y retrouver l'enfance avec de grandes taches bleuies de mer et de larmes, avec le souffle du vent et du temps" (In one of the first pictures I painted, I ransacked my memory to find my childhood with large blue strokes of sea and tears, with the breath of wind and time) (23–24). During a particularly difficult period of her life, she created art that reflected her pain: "C'est là que j'ai peint mes peintures les plus mordantes. Comme des plaies qui se cicatrisent et qui grésillent. On voudrait que la douleur s'arrête mais on sait qu'elle apporte aussi quelquefois, l'espérance de l'oiseau qui s'envole, juste le temps de la prochaine blessure" (This is where I painted my most powerful paintings. Like wounds that heal and sizzle. I would like the pain to stop but I know that it also sometimes brings the hope of the bird that flies away, just until the next injury) (52). That she is able to find hope in the wounds through creativity suggests the healing power of her art, highlighting the multiple functions of creative work for the artist.

While painting allows her to remember, her will to create was weaponized and used against her under the dictatorship. When she is questioned by the police and subsequently imprisoned, they mutilate her hands as a form of punishment; yet, "Même au milieu de mes délires et mon agonie, j'ai toujours su que mes mains affreusement mutilées pourraient encore servir. Je sentais à la pointe de mes doigts le flot des couleurs, la déban-dade des formes, la douleur des pinceaux ; mais ce bandage sur mes yeux me rendait folle d'angoisse" (Even in the middle of my delusions and my agony, I always knew that these terribly mutilated hands could still serve me. Through my fingertips, I could sense the flow of colors, the fading of forms, the pain of the brushes; but this bandage on my eyes made me crazy with anxiety) (57).

Though she might be misunderstood as a woman artist, the police understand the dynamic all too well, which is why they choose to pun-ish her by mutilating her hands. "Ma seule rencontre avec la souf-france physique pourrait être qualifiée de futile" (My only encounter with physical suffering could be called futile), she says, because despite her refusal to comply with the police orders, and despite how severely they torture her, they do end up finding her lover, Léo (56). She pays severely for being noncompliant with those in authority. The violation of her hands and her eyes compromises Marie-Jeanne's ability to create. Although she eventually regains control of her hands, the mutilation of her eye lasts for the remainder of her life, resulting in the *œil-totem* the title refers to. Marie-Jeanne's relationship to painting makes the violence that she is subject to all the more tragic as it deals a blow to her ability to work as an artist.

As we will see later with Kettly Mars's character Marylène in *Je suis vivant,* who is also an artist, Marie-Jeanne's relationship to her art trans-forms over the course of her life. Creativity takes on a life of its own and consumes her: "Personne n'a compris que ma peinture me dévorait tout entière et que je ne souhaitais aucune entrave à cette passion pour moi si péremptoire" (Nobody understood that my painting devoured me whole, and that I did not want anything to hinder this passion that was for me so peremptory) (52–53). Marie-Jeanne regularly invokes painting as a metaphor for various parts of her life. She connects her work as an artist to discrete moments that have positive and negative connotations—her trauma with the Marines, remembering the life of a friend, her sex life. The figurative brush strokes she uses to tell stories about her past are also the strokes of her artist's hand. People around Marie-Jeanne—especially her children—misunderstand her relationship to her art. As a mother, she is not afforded the luxury of abandoning everything for a creative life, and, when she attempts to do so, her children cannot forgive her.

Marie-Jeanne interacts with various aspects of herself and expresses her creative identity through her recollections: "on the inner screen of aging, these shadows—memories of younger selves, anticipation of older selves—meet, conflict, interact. Separation and continuity are the source of tension that helps us accommodate change. Incorporating previous states, we become the sum of what we have been. It is, paradoxically a permanently inchoate process."[46] Painting operates as one metaphor within this inchoate process, allowing Marie-Jeanne to use her creative expressions as a form of self-representation and visioning of the world. Explaining her attitudes toward order, Marie-Jeanne states: "Je déteste qu'on me dicte quoi faire, qu'on soit militaire ou médecin" (I hate being told what to do, whether by a military man or a doctor) (57). Like the "disorderly women" Glover describes, Marie-Jeanne thwarts the conventions of Haitian womanhood.

Aging and Interiority

Interiority, defined by Kevin Quashie as "the quality of being inward," is one of the hallmarks of Black feminist literature.[47] The interior represents "the inner reservoir of thoughts, feelings, desires, fears, and ambitions that shape a human self."[48] As a Black feminist preoccupation, the interior can serve as a guide to Black women's lived experience that is unmolested by respectability or other conventions of the social world. The interior gives the reader of *L'œil-totem* a proximity to the inner workings of Marie-Jeanne's mind. It is because of her inner thoughts, feelings, sensations, and anxieties that the reader apprehends how old age registers mentally and materially. As such, Marie-Jeanne is an alluring example of what Quashie deems "the agency of paying attention, asking questions, and considering."[49] Whenever Marie-Jeanne pays attention to the process of aging, it is about how old age is lived in her own body *and* how it is interpreted by others around her. Marie-Jeanne's interiority responds to Anca Cristofovici's invitation "to consider aging not only as an extension of our lives in time, but also as an extension of our understanding of who we are and how we relate to others."[50]

When Marie-Jeanne thinks to herself that "la vieillesse ne se cache pas dans le sang qui coule trop clair dans la vie qui s'en va au compte-goutte, avec chaque souffle volé au papillon qui passe, avec chaque filet de regard qui s'affole sur un rayon de pluie" (old age does not hide itself in the blood that flows too clear in the life that is dripping away, with every breath stolen from the passing butterfly, with every glance that panics upon seeing a ray of rain), she is reflecting on the visibility of old age to the person experiencing it and to those who surround her (20). Just as old age cannot hide from others, Marie-Jeanne does not attempt to hide it from the reader. For this protagonist, feminine aging is not a taboo subject; rather it is one that she regularly mulls over with transparency. Thinking deeply about what it means to grow old and what is lost in the process, Marie-Jeanne's poetic language captures her ruminations. Her references to blood and breath connect to the materiality of the body; they also reinforce that the imminence of death is ever looming for the elderly.

Marie-Jeanne describes aging as a dynamic process, and she is acutely, at times painfully, aware of how that process occurs in her body. But there is also, in these interior thoughts, a sense of fatigue with growing old. She longs to escape from the monotony of her day-to-day life. As she watches more of her friends succumb to death, Marie-Jeanne finds herself less eager to meet each passing day: "La vieillesse c'est ne pas pouvoir toujours répondre à cette question, par oubli, par lâcheté, par lassitude. Et tout simplement aussi parfois parce que l'envie de me réveiller ailleurs entrave mon sommeil" (Old age is not always being able to answer this question, because of forgetfulness, cowardice, weariness. And quite simply sometimes because the desire to wake up elsewhere hinders my sleep) (20).

Marie-Jeanne's rich inner life, her interiority, exhibits an ability to question her own thoughts and beliefs, to look for other worlds, realities, and possibilities beyond what she knows. In this, too, I read the contours of her interior life as a Black feminist response to the monolithic view of aging. Within this inner monologue we notice that Marie-Jeanne is explicit about feminine aging—she viscerally experiences her body's limitations and discomforts; and, whether she is contemplating moving with difficulty or going through menopause, her detailed descriptions are assiduously embodied. "La ménopause d'abord, avec sa gueule de 'Que tu veuilles ou non, me voici!' ses jeux de fibromes et de cycles déréglés, son sang aux couleurs stériles, ses crises et ses élans, sa façon bien à elle de te faire comprendre qu'elle est là" (Menopause comes first as if screaming, "whether you like it or not here I am!" The interplay of fibroids and irregular cycles, of blood in a sterile color, of fits and starts, its way of its own to make you understand that it has arrived) (77). Her thoughts to herself about what it means to grow old are often punctuated by insightful comments about what it *feels like to grow old*:

Aujourd'hui—point parfois nébuleux à définir entre hier et demain—voilà que ce corps voudrait m'imposer des limites ! . . . La vieillesse c'est suivre la décadence de son corps ami déloyal avec qui on a partagé trop d'aventures pour lui tenir longtemps rigueur.

(Today—sometimes a nebulous point to define between yesterday and tomorrow—here is my body wanting to impose limits on me! . . . Old age is like following the decadence of your disloyal friend, your body, with whom you have shared too many adventures to hold that against it for a long.) (77)

Here Marie-Jeanne's reference to her body in terms of betrayal evokes duplicity because she never knows what to expect from it now. That she sees her body as an old friend who begins to betray her suggests a split between her mind and her body—a familiar relationship that becomes increasingly unfamiliar.

Another way that Marie-Jeanne frames aging in her mind is through community. Thinking about the people around her whom she has lost over the years, she laments the invasiveness of death that keeps snatching her friends and family, that to be elderly is to experience continual loss. In these thoughts, she reinforces Cristofovici's observation that, "as a rule, loss and mourning accompany the discourse of aging":[51] "Nous ne savons pas compter la mort, dit le poète. Il me semble depuis quinze ans que je vis avec eux. Comment les compter sans me considérer moi-même comme l'un d'entre eux, oublié dans un monde où les gens à qui parler sont tous partis. Je ne vais plus aux funérailles" (We do not know how to count death, says the poet. It seems to me that I have lived with them for fifteen years. How can I count them without seeing myself as one of them, forgotten in a world where people to talk to have all gone. I don't go to funerals anymore) (50).

Death appears imminent to Marie-Jeanne, and she sees it as the only thing that will separate her from her home: "Ce lieu est mon domaine conçu pour rêves fous, pour œil-totem, cœur déjoué, sexe affamé. Madame Karolis ne peut se payer le risque d'être malade. La mort seule peut la déloger" (This place is my domain constructed for crazy dreams, for the totem eye, for a heart without joy, and for a famished sex. Madame Karolis cannot run the risk of being sick. Only death can dislodge her) (99). Her sense of connection to the material space she inhabits and her determination to never leave it assert one of the greatest challenges of aging: too often, elderly people are uprooted and displaced against their will.

Marie-Jeanne's acts of remembering take on a different tone when, early in the novel she relates a childhood encounter with the Marines that leaves a traumatic imprint and illustrates how history, gender, and power collide in her life. This example reminds the reader that the US Marine Occupation had insidious effects on Haitian girls and women and that even children were not spared from the intrusion of the foreign military occupation. The period of the occupation is especially relevant in the context of Haitian feminism. According to Danièle Magloire, the development of Haitian feminism can be linked to the resistance to the US Occupation of Haiti (1915–34), when "des Haïtiennes, issues de la petite bourgeoisie et de la bourgeoisie, se sont mobilisées dans les villes pour contester cette 'domination totale,' comme le faisaient déjà des groups de paysans et paysannes en armes. En lien avec cette résistance à l'Occupation, mais de manière autonome, ces femmes vont constituer une antenne locale de La ligue international des femmes pour la paix et la liberté" (Haitian women, from the petite bourgeoisie and the bourgeoisie, rallied in the cities to challenge this 'total domination,' as groups of armed peasants were already doing. In connection with this resistance to the Occupation, but autonomously, these women created a local branch of The International League of Women for Peace and Freedom).[52]

It is in this light that we can understand Marie-Jeanne's feminist consciousness and that of her aunt whose description resonates with the type of activist woman Magloire discusses. Furthermore, and as Magloire also points out, among the organizing efforts of these first feminists was the need to address "les agressions sexuelles perpétrées par les Marines envers les femmes et les filles . . . Ce faisant, les Haïtiennes se sont posées comme sujet politique affirmant leur agentivité" (sexual aggressions against Haitian women and girls perpetrated by the Marines . . . As such, Haitian women positioned themselves as political subjects affirming their agency).[53]

As a young child of seven or eight, Marie-Jeanne becomes an example of the sexual violation of Haitian girls during the Occupation. Her traumatic encounter with Marines occurred while she was walking through her neighborhood with her siblings and cousins: "Quand je vois les Marines, il est trop tard pour rebrousser le chemin. J'aurais pu le faire mais je ne veux pas déclarer ouvertement ma peur" (When I see the Marines, it is too late to turn back. I could have done it but I don't want to openly declare my fear) (25–27). Even at such a young age, she is immediately aware of the threat that the US Marines pose and the hypocrisy of the imperial exercise at work.[54] She says, "Il m'attire tout contre lui et me donne un baiser de bête enragée, je sens sa langue m'insulter tandis que ses mains remontent ma jupe et me touchent avec brutalité . . ." (He pulls me towards him and gives me the kiss of an enraged animal, I feel his tongue insulting me while his hands move my up skirt and touch me brutally . . .) (26). Because of the ellipsis, we as readers do not know exactly what happens next, although we can draw conclusions from Marie-Jeanne's retelling.

The white soldier's digital penetration of little Marie-Jeanne is an instance of sexual violation that traumatizes her for life: "Ne pourras-tu donc jamais oublier les doigts de ce blanc dans ta chair?" (Will you ever be able to forget the fingers of this white man in your flesh?) (18). This childhood sexual trauma also has a negative impact on her sexual relationships when she is a young woman. Reflecting on the incident, she describes it as "cet après-midi d'avril 1916, un jour de vent persistant et doux. Un jour qu'on ne raconte pas aux grandes personnes pour que la douleur n'en devienne pas plus forte, et que l'humiliation ne grandisse pas davantage" (that afternoon in April 1916, a day of persistent and mild wind. It is a day we never tell the grown-ups about so that the pain doesn't get stronger, and the humiliation even greater) (24). The children do not share what happens with adults because they understand the presence of the Marines as a form of structural violence.

But remaining silent exacerbates Marie-Jeanne's feelings of shame. As readers bearing witness to this violated child's pain, we see how shame infiltrates the lives of survivors, especially when they are children who do not understand what is happening to them. Many decades later, shame and fear continue to calibrate Marie-Jeanne's memories of the incident: "Quelquefois quand ma mémoire se fait complice de ma honte, elle ne garde de cette journée que l'écho des voix bouleversées et sourdes de mes sœurs et mes cousins, le bruit des feuilles et des branches contre les tôles et sur le pavé, et les reflets d'un visage rubicond" (Sometimes when my memory is an accomplice to my shame, it recalls of this day only the echo of the horrified and muffled voices of my sisters and my cousins, the noise of leaves and branches against sheet metal and on the pavement, and the reflections of a ruddy face) (24). Marie-Jeanne's awareness of how this trauma affects her further shapes her subjectivity. She understands that this violation is sexual abuse, that it occurred because of a power differential, and that by remaining silent she is sparing her parents a greater humiliation while they themselves are the victims of American empire. Even the placement of this story—early in the first chapter—where it appears freely associated with her painting, confirms that trauma informs how she becomes who she is.

Peppered throughout Marie-Jeanne's interior monologue are rhetorical questions that she both queries herself and imagines others asking. In a

long passage about one of her first lovers, Bernard, she imagines him interrogating her about that traumatic encounter during the Occupation and
its lasting effects on her mind. He is noticeably dismissive of the wounds
of sexual abuse on her mind and body: "Oui, je sais qu'un événement
tragique t'est arrivé, lors de l'occupation américaine, mais n'est-il pas
devenu, lui aussi, au fil des ans, une arme de plus à utiliser dans ta quête
de la démesure?" (Yes, I know that a tragic event happened to you during
the American occupation, but has it not also become, over the years, one
more weapon to use in your quest for excess) (75).

The childhood encounter with the Marines also foreshadows Marie-
Jeanne's recollection of her time in prison, because of which she suffers
from ongoing post-traumatic stress disorder and sustains a lasting injury.
The reader wonders how much and what Marie-Jeanne will share with
her grandson about this past, about the memory of the prison that is
heavy for her to carry. What interests me about Marie-Jeanne's relationship to memory is how well it evinces a "shifting I" outlined by M. Jacqui
Alexander in *Pedagogies of Crossing* when she describes the relationship
between voice and memory. According to Alexander, "Modulations in
voice, therefore, are an opening that permits us to hear the muse, an
indication of how memory works, how it comes to be animated."[55] I read
Marie-Jeanne's ruminations about how memory works, and traumatic
memories especially, as grounded in an understanding and privileging
of her own voice. Moving somewhat quickly from one memory to the
next, Marie-Jeanne's interiority indicates that, for an aging woman, paying attention to where your mind goes is a form of agency, even when you
cannot control the flow of those memories.

Alongside this nuanced portrait of our unconventional elderly heroine
is how the aging subject sees herself in relation to how the world sees her.
Building on Glover's point that nonbelonging can be a sign of resistance, I
read Marie-Jeanne's refusal to be what her children want her to be as both
resistance and determination. As I discuss earlier in this chapter, one of the
driving conflicts of the novel is the strained relationship between Marie-
Jeanne and her children. Meditating on why this relationship is so fraught,
Marie-Jeanne wonders if her frustration might be linked to her affinity
for Tante Clara, who her mother criticized for not caring about children.

J'apprends à vivre avec ces malaises que sont mon fils cadet et ma fille unique.
Mais je me demande de plus en plus si j'aurai jusqu'au bout le cynisme néces-
saire pour considérer Daniel et Josie comme mes enfants alors que mon mépris
et ma colère augmentent . . .

(I am learning to live with the discomfort that my second son and my only daughter are to me. But I wonder more and more if I will have until the end the cynicism necessary to consider Daniel and Josie as my children as my contempt and anger increase . . .) (47)

Increasingly resentful of how her children treat her, Marie-Jeanne mulls over why their relationship devolved into such acrimony. The passage above manifests her ability to lean into the discomfort and wonder what it means about her; she demonstrates the kind of willingness to be self-critical that emanates from a curious mind. Far from being fixed in her ways even as an octogenarian, Marie-Jeanne's attention to her interior becomes an opportunity for self-reflection and critique. Her interiority unveils her capacity to consider her own contributions to the soured relationship and find ways to explain it other than only blaming the disconnect on her children.

Similarly, Marie-Jeanne's inner thoughts about her grandson's opinion of her display the same awareness of how she is seen by others that we saw in relation to her neighbors and children, what Lorde calls "watchfulness." The reader cannot help but notice how often Marie-Jeanne wonders what Dimitri thinks about her. On the one hand, she imagines that he sees her as little more than an "eccentric grandmother." But in describing herself with "deviance that amuses rather than shocks" she acknowledges how she playfully relates to her grandson. The cross-generational relationship between Dimitri and his grandmother can be read as a critique that counteracts the exclusion of the elders from other parts of society. The pair's relationship is animated by the idea of transgenerational sharing and transmission.[56] As I show later on in this chapter with Sophonie and Antoinette in *Kasalé,* we see that Dimitri is the only one positioned to carry on his grandmother's legacy and memory. A similar dynamic unfolds in *The Infamous Rosalie* in which the older women pass on the memories of life under slavery to the young protagonist.

As an example of the protagonist's acute "sense of self-regard," Marie-Jeanne's awareness of how others perceive her (what I have been referring to as her watchfulness) activates the novel's Black feminist critique. Not only is her sense of self-regard informed by how she sees herself, but she is also deeply critical of how others see her. Just as the name Madame Karolis signifies the neighbors' opinion of her, she shrewdly observes, "ma fille pose sur mon pays un regard made in US" (My daughter looks at my country with a perspective that is "made in the USA") (104). Marie-Jeanne's judgment is instructive insofar as it reminds the reader that migration is not the goal for every Haitian. Her recognition of how often a "made in the USA" perspective harmfully looks down on Haiti is without question informed by her experience living under the occupation during her youth. The authors of *Gender, Social Inequalities, and Aging* point out that "ageism is unique from all other oppressions because we shall all become old. . . dependency in old age may not be bad, provided one has control over their own care."[57] *L'œil-totem* amplifies how dependency in old age unfolds for an elderly Haitian woman artist who must negotiate relationships with her community and her children. Trouillot does not merely expose the problems with how the elderly are mistreated but, through careful attention to Marie-Jeanne's interior life, invites the reader to pose ethical questions about the experiences, emotions, negotiations, and knowledges of an octogenarian.

A Relational Ethic of Intergenerational Connection

As the second narrator of *L'œil-totem,* Dimitri, in his perception of his grandmother, provides an important vantage point of how Marie-Jeanne is seen by others. Trouillot's use of a double-voiced narrative structure with alternating chapters reinforces the importance of relation and recognition in a Black feminist ethic. This relational dynamic introduces ethical questions about the position of the elderly in society. Offering a point of view that is different from yet sympathetic to Marie-Jeanne, Dimitri's perspective shows how the younger generation, which does not have the same responsibility as the generation in between, encounters the elderly.

The narrative structure of *L'œil-totem* suggests that an ethic of care and connection is necessary for Marie Jeanne's survival, especially when family tensions arise. A telling example is when Dimitri's parents urge him to convince Marie-Jeanne to leave the house. They attempt to use the close relationship between grandmother and grandson to their advantage and essentially have Dimitri do their bidding: "Mais toi Dimitri tu devrais essayer de la convaincre qu'elle ne peut continuer à vivre dans ce quartier de plus en plus insalubre et dangereux" (But you Dimitri should try to convince her that she cannot continue to live in this increasingly unhealthy and dangerous neighborhood) (32). But when Dimitri explains to his parents what he and his grandmother are doing, he emphasizes collaboration and connection: "Actuellement, elle et moi travaillons à reconstituer l'arbre généalogique de la famille depuis l'aïeul Joseph Thévenot" (She and I are currently working on rebuilding the family tree, starting with our ancestor Joseph Thévenot) (37). He is clear about his mission with his grandmother and what he hopes to achieve through their work together, and he also seems inclined to protect his grandmother from her children (his parents and aunts). Whereas Dimitri listens to stories about the jar with interest, the other family members are further perplexed and annoyed by the mystery that lies at the heart of the novel: where is the treasure-filled jar that Marie-Jeanne fixates on, and why is it so important to her?

Through Dimitri's eyes we experience the tension between generations and the possibility for a different relationship in the future. Marie-Jeanne shares the family history with Dimitri and insists that he transcribe the genealogy. Dimitri learns from and appreciates his grandmother in ways he had not anticipated. Their exchanges are often humorous and charming, conveying an easy rapport across generations. She berates him for his ageism: "Ne me traite pas en vieille femme sénile, Dimitri, ne m'enlève pas une parcelle de vie, fut-elle douloureuse" (Do not treat me like and old senile woman, Dimitri, do not take one bit of life away from me, be it ever so painful) (40). Her chiding stems from her commitment to living as fully as possible, no matter her age.

And Dimitri understands that he should not try to discourage her. His words make clear that, unlike his parents, he admires her determination: "Du haut de leurs 88 années d'existence, les yeux de Marie-Jeanne me transmettent clairement leur détermination et me mettent en garde contre toute interférence" (From the height of their 88 years of existence, the eyes of Marie-Jeanne transmit clearly to me their determination and put me on guard against any interference) (35). He looks at his grandmother, sees her determination, and understands that he must not interfere with her will. He looks at her and *sees* her. Dimitri cares deeply about his grandmother and her fate in the home she lives in, a concern that relates to her age but also shows that he cares about her emotional state: "je ressentais si souvent au cours de la semaine l'angoisse de la retrouver blessée ou boule-versée, en choc ou en délire, malheureuse ou sénile" (I felt so often during the week the anguish of finding her hurt or upset, in shock or delirium, unhappy or senile) (35). His concerns for her safety above all else contrast starkly with his parents' preoccupation with the land and the home.

Together, grandmother and grandson pore over the genealogic documents and their creation of the archive that strengthens and preserves familial bonds. Their partnership is grounded in this work of preservation and memory. I am especially interested in their rapport as an example of Black feminist relation because it, too, pivots on memory, connection, and movement. The stories Marie-Jeanne tells Dimitri reveal her investment in safekeeping family histories. For her, the intergenerational relationship with Dimitri helps to combat a sense of alienation, establishes the possibility of preserving and continuing her legacy, and offers a unique perspective that is infused with life.

The extent to which Marie-Jeanne's relationship with Dimitri diverges sharply from her relationship to others is shown especially in how her attachment to the jar that she is searching for is a source of frustration for people around her. Dimitri's aunt Josie expresses to him her exasperation with her mother in no uncertain terms:

> Ne me dis pas qu'elle n'a jamais mentionné la fameuse jarre, elle qui me parle que de ça. J'ai grandi avec cette obsession de ma mère. Elle lui a sacrifié sa famille, d'abord Papa, puis nous, ses enfants . . . La jarre de maman a envahi notre espace et notre enfance. La maison elle-même n'était importante que parce qu'elle pouvait cacher cette fameuse jarre. Seule sa peinture, autre obsession de ma mère.

> (Do not tell me that she never mentioned the famous jar, she who talks to me only about that. I grew up with this obsession of my mother's. She sacrificed her family, first Dad, then us, her children . . . Mom's jar invaded our space and our childhood. The house itself was important only because it could hide this famous jar. Only secondary to this was her painting, another obsession of my mother.) (41)

Tante Josie sees Marie-Jeanne's "obsession" as an intrusion and "invasion" of the family. Marie-Jeanne's children's contempt for the jar, which to her functions as a sacred object but which they see as a product of her imagination, manifests in their comments that range from disregard to disdain (41).

The children's feelings toward their mother stem from perceived neglect. By showing the disconnect between what the children expect from a mother and how their mother chooses to live her own life, *L'œil-totem* enacts an important feminist critique in which motherhood is not the most significant role in a woman's life. Marie-Jeanne is following her aunt's legacy. Despite the fact that, unlike Tante Clara, she became a mother, she has not allowed the primacy of motherhood to dictate her existence. It is hard to overstate how unconventional it is for a woman of Marie-Jeanne's generation and age to behave this way. Her determination to assert her own autonomy independent of her children should be read as a feminist impulse. It is also one that resonates with Glover's contention that, for disorderly women characters, an ethic of self-regard unconventionally privileges the individual over the community.[58] Part of privileging of the self requires rethinking and often resisting the heteropatriarchy of normative family structures requiring women to be mothers a priori. While Marie-Jeanne does not go as far as Tante Clara in this regard, her uneasy relationship with her children counters a static view of motherhood.

But, as I pointed out in my readings of Régine Romain's photograph *Mama Ginen* and my invocation of Lorde's "Age, Race, Class, and Sex" essay, the other side to consider being looked at is an awareness of how others look at them. The result is an elderly double consciousness. To take it even further, the intensity of the external gaze (being looked at) also triggers the internal gaze (interiority), causing the older woman to look for other possibilities (worlds). Whether it is her grandson, her children, or the people in her neighborhood, Marie-Jeanne is keenly aware of others' perceptions of her. Without access to her interior, the reader would not understand how profoundly complex her evaluation of these interactions is. After one session with Dimitri, she wonders, "Où es-tu parti Dimitri? si je t'ennuie, tu le déclares carrément, mais ne me reste pas en silence à me regarder avec des yeux à demi morts" (Where are you, Dimitri ? If I bore you, tell me clearly, but do not stay there in silence looking at me with half dead eyes) (37). The activity of the interior that we witness in Marie-Jeanne reflects her fears, insecurities, evaluations, and judgments of others. The power of her interiority lies in her ability to see the world for herself and articulate it on her own terms.

Sex and the Elderly Citizen

Marie-Jeanne relates to her own body not only as a site of physical aging but also as what was once a locus of pleasure. She speaks openly about sex with various men, so much so that that her children berate her for impropriety. Again, the older generation is seen as more sexually liberated, defying convention. Sex and sexuality play an operative role in how Marie-Jeanne self-actualizes, showing that "the terms of her self-regard are sexual," as is true of the protagonists Glover examines in *A Regarded Self*. As an elderly woman, her relationship to sex is yet a further example of her radical unconventionality, especially for a woman of her generation.[59]

Of the protagonists that I examine in this chapter, Marie-Jeanne is the most explicit about sexual pleasure and the importance of her sexuality, in terms of both how it has influenced her life and how others perceive her. The materiality of her body is communicated in scenes about sexual desire and old age. These two modalities are not often placed together, but an intersectional perspective allows us to hold them together. Further, her sex life is another area in which we discern Marie-Jeanne's hatred of being told what to do. Put simply, Marie Jeanne insists on being a sexual being. In her explicit embrace of her sexual self, she discusses her sexual experience in detail, lists her lovers, and considers what each of these men has meant to her. Just as she is aware of her own desire for pleasure and companionship, she understands how others see her and judge her as a result. Much of this judgment comes from her children, who are unable and unwilling to see their mother as a sexual subject. Of her daughter Josie, Marie-Jeanne thinks to herself, "Josie qui persiste à ne voir en moi que la femme de son père affirme que je vis depuis plus de quarante ans dans le péché" (Josie, who insists on seeing me only as her father's wife, says that I have been living in sin for more than forty years) (52).

Marie-Jeanne's frank way of talking about sex and pleasure becomes apparent at the beginning of the novel as she discusses her first sexual encounter and reveals that it took her ten years to discover the pleasure of orgasm. Recounting her experience with the first man she married, she mentions his foul-smelling penis and testicles: "Monsieur Dorcil a peur de perdre sa virilité en se lavant trop souvent les testicules. Monsieur Dorcil fait l'amour comme on se gratte et il m'a fallu attendre dix ans et cinq amants après sa mort pour comprendre la beauté du délire" (Mr. Dorcil is afraid of losing his manhood by washing his testicles too often. Mr. Dorcil makes love as one scratches an itch, and I had to wait ten years and five lovers after his death to understand the beauty of ecstasy) (16). The "beauté du délire" that Marie-Jeanne refers to is explicit in naming how long it took for her to orgasm and the beauty of that experience. Later on, while narrating her experience with another lover that leads to her arrest, she is again unequivocal about their passionate lovemaking: "quand nous avions le temps, Léo Blanchard et moi on s'aimait avec folie" (when we had the time, Leo Blanchard and I made love madly) (54). That Marie-Jeanne's repeated references to her sexual pleasure and desire mark her as unconventional in the context of her time and generation should prompt us to wonder why we do not see older women as sexual subjects. None of her comments are shocking; rather, they invite us to question how we are accustomed to thinking (or not thinking) about the elderly as sexual and sensual.

As an erotic subject, Marie-Jeanne strays from the model of Caribbean womanhood described by Mimi Sheller that demands women to "perform normative scripts of sexual citizenship such as the good mother, the respectable woman, the worthy Christian . . . which involved the harnessing and simultaneous disavowal of the erotic potential of the body."[60] This is clear as Marie-Jeanne underlines her family's refusal to accept her as a sexual being.

> Après dix-huit ans d'habitude conjugale, personne ne comprit ma décision de vivre seule *au milieu des plus fortes passions.* Personne ne m'a pardonné surtout de ne pas avoir caché *mes liaisons,* d'avoir aimé ouvertement Carlo, Bernard, Frédérique, Maurice, Léo, ces hommes qui ont partagé avec moi, à chacun leur façon, leur humanité. Personne n'a compris que ma peinture me dévorait tout entière et que je ne souhaitais aucune entrave à cette passion pour moi si péremptoire. Tous ces hommes d'ailleurs—sauf Frédérique—s'accro-chaient à la vie par une force plus exigeante que le lien qui les unissait à moi.

> (After eighteen years of married life, no one understood my decision to live alone in the middle of my strongest passions. Most of all, no one forgave me for not hiding my sexual liaisons, for having openly loved Carlo, Bernard, Frederick, Maurice, Leo, those men who shared with me, each in their own way, their humanity. No one understood that my painting was completely devouring me and that I did not want any hindrance to this passion which was for me so peremptory. Incidentally, all of these men, except for Frederique, were clinging to life by a force more demanding than the bond that united them to me.) (52–53)

As we will see in chapter 3 on the ethical-erotic, sexual desire for Marie-Jeanne is linked to her identity as an artist. Each of the men she names as her lover is also an artist—we learn that Bernard is a musician and Carlo is a poet—further reflecting how sex and creativity are coupled in her life. I read Marie-Jeanne's first-person account of the connection between her sexuality and her art as a Black feminist position that refuses to capitulate to the respectability demanded of women her age, especially by their own families. Instead, she revels in the intimate nature of cre-ativity for the woman artist whose sexual proclivities link to her art. The relationship between Marie-Jeanne's identity as an artist and as a sexual being reinforces the idea of world-making essential to a Black feminist ethic. She makes art and she makes love; the two complement each other and can even be substituted for one another. An important part of *L'œil-totem's* contribution as a Black feminist text is that it tells one woman's story of how sex and art converge in a woman's life, despite the com-munity's refusal to see her as either a sexual being or an important artist.

What are we to make of Marie-Jeanne's determination to belong, to remain planted, and to refuse the role and place that her children designate for her? Is her refusal to comply with what is expected of women in her

age group all that qualifies *L'œil-totem* as a Black feminist text? To answer
that question, we can "take as given Black feminist inquiry as a site of critique that challenges monolithic notions of Black womanhood" as Valerie
Smith instructs in *Not Just Race, Not Just Gender*. In this light, Trouillot's
portrayal of an unconventional older woman accomplishes several goals.
First, the story itself removes this older woman from obscurity, thus asking the reader to take age into account in applying an intersectional lens.
Second, in its razor-sharp focus on Marie-Jeanne's interiority, *L'œil-totem*
reveals how the inner lives of older women have been neglected in feminist discourses. Third, Marie-Jeanne's watchfulness showcases an elderly
woman still in search of a world beyond the restrictions of what others
deem as appropriate. A reading informed by the theory of intersectionality illuminates how Marie-Jeanne's lived experience as an older woman is
constantly in negotiation for her and for those around her.

Marie-Jeanne la marginale

Trouillot describes Marie-Jeanne as "une marginale, une femme non-pas
insouciante, mais certainement indifférente parfois aux regards que les
autres posent sur elle" (a marginal person, a woman who is not entirely
carefree, but certainly indifferent at times to the looks others turn on
her).[61] The more she ages, the more the protagonist of *L'œil-totem* remains
indifferent to how others see her. Even with her pronounced "sense of self-
regard," for the protagonist of *L'œil-totem*, the aging process brings pain,
reflection, and regret; still, despite its difficulties, it would be incorrect to
say that Marie-Jeanne's experience of old age is only negative. Whereas
she may appear invisible and forgotten by her children, for her grandson
and for the reader, she occupies the center stage.[62]

Also at stake in this examination of aging and ethics is how the elderly
are (or are not) treated in an ethical fashion. The *fanm se kajou* proverb
suggests that as women age, they "get better." But does this place they
hold in the cultural imagination ring true for how they are treated by
others? From the neighbors on the street who refer to her as Madame
Karolis to her own children, it is clear that she is not venerated in the
way that we traditionally think of our Haitian elders. When she hears,
"Madame Karolis *zo granmoun pa pran*. Reste sagement dans ton lit ou
sur ta dodine. Ne t'amuse pas à fouiller la terre pour chercher la jarre.
Laisse dormir le passé. *Wa tonbe sou zo grann ou wi*" (Madame Karolis,
the bones of an old person cannot stand. Stay wisely in your bed or on
your rocking chair. Do not try to search for the jar. Let the past sleep. You

will fall on the bones of the dead, yes), it is both a rebuke and a judgment (76)—a rebuke for not staying in her place as an elderly woman, a judgment for refusing to accept immobility as a mode of being.

Mobility is important because it reminds us that age, like other categories of identity is not a fixed referent. Marie-Jeanne was never meant to survive. Like her executed Haitian namesake foremother, she is an aberration to those around her. If she does survive, it is despite the forces at work against her. Just as she declares in the novel's first paragraph, "je ne bougerai pas d'ici" (I will not move from here), refusal marks her character. The critique of how the elderly are treated within the family unit and the ethical questions that follow from this cause the reader to take note of the ways the social value and agency of the elderly deteriorate as they age, even though their own will does not.

Along with how beautifully it displays the author's rapt attention to the interiority and subjectivity of an elderly woman, perhaps one of the greatest achievements of Trouillot's portrayal of Marie-Jeanne is that, though she may be a problem character, she is not a problem to be solved. From a narrative standpoint, Marie-Jeanne's idiosyncrasies and disregard for convention are never fixed for her family or the reader. Just as Glover suggests in her study of disorderly protagonists, or difficult Caribbean women characters determined to place their own individual needs over those of the community, Marie-Jeanne adopts an ethic of refusal vis-à-vis those around her. After all, as Marie-Jeanne explains in her own words, "la vieillesse c'est une chanson inachevée, c'est ce sentiment d'urgence qui vous tient à la gorge alors que vos pas s'alourdissent et que le temps canaille s'enfuit avec le vent" (Old age is an unfinished song, it is this feeling of urgency that holds you by the throat as your steps get heavier and that scoundrel time flees with the wind) (78). Aging is a song that has not yet ended, and the duration of the process and the uncertainty of the outcome are vivid for the person experiencing it.

Kasalé: A Vodou Ethic of Care

While *L'œil-totem* presents an elderly woman with a refined sense of self-regard buoyed by the intergenerational relationship with her grandson, *Kasalé* espouses a Black feminist ethic of care rooted in Vodou to demonstrate how, to borrow from Jacqui Alexander, "the ethics of spirituality inform daily life."[63] Published in 2003, Kettly Mars's first novel is set in the community of Kasalé, a small village just outside of Port-au-Prince on the main road to southern Haiti. The two protagonists, Antoinette/

Gran'n and Sophonie function as a pair with a spiritual connection that highlights how bonds between women can be stronger than familial ties. Their relationship reinforces the idea that for Black women, "female relationships are an essential aspect of their self-definition," as many Black feminists have explored.[64]

Kasalé is a close-knit community that is vulnerable to the actions of the nearby city including the machinations of rapid political changes under the dictatorship. Set during the 1970s, the novel introduces the reader to a Duvalier-era *lakou* (communal yard or family courtyard) where the community of houses are set up around the *cachiman* tree. That this particular lakou was once the Salé plantation further endows it with a historical significance linked to slavery,[65] but the context of the dictatorship is especially noteworthy when we understand how Dr. François Duvalier deployed Vodou tropes to maintain control. Keeping in mind Alessandra Benedicty-Kokken's observation that, "as generally known, the Duvalierist government nurtured certain narratives of Haiti—one associated with its revolution and another related to Vodou as the folk religion that lent 'authenticity' to a specifically Haitian national expression," the manipulation of the national religion as a means to serve political ends of *la terreur* begins to seep into the context of the novel.[66] Antoinette's determination to serve the spirits is equally important in this regard because it is a refusal to cede the ownership of the religion to the regime since "after the Duvaliers, Vodou became associated with the grotesque tyranny of Duvalierism."[67]

Mars's use of the lakou initiates the reader into a profoundly social and spiritual narrative with two Black women at the center. Antoinette's relationship with Sophonie and to Vodou exemplify what Alexander references in her recognition that, "African-based cosmological systems are [. ...] manifestations of locatedness, rootedness, and belonging that map individual and collective relationships to the Divine."[68] According to the logic of Vodou, the overlap of social and spiritual worlds in the lakou constantly informs daily life. As the religion scholar Claudine Michel explains, "Lakou, as social milieu, remains ever so present in modern Haiti, in both rural and urban spaces. Real or imagined, today's lakou(s), are relational spaces that ensure participation and ownership in communal affairs."[69] Within this relational space, women, men, children, elders, and ancestors gather together.

And the lakou functions as more than a physical space; as Charlene Désir further clarifies, "the lakou is more than a community; it is a theoretical and social framework and an integral part of the social fabric of Haiti. Within the community, there is a poto-mitan (the center post) that brings strength to all parts of the surroundings, including all aspects of family and community life."[70] My analysis of *Kasalé* considers how Antoinette operates as a poto-mitan within this network. Though she is integral to the community's social fabric, and at the center of the story, she is still peripheral to the social dynamics and relationships within the lakou. When viewed in this way, *Kasalé* helps to demystify the figure of the poto-mitan and lays out some of its drawbacks for elderly women. I identify this circumspection toward the figure of the poto-mitan as a Black feminist position that refuses homogenizing taxonomies that fix Black womanhood into a single frame. It also probes what the figure of the poto-mitan has to offer beyond a symbolism. I wholly agree with Sabine Lamour, who smartly maintains that feminist scholars must interrogate what she calls the "obligations morales de renoncement et de don de soi" (the moral obligations of renouncement and gift of self), a tendency that cleaves to the poto-mitan regardless of geographic location.[71]

Essential to this analysis is how Antoinette's identity as a *Vodouizan* (Vodou practitioner), a *mambo* (Vodou priestess), and a healer determine her relationship to those around her. For this protagonist, Vodou is a way of life that influences her interactions with humans and nature, as well as her understanding of herself. Because African-derived religions like Vodou are "belief systems [that] place emphasis on the presence of the ancestors, spirits who guide and protect living beings in the physical realm," we know that as an elderly woman Antoinette will soon transition to join the ancestor spirits.[72] Her imminent death presents a spiritual task to fulfill; unless there is a new initiate to serve the spirits after her death, the practice of Vodou in Kasalé will die.

Fanm se poto-mitan: Vodou Symbol and Black Feminist Foil

In her foundational essay, "Fanm se Poto Mitan: Haitian Women, the Pillar of Society," Marie-José N'Zengou-Tayo contends that despite the ubiquity of the poto-mitan proverb from which she derives the title, Haitian women have not been recognized for their vital role in society. If, following N'Zengou-Tayo, we affirm the idea that "the Black peasant woman represents the nation's resilience," then Antoinette can be analyzed in terms of her ability to withstand adversity against all odds.[73] But in my view, examining Antoinette through the prism of resilience reveals some of the grating limitations of the trope itself. As a representational practice, the poto-mitan relies on the enduring strength and isolation of Haitian women, yet, too often it fails to account for how Haitian women operate as a collective and in collaborative ways. Darline Alexis critiques monolithic constructions of the poto-mitan figure that deny how it operates beyond the singular. As Alexis insightfully explains, many have embarked on descriptions of Haitian women as poto-mitan, deploying the central pillar of the Vodou temple as a metaphor, but few have grappled with the multiple figurations of these temples, some of which require more than one central pillar.[74] How can an examination of the architecture of the temple as one requiring the strength of multiple pillars upend our rigid views of Haitian womanhood? What happens to the reality of connection, collaboration, and collectivity that characterize life for many Haitian women when we rely so heavily on the singularity of the poto-mitan?[75]

These questions are especially important when we take into consideration Vanessa Valdés's argument that African diasporic religions "provide alternative models of womanhood that differ substantially from those found in dominant Western patriarchal culture" because, in this case, the use of the poto-mitan leitmotif has become equally restricting.[76] What happens when an esteemed symbol confines and restricts? What is needed is a theorization of the poto-mitan that includes attention to individuated personhood within the collective, a perspective similar to what Karen McCarthy Brown attempts in *Mama Lola,* in which poto-mitan "refers to a worldview wherein peasants are the central post holding up Haiti's ability to function as a nation, as communities and as households, or the central axis around which all activities originate and find support. It refers to the concept of building personhood, not as separate individuals but as a people situated within the collective consciousness of Haitian society."[77]

By dislodging the poto-mitan from having an exclusively gendered focus, Brown rightfully invites us to see beyond its singular meaning. Subjecting the poto-mitan to Black feminist scrutiny allows us to move beyond a framework that renders Haitian women solely as women who must give and sacrifice to uphold the community. This is what Sabine Lamour critiques when she describes the tendency to see the poto-mitan as "femmes débitrices de leur groupe social . . . Mère Courage toujours prêtes à se sacrifier pour leur entourage" (women who are the debtors of their social group . . . a Mother Courage always ready to sacrifice herself for those around her).[78] Eternally sacrificial, strong enough to hold up her entire community, the poto-mitan is a trope that deserves more critical attention in formulations of Haitian womanhood.

Kasalé's poto-mitan is ninety-year-old Antoinette, one of the novel's two protagonists as well as its moral center. Antoinette is quiet. In contrast to Marie-Jeanne, who boldly lives her life with a seemingly endless stream of chatter enlivening her interior, Antoinette moves through the world in measured restraint. She much prefers communing with spirits and nature to interacting with people. Mars's attention to Antoinette's interior is consistent with her overall style, which, Joëlle Vitiello has noted is "précise à la fois poétique et décapante, revête aussi un aspect réaliste en ce qui concerne des descriptions de situations quotidiennes (émotions et actions) au sein de toutes classes sociales" (precise, both poetic and scathing, [and also offers a] realistic aspect with regard to descriptions of everyday situations (emotions and actions) within all social classes).[79]

Although Antoinette represents the center of the novel, she seems isolated throughout. Her perspective highlights the distancing effects of the poto-mitan because of which the elderly can live in isolation from the social bonds that are especially crucial later in life. Could it be that the weight that she carries is a bit much for Antoinette's frail shoulders? Just as Trouillot's commitment to the interiority of her elderly protagonist reveals the challenges that come with age, Mars's portrayal of Antoinette highlights the limits of the poto-mitan status in one woman's life. My analysis of *Kasalé* explores how the simultaneity of Antoinette's condition as an older woman and a Vodouizan shapes her lived experience and endows the sturdy structure of the poto-mitan with more complex meaning. When another relative, Esperanta, refers to Antoinette as "la doyenne de la cour" (the most esteemed inhabitant of the compound), she notes Antoinette's importance within the community (190). Being recognized as the "doyenne" means she is respected by all although she seems not to be active in the quotidian social life of the community. It also acknowledges that within the traditional system, Vodou functions "as a sort of juridical system," in which the dealings of the community are under her authority.[80] But despite her role as the doyenne, Antoinette seems exterior to much of the goings-on in the lakou. Whether it is the chatter of the women at the market, the activity of people washing in the river, or any of the other day-to-day activities that define life in Kasalé, she lurks on the periphery of the lakou conversations and activities.

Antoinette operates in a realm of her own that is largely private, deeply spiritual, and strikingly quiet. Here I invoke quiet in the same way that Kevin Quashie does in his engrossing study, *The Sovereignty of Quiet*, in which he posits that "quiet is the subjectivity of the one."[81] While Quashie's use of quiet hinges on "the one," because *Kasalé's* elderly protagonist is a woman on her own quietly serving the spirits, she is not entirely alone. For Antoinette, the spirits, gods, and ancestors are her constant companions. The definitive role that Vodou plays in her life furthers Vanessa Valdés's point that for many Caribbean women writers, spirituality is "fundamental in the subject formation of their protagonists," a dynamic that Mars brings even further by offering two markedly different protagonists for whom their subject formation pivots on knowledge of the traditional religion.[82]

This attention to religion as a constitutive part of identity is impactful especially when we consider, as Yanick Lahens has rightly argued, that Vodou, "dévoile une dimension du vécu non prise en compte par l'intersectionnalité, mais un des lieux de pouvoir de la femme dans la culture populaire" (reveals a dimension of lived experience that intersectionality does not take into account, but one that is an important site of power for women in Haitian culture).[83] In *Kasalé* the added dimension of Vodou operates multiplicatively along with Antoinette's age, race, class, and gender. Antoinette's devotion to Vodou informs every aspect of her life; looking at her through the lens of the poto-mitan requires that we account for the spiritual origins of the term (which many scholars abandon to focus on the gendered dimensions). Reading the poto-mitan as the "knitting together of mind, body, and Spirit" conceptualized by M. Jacqui Alexander generates a more robustly intersectional appreciation of how gender, age, and religion combine in Antoinette's life.[84]

As one of the most enduring archetypes of Haitian womanhood, the ubiquitous figure of the poto-mitan recurs across genres, disciplines, and forms of expressive culture. In her essay "Papa, Patriarchy and Power: Snapshots of a Good Haitian Girl, Feminism, and Dyasporic Dreams," Gina Athena Ulysse writes, "I grew up with the knowledge that women in my culture were the *poto-mitan* of their families. I was choosing another way."[85] I interpret Ulysse's anti-poto-mitan stance as her longing for a model of Haitian womanhood that nuances the fixed idea of the central pillar. Ulysse's discomfort with the poto-mitan can be attributed to its fixity—a rigid central pillar that speaks to the ways in which women manifest various burdens in society. The pillar is hardened, set in stone, and firmly entrenched. Rather than discard the figure of the poto-mitan altogether, I am interested in how it might be reconfigured, reformulated. Or, as Omi'seke Natasha Tinsley asks, "What if . . . the idea of woman-as-poto mitan can be recurved into something that Haitian women can actually lean on?"[86] In my view, the alternative to the poto-mitan is a model of Black feminism that is constantly in negotiation. Similarly, I contend that a Black feminist ethic demands that we interrogate and theorize the figure of the poto-mitan in more complex ways by questioning what it means for the woman who inhabits the role. What does it *feel like* to be a poto-mitan, or what kind of ethic can emerge from the poto-mitan? How does bearing the weight held by the central pillar influence female subjectivity? Returning to Glover's convincing arguments in *A Regarded Self,* we can also note that the poto-mitan's position as the one on whose shoulders the entire community rests leaves little room for the expression or elaboration of her individuated self. Her primary obligation must be to the community she holds up. In other words, a poto-mitan can be only that—a pillar of the community and not an individual who is at liberty to privilege her own needs, nurture her sense of self, or exist outside of a "communal project."[87]

Still, those committed to deploying local concepts to theorize gender might wonder, what is the problem with the title of *poto-mitan?* As I have pointed out elsewhere, when the poto-mitan becomes shorthand for Haitian womanhood represented in its entirety, it becomes a stereotype that can flatten the human aspects of Haitian women's lives and deny the ways in which Haitian women are plural.[88] It deceives us into thinking that a single metaphor, symbol, or figure can capture the essence of Haitian womanhood. When viewed as the pillars of society, Haitian women are expected to uphold those around them, to do an extraordinary amount of labor that is physical, spiritual, and/or emotional, and to be the steadfast keepers of tradition. The manifold iterations of the use of the poto-mitan to signify Haitian womanhood confirms how widely this signifier is deployed. For many critics, the idea of the Haitian woman as a poto-mitan is often a foregone conclusion. Marie-José N'Zengou-Tayo is far from alone in her use of the poto-mitan formula, which she uses to frame her arguments about the role of women in Haitian literature. Fiction writers Louis-Philippe Dalembert and Lyonel Trouillot also use the poto-mitan trope to describe the significance of Haitian women writers in their study *Haiti: Une traversée littéraire,* writing that "on sait le rôle joué par la femme dans la société haïtienne, dont elle est, pour reprendre une métaphore vaudou, le Poteau-mitan" (we are aware of the role played by the woman in Haitian society, who is . . . to use a Vodou metaphor, the poto-mitan).[89] Dalembert and Trouillot's certainty of the role suggests that, for them, the prominence of the poto-mitan is undeniable. As these examples indicate, it is well-established not only that Haitian women are portrayed as poto-mitan but also that the poto-mitan can operate as a generative critical frame for analyzing Haitian womanhood.[90]

Building on Darline Alexis's argument, I want to probe the problem with the title *poto-mitan* by focusing on its singularity or singular nature. What interests me is how the figure of the poto-mitan, borrowed from Vodou epistemology, actually sheds some of its original meaning when blindly applied to gender identity. Despite the fact that many Vodou temples have more than one central pillar, the term has come to be associated with individual women as the sole bearers of the title.[91] This individual notability contradicts the collectivity associated with Black feminism. A Black feminist poto-mitan would acknowledge the need for the pillars to be surrounded, supported, and upheld by others. Elsewhere I have questioned the utility of the poto-mitan construction for how it limits Haitian women to a singular role that can problematically perpetuate the myth of the strong Black woman.[92] Since the publication of Michele Wallace's *Black Macho and the Myth of the Superwoman* (1979), there have been numerous Black feminist theorizations of how strength and resilience restrict Black female subjectivity. Patricia Hill Collins's "Mammies, Matriarchs, and Other Controlling Images," for example, invites us to carefully contemplate the limitations and the risks of cleaving to images of strength and endurance to imagine and represent Black women. In a similar vein, my critique of the poto-mitan is that it can romanticize Haitian women's suffering in the same way that the resilience trope operates. As Edwidge Danticat has pointed out, "Yes, Haitians are resilient, but that does not mean that they can suffer more than others."[93] My problem with deploying the poto-mitan as a primary lens for theorizing Haitian women's lived experience is that it signifies little else than strength and resilience. The subsequent readings of *Kasalé* posit that by focusing on the relational and spiritual dynamics between Sophonie and Antoinette, Mars offers a Black feminist revision of the poto-mitan figure that contravenes its potentially totalizing discourse. As we saw in *L'œil-totem,* in *Kasalé* Mars's dedication to the interiority and subjectivity of her elderly protagonist discloses to the reader "what else" Antoinette is and might be "other than old." Kettly Mars thus imbues the aesthetic character of the novel with a Vodou ethic that is in productive dialogue with Black feminism.

Serving the Spirits with Gran'n

As a Vodouizan who is also a mambo, Antoinette challenges the declining practice of Vodou in a community that has moved away from the traditional religion because of the encroachment of Christianity in various forms. The action of the novel centers Antoinette's spiritual journey and the development of her relationship with Sophonie. Built around the familiar structure of the quest narrative, *Kasalé* follows Antoinette's pilgrimage to fulfill a spiritual mission, as well as Sophonie's path to becoming a Vodou practitioner. Their double paths are inextricably intertwined—one woman is at the beginning of her spiritual journey and the other at its earthly conclusion. Antoinette is aided in her quest by Sophonie, who is anointed by the spirits, though she does not fully realize what this means; the novel thus charts the process of spiritual awakening and religious education for the younger woman. Antoinette's continuous overlapping of the spiritual and natural worlds underscores Vodou as more than a religion; it is indeed a way of life. Outlining this aspect of Vodou as a way of life, and fundamentally linked to purpose, Claudine Michel explains, "le Vodou repose sur une vision globale du monde, qu'il est un système compréhensif qui façonne l'expérience humaine de ses adeptes dans leur quête spirituelle et leur désir de bien remplir leur mission terrestre" (Vodou is based on a global vision of the world, it is a comprehensive system that shapes the human experience of its followers in their spiritual quest and their desire to fulfill their earthly mission).[94]

Shortly after *Kasalé* begins, the fall of the cachiman tree acts as a portent symbolizing a spiritual mission that must be fulfilled. When Antoinette sees that the cachiman has fallen, she almost falls down herself: "Le cachiman blessé entra dans le champ de vision de Gran'n au moment où elle se retournait. Un sursaut faillit renverser la vieille. *Oh! Oh! Oh! Rete! Sa'm wè la'a? Oh! Oh! Oh!* Elle ne put articuler un mot de plus" (The wounded tree entered into Gran'n's field of vision as she turned around. A jolt almost toppled the old woman. Oh! Oh! Oh! Stop! What do I see there? Oh! Oh! Oh! She could not utter one more word) (12). This event registers as a spiritual crisis and a foreshadowing event. Antoinette's body mirrors the action of the fallen tree, affirming the connection between them. Expressing her shock in Kreyòl, she questions what she sees in front of her and asks that everything around her stop. According to Vodou's spiritual logic, the fall of the cachiman tree signals to Antoinette the imminence of her death and calls for the construction of the temple: "Mais Antoinette, devant la déroute du *cachiman,* réalisa ce matin-là que le temps prenait un virage. Elle comprit que comme l'arbre déraciné, sa vie ne tiendrait plus longtemps" (But Antoinette, faced with the destruction of the cachiman tree, realized that morning that time was taking a turn. She understood that, like the uprooted tree, her life would not last much longer) (13). Interestingly, there are several parallels between Antoinette and the tree, which sits in the middle of the lakou: she is the center of the novel, she is an upright symbolic pillar of the community, and she has a significant spiritual role in the lakou.

Kasalé pays respectful homage to Vodou, which at the time the novel was set was "disappearing." Joëlle Vitiello convincingly asserts that "*Kasalé* est aussi une réponse, féminine à *Gouverneurs de la rosée* de Jacques Roumain" (*Kasalé* is also a female response to *Masters of the Dew* by Jacques Roumain), especially for how it also thematizes an environmental concern related to water.[95] But unlike its literary ancestor and intertextually linked "peasant novel" *Gouverneurs de la rosée* (*Masters of the Dew*) (1946), *Kasalé*'s depiction of Vodou and its role in the lives of rural Haitians moves beyond spectacle and simplification.[96] Mars holds the traditional religion in high regard and seeks to pay homage to Vodou through her writing: "Je voulais représenter le côté humain du Vodou, une religion *qui est un miroir pour le peuple haïtien*" (I wanted to represent the human side of Vodou, a religion that is a mirror of the Haitian people).[97] The idea of Vodou as a mirror of the Haitian people is, for scholars of the religion, rich with meaning. By this I mean that Mars's choice of a mirror as symbol also has a spiritual connotation: in her study on the ritual use of mirrors, Kyrah Daniels persuasively argues that "the ritual use of mirrors as mortuary arts signals the omnipresence of ancestral spirits and the importance of sustaining lines of communication between visible and invisible worlds."[98]

For the Vodou practitioner, serving the spirits relies on this dialectic of visible and invisible worlds. One interacts with the visible world knowing that there are always invisible forces at work. What you see is regulated by what you cannot see. In this context, looking for other worlds is a framework in which visible and invisible worlds exist side by side. If Antoinette emblematizes Vodou as a reflection of Haitians, she also serves as a reminder that most of the other characters in the novel are alienated from the religion, and thus alienated from themselves. Kasalé becomes a place without memory, without roots, bereft of sacred knowledge. Sophonie and Antoinette are the rare exception to this alienation, and their relationship allows us to witness the transmission of Vodou as a belief system and spiritual practice from one generation to the next in order to countervail its decline.

Because Antoinette's relatives are alienated from the practice of Vodou, she must find someone else through whom the tradition can be carried on. But she cannot just find the person herself—she must pay attention to whom the spirits designate. As Sophonie begins to share her dreams with Gran'n, the older woman understands more clearly that she will in fact be the one through whom Vodou will survive in Kasalé. The reader learns of this dream as soon as the story begins: "Cette nuit-là, Sophonie tomba grosse au plus fort de l'averse. Un rêve liquide posséda son corps au moment où la rivière débordant de ses berges déracinait le cachiman sur l'arrière-cour de Gran'n. Elle se souvient seulement d'une cascade humaine déferlant sur son cri, martelant son ventre, pilonnant ses fesses, comme le courant énervé, quand il bute contre les roches dans une rage d'écume" (That night Sophonie suddenly became pregnant in the depths of the downpour. A liquid dream possessed her body as the river overflowing its banks uprooted the cachiman in Gran'n's backyard. She only remembers a human waterfall surging over her cry, pounding her stomach, pounding her buttocks, like the angry current, when it stumbles against the rocks in a rage of foam) (7). This introductory paragraph immediately connects Sophonie, Antoinette, and the nature that surrounds them in a gushing flow of words. Unbeknownst to her, the "rêve étrange dont les images vivaces ne quittaient pas son esprit" (strange dream whose vibrant images would not leave her mind) marks the dawning of Sophonie's relationship to the spirits, a relationship which Antoinette will be essential in helping her to develop (7).

Antoinette and Sophonie's connection has a spiritual significance that is also gendered and highlights Vodou as a unique source of power for women. Together they embody Karen McCarthy Brown's insistence that, "Vodou empowers women to a larger extent than the great majority of the world's religious traditions. As Haitians struggled to survive and adapt both during and after slavery, women gained social and economic power, gains that are mirrored in the influence of women within Vodou."[99] One of the reasons women are able to thrive as practitioners and priests of Vodou is that the religion offers more leadership opportunities and more capacious definitions of womanhood than do Western religions. By passing on her sacred knowledge to Sophonie, Antoinette positions the younger woman to tap into a form of empowerment that is spiritual and sacred. As she moves toward locating that power within herself, Sophonie demonstrates Vodou's power as both individually and collectively significant. The women's spiritual friendship thus effectively manifests M. Jacqui Alexander's beautifully articulated observation that "we are connected to the Divine through our connections with one another."[100] Antoinette and Sophonie's connection to Vodou is a divine partnership that binds them to one another in this world and beyond.

Embodied Elders: Old Age and the Female Body

As we saw in *L'œil-totem,* an elderly woman must reckon with her aging body each day. The body is a constant referent offering both a point of contact and a process of negotiation for the older person. Through the creation of an embodied discourse, Mars foregrounds the toll that aging takes on the body. Our first introduction to Antoinette highlights her bodily functions, which in old age gain acuity: "Gran'n raclait de sa gorge les mucosités accumulées pendant la nuit" (Gran'n cleared her throat of the phlegm accumulated during the night) (9). Here we see a woman whose first movement of the day connects her to an aging self as she evaluates how her older body feels.

Antoinette's aging body rapidly declines from the beginning of the novel to the end, which concludes with her death. Almost every description of her body highlights her age and her relationship to it. In one particularly striking scene, she climbs up the mountain with Sophonie, inching towards the *kay-miste,* a small family temple that they must erect before her death in order to honor the spirits. She is unable to complete the journey because of her frail and aching body, her physical strength undermining her spiritual strength.

The scenes portraying the women's expedition up the mountain radiate many of the tenets of a Black feminist ethic of care and connection in which we see a younger woman guided by the concern for her elderly spiritual guide. Their sojourn to Terre-Rouge is a journey within a journey, highlighting the novel's quest motif. It is significant for a few reasons: it displays the fragility of Antoinette's body, it affirms her connection to the land, and it cements the bond between the two women: "Au fur et à mesure de son avancée, elle se rendait compte des ravages du temps dans son corps. Elle n'avait pas eu l'occasion, depuis longtemps, de mettre ses forces à l'épreuve. Tout son être fondait dans une grande faiblesse. Ses jambes pesaient lourd, tellement lourd" (As she advanced, she became aware of the ravages of time in her body. She hadn't had the opportunity to test her strength in a long time. Her whole being melted into great weakness. Her legs were heavy, so heavy) (110). Her myriad aches and pains amplify the toll of old age on Antoinette's elderly body. Antoinette had not tested her strength in a while, which confirms her quotidian inactivity or insufficiency of activity that distance her from her aging body.

Antoinette's relationship to her body can help us to think differently about the spiritual and material realms she inhabits because framing aging as an embodied experience brings into relief its omnipresent spiritual significance. As M. Jacqui Alexander argues, we must "understand spiritual work as a type of bodily praxis, as a form of embodiment."[101] Importantly, Antoinette's relationship to the spirit world as a Vodou practitioner does not take her body for granted. The sense of balance upheld in Vodou encourages integration of body and spirit, creating this kind of bodily praxis. When we consider Alexander's approach to the body as "a meeting ground" for the sacred, the difference between how others perceive Antoinette's body and how she perceives it herself is stark.[102] As a woman who is spiritually astute and who has achieved balance, Antoinette situates her body in a larger metaphysical field.

The aging body is also made present through the younger woman's observations. By looking carefully at Antoinette, Sophonie understands more about how the aging process affects the older woman: "Chaque matin pareil, les bruits du vieux corps de l'aïeule réglaient le réveil de Sophonie" (Every morning was the same, the sounds of the old body of her elder ruled Sophonie's awakening) (10). Sophonie is keenly aware of how Antoinette's body moves and interacts with the world around her. She sees her difficulties and worries that Antoinette's time on earth is waning. She looks at the knots in her hands and fears that the end is near. Sophonie views Antoinette with care and tenderness as she contemplates the imminent loss of her mentor: "Gran'n paraissait fragile comme le papier fin dont les garçons confectionnent des cerfs-volants au temps de carême. Objets graciles, mais capable de monter très haut dans les airs, de chevaucher les vents fougueux du ciel" (Gran'n looked fragile like the thin paper kites that boys make during Lent. Slender objects, but able to climb very high in the air, to ride the fiery winds of the sky) (38). Antoinette's vulnerability affects Sophonie, but for the younger woman, the attrition on the older woman's body does not compromise its strength. The metaphor of the kite used during Lent speaks to how much Antoinette endures, all the while connecting her to a spiritual season and celestial significance. On the one hand, this view maintains the power of resilience as a marker for aging bodies, but, when juxtaposed with Antoinette's lived experience of her own body, her unequivocal resilience is thrown into question.

A nonagenarian and doyenne of the lakou, Antoinette represents a way of life tethered to past traditions. She is tellingly described as "Antoinette, que toutes les générations confondues appelaient Gran'n, comptait au moins quatre-vingt-quinze années. Elle ignorait sa date de naissance, ne savait ni lire ni écrire" (Antoinette, who all the different generations referred to as Gran'n, was at least ninety-five years old. She did not know her date of birth, and did not know how to read or write) (13). But despite her inability to read and write, she is the most knowledgeable character in *Kasalé*, reinforcing the value of her well of sacred knowledge. As a Vodouizan, she serves the spirits with fervor, despite her social understanding of how Vodou is marginalized and denigrated in the community.

Oui vrai, elle avait roulé sa bosse par-ci et par-là durant sa longue vie. Partout où appelait le service des lwa. Hounsi de son état, servant des mystères, dotée du don de guérison, elle avait parcouru vallons, mornes, contrées froides et brûlantes. Beaucoup d'amis, serviteurs comme elle, fleurissaient son souvenir. Mais toujours ses pas la ramenaient vers Kasalé, son commencement, sa fin. En ce lieu sommeillait sa mémoire, sous chaque arbre, chaque rocher fiché dans les mornes, dans chaque crevasse, chaque trille d'oiseau. Ici, dans la terre froide du *lakou* où reposaient tant de familles.

(Yes truly, she had gotten around during her long life. Wherever service of the *lwa* called. Hounsi of her stature, serving mysteries, endowed with the gift of healing, she had traveled valleys, hills, dreary, cold and burning lands. Many friends, servants like her, flourished in her memory. But her steps always brought her back to Kasalé, her beginning, her end. In this place her memory slept, under every tree, every rock pressed into the hills, in every crevice, every trill of a bird. Here in the cold earth of the lakou land where so many families lay.) (13)

This passage, laced with a Vodou ethic of what it means to be alive, exalts Antoinette's connection to the land, reveals her thoughts about death and aging, and affirms her spiritual authority in the community. In her comprehensive study *Divine Horsemen: The Living Gods of Haiti,* Maya Deren characterizes this ethic as an eternal chain: "the entire chain of interlocking life links—life, death, deification, transfiguration, resurrection—churns without rest through the hands of the devout. None of it is ever forgotten: that the god was once human, that he was made god by humans, that he is sustained by humans."[103] Antoinette's participation in this interlocking chain of life means that even after death she will remain present in Kasalé.

But, as I noted earlier, the reverence and deference directed toward Antoinette also isolate her. Her place as an elder isolates her from the other members of the community. She is revered but still kept at a distance. Looking at how much is said *about* her rather than *to* her further reveals this dynamic: "Cette histoire du cachiman et d'Antoinette, la famille et les anciens de la cour la connaissaient. Elle était une sorte de légende, un mythe auquel plus personne ne croyait, sauf quelques d'antan qui savaient que le commerce des esprits continuait" (This story of the cachiman tree and Antoinette, the family and the elders of the compound knew about it. It was a sort of legend, a myth that no one believed, except a few from yesteryear who knew that the belief in the spirits continued) (14). That everyone in the community is aware of the myth yet refuses to believe it stems from the faded relationship to sacred knowledge in the lakou. One of Mars's achievements in the novel is that she shows how the twenty-first-century vilification of Vodou occurs even in small communities. Antoinette, despite her age as someone who should have earned the right to practice whichever religion she pleases, is nonetheless aware that she must keep a part of her identity as a Vodouizan hidden from those in the community.

Not Blood, but Chosen: Spiritual Kinship between Women

Much of *Kasalé* is also about the budding, and eventually intimate, relationship between Antoinette and Sophonie, the novel's other protagonist, who becomes Antoinette's mentee and initiate into the traditional religion. Cross-generational companionship allows Antoinette to realize her end-of-life mission. As I noted in my analysis of *L'œil-totem*, connection between older women and younger people (both within their families and outside) is life-affirming. How we understand the relationship between Antoinette and Sophonie connects to how age operates in the novel through both contrasts between them and their closeness.

Theirs is an undeniably intense bond endowed with a transcendent, spiritual significance. As Antoinette explains to Sophonie, "Tu ne descends pas de mon sang, mais ils t'ont choisie. Car rien ne se fait pour rien dans cette vie" (You are not from my blood, but they have chosen you. For there is nothing in life that is done for no reason) (59). Antoinette's words leave an indelible imprint on Sophonie: "Le discours de la vieille coulait comme une douce pluie sur l'inquiétude de Sophonie" (The old woman's speech flowed like a soft rain onto Sophonie's worries) (60). For Sophonie, Antoinette is a comfort, an anchor, and a bond to a community that still has yet to welcome her. Their intimacy becomes a form of belonging through which the two women find a place together. The ethic of care that regulates their interactions relies on what is spoken and unspoken between them, as well as what is invisible and visible because it is an encounter rooted in Vodou.

In addition to the precise spiritual instruction of how to serve the spirits and discern what they are saying, Antoinette also shares the history of the lakou with Sophonie. When Sophonie asks her why the members of the community no longer serve the spirits, Antoinette explains that the loss of Vodou is a result of religious persecution; she offers historical background about how Vodou has been demonized as well as how Vodouizan are marginalized for their beliefs. By naming the fraught context in which Vodouizan practice their religion, Sophonie learns the importance of Antoinette's heritage, which is increasingly threatened by the negative perceptions of Vodou.

The intimate bond between the women beautifully extends beyond their mutual devotion to Vodou. When Sophonie shares a dream that she has about Antoinette, the older woman is touched: "Sophonie étonnée vit la vieille sourire largement. Une joie profonde lui était dans les plis du visage. Antoinette semblait rajeunie. Elle souriait, gencive dehors. Les feux de la lampe semaient des étincelles dans ses yeux" (Sophonie was astonished to see the old woman smile widely. A deep joy was folded into her face. Antoinette seemed rejuvenated. She smiled so broadly her gums were visible. The lamp fires sparkled in her eyes) (131). The attentiveness that characterizes Antoinette and Sophonie's dynamic reveals a special, sacred bond. The women listen to each other, care for each other, speak carefully to one another, and spend much time thinking about one another. On one level, this intimacy is born of Antoinette's need to induct Sophonie into Vodou before her death. But, for our purposes, it goes far beyond the passing down of Vodou epistemology. Their relationship articulates a Black feminist ethic of care because we see how their encounters transform each one for the better.

The depth of the two women's connection is powerfully rendered when Antoinette's life comes to a gradual end. As Sophonie watches over the older woman hovering between life and death, she attends to Antoinette in a way that enacts the dynamics of the wake described by Christina Sharpe in her book *In the Wake: On Blackness and Being;* that is, she "tends to the dying," vigilantly caring for and defending the older woman, even in death.[104] As she sits with dying Antoinette, Sophonie attends to her needs "to ease [her] way, and also to the needs of the living."[105] The wake, as Sharpe masterfully articulates it in her study, is tending to and watching for death. This vigilance is a condition yoked to the afterlives of slavery, which cause the specter of death to recur across space and time. The wake helps to negotiate the past and its recurrence in the present. Both Antoinette and Sophonie anticipate the older woman's death, effectively placing them in the wake. For Antoinette, this anticipation begins the moment the cachiman falls. She thus enters into the dynamics of the wake—a watchful, attentive state of anticipating death—from the novel's beginning. But an important part of the watchfulness necessitated by the wake is a kind of looking that "makes ethical demands on the viewer; demands to imagine otherwise."[106] Equipped with the knowledge of Vodou, in which life and death are eternally linked, Sophonie's watch over the dying Antoinette takes on a different meaning. In *Kasalé,* that otherwise imagining occurs through their transcendent spiritual relationship, as well as in the investment in the future manifested in their intergenerational spiritual friendship.

The idea of the future inhabits Sophonie and Antoinette's relationship; the younger woman will preserve the practice of Vodou and pass it down to the next generation. It is also present in Sophonie's biological son, Jasmin. With the entry of Jasmin, Mars uses a single moment in the final scenes of the novel to point to the future. Answering her son's questions about death, Sophonie begins to transfer the sacred knowledge that Antoinette has already passed down to her.

> Jasmin, lorsque Gran'n et moi nous saluons les esprits, quand ils nous parlent dans nos rêves, c'est une façon pour nous de ne pas oublier nos racines. Ces gestes nous viennent naturellement, ils nous réconfortent. Souvent, nous ne savons plus qui nous sommes. Cette ignorance nous fait peur, nous rend méchants. L'éternel dans sa sagesse laisse le choix à l'homme ... de servir les bakas ou les bons anges. Ceux qui disent que nous faisons mal ont simplement peur de notre vérité.
>
> (Jasmin, when Gran'n and I greet the spirits, when they speak to us in our dreams, it's a way for us not to forget our roots. These gestures come naturally to us, they comfort us. Often, we do not know who we are anymore. This ignorance scares us, makes us mean. The eternal in its wisdom leaves the choice to the man . . . to serve the *bakas* or the good angels. Those who say we are doing harm are simply afraid of our truth.) (225–26)

In this exchange with her son, Sophonie dispenses key elements of Vodou practice as well as a keen reflection on the conflict between the different religions in Haiti. The implication here is clear: although Gran'n had no biological heir through whom to pass down her sacred knowledge of Vodou, Sophonie can and begins to do so long before her own death.

Despite the somber intimacy of Sophonie keeping wake over Antoinette in their final moments together, Antoinette's actual death is never described in the novel. Instead, we have this scene between Sophonie and her son, and there is a description of nature in which we see what Kasalé looks like on the morning of Antoinette's death. The older woman's entry into the realm of the ancestors is treated as separate, sacred knowledge imbued with a natural significance.

Antoinette and Sophonie's bond grounds the story of *Kasalé* in the spiritual lives of two Black women from a small community. But they are not mere symbols like "the Black peasant woman [who] represents the nation's resilience" described by N'zengou-Tayo. How they relate to one another and to Vodou demonstrates that religion serves as an intimate and vital point of connection across generations. Their relationship is characterized by a Vodou ethic of care, intimacy, and balanced integration of the physical and spiritual worlds. If Antoinette is to be remembered and cared for in her final days, it is only because of her relationship with Sophonie. If Vodou is to survive in Kasalé, it is only because of the intimate bond between these women. Devotion to Vodou creates a sacred intimacy between them, and the care that Sophonie lavishes onto her elder spiritual mother flourishes because of the religion. The women represent two models of spirituality; reminding us of Ulysse's point that "in spite of the simple narratives that tend to reduce us to singular notions, we are and have always been plural."[107] Here we have two women whose deeply rooted faith in Vodou and paths to following the religion are radically different from one another.

In the emotional scene, just prior to Antoinette's transition into the ancestral realm, we see how Sophonie and Antoinette's relationship has evolved and how they are eternally and ethereally linked through Vodou. The novel ends just as Antoinette's life does, highlighting her prominent role in the entire story. Yet, in Sophonie her legacy lives on. The bond between the women transcends time, blood ties, and ultimately the realms of life and death, the visible and the invisible. The elderly woman's passing facilitates Sophonie's entry into Kasalé, where she was previously ostracized but is now empowered by the Sacred. Or, to conclude with the words of M. Jacqui Alexander on the collective power of the sacred: Sophonie has begun to do the "spiritual work" or "praxis of the Sacred" that "inheres the lived capacity to initiate and sustain communication and human consciousness, to align the inner self, the behavioral self and the invisible . . . confronting an engagement with the embodied power of the Sacred."[108]

Stories to Pass On: Memory and Slavery in *The Infamous Rosalie*

I have spent most of this chapter with the examples of elderly women in *Kasalé* and *L'œil-totem*. I now briefly turn to offer a discussion of how age figures in relation to the history of slavery in Évelyne Trouillot's novel, *The Infamous Rosalie*. Whereas the first two novels represent elderly women who are underappreciated in their communities, *The Infamous Rosalie* is a counterexample expounding on how elderly women shape future generations in explicit and implicit ways. At the same time, it relays the toll of slavery's violence on older women who still hold memories of their past before bondage. In this way, the novel continues the dynamic that I began to delineate in the two previous examples where the elderly women actively pass something on—family history in one case, and sacred knowledge in the other—to their younger companions.

The Infamous Rosalie is a coming-of-age story about a young Creole woman named Lisette, who evolves from being a naive enslaved domestic to a radicalized Maroon. Often compared to Toni Morrison's novel *Beloved*, *The Infamous Rosalie* painstakingly renders the everyday violence of life under chattel slavery by relating the story of women living on the Fayot Plantation prior to the beginning of the Haitian Revolution. By foregrounding the quotidian brutalities and human atrocities of life on the plantation, *The Infamous Rosalie* stands as an important example of the machinations of race, gender, sex, and power at work in 1750 Saint-Domingue. Renée Larrier convincingly situates the novel in a cadre of narratives by Caribbean women that "locate the normative femme as a Black woman and narrate enslaved women's agency and subjectivity in a world of racial oppression and gender violence."[109] As a Creole, Lisette was born in Saint-Domingue, unlike the female ancestors to whom she constantly refers in the novel—her mother Ayouba, aunt Brigitte, grandmother Charlotte, and godmother Ma Augustine. These four older women survived the trans-Atlantic slave trade via their passage on the *Rosalie,* the ship for which the novel is named.[110] For the purposes of this chapter, I am interested in how Lisette's elders help to shape the evolution of her liberated consciousness. This interaction once again reveals that, in the context of aging, a Black feminist ethic of care pivots on the kind of encounter required in order to see the elderly as *more than just old*. The lived experience of these older women is one of the few remaining links to their African heritage and ancestry. Each of them expresses that connection differently: Ma Augustine through her stories, Tante Brigitte through her knowledge of nature, and Grann Charlotte through her use of material culture and memory.

Although she did not live through the violence of the Middle Passage herself, Lisette is a secondary survivor of this trauma. The older women recount stories about the ship itself and the life in the barracoons that preceded it. For Lisette, the inherited memories of the Middle Passage commingle with her lived experience of life on the plantation: "In my sleep I struggle against miasmas and stagnant waters, barracoons and the steerage of ships, the growl of dogs, bodies too hot and damp, the sound of bludgeons" (12). At first, she is eager to escape these inherited memories: "My youth wants to erase the stories of *The Infamous Rosalie* and the barracoons, to lift off this weight that clouds my vision whenever I try to dream" (64). In her psychic space Lisette moves fluidly between the past and the present. While she dreams, she is unable to distinguish one from the other; all of the temporal spaces collide. Lisette's relationship to the past is pregnant with fear and longing: "I feel the need to touch my talisman, to see these things that link me to Grandma Charlotte, to my mother, whom I didn't know, and to this great-aunt Brigitte they spoke so much about to me. I suffer from all the mysteries that surround me, from the stories that reveal themselves as pain comes and goes, from the days ahead that seem to extend immense tentacles of despair and anger" (21). These inner thoughts reveal a relationship to time in which she is suspended between the past and the present, wanting to put hope in the future but unable to imagine a future free from slavery.

Using the lens of history, Saidiya Hartman eloquently captures the kind of pain Lisette experiences: "this pain might best be described as history that hurts—the still unfolding narrative of captivity, dispossession, and domination that engenders the Black subject in the Americas."[111] It is a temporal understanding that painfully connects the past, present, and future even if the past is made up of indirect experiences. The stories of the past operate as more than an invocation of the oral storytelling tradition; they are also fodder for and eventually the catalyst of Lisette's future path as a Maroon. Hearing Grandma Charlotte's story endows her with an ethical responsibility. Parsing the interplay between ethics and responsibility Mariangela Palladino argues that "to tell a story implies responsibility for both the teller and the receiver: whoever narrates is responsible toward those who listen or read; those receiving the story are given a responsibility; a demand is made that they deal with that is being told . . . By learning a story we are introduced to another world."[112] In the Haitian context, this sense of responsibility is dynamically rendered through the folk traditional use of "krik, krak" a form of call-and-response requiring active listening. Before beginning the story, the giver of the tale asks, "Krik?" and in order to signal her willingness and readiness to receive it, the hearer responds, "Krak!" This call-and-response ritual acts as a vocal confirmation of the responsibility Palladino mentions. In *The Infamous Rosalie,* the older women's stories eventually propel Lisette into a life of fugitivity and freedom.

Trouillot's use of the foremothers' stories as an integral fabric in the tapestry of Lisette's life weaves her experience in the present into a continuous historical narrative. Remembering a conversation with her grandmother just before Grandma Charlotte died, Lisette recalls the older woman's parting words: "'I'm leaving you in your godmother's care,' Grandma Charlotte had told me before she died. 'She's a ship sister, an Arada woman like us. She knew your great-aunt Brigitte well.' The name of my great-aunt is itself a talisman, as powerful as the one she gave me. I hang onto it in moments of despair, when I'm about to succumb to my sinking morale" (11). Interestingly, the name Brigitte also parallels Gran Brijit in the Vodou pantheon, who, as Kyrah Daniels describes her, "sleeps with the book of the Dead under her pillow and the Book of Life as a journal on her nightstand [. . .] she reminds the ancestral elders to watch over the children they left behind."[113] Connection to the older generation protects, inspires, and motivates Lisette in her quest for freedom, making it possible for her to imagine her life differently. Standing on the shoulders of these female ancestors, Lisette offers her daughter the same powerful legacy. To be an Arada woman is to understand the power of this heritage; despite the daily indignities of slavery, Arada women refuse to accept as routine its dehumanization and degradation. Through small acts of recognition and resistance, they piece their personhood back together.

Throughout *The Infamous Rosalie*, Évelyne Trouillot explores different manifestations of women's agency on the plantation through the female characters that surround Lisette. As Trouillot explains in the afterword, her archival encounter with an Arada midwife inspired her to write *The Infamous Rosalie*. After reading about the midwife in *La Révolution aux Caraïbes*, an archival history of slavery and resistance in the Caribbean, Trouillot was so moved that she used the novel to stage such an encounter for the reader. The woman's story includes the trial where she stands accused of killing numerous infants. During the trial, the midwife reveals a necklace made of rope with seventy knots, and she confesses that each knot represented one of the seventy babies she had killed at birth. She explains her defiant actions: "to remove these young creatures from the shameful institution of slavery, I inserted a needle in their brain through the fontanel at the moment of their birth" (131).

The Arada midwife who Tante Brigitte's character is based on is an example of gendered resistance, embodied agency, and reproductive liberation. Her case shows how enslaved women were involved in circuits of resistance ranging from poisoning their masters in the kitchen to killing their own (and others') children at birth. It should be noted that her inclusion in the archive can be contrasted with the exclusion of women in general from the histories of the Haitian Revolution. Trouillot's use of the story functions as a form of historical recovery.

The focus on reproduction and reproductive freedom as a site of resistance exists along the continuum of female-centered agency that Trouillot highlights in the novel. The characters in *The Infamous Rosalie* remember Brigitte's reproductive radicalism and, through the material object of the talisman that Lisette is determined to hold onto, also manage to memorialize it in the present. At the same time, reproductive freedom and female agency operate differently in Lisette's life by the end of the novel when she too is pregnant. By choosing to become a Maroon and to keep her child, to whom she whispers, "Creole child who lives in me, you will be born free and rebellious, or you will not be born at all," Lisette accepts and revises the heritage of reproductive freedom that she is born into (129).

The collaboration among the women who help to inspire Lisette's future relies on the encounter with their stories and their memory. The Black feminist ethic that unfolds in *The Infamous Rosalie* establishes the value of Black women's connection to one another for creating better futures. Just as the novel also helps to underscore Mimi Sheller's point that "gender and sexuality . . . were not peripheral concerns; they were central to the practice of slavery," it shows how enslaved women made use of gender and sexuality to create new possibilities for their embodied freedom.[114]

Enslaved women and their stories structure the plot of *The Infamous Rosalie* as their experiences with slavery are transmitted orally from one generation to the next. There are the moments that Grandma Charlotte and Ma Augustine share and there are others that they "have shrouded in mystery" (30). The older women choose to hide some of the details of the history from Lisette in order to protect her. Realizing the power of their sacred memory, they choose to offer their stories to her only at what they deem will be the appropriate time: "What does their silence mean—this silence that intrigues and confounds me? I try to make up for it by gathering the small bits of information that I collect here and there from Grandma Charlotte and Ma Augustine over the years" (30). When Grandma Charlotte does share, as in the passage below, the exchange between the younger woman and her grandmother follows the cadence of call-and-response ritual by which Lisette must ask for the story to be told. The grandmother's decision to share is not simply based on tradition; she really would prefer not to repeat the stories and revisit the past: "After starting to tell the story, Grandma Charlotte always respected a moment of silence. I appreciated this pause, *which brought us together* and gave me permission to choose my story for that day. Grandmother would agree to my request except when I demanded she tell Brigitte's story or the one about the barracoons that she was keeping for a special day, a day still to come" (24).

How the stories move from Grandma Charlotte to Lisette is determined by the older woman's perception of Lisette's state of mind. She is sensitive to the need for Lisette to evolve. An ethic of care undergirds her decision to reveal the more painful memories. As we saw with Dimitri, but in reverse, there is a desire to protect that stems from an ethic of care. The exchange takes on a ritualistic air as Grandma Charlotte pauses, a pause that Lisette understands as a signal for her to choose the story. But the pause can also be read as the older woman's reverence for what she is about to share. She pauses so as to honor the sanctity of the ancestors whose story she tells, to acknowledge the dignity of those who came before her. Trouillot's attention to the stories themselves and how they are told has a metatextual significance that pulls the reader into a personal ethical pause for reflection.

Grandma Charlotte died before seeing Lisette realize her destiny as a Maroon. Her death is a formative experience in Lisette's life that takes an exacting toll: "I was fourteen years old when Grandma Charlotte died, *old and weakened, helpless* in the face of the smallpox that killed her. Slavery had depleted my grandmother's reserves of joy and tenderness. She has only her anger and pride left. I learned to respect the distance she imposed on everyone who got close to her, but I knew that I was her most prized possession in the world" (31). Defeated by slavery, Grandma Charlotte's diseased, old, and weak body is stolen for a second time. This time her life is snatched from young Lisette for whom the elderly grandmother was a rare biological connection and unique touchstone to her dead mother. But her spirit lives on in what she told Lisette. We encounter the old grandmother's lasting significance in these stories that Lisette incessantly replays in her mind. For example, Grandma Charlotte responds to Lisette's request for her to tell the story about *The Infamous Rosalie:*

One day, I promise you, I'll tell you about the barracoons; one day, when you'll need wings to carry yourself beyond the present moment. One day, *when your need will be greater than my fear of going back there in my memory.* But not today . . . On the ship I experienced a night I had never known, a night with no sky, no stars, no breeze; with bodies huddled against each other; without love or passion; with odors and movements stripped of their intimacy; with linked embraces and never-ending moans. Imagine a night when you can't count the stars because above you is nothing but a wooden ceiling. In place of windows were panels. In place of a universe was steerage. At night our bodies and minds do not rest, and shadows heighten the sense of turmoil caused by flesh pressing into flesh. You spend several days with your breath in tune to that of your companion in chains when you realize her breathing has ceased and that you're bound to a nearly rigid corpse. And no one hears your scream; it resonates only in your heart . . . For there are hundreds of screams that mask your own. (25)

Trouillot connects Lisette's story to a generation of women that came before her, constructing a female genealogy that begins long before the Middle Passage. By picking and choosing what to tell Lisette, the godmother and grandmother negotiate the wounds of memory until they no longer can. Grandma Charlotte's promise to tell Lisette "one day, when your need will be greater than my fear of going back there in my memory" suggests that her decision is guided by selfless love. Here love emerges as an ethic that informs the choice. The more painful the memories of the past, the more fearful she is of revisiting it. But at the same time, her promise to tell her "one day, when you'll need wings to carry yourself beyond the present moment" suggests that this same pain, while it might be difficult for Lisette to hear, will ultimately lead to her radicalization. According to this logic, the pain of the past can inspire the action of the future. Enduring the painful memory is a calculation that Grandma Charlotte must make in order to free Lisette. Her godmother explicitly tells her stories about the past so that she may imagine a different future for herself, which evinces a Black feminist ethic at work in the novel's logic for how characters make decisions about their lives.

The Infamous Rosalie can be read through Gina Athena Ulysse's theory of rasanblaj for how it demonstrates the determination of the enslaved to gather and to perform ceremonies in defiance of plantocracy rules, as well as how Lisette assembles the stories of the elders to imagine a different world for herself. Under the Code Noir, any gathering of the enslaved was a radical act. Trouillot reveals how the desire to live and assert one's basic humanity despite the horror of the slave system pushes the enslaved to gather, to tell, to share, and to protect one another. The entire novel carefully attends to the humanity and dignity of the enslaved. The enslaved people in *The Infamous Rosalie* fall in love and make love. They argue, they question, they gather, and they plot. They dance, pray, play games, laugh, and flirt. In this way, the novel effectively champions what Mimi Sheller denotes as "the full humanity of gnarled hands and hardened feet, dusty earth and ancient trees, and the erotic actions . . . of walking, dancing, writing, speaking, singing, drumming, and serving the spirits."[115]

The novel is set almost forty years prior to the beginning of the Haitian Revolution and is mainly concerned with the daily ignominy of life on the plantation. However, while reference to independence is not explicit, *marronage,* the process of extricating oneself from slavery through flight, alludes to the freedom in Haiti's future. I understand the act of *marronage* as one of the first manifestations of rasanblaj, defined by Ulysse as "an assembly, compilation, enlisting, regrouping (of ideas, things, people, spirits. For example, fè yon *rasanblaj,* do a gathering, a ceremony, a protest)." The term *rasanblaj* offers a unique Black feminist lens through which we can analyze this practice.[116] Because rasanblaj is also "inherently polysemic" as well as a "method, a project, a process" it is a fitting frame for analyzing *The Infamous Rosalie,* which is also a story about how the network of Maroons and enslaved people on the plantation began to work surreptitiously to undermine the machinations of the plantation life and begin the process of liberation that will eventually lead up to the Haitian Revolution. Responding to "the call of the forest," the enslaved run toward freedom, fleeing captivity, and defying their chains.[117] The women who surround and inspire Lisette are a force in her life that also manifest rasanblaj. As such, rasanblaj informs the trajectory of Lisette's life: it is the regrouping of ideas passed down to her from the older women who figure prominently in her interiority, and it is the process of resistance unfolding in Saint-Domingue during the "temps de l'empoisonnement," when poisoning was rampant in the homes of the slaveholders.

Since Lisette is the first-person narrator of *The Infamous Rosalie,* hers is the only perspective we have on the elderly women who are nonetheless central to the story. When she first mentions Grandma Charlotte, it is years after the older woman has died: "'I'm Sarah's Negress,' I said one day long ago, when Grandma Charlotte was still alive. Back in our shack, she slapped me in the face. 'I don't want you ever to think that thought again, Lisette. Arada women belong to no one'" (4). Lisette immediately associates the old woman's slap with the violence she is always subject to as an enslaved girl: "I have a long history with beatings, enough to know them well and to mistrust them. Even in my privileged position working for Mademoiselle Sarah, I was never protected . . . Ten, twenty, even fifty lashes for the worse offenses—the whip and I share a long history of blows and evasions, of crashes and missed encounters . . . The whips traces aren't visible: they've lodged in the hollow of my hand, and I feel as if my guts are dragging under my feet, though no one can see them" (5). She understands the slap as an extension of that violence even if it stems from a totally different logic. After a lengthy reflection on what it means to bear the weight of these different blows, Lisette returns to the nature of Grandma Charlotte's slap by connecting it to a lesson the older woman attempted to convey.

> But on that long-ago day, when Grandma Charlotte was still alive, the slap of her hand left its mark on my cheek. It gathered the pitfalls of my hidden desperation: the scattered bits and pieces of my shame, the urge to express my anger and the morsels of my tears and my betrayal, and it wove them all together in a single brusque movement more powerful than the whip. I still feel the sharp stinging sound coursing through me, her disdain for my unease and fear, her lack of pity for my bowing and scraping. I rest on the wings of that gesture whenever my knees refuse to bend to refresh my pupils in the darkness of their truth. (5)

By calling the old woman's slap a "gesture" with "wings" that remains with her years after it occurs, Lisette delineates how the isolated acts and words of her elders fashion her identity. It is equally important that the moment of the slap triggers a pause for the protagonist to compare the violence of her enslaver to her grandmother's sharp blow. As Lisette looks at these two situations, the reader is drawn into her ethical inquiry: does the grandmother's violence sting more or less because she is a loved one? Grandma Charlotte's admonishment is telling, considering that she is "an Arada woman who was the house cook until she died of smallpox," which means that her oppressors considered her to be loyal, trustworthy, and devoted to their service (6). But it is she who gives her granddaughter the talisman Lisette wears, which shows that despite her appearance of fidelity and compliance, she actively resisted the Code Noir. For Lisette, the talisman becomes "a way to remember Grandmother Charlotte and the mother [she] never knew" (11). The talisman serves as a point of lasting connection between Lisette and the women who came before her and serves as a spiritual guide.

In addition to the women who have joined the realm of the ancestors, Lisette's rasanblaj of Black women elders also includes Ma Augustine and Ma Victor. Ma Augustine in particular "all by herself stands for Grandma Charlotte, my great-aunt Brigitte, and all [the] ancestors who died in the prime of their lives" (23). The collective voices of these women—both the living and the dead—churn in Lisette's mind and spirit and eventually pave the way for her to escape and become a Maroon. The stories from the older women never obscure the violence of their experience; they understand the importance of conveying every detail. It is equally important that the stories Grandma Charlotte and Ma Augustine tell are not only about bondage but also about freedom. As Grandma Charlotte recounts:

> Ayouba, your mother, had not yet understood the meaning of her destiny when the horror began. We were about twenty people, young men, beautiful and strong, young women, full of life, with high and beautiful chests, laughing eyes, and promising hands. Free. Brigitte could have told you how we were captured, how we resisted. Me, I only want to remember the simple joy that existed before, before the smell of those waves, those winds, and the sand moving beneath our feet. I don't just want to remember sand dunes and the bare shoulders of slaves. I want to think about the time before the kidnapping, before *The Infamous Rosalie*. Because afterward I'll have nothing warm to hold in my memory, except the weight of your hand against my cheek and the day of your birth. (24)

Here Grandma Charlotte develops her own theory of remembrance. She does not want to relive the passage and the barracoons because she prefers to cling to her memories of freedom. For an enslaved woman, there is a cost to remembering, to recalling, and to reliving the violence of slavery. From this perspective Lisette is in a position of privilege, which affords her the luxury of the listening to the story without being triggered.

When Grandma Charlotte eventually does tell Lisette about the barracoons, it is in response to the young girl's acceptance of a gift from her "mistress," and the elderly woman's goal is to propel the younger woman toward resistance as a radical future, even if it does not occur until after her death. Concerned that Lisette is taking pleasure in one aspect of her enslaved existence, the grandmother seeks to correct this egregious misstep. Her telling of this story follows a cadence different from her telling of the other stories. As Lisette describes her, "My grandmother's voice sounded different; no doubt it was my fear of what was about to happen that made her voice sound like the tolling of a bell. Grandma Charlotte began slowly and spoke without pause, as if she had chosen her words a long time ago" (77). We can contrast the story of the barracoons with the previous passage about the slave ship. For Grandma Charlotte, there is an important distinction between the two that is further evidenced in the text by how the story is told. Lisette notices the difference: "Grandma spoke in a monotonous tone of voice, which was unusual, for she was always so incisive with her words and gestures. Her voice stung me, and sitting at her feet, I didn't dare move. My eyes glance at her face now and then, but I would quickly look away out of modesty in the face of this distress that preceded my birth" (78). I will quote this passage at length here because it illustrates my final point for this section:

> This whole story is like a vast wound. Some parts of it bleed more than others. There are more recent marks, not as fatal. Then there are old wounds that have stopped bleeding but have filled the entire body with a smell of rotting flesh. From time to time this stench rises to the surface with a whiff of decaying bodies, masking makeshift lies, baskets woven with happiness bought on credit. The time of the barracoons is a festering wound deep in the bones, a humiliation for all to see. When one has experienced this kind of humiliation, defeat can call your name at any time and undo your memory . . . Listen to the story of the barracoons! Perhaps one day we'll no longer be talking about any of this. Perhaps one day we'll no longer even remember this word; it will have perished with those of us who bore its mark—but the shame will remain until we root it out . . . I've already told you about the slave ship, the ship's steerage, the ship's hold and the sea. There are some who found the days of the crossing to be the most horrible and painful. But for me the barracoons are the wound that will always bleed deep inside me. That was when I knew for sure that a large part of me had been buried. (77–78)

Grandma Charlotte's metaphor of the wound to keep the story captures the unrelenting pain of her experience. As she tells the story, she refers to parts of her mind, body, and soul demonstrating a holistic knowledge of her lived experience. She acknowledges that for others the barracoons may not be the worst part of slavery but makes it clear that for her this was the defining moment of terror. It marked a critical moment in her identity because at this point she "knew for sure that a large part of me had been buried." This observation references the moment of capture as a constitutive and transformative event in her life, one that would alter her identity and seal her fate, so to speak. It also helps to explains her determination to cling to her identity as an Arada woman. Grandma Charlotte's insistence upon her own memory of humiliation and that of others also makes an important point about the individual memory of enslaved people that we do not have access to.

In Grandma Charlotte and Ma Augustine, we see how elderly women intentionally produce and share knowledge that impacts, inspires, and transforms younger generations. In the specific context of enslavement, the value of these women in the community as arbiters of wisdom gives birth to freedom as a radical possibility. As an example of the multivaried meanings of rasanblaj, *The Infamous Rosalie* attests to the possibility for life—inspired by the wisdom and care of the grandmothers—in the dehumanizing context of slavery.

Gran moun se moun

While race, class, sexuality, and gender are unquestionably foundational in Black feminist analysis, less attention has been given to age as a category in the intersectional framework. Especially when we consider how aging operates as another site of marginalization and a marker of difference, its import for feminist analysis should not be ignored. The perspectives on feminine aging vary in these novels, depending on the social networks of the women in question, but when viewed in relation to one another, they seem to tell us that aging is who you share it with. For Marie-Jeanne, Antoinette, Grandma Charlotte, and Ma Augustine, the communal bond of their connections sustains them and enables them to live fuller lives.

That same communal bond also allows their stories and legacies to live on after death. Looking at these elderly women in relation to the pairs presented in this chapter, we see how "the dramas of encounter and recognition" endow representations of aging with added meaning.[118] Through purposeful sharing of their knowledge, memories, religion, and lived experience with younger people, these characters pass on traditions and the remembrance of past events from one generation to the next—a perspective of relational dynamics that importantly refuses to eclipse the experience of the older person with the perspective of the younger.

Even apart from their relationships to the younger generation, Marie-Jeanne, Antoinette, and Grandma Charlotte are rendered as elderly women with contributions to make to the world and with their own unique vantage points. *Kasalé, L'œil-totem,* and *The Infamous Rosalie* illuminate the relationship between gender and age for Haitian women in different contexts, of different social status, and during different time periods, reminding us that as they grow older, Haitian women's experiences are enmeshed in a host of ethical dynamics. In the village of Kasalé for a poor Vodouizan for whom serving the spirits is what is most important, in the urban setting of Port-au-Prince for a middle-class woman whose home means everything to her, and on a plantation in Saint-Domingue prior to the beginning of the Haitian Revolution, we see how aging is gendered and has multiple significations that ask us to attend to how we actually value the elderly.

Dedicated to a sense of history and interiority, these elderly protagonists reveal the difficult truths that women's lives do not always matter for those around them, even when the conventional cultural wisdom suggests otherwise. Whether it is as a spiritual leader who passes down the tradition of serving the spirits or a grandmother who painstakingly shares her archive of family lineage with the next generation, these women are examples of how the elderly contribute to society, overcome obstacles, and beget meaningful legacies. And, even more, the narratives affirm elderly women as living, breathing, feeling subjects with rich interior lives that far surpass the sum of how others see them.

Through these elderly women we thus witness the richness of the human experience that spans several decades. Their presence as subjects is a representational practice with ethical implications for literary representations of women asking us to see what they are other than old. As we witness the importance of mobility in how these women move in time and space and relate to others, we also observe more contours of their humanity than stagnant views of the elderly allow for. The idea of movement or mobility recalls the importance of aging as an experience that is material, physical, and embodied. As we saw throughout this chapter, embodied aging is also on display when elderly characters interact with their bodies both in terms of pain and pleasure.

By devoting pointed attention to how gender impacts age in the lives of Haitian women, Trouillot and Mars highlight the ethical problems that arise as women grow older, offering new insights into how intersectionality operates as an optic in Haitian society. Again, it is important to note that none of these women are conventional with respect to interaction with aging. They resist convention and agitate the expectations of those around them, whether by talking about sex, by unswervingly serving the spirits in a community that denies the importance of Vodou, or by passing on a treasured and outlawed talisman to the next generation in defiance of colonial law.

In these ways, the vision of aging presented in *L'œil-totem, Kasalé,* and *The Infamous Rosalie* disrupts the reader's assumptions about what it means to be and to grow old. Although their interior monologues show us that the elderly protagonists are aware that society sees them as fixed and static, in their relationships to others, as well as their social and familial status, they divulge aging as a complex intersection of race, class, and gender as well as other markers of identity. Through these representations of aging, the authors challenge the reader to consider how aging is processed in the mind, body, and spirit, while providing depth, color, and nuance that centers elderly women as embodied subjects.

By paying attention to the interior lives of these characters through the use of narrative structure as well as the plots of the novels, Trouillot and Mars ask the reader to contemplate the ethical dimensions of writing about elderly women protagonists. The interiority of these much older women reveals a treasure trove of active thoughts, emotions, physical bodies, and spiritual practices, and memories. The quiet of their lives does not negate the activity of their minds and spirits. Conventional and unconventional in their own ways, they operate according to some enduring tropes but also challenge them, and they are often in contradiction with what society tells us them that they ought to be.

The title of this chapter, *Gran moun se moun,* invokes the personhood of aging people, naming them as subjects and affirming their humanity. My argument that age should be theorized as operative in our discussions of intersectionality turns to voice and visibility, connection and mobility, seeing and looking, because we have to see how these women are made legible in society and examine when their voices can be heard. Looking at how the narratives are constructed, it is clear that the voices of the women are more present in their minds than as audible forces in the world around them. In the case of Grandma Charlotte, it is the memory of her voice presented through Lisette. Marie-Jeanne is aware of how she is seen by her children but does not say anything to them about it. Similarly, Antoinette observes the behavior of people in the lakou but never challenges them directly. For each of these intrepid protagonists, their interiority provides insight into their understanding of (and disagreement with) how others see them.

In many ways, the elderly women in *Kasalé, L'œil-totem,* and *The Infamous Rosalie* are simultaneously central and marginal figures in the social worlds they inhabit, just as their centrality to the novels' plots contrasts with how they are seen by other characters. It is this dynamic in particular that calls for ethical reflection from the reader. The protagonists' relationships demonstrate that the dichotomy between old and young is ultimately a false one. The closeness between Sophonie and Antoinette, Dimitri and Marie-Jeanne, and Lisette and Grandma Charlotte, Ma Augustine and Ma Victor exemplifies intimate intergenerational connections. The Black feminist ethic at work in these novels emphasizes the importance of intergenerational dialogue and relationship as a way for the elderly to survive and be intimate.

Also, by exploring subjectivity from the vantage point of elderly women, *Kasalé, L'œil-totem,* and *The Infamous Rosalie* make important and necessary Black feminist interventions and ask us how we deploy intersectionality as an optic. Why are we not factoring age into our frames of analysis? Stories of aging offer insight into how marginal figures of society are pushed yet further into the margins as they age, but these novels put pressure on that impulse by offering singular relationships of love and care to enliven the ways these women interact with others and create lasting legacies. In content and form, these narratives display the complexity of elderly women and how they are often rendered invisible to those around them. Further, the ethical questions these texts engage expand feminist attention to personhood to include aging women. A feminist perspective on aging should consider the ways that elderly women are subjects and agents in their lives, able to make decisions about their mobility and have a stake in the communities they live in.

According to Paulette Poujol-Oriol's daughter, the scholar Claudine Michel, until her death in 2011, Poujol-Oriol often repeated that "la vieillesse est un naufrage." Old age is a shipwreck, one that leaves the elderly lugubriously alone despite the professed commitments of a cultural tradition that highly esteems them. I began this chapter with a consideration of a photograph of an elderly woman in Régine Romain's collection "Ayiti: Reaching Higher Ground." The subject of that photograph, Mama Ginen, reaches for higher ground by looking, surviving, and refusing. In her pointed look of refusal, I also see an ethic of survival, a determination to survive on her own terms. Her survival is to a large extent made possible by what she refuses to do and be for others, like the willful, disorderly, and unconventional protagonists in these novels. Taken together, the host of textual meanings that *Kasalé, L'oeil-totem,* and *The Infamous Rosalie* generate affirms the importance of aging subjectivities within a Black feminist ethical stance.

3   The Ethical-Erotic

Sex and Intimacy

> Mais ce n'est pas évident d'écrire l'érotisme quand il s'agit de corps noirs. Beaucoup de projections fantasmatiques y sont associées. Nous-mêmes avons intégré un certain nombre de représentations sur notre propre corps. Comment mettre ce mécanisme du désir, de l'érotisme—qui est quand même une des choses importantes de la vie—en écriture?
>
> (But when it comes to Black bodies, it's not easy to write eroticism. There are so many projections of fantasy associated with it. We ourselves have internalized a number of representations about our own bodies. How can we put this mechanism of desire, of eroticism—which is still one of the important things of life—into writing?)
>
> —Yanick Lahens

FOR THE 2017 celebration of International Women's Day, Haitian popular singer Rutshelle Guillaume posted a message on her social media accounts extolling the indomitable power of women. The caption beneath the post read: "Chères femmes, Combinons nos forces, élevons-nous les unes les autres au lieu d'être le pire démon, l'une pour l'autre. Je veux que vous atteigniez la grandeur et surmontiez vos obstacles. Restez sans peur et faites-leur savoir que vous êtes une reine VICTORIEUSE!" (Dear women, let us combine our strengths, lift each other up instead of being the worst demon for each other. I want you to reach greatness and overcome your obstacles. Stay fearless and let them know you're a VICTORIOUS queen!)[1] Guillaume's words of solidarity and encouragement were intended to communicate strength, power, and possibility. Along with the message was a beautiful photograph displaying the bodies of two Black women's naked torsos entwined with one another. Despite the meditation on female empowerment, unity, and sisterhood, it was this alluring image that generated the most interest and discussion in the days that followed. The stir that the photograph caused appeared to be owing to the fact that it featured two naked women, Guillaume and the actor Anyès

Noel, seemingly wrapped in a loving embrace. To many it was unclear how the sensuality and intimacy radiating from the intertwined women linked to the message of solidarity. Guillaume's post and the reactions to it reinforce Mimi Sheller's observation that "Caribbean popular sexualities, then, are always political acts operating in a politicized context."[2]

The message of empowerment that Rutshelle Guillaume communicated in the post is consistent with the themes of her songs that include topics such as love, relationships, and romance. In the post, the use of "victorious queen" echoes her song "Victorious" on the album *Rebelle,* in which she writes about the power of women to overcome. Guillaume uses her music to speak out about justice, choice, and liberation, all in relation to women's sexuality. In doing so, she often pairs gorgeous, sensuous melodies with difficult subjects. "Victorious" is about a survivor of domestic violence celebrating the end of her relationship with her abusive partner. "Je ne suis l'esclave de personne" "je dis non à ton malheur" (I am no one's slave. I say no to your misfortune). In the song "Je suis," Guillaume names and celebrates the different parts of her identity, acknowledging her multiple roles: "Je suis l'enfant prodige de ma ville, l'ambassadrice de mon pays / Je suis le dream come true de ma famille / La mère chérie de ma fille / Je suis représentante des fanm vanyan, modèle typique des femmes creoles" (I am the child prodigy of my village, the ambassador of my country, I am the dream come true of my family, the beloved mother of my daughter, I am the representative of the brave women, the typical mode of creole women). By explicitly naming who she is, she asserts her own identity in her terms.

In a similar vein, "Kite M Kriye" (Let Me Cry) takes a multifaceted approach to emotional interiority. The song is about a woman's anguish, anger, and deeply felt emotions whether she is crying out for love, against injustice, and for autonomy. The lyrics of the song culminate in a list of occasions and reasons that she cries out:

Mkriye lem revolte
Mkriye lem boulverse
Mkriye lem ap priye
Mkriye pou mwen bliye
. . . .
Mkriye se anba jem dlo ap koule e li tou seche
Mkriye pou sak gadem
Mkriye pou sak pa regadem
Mkriye le la sosyete anvi foure dwet nan jem

Mkriye lem maltrete
Mkriye lem pa trete.

(I cry when I revolt
I cry when I am overwhelmed
I cry when I pray
I cry to forget
I cry when tears stream from my eyes and when they are dry
I cry about my own business
I cry about what is not my business
I cry when society wants to
I cry when I am mistreated
I cry when I am not treated.)[3]

Guillaume's ongoing expressions of sexual liberation, rage, betrayal, and despair demand that we engage the ethical and the erotic together, not as either/or but as both/and. Viewed in this light, we can understand Guillaume's songs, which deploy the erotic for ethical reflection, as a Black feminist intervention acknowledging the multiplicity of Haitian womanhood.

As a well-known contemporary artist who combines *konpa, rara,* and other genres like jazz and pop, Guillaume presents one perspective of how the erotic manifests in today's Haitian audioscape. Her music is powerfully sensual. The erotic nature of her songs manifests in form as well as content. By beginning this chapter with Rutshelle Guillaume, my goal is to call attention to how the themes of intimacy, sexuality, gender, and sensuality circulate in Haitian society in a medium different from literature. One of my primary arguments in this book is that exploring a Black feminist ethic requires considering how different genres and mediums relate to one another. In this regard, popular culture is an important point of entry that is especially relevant in the contemporary moment.[4] Haitian soundscapes offer a way to hear what is alive in society through the voices of popular singers. They also influence how recurrent themes circulate in the popular imagination. Guillaume's music is noteworthy in the context of this book for how she situates Haitian womanhood by invoking tropes such as "fanm vanyan" and "fanm poto-mitan" then reconfigures their meaning for 21st century purposes.

In this chapter I draw from a long tradition of Black feminist analyses of sex and sexuality from the Caribbean and beyond. The chapter builds on scholarship by Caribbean feminist scholars such as anthropologist Lyndon Gill, who in *Erotic Islands: Art and Activism in the Queer Caribbean,* makes the case for an ethical approach to theorizing sex and sexuality.

Inspired by self-described lesbian warrior poet and essayist Audre Lorde's canonical essay, "The Uses of the Erotic: The Erotic as Power," Gill re-conceptualizes the erotic in terms of love, justice, and care by mining the "interrelated conceptualizations of the political the sensual, and the spiritual."[5] His project aligns directly with how I articulate what I will refer to here as "the ethical-erotic." I define the ethical-erotic as a frame-work for seeing sexual intimacy beyond the physical act that looks at the creation of intimacy through looking, talking, and touching. If an ethical approach asks *who are you?* then the ethical-erotic asks *who you are as a desiring sexual subject?*

What is the role of ethics in erotic representations of sex and sexuality? How can we think about sex and sexual dynamics erotically *and* ethically? How can we imagine new forms of agency that begin with the erotic, sex, and pleasure? These are the kinds of questions that interest me here. The field of sexology, which contemporary Caribbean activists and scholars have begun to invoke in discussions of sex and sexuality, helps us to imag-ine what the ethical-erotic might look like.[6] Namely, the sexologist bill of rights avers that safety and pleasure *should* be central to how we think about sex whether it is relationally, politically, spiritually, or socially. In this chapter I deploy the ethical-erotic as a way to analyze how representations of sexual relationships display the social, sensual, physical, and psycho-logical aspects of sex. My view acknowledges sex as a multidimensional and multiaffective act that generates a range of feelings associated with pleasure and desire. My approach to sex and intimacy also foregrounds pleasure, autonomy, agency, play, and passion, which, when taken together, help to map the erotic subjectivities of the characters I examine.[7]

It is with this approach in mind that I analyze a series of relation-ships in Kettly Mars's *Je suis vivant* (2015), Yanick Lahens's *Guillaume et Nathalie* (2013), and Évelyne Trouillot's *The Infamous Rosalie* (2004) and *L'oeil-Totem* (2006). I argue that sex and sexual dynamics in these novels deploy narrative techniques, logics of intimacy, and descriptions of the physicality of sex in ways that establish the ethical-erotic. There are three components in my conceptualization of how the ethical-erotic functions in these novels: first, it allows erotic subjectivity to flourish, second it foregrounds intimacy, and third it pays attention to dialogue and discourse as crucial in sexual relationships. Dialogue and discourse as I approach them refer to spoken acts (talking) as well as nonverbal exchanges like looking and touching.

To be clear, the idea of "sexual morality" narrowly construed is not what interests me here. Earlier in this book I identified the distinction between ethics and morality; it is worth noting again, especially given the scope of this chapter. In addition to Chielozona Eze's useful point that "whereas morality might be personal, ethics is always about the quality of one's relationships with others," I also find Colin Dayan's distinction instructive for my purposes. Ruminating on the difference, Dayan writes, "I have always thought that morality is not ethics . . . Ethics takes on for me a meaning that is less abstract. It has to do with locale, the proximity of one creature to the other or how an individual relates to what is not familiar. To be ethical in this sense, is to locate oneself in relation to a world adamantly not one's own. Whereas morality is an austere experience of non-relation, ethics demands the discomfort of utter relatedness."[8] Because ethics as I conceptualize it is about the quality of one's relationships with others, it lends itself well to thinking about the erotic. Following Dayan's description of ethics as proximity, I am interested in the ethical-erotic as an optic for how sex is described, referred to, and engaged in.

This view is especially important when we consider that Black feminist analyses of sex have often focused on violence and violation.[9] Black feminist scholars have been instrumental in acknowledging that sex is a theme often paired with violence. Mary Helen Washington identifies this combination as pleasure and danger: "if pleasure and danger are concomitant aspects of sexuality, it seems clear . . . that Black women writers have, out of historical necessity, registered far more of the latter than the former."[10] In my own scholarship I have used representations of sexual violence as a point of departure for locating rape narratives that foreground survivor subjectivity so as to shift discourses of sexual violence. My book, *Conflict Bodies: The Politics of Rape Representation in the Francophone Imaginary*, offers a set of strategies for reading rape that places the embodied experience of survivors at the center. Going all the way back to the origin myth of Haiti in the legend of Sor Rose, whose story "depends for its force on rape," I read works like Marie Chauvet's *Colère* and Kettly Mars's *Saisons sauvages* as examples of how sexual violence in Haitian literature is often linked to the political context.[11] By contemplating what sexual violence means for the survivor rather that what it symbolized for the nation, I purposefully shifted the discourses enshrouding rape culture.

In *Looking for Other Worlds*, by contrast, I focus on love, care, intimacy, and tenderness in order to offer a counternarrative. I am interested in a different angle that moves away from sexual violence (which is about power and control) to the act of sex itself. My view is that now, a few decades after Washington's observation about the entwined nature of pleasure and danger, we need a Black feminist ethic that pivots from danger (without, of course, denying its existence) toward pleasure. By decoupling sex and violence, I aim to posit one way to move toward an ethical-erotic in which safety, pleasure, and play are signs of intimacy.

Guided by the notion of sexual rights, sexual ethics as I map it here takes into account sexual freedom, sexual autonomy, integrity and safety, sexual equity, and sexual pleasure. Through my use of the ethical-erotic, I take seriously Jennifer Nash's directive to engage alternative affects, specifically the emotions associated with love, from the defensiveness that can hinder the Black feminist project. To investigate the contours of love and pleasure, I am interested in the intimacy and fulfillment that these characters derive from their sexual relationships. For protagonists in *Guillaume et Nathalie, Je suis vivant,* and *The Infamous Rosalie,* desire is a transformative force that can result in fulfillment and freedom. Intimacy is a motor that leads to more pleasurable sexual relations for the characters of these novels.

Lyndon Gill's concept of erotic subjectivity is useful for examining literary representations of sex while also highlighting ethics. As Gill explains, "Erotic subjectivity is at once an interpretive perspective and a mode of consciousness; it is both a way of reading and a way of being in the world."[12] When deployed as "an interpretive frame that highlights the spectacular and quotidian interworking of the political, the sensual and the spiritual," erotic subjectivity has much to offer for the analysis of literary texts in which desire can be a source of subject-making.[13] The ethical-erotic framework instructively wrests interpretations of sex and sexuality from singular, homogenizing frameworks and relies rather on a combination of factors.

Erotic subjectivity is central to my argument that these three novels present sexual relations as inextricably bound to a broader view of intimacy. By using erotic subjectivity as a lens, I intend to show how people experience sex as a multifaceted and multisensorial experience. Erotic subjectivity, which includes erotic agency, operates as an alternative framework for understanding how sex, power, and ethics correspond, overlap, and interrelate.

In accord with this approach, I am drawn to sexual acts to look at how pleasure, practice, and play function as tropes of intimacy that foreground erotic subjectivity of the characters in the novels. If, as Joanna Zylinska suggests in *The Ethics of Cultural Studies,* "ethics emerges from the lived experience of corporeal, sexual beings," then the erotic has much to offer in the elaboration of a Black feminist ethic.[14] While feminist discussions about the centrality and the politics of intimacy often remind us that intimacy should not be confined to the personal realm because it is also deeply political, I want to dwell nonetheless on personal, private, quiet moments in these novels. By exploring how intimacy figures within a private realm, my examination of erotic subjectivity draws heavily on such moments between couples.[15]

Especially in the sensual sex scenes, the logics of intimacy point to an ethical-erotic that takes us beyond the physical act of sex itself, closely following Audre Lorde's point that the erotic is "the power which comes from sharing deeply any pursuit with another person."[16] What Lorde makes abundantly clear, and what Caribbean scholars such as Vanessa Valdés have subsequently excavated, is "the erotic as an energy that empowers women, as natural to their being, something separate from the expression of sexuality, with either men or women."[17]

Throughout this book we see that Trouillot, Mars, and Lahens make narrative and stylistic choices that are informed by ethical questions. By experimenting with narration, these authors convey a sense of intimacy that extends to the reader's relationship to the narrator and the characters themselves. The Black feminist poetics they deploy to represent sex in *Je suis vivant, The Infamous Rosalie,* and *Guillaume et Nathalie* place the readers and characters in an intimate embrace, creating an ethical-erotic dialogue. We as readers are invited into the relationships, and, as we observe them, we are also called to consider our own relationships to the text and to others. While sex and sexuality can be configured in terms of power and oppression, freedom and liberation, focusing on the erotic yields a perspective that is profoundly relational, more intimate, and ultimately more spiritual.

Sex and Sexuality in Haitian Literature

Analyses of sexuality in Haitian literature can be situated in the larger context of the Caribbean, where expressions and theorizations of its meanings have been particularly robust. Caribbean scholarship on sexuality includes pioneering studies by M. Jacqui Alexander, Rhoda Reddock, Omi'seke Natasha Tinsley, Rosamond King, and Mimi Sheller, to name but a few. Among the groundbreaking texts by Caribbean feminists in this area, Omi'seke Natasha Tinsley's *Thiefing Sugar: Eroticism Among Caribbean Women* investigates how women loving women utilize poetic language and garden metaphors to express desire. Encouraging her readers to look to nature for metaphors about sexual desire, Tinsley's work demonstrates what it looks like to unearth the hidden pleasures of a text. *Thiefing Sugar* includes a chapter on nineteenth-century Haitian author Ida Faubert, one of the country's earliest poets, who "belonged to the first generation of Haitian elite women [who] pioneered a tradition of female intellectual production that professed its feminism—but did so under (flower) cover."[18]

By explicitly linking the development of a Haitian feminist intellectual tradition to a larger discourse of queer sexuality, Tinsley provides a different angle from which to understand feminist genealogies in Haiti. She sees Haitian feminism as a precursor to discussions of same-sex-loving people because, "in its tactical self-veiling, Haitian feminist expression emerged as a symbolic forerunner of Caribbean same-sex discourses, a sparse tangle of voices strategically placed between hidden open spaces."[19] More recently, Tinsley's study *Ezili's Mirrors* is a daring examination of the relationship between sexuality, the erotic, and Vodou that asks the reader to imagine the iterations of the goddess Ezili as a sexed, trans, queered body. Identifying Ezili as "the prism through which so many contemporary Caribbean authors were projecting their vision of creative genders and sexualities," Tinsley draws from various forms of cultural production to make her provocative points.[20]

Regarding the linkage of these concepts with Vodou, scholars such as Cécile Accilien explain, "Vodou exists in tension with other elements of Haitian culture and society; its authorization of gender fluidity and the free expression of same-sex desire collides with the global context in which Haitian culture and society have developed."[21] And while these scholars have generated a rich body of work that unites Vodou epistemologies with sexuality studies and fluid sexuality, my work departs from the tendency to locate the sexed Haitian body exclusively in relation to the practice of serving the spirits. What interests me for the purposes of this chapter are the material bodies, variegated feelings, intimate actions, and tender emotions of Haitian couples. Like Tinsley, I noticed that these authors articulate "many kinds of desires, caresses, loves, bodies, and more," and I want to dwell on the erotic poetics through which these touches emerge.[22] At the same time, following Gill's call to embrace the sensual-political-spiritual in our analyses of the erotic, my attention to these touches moves far beyond the physical.

The novels that I examine foreground the quiet and quotidian unfolding of Black love. Even so, it must be noted that, as Mimi Sheller explains, "sexuality is rooted in place, politics, relations of power."[23] As each of these relationships makes clear, place adds context and meaning to these

expressions of sexuality. Marylène and Norah in the comfort of the bourgeois home, Guillaume and Nathalie in the throes of passion in a Pacot
apartment, Lisette and Vincent making love in the thick of the forest—
these love scenes ask us to imagine sexual relations as unspectacular, tenderly mundane, and quietly intimate, no matter the surroundings. The
ethical-erotic offers a point of entry for imagining Black love on its own
terms rather than for what it tells us about home, nation, and sexuality.
Here I want to actively imagine Black love and its related terms differently.
It is an impulse that pursues Yanick Lahens's statement in the epigraph
of this chapter: "Mais ce n'est pas évident d'écrire l'érotisme quand il
s'agit de corps noirs. Beaucoup de projections fantasmatiques y sont asso-
ciées" (But when it comes to Black bodies, it's not easy to write eroticism.
There are so many projections of fantasy associated with it).[24] What I
hear in Lahens's statement is that the problem of global anti-Blackness
has both implicitly and explicitly conflicted with our ability to fully and
freely pursue the manifold uses of the erotic in expressive culture. This is
of course because narratives of stigma, deviance, and violence too often
cleave to representations of sex and the analyses of them. We can note,
as Rosamond King does, how sex is present alongside its simultaneous
stigmatization and that, "in spite of, and perhaps because of this legacy,
sex and sexuality appear and reappear in the literature as tools of pleasure
and politics, oppression and liberation."[25]

History shows that since the colonial era, sex and power have intertwined in ways that were often marked by violence. Perhaps in some part
due to this fraught history, in the specific case of Haitian literature, more
attention has been given to sexual *desire* than to the act of sex itself.
Sexual desire has been depicted in Haitian novels as early as 1929 when
Cléante Desgraves Valcin wrote about clandestine lovers in her novel *Cruelle destinée.*[26] It is telling that the first novel written by a Haitian woman
approached desire in ways that invite a reflection on the point where
ethics and erotics meet. Later in the twentieth century, Marie Chauvet
described the daily longings and frustrations of a forty-year-old woman
through her interior life in *Love, Anger, Madness* (1968). At the time
of publication Chauvet's portrayal of one woman with repressed sexual
urges and explicit fantasies was considered wildly audacious. As Paulette
Poujol Oriol pointed out, this moment can be considered a turning point
for the proclamation of female desire in Haitian literature: "Après Marie
Vieux, aucun sujet n'était plus interdit aux romancières haïtiennes" (After
Marie Vieux, no subject was forbidden to Haitian women novelists).[27]

Writing about sexual desire is of course not limited to Haitian women writers. For authors like Danny Laferrière, sex is a trope that emerges in themes as disparate as sex tourism by white women looking for young Black men in Haiti to the figure of the Haitian gigolo living in Montreal.[28] One of the most common figures of Haitian literature exists in the sex worker, recurring across generations, ranging from Jacques Stephen Alexis's novel *L'espace d'un cillement* (1959), which features a prostitute seeking to find a different way of life, to Makenzy Orcel's (2017) *Les Immortelles*, set in post-earthquake Haiti. But critical work on Haitian literature repeatedly invokes the difference in how women writers explore themes related to sexuality. Analyzing how sexuality figures in Haitian literature written by women, as opposed to men, Lahens identifies an approach to desire that differs from canonical novels such as *Gouverneurs de la rosée* and *Compère Général Soleil*.

> Celle-ci n'oscille pas dans ces textes comme les hommes ont voulu nous la présenter entre la sexualité éthérée d'Anaïse et de Claire-Heureuse et la sexualité quelquefois débridée du géo-libertinage de Depestre. Ce qu'elles [les écrivaines haïtiennes] proposent, c'est au-delà des difficultés liées à l'apprentissage, à la découverte de cette sexualité son approche tranquille et sereine.[29]

> (In these texts sex does not operate as men wanted to present it to us—oscillating between the ethereal sexuality of Anaïse and Claire-Heureuse and the sometimes unbridled sexuality of neo-libertinism of Depestre. What they propose goes beyond the difficulties linked to learning about sex, to discovering in sexuality, a calm and serene approach.)

As the critical work by Poujol Oriol and Lahens highlights, the theme of sexual desire in Haitian literature reached new heights in the twentieth century. Cleante Desgraves and Marie Chauvet set a powerful precedent for the unbridled exploration of women's sexual selves. My study proceeds in a different direction by offering a Black feminist ethic rooted in love, intimacy, and care as a lens for parsing representations of sex. The ethical-erotic is a Black feminist approach to sex in which care, intimacy, and agency flourish and thrive. As a critical framework, the ethical-erotic presents an opportunity to focus on "sexuality not as identity, but as praxis, something constantly constructed and reconstructed through daily actions" as Omi'seke Tinsley suggests we should in *Thiefing Sugar*.[30] Like Tinsley, I am interested in daily actions like looking, talking, and touching as signs of intimacy.

The erotic as it figures in *Je suis vivant, The Infamous Rosalie,* and *Guillaume et Nathalie* displays an intricate network of intimacy in which desire and pleasure are constantly in play. What is the role of sexual ethics in these novels? How do these authors introduce sexual activity as a way to pose moral questions to individuals and society? By engaging with taboo representations of sexuality in variegated manifestations, these authors defy the constraints of social mores and elaborate a more liberatory sexual ethics.[31] At the same time, they prompt us to challenge conventions of what kind of sex is acceptable, with whom, when, where, and how. Mars and Lahens create female characters who are sexually empowered *and* disempowered, who express their longing openly, whose approach to sex is profoundly nuanced, and who embrace the contradictions of their sexual predicaments. Taken together, scenes of sexual encounters set the stage for a rigorous questioning of sexual convention, the power dynamics within sex, and accepted ideas of the role sex plays in the lives of all people.

These examples of sexual encounter establish erotic subjectivity as an ethical stance. Focusing on erotic subjectivity raises ethical questions because of how autonomy, pleasure, and individuation combine. Again, it is important to note that erotic subjectivity as I understand it here depends on autonomy and agency. That is, to what extent are the protagonists allowed to realize their own visions of sexuality, to express their desire as they choose, and to act on it without the influence of others?

Describing the possibilities to be found in theorizing erotic agency, Mimi Sheller posits in *Citizenship from Below: Erotic Agency and Caribbean Freedom* that "erotic agency [is] a renewed theory of embodied freedom."[32] As a theory of embodied freedom, erotic agency signals the ability to control what one does with one's body, when, and with whom. Embodied freedom suggests that the body can be a point of departure *from* which and *through* which liberation is realized. The analyses that follow show how freedom is central to the characters whose sex lives Mars and Lahens depict. How can they be free to express their desire to and for one another? How do they freely follow the paths of their pleasure and desire? First in my analysis of *Je suis vivant,* I consider how same-sex desire becomes a space of care, intimacy, and freedom in sexual expression despite containment. Second, I read Lahens's novel *Guillaume et Nathalie* as a literary meditation on the necessity of romance to create new narratives of post-earthquake Haiti. For the characters in *Je suis vivant* and *Guillaume et Nathalie,* sexual activity becomes a way to express the fullness of their personhood as desiring, feeling, and thinking subjects. Finally, I turn to Lisette's relationship with Vincent in *The Infamous Rosalie* to show how their relationship puts the protagonist on a path to freedom. As an example of erotic agency in the context of the plantation's violent subjugation, *The Infamous Rosalie* emblematizes Sheller's formulation of erotic agency as a vantage point from which to explore "alternative ways to think about the self, the social, and the sacred; agency structure, and the metaphysical; autonomy, subordination, and divinity; and the body, the state, and the spirit."[33] For each of these novels, I pursue the ethical-erotic as a Black feminist framework invested in exploring how looking, talking, and touching show us the characters' identity as sexual subjects.

Same-Sex Desire and Fulfillment in *Je suis vivant*

Kettly Mars's *Je suis vivant* (2015) is a family drama that takes on the fraught subject of mental illness. The novel tells the story of the bourgeois Bernier family living in the suburbs of Port-au-Prince and what happens when eldest brother Alexandre, a man battling schizophrenia, returns to their household. After the 2010 earthquake, the upscale psychiatric home where Alexandre has lived for forty years closes permanently, and he is suddenly sent home. The Bernier household is made up of the mother, four adult children two of whom have spouses, and the staff of domestics. Éliane is the eighty-six-year-old matriarch who still mourns the loss of her deceased husband, Pierrot. The oldest daughter, Marylène, is an artist who had moved to Belgium for her education and career but returned to Haiti decades later. Next in age is Alexandre, who at the age of eighteen was sent to live in a home for the mentally ill. Grégoire, the third child and second son, assumes much of the responsibility for his brother's care later in life. Finally, Gabrielle is a stereotypical youngest child whose childhood was dominated by her brother's illness.

Each of these characters, along with their spouses and people who work in their house as staff, reacts differently to the reintegration of Alexandre into the household. Set entirely inside the Bernier home, *Je suis vivant* is a domestic novel preoccupied with the insularity and interiority of one family. As a story about Alexandre's schizophrenia and its effects on his family, the novel reveals the toll that mental illness takes on the individual as well as on other family members.[34] Narrated in the voices of each family member, as well as Norah and occasionally their servants Livia, Anna, and Ecclésiaste, *Je suis vivant* is a polyphonic narrative that looks at how different family members see (and fail to see) each other.

Written in Mars's trademark style that is intensely attentive to detail *Je suis vivant* conveys myriad issues in the context of a single family.³⁵

The subplot that most interests me for the purposes of this chapter is about two women who fall in love: Marylène, the eldest daughter, and Norah, a younger woman who initially poses for Marylène—a rapport that signals an unequal power dynamic from the start. Theirs is one of a few woman-loving-woman relationships in Haitian literature written with such care, nuance, and balance. Marylène's sense of her sexuality is complicated from childhood through adulthood. When she lives in Belgium as a student and then as an artist, she experiences a series of difficult romances with men. Upon her return as a sixty-year-old woman she finally expresses the fullness of her sexuality—desire, preferences, and appetite—within the confines of the Bernier home.

In some ways, Marylène's sense of liberation upon coming home appears to counter the idea that queer Caribbean people are only free to be what Nadia Ellis suggestively calls "out and bad" in their hostlands and that nonheteronormative sexuality is generally hidden in the lives of Caribbean people.³⁶ This appearance seems to be further supported in that nowhere do we see Marylène cast as what M. Jacqui Alexander calls "a dutiful daughter jeopardizing middle-class respectability."³⁷ But the text clearly indicates that Norah never leaves the Bernier home, or even Marylène's room there. This confines and contains their relationship and suggests that Marylène keeps her lover hidden.

As the firstborn daughter in a bourgeois family, Marylène is a woman-loving-woman for whom sexuality is a vexed site of freedom from the restricting respectability politics of her class. Following M. Jacqui Alexander persuasive argument in *Pedagogies of Crossing* that "women's sexual agency and erotic autonomy . . . pose a challenge to the ideology of an originary nuclear heterosexual family that perpetuates the fiction that the family is the cornerstone of society," we notice how few representations of sex and sexuality explicitly engage with women's pleasure and desire on their own terms.³⁸ Marylène troubles this dynamic by embracing Norah within the context of her nuclear heterosexual family. Their coupling threatens the Bernier family's heteronormative patriarchal structure all the more because it occurs within the house, compromising the family's vision of hetero-patriarchal respectability.

Marylène and Norah's relationship also demonstrates how class and age figure in woman-loving-woman relationships, illuminating the necessity for an intersectional approach. If I read much of their relationship through the lens of M. Jacqui Alexander's *Pedagogies of Crossing* it is because this text exacts an intervention that, in the words of Alexis Pauline Gumbs, "works to create textual possibilities for inquiry well beyond individual scholarly authority" and ultimately encourages us to move beyond and through boundaries of thought and theorizing.[39]

I use the term *woman loving woman* rather than *queer* or *lesbian* because this characterization is more consistent with the lexicon of sexuality in contemporary Haiti.[40] The official website of *Kouraj,* an organization that advocates for the rights of LGBT people, notes that "M Mouvement" is a better descriptive for gay and lesbian people in Haiti.[41] Although some theorists of queer Caribbean studies have contested the utility of the term *queer* in the context of these islands, they nonetheless identify its necessity. In the specific example of Haiti, *LGBT* and *queer* are not used with the same frequency or specificity as "M Mouvement." Explaining this, Thérèse Migraine-George writes that M Mouvement is "based on the Kreyòl terms *Masisi, Madivin, Makomer,* and *Mix,* which . . . more accurately reflect the complex reality of same-sex practices in Haiti while resisting Western-imposed gender and sexual norms."[42]

Through her characters' embrace of sexual fluidity and ambiguity, Kettly Mars illuminates the limitations of assigning fixed referents for desire. As her protagonists move between sexual partners, what matters is not the sexuality or the gender of the two partners but rather the desire and the pleasure they derive from one another, regardless of how they choose to identify. Still, when we understand queer in the terms that José Esteban Muñoz offers as "that thing that lets us feel that this world is not enough," it is clear how Muñoz's acknowledgment of the need for other worlds evocatively connects to my organizing frame for this study.[43]

I am nonetheless drawn to definitions of queer that can productively generate and accommodate a more expansive range of meaning. This is what Moya Bailey proposes by using the term to signal "the qualitative position of opposition to presentations of stability—an identity that problematizes the manageable limits of identity . . . Queer involves our sexuality and our gender, but so much more."[44] *Je suis vivant* demonstrates how Mars stretches structures of desire to accommodate a range of sexual praxis.

Of course, an intersectional analysis of how sexuality informs the lives of Haitian same-gender-loving people must account for the differences dictated by class. In her study of Haitian film, Cécile Accilien smartly offers the following: "As Charlot Jeudy, president of KOURAJ, an organization fighting for LGBTQ rights in Haiti, observes, homophobia is a severe problem in Haiti, one that affects every element of society, although it must be noted that, as in other aspects of Haitian culture, the disparity between rich and poor is clear. There is a divide between LGBTQ people who have power, who generally live in Port-au-Prince, the capital, and those who live in rural areas and are struggling to survive."[45] Accilien goes on to note that in the upscale suburb of Pétionville, many LGBTQ people will informally gather for dinner parties, at restaurants and beaches, highlighting how class and sexuality move through space and place. In other words, and as Vanessa Agard-Jones makes clear in her work on same-sex relationships in the French-speaking Caribbean, LGBTQ "people cannot be reduced to victimized subjects living in a universally homophobic place."[46] We must regularly return to this point and use it to anchor our analyses of same-sex relationships in the entire region, especially if we are to "remember the Caribbean not as a generality but as a complicated specificity."[47] Put differently, the local context highlighted in each of these novels should also lead us to make sense of the variegated machinations of sexuality in the quotidian life of ordinary Haitian people.

Je suis vivant departs significantly from Mars's earlier novels for how it conveys sex primarily in relation to intimacy and care.[48] The novel displays modes of intimacy that are based in feeling, thinking, and seeing, especially through the character of Marylène Bernier. That Marylène appears to be the only character who seems to have meaningful sexual autonomy is significant. As she ponders her relationship to sex and her own desire, we notice that she is one of the few characters engaging in this type of self-reflective inquiry. How she interacts with her sexual drive and the flows of her desire are also situated in the context of her art and creativity. Marylène exemplifies how belonging in the family is configured for a middle class, Black woman with same-sex desire; and it is particularly important that her sexual agency serves as a form of connection and affiliation rather than alienation. The relationship between Norah and Marylène shows how social and sexual relations combine for women who love women. Below we see how their relationship is forged not only through the physical but also through their conversations; and through it all, visual art operates as a connecting force between them. As we saw with Marie-Jeanne in *L'œil-totem*, art and creativity inform how the ethical-erotic infuses Marylène and Norah's relationship. Through Norah and Marylène's same-sex love story, Mars questions the limits of the hetero-patriarchal model offered by the family metaphor central to the architecture of the novel. She also exposes the silences that surround same-sex relationships by limiting the women's relationship to the home.

I also read Marylène's story in light of Rosamond King's point that same-sex-loving women are at once invisible and hyper-visible. Although

Marylène's love for another woman is noticed by all the members of her household, it is never openly commented upon. They see it, but do not speak about it to her, thereby replicating social silences. Although, the two older women, Éliane and Livia, are to an extent exceptions to this silence, their concern is more about Norah in terms of class, not sexuality.

This Bernier family dynamic mirrors how patterns of visibility and invisibility play out regularly in the lives of same-sex loving people throughout the Caribbean and shows how "desire and gender expression can be absorbed by prevailing norms which is why they are rendered easily invisible."[49] King's study *Island Bodies* effectively deconstructs the myth of invisibility of Caribbean lesbians, reminding us that the realities of Caribbean sexuality "are so flexible."[50] King's insistence on the agency and autonomy of Caribbean people is instructive because it also points to an ethical position. For King, "the power of desire is a motivating force for individual fulfillment," and in *Je suis vivant* we see how this unfolds because the characters are on quests for individual fulfillment that, with the exception of Marylène, go unrealized.[51]

Although each family member, and several people related to them, tells his or her story, Marylène's voice recurs most often, and her background story is the most detailed. Early in the novel, she divulges the extent to which sexual desire has regulated her life since her teenage years.

Y a-t-il eu un moment de ma vie où je ne courrais pas après un homme? J'ai cherché l'amour et la voix d'un homme pour remplir mes quatre murs. Parce qu'une femme se doit d'avoir un homme dans sa vie, dans sa peau. Un homme à soi, un chasse-solitude. Un ami qui ne le restera pas longtemps, un amant en devenir . . . Ce besoin d'un homme peut devenir une obsession. Un homme ou la perte de sens de tout. (59)

(Had there been a time in my life when I wasn't running after a man? I sought the love and the voice of a man to fill up my four walls. Because a woman must have a man in her life, in her skin. A man of her own, someone to chase away loneliness. A friend who will not stay long, a lover in the making . . . This need of a man can become an obsession. A man or the loss of all meaning.)

Marylène's idea that "une femme doit avoir un homme dans sa vie" acquiesces to gendered social codes that require women to have men in their lives to achieve fulfillment. Her acknowledgment of this dynamic intrigues us when we consider how she will later choose a woman rather than a man as her lover, a development in her sex life that I read as an example of Marylène becoming freer. After all, and as Vanessa Valdés has observed, "broadening one's sexual preferences and practices . . . [can serve] as a reminder to that person that s/he remains a free being."[52]

Marylène's reference to "mes quatre murs" can be read in sexually explicit terms. Without expressing overtly that she was soliciting lovers, the walls she mentions, combined with wanting a man "in her skin," have a sexual connotation; the man could be entering the walls of a bodily orifice, penetrating her vagina. Still, the opacity of the reference means that she could be referring to the other aspects of herself in which desire lives— her spirit, her soul, her emotions. The latter reading suggests a spiritual, sensual, and physical sensation that aligns with the ethical-erotic. Both readings "mes quatre murs" suggest that the erotic is interchangeable in its physical and psychological elements.

An appetite for sex pursues Marylène throughout the course of her life and eventually emerges as a replacement for her creativity. As we saw in the previous chapter with Trouillot's *L'œil-totem,* the connection between women's creativity and sexuality plunges the reader into a deep reservoir of meanings. By drawing a parallel between sex and artistic praxis, Mars and Trouillot link sexual acts to autonomy and agency, in a sense comparing the ability to create through art to the ability to create through sex. This world-making impulse is especially important in that it refers to sex as creation without foregrounding procreation. It is a perspective that reinforces Jafari Allen's insightful point that "to talk about sexuality, therefore, is to talk not only about the everyday lived experience of the sexual(ized) body, but also about the imagination, desires, and intentions of the sexual(ized) subject."[53] By naming her intention to use sex to fill a creative void, Marylène alludes to the uses of the erotic. When Marylène reveals that she has had an abortion, the importance of sex as creation for creativity's sake rather than for procreation further dislodges sexual acts from hetero-patriarchal reproductive agendas. Again, while the family is at the center of the story, Mars finds ways to destabilize and interrogate its dominance, leading the reader to pose ethical questions about how families operate, communicate, and interact.

When Marylène discloses her sexual history, she does so nonchalantly, referring to "quelques amants pour tuer le temps quand la peinture se refusait à moi. Une femme qui peint, ça excite la curiosité des sens" (a few lovers to kill the time when painting eluded me. A woman who paints excites the curiosity of the senses) (60). Art is essential in her life: she prefers art to sex, but, in periods where she lacks creativity, she can replace the need to create with sexual activity, filling up the artistic void with erotic pleasure.

This revelation tells us first that there was a time when art was more important and more fulfilling than sex for Marylène. Second, it shows how aware she is of her positionality as a woman artist. Third, it ties sensuality to artistry; that is, she is aware of how her work as a painter is sexually exciting for the people with whom she has sex. And yet there is a dual referent at work because Marylène could also be describing how painting excites her own senses, not only those of her lovers. Her connecting of sexual appetite and creative praxis identifies sex as a generative, productive, and creative force that moves far beyond the body.

The interweaving of Marylène's creative and erotic lives is brought into greater relief after she meets Norah. In the course of the novel, their relationship further develops the sensual rapport between art, sex, and intimacy. Audre Lorde brilliantly captured this dynamic between creating and feeling in the context of the erotic. Her point that "the erotic is not a question only of what we do; it is a question of how acutely and fully we can feel in the doing" further illuminates Marylène and Norah's relationship to the ethical-erotic.[54] Through Marylène's heightened awareness of how her artistry and sexual pleasure overlap, Kettly Mars asks the reader to contemplate sex as a form of creativity, an artistic sensuality. It also confirms Mars's disclosure to Nadève Ménard: "La sensualité est ce que nous sauve de nous-même et des autres . . . La sensualité n'est pas que sexuelle" (Sensuality is what saves us from ourselves and from others . . . sensuality is not only sexual).[55]

Marylène's decision to invite Norah into the family home should also be read as a refusal to abide by bourgeois codes of respectability dictated by her class. At the same time, the two women remain entirely in the home or in Marylène's room, and so taking intersectionality into account helps to parse the ways that "class can sometimes protect those who are gender nonconforming."[56] Marylène's relationship to her sexuality and how her family perceives it is consistent with how same-sex desire can function as an open secret in some Caribbean societies. Describing this feature of Caribbean social life, Yolanda Martinez-San Miguel explains that "the degree of publicity or discreetness about someone's sexual preferences is more important than the actual sexual practice."[57]

Marylène and Norah are very discreet: that their relationship takes place entirely behind the closed doors of the Bernier home reminds the reader of the limits placed on women's open expressions of their sexuality. Also, the stately nature of the Bernier home should not be lost on us. Its stunning architecture is referenced throughout the novel. The significance of that architecture (the home is one of the few structures that remained entirely stable during the thirty-five second earthquake) is both literal and figurative. When we understand that, as Imani Perry writes, "patriarchy is the foundational structure for gender domination," feminist analysis helps us to see how the structure of the Bernier house was physically oppressive to Marylène while she was coming of age.[58] Now, years later, and after the physical house endured despite the earthquake that levelled so many buildings in Port-au-Prince, this house has become an enclave where she and her lover do as they please away from the penetrating glare of society.

"Through an Erotic Looking Glass"

The poetics of lovemaking in *Je suis vivant* represent sex with careful attention to the women's individual bodies coming together and the erotic pleasure they derive from it. Examining their exchanges "through [an] erotic looking glass," as Lyndon Gill advises, we see that they unfold in ways beyond the physical.[59] This is especially enriching when we take into account Mars's writing style, which as Joëlle Vitiello has observed, is scrupulously attentive to detail: "L'auteure est particulièrement attentive aux détails (olfactifs, visuels, physiologiques, et psychologiques) qui lui permettent de donner corps à ses personnages et à leurs dilemmes de façon crédible, presque cinématographique" (The author is particularly attentive to details [olfactory, visual, physiological, and psychological] which allow her to give substance to her characters and their dilemmas in a credible, almost cinematic way).[60]

When Norah first enters Marylène's life, it is to pose as a model, a decision that the latter refers to as uniquely important in her life:

Je devais bien confirmer à Norah qu'elle pouvait venir poser pour moi ou bien lui dire que je n'avais plus besoin de ses services. Cette décision m'a semblé l'une des plus importantes que j'ai eu à prendre depuis très longtemps. Comme celle de divorcer après dix années de vie conjugale. Depuis qu'elle pose pour moi, je pense trop souvent à Norah. Je m'y attendais un peu mais je suis quand même désarçonnée par l'effet qu'elle me fait.

(I had to confirm with Norah that she could come over to pose for me or tell her that I no longer needed her services. This decision seemed to me one of the most important I'd had to make in a very long time. Like divorcing after ten years of married life. Since she poses for me, I think too often about Norah. I was expecting it a bit, but I'm still thrown off guard by the effect it has on me.) (89)

At the time of their initial encounter, Marylène's desire for the younger woman takes her by surprise, although she quickly welcomes it. Contemplating her attraction to Norah, her thoughts move to the younger woman's body with curiosity and eager desire. She focuses first on Norah's eyes, searching for more behind them:

> Elle a des yeux qui dévorent tout autour d'elle, moi y compris. Elle a le cou parfait, les lèvres parfaites, une peau parfaite. Sauf ses doigts qui sont rudes, ils n'ont aucune douceur, leurs jointures sont noueuses, la peau de ses mains est sèche et secrète. Des mains d'une femme aux abois qui se cache derrière un faciès de vingt ans. Je me demande quel est son âge réel.

> (She has eyes that devour everything around her, including me. She has a perfect neck, perfect lips, perfect skin. Only her hands have no softness in them: she has rough fingers and knotty knuckles, the skin of her hands is dry and secret. She seems to have the hands of a beleaguered woman hiding behind the face of a twenty-year-old. I wonder what her actual age is.) (90)

Marylène first looks at Norah through the eyes of an artist, noticing her perfectly shaped neck and imagining the texture of her soft skin. Before she ever paints, undresses, or makes love to Norah, she paints her with her eyes and a devouring look of her own. Marylène's assessment of Norah's body begins with her eyes and travels down to her hands; the eyes that see and hands that do mark the body's agency. By noticing the roughness of her hands, Marylène connects Norah's body to her class status. She also asks herself questions about the meaning of Norah's presence in her life in relation to other parts of her life: "Elle est entrée dans ma maison et dans ma vie en même temps qu'Alexandre. Pourquoi ? Je suis presque vieille, j'ai plein de cheveux blancs, j'ai toujours été hétérosexuelle. Pourtant elle me fait le même effet que me ferait un homme, quand j'aimais encore l'odeur des hommes" (She entered my home and my life at the same time as Alexandre. Why? I am almost old, I have lots of white hair, I've always been heterosexual. Yet she does the same thing that a man would do to me, when I still loved the smell of men) (89–90). In her mind Marylène connects Norah's arrival to her brother's reentry into the Bernier home, marking two life-altering moments. By linking the two, she suggests that something about Alexandre's return leads her to think differently about her own desire. Could it be that Alexandre's return to the home introduces the possibility of other worlds, worlds very different from the one the Berniers were imagining as their future? Does the abrupt change in the family situation free Marylène to think about what else in her life could be subject to change?

When Marylène describes Norah, she notes not only how she *sees* her (and interestingly a focus on Norah's eyes demonstrates an interest in what and how *Norah sees*) but also how she *feels* describing the smoothness of her skin as well as her rough hands and fingers. The descriptions highlight desire as multisensorial and multiaffective. Desire is not relegated to physical attributes; it also searches for what lies behind the desired subject. Marylène's look at Norah mirrors the younger woman's because, just as Norah "devours everything around her," Marylène seems to be doing the same as she studies Norah. At first, Marylène's rigidity in her view of sexuality as either heterosexual or not reveals an inability to think in fluid terms about sexuality despite what desire causes her to feel. Eventually, however, she will act on her attraction to Norah and the two of them enter into a consensual relationship.

The portrayal of Marylène and Norah's relationship confirms that "heterosexuality is far from universal in the Caribbean," because it also shows that for the Bernier family Marylène's desire is in fact neither spectacular nor deviant.[61] The outrage does not come from the circumstance that they are women desiring one another, but rather from the class dynamics of their relationships.

Seeing Norah

I have spent much of this section discussing Marylène as the character whose sexuality and sexual relationships we analyze, but I now want to turn Norah. Interestingly, and I think tellingly, Norah is the only character in the novel who is on the outside of the family; even the people who work as domestics in the home are interior to the Bernier household where they have lived for years. Norah narrates four chapters in *Je suis vivant*. She sees a sexual relationship with Marylène as inevitable and thinks extensively about what the terms of their sexual encounter will be: "Marylène m'a prise de court. Bien sûr, je savais qu'elle n'aurait pu résister longtemps encore à la tension sexuelle qui grandissait entre nous" (Marylène caught me off guard. Of course, I knew she couldn't resist the growing sexual tension between us for long) (152).

We learn much about Norah's state of mind and her sense of self in relation to Marylène as their love story unfolds. Norah begins to derive her own sense of pleasure from the moments they share in the studio, enjoying the touches of Marylène's artist hands on her body, and the smells of the studio. She is enticed by the idea that posing as a model for Marylène will connect them forever: "Ces toiles me lien en quelque sorte à Marylène, elles nous tiennent dans une complicité exaltante" (These paintings link me in a way to Marylène, they hold us in an exhilarating complicity) (153). Norah takes great pleasure in being seen, valued, touched, and affirmed by Marylène. Her sense of self blooms under Marylène's artistic touch. The pleasure she derives from the art and from being a model foreshadows the intense sexual pleasure that she will experience: "J'aime venir à mes séances de pose, c'est la chose la plus géniale qui me soit arrivée dans ma vie" (I love coming to my modeling sessions, it is the most wonderful thing that has happened in my life) (153).

When the women make love for the first time, it comes as a surprise to the reader and also to Norah, who had expected that she would be the one to make the first move. Norah describes the unfolding of their first sexual encounter, and the reader experiences Marylène's pleasure through her eyes.

Marylène s'est approchée de moi. Je posais, assise sur mon tabouret . . . Elle étudiait de près mes traits, mes yeux, mon nez, ma bouche . . . Mais cette fois elle avait un autre visage. Elle s'approcha de moi comme une automate, le regard fixe. Elle fit glisser la bretelle de mon corsage sur mon bras, je ne portais pas de soutien-gorge, elle se pencha et posa un baiser sur mon épaule. Et un autre, et un autre encore, en montant vers mon oreille. Et soudain, comme possédée, elle couvrait mes lèvres de ses lèvres. De léger spasmes lui traversaient le corps. J'ai cru entendre une plainte monter à sa gorge. J'ai penché la tête en arrière et j'ai fermé les yeux pour goûter à sa langue et lui offrir mon avenir.

(Marylène approached me. I was posing, sitting on my stool . . . She was studying my features closely, my eyes, my nose, my mouth . . . But this time she had another face. She approached me like an automaton, her gaze fixed. She slid the strap of my bodice over my arm, I wasn't wearing a bra, she leaned down and kissed my shoulder. And another, and another, going up to my ear. And suddenly, as if possessed, she covered my lips with her lips. Slight spasms rippled over her body. I thought I heard a whimper rise in her throat. I tilted my head back and closed my eyes to taste her tongue and give her my future.) (154)

In this detailed love scene, the women move from the artistic activity to sexual activity. It is a ritual that they have enacted many times with Marylène looking, touching, and evaluating Norah, then re-creating her likeness on the canvas. These sessions had been charged with erotic energy long before the women sexually explored one another's bodies. Artistic creation becomes a sexy metaphor for creating physical pleasure. Their looking, touching, and talking eventually lead to sex. The women's pleasure also follows the familiar pattern that I frame as the ethical-erotic, reminding us that even though erotic acts are more than sex, they include sex. Told from Norah's perspective, this scene foregrounds her erotic subjectivity as we note a progression from the pleasure she takes in being in the art studio and being a model to the pleasure she receives from Marylène's body, and then her decision to "offrir son avenir" by offering the pleasure on her own.

The beginning of the sexual relationship inaugurates a new phase for both women. Their touches grow longer, their talk expands and deepens, and their looks hold and linger. After the initial kiss, they quickly move into the next phase of their relationship: "Et puis les choses sont allés plus vite. Nous étions soudain nues. Le canapé était comme un îlot au milieu d'une mer déchaînée de couleurs où nous avions pris refuge. Marylène ne se lassait pas de toucher mon corps, de le palper, le caresser . . . Ses seins son petits et ses mamelons énormes. Je les ai goûtés à pleine bouche" (And then things went faster. We were suddenly naked. The sofa was like an island in the middle of a raging sea of colors where we took refuge. Marylène never tired of touching my body, touching it, caressing it . . . Her breasts are small and her nipples huge. I tasted them fully in my mouth) (154). The chapter ends abruptly here, and Mars leaves the reader on a precipice of the women's pleasure.

The island and ocean metaphors in Norah's description of how they fall for each in their lovemaking reflect that, for sexually fluid women, waters offer a rich metaphor for sensually capturing their waves of pleasure, as Omi'seke Tinsley' successfully conceptualizes in "Black Atlantic, Queer Atlantic." The sofa that turns into a boat and holds Marylène and Norah as they enjoy each other's bodies speaks "to the possibilities of and limits of fluid erotic identities in the Caribbean and to crosscurrents of complexities."[62] Together these lovers find an ocean that serves as a refuge despite the sea raging around them. Swallowed up in one another's pleasure, they float to a different place from the rest of the Bernier home.

In my view, the way that Norah's story unfolds encourages the reader to sympathize with her and see the story through her eyes, even though we see how she is *seen* before we *see* her. It is important that this young woman from a poor neighborhood tells us from her perspective how she understands the Bernier household. Through Norah, Mars reinforces the need for intersectional analyses of sexuality because, unlike Marylène, who comes from a wealthy background, Norah is further marginalized for being economically disadvantaged. When she enters the Bernier home for the first time, Norah has a sharp critical eye and makes quick judgments of her own. She is the character about whom we learn the most in the shortest amount of time: "Je ne lui ai pas dit que j'habitais sous une tente, tendue sur la toiture cassée de la maison de mon oncle où je vis, dans un quartier, disons populaire" (I did not tell her that I lived in a tent, stretched out across the broken roof of my uncle's house in a neighborhood we could call common) (106). This revelation is not only about class but also about how the earthquake aggravated class inequalities, leaving the more vulnerable population even more vulnerable.

As Marylène appraises her physical appearance, Norah also looks at the older woman: "Elle n'est pas vraiment laide. Plus jeune elle attirait sûrement l'attention pour des raisons difficiles à définir comme l'intensité de son regard doux et sauvage. Ses grosses fesses et sourcils épais qui étonnent. Mais cette coupe de cheveux, ces tee-shirts informes, ces pantalons trop grands . . . qu'est-ce qu'elle essaie de cacher?" (She is not really ugly. Younger, she surely attracted attention for reasons that were difficult to define, such as the intensity of her soft, wild gaze. Her big buttocks and thick eyebrows that amaze. But this haircut, these shapeless T-shirts, those pants that are too big for her . . . what is she trying to hide?) (107).

These observations reveal Norah's introspective nature and a curiosity about Marylène that eventually develops into care. Again, as we saw in the previous chapter, the exterior gaze renders her as object, whereas her interiority reveals a woman with enough of a sense of self-regard to critique others' opinions of her: "Depuis l'adolescence j'ai dû suivre en étant intelligente et bien roulée. Deux qualités qui inquiètent les hommes et les femmes; qu'ils ont besoin de dissocier chez une femme. Sois bien roulée et tais-toi. On ne m'en demande plus. Trop d'intelligence chez une femme menace la sécurité publique" (Since adolescence I had to go with being smart and voluptuous. Two qualities that disconcert men and women; that they need to separate from each other in a woman. Be voluptuous and shut up. They do not ask more from me. Too much intelligence in a woman threatens public safety) (121). Norah's evaluation of how she is seen by others is insightful and sardonic. Her perspicacity and frank way of speaking further endear her to the reader. Through her interiority, we can glean more about who she is than we can from her interactions with others. How then do our key words of recognition, questioning, and relation function for this character? We know that looking and being looked at inform the frame of recognition. Like Marie-Jeanne in chapter 2 and as we will see with Titi and Sorel in in chapter 4, Norah is profoundly aware of how others look at her. But in this case, looking does not always lead to recognition. Rather, it shows us that, as we saw in Tina Campt's *Looking for Images,* to be looked at is not the same as to be seen. Norah is a subject intent on moving beyond the reductive ocular logic of a surface look.

The nuance that I am parsing here is eloquently captured in *Why Haiti Needs New Narratives,* in which Gina Athena Ulysse contemplates the irony of Haitian women's (in)visibility. She also posits the importance of voice and visibility in Haitian representation, explaining how the logics of visibility intersect with gender in paradoxical ways: "The world has watched Haiti's most vulnerable women survive quake, flood, cholera and homelessness . . . yet those women still feel invisible. What will it take for them to be seen and heard? 'Nou pa gen vizibilite.' We don't have visibility, Mary-Kettley Jean said . . . Her words are ironic."[63] The Kreyòl phrase translates as "we do not have visibility." They do not have visibility; but this is not the same as being invisible. Visibility is something one can possess, and thus it is also about power.

Like the real-life Mary-Kettley Jean, whose voice Ulysse amplifies in her chronicle, the fictional Norah is a woman who survived the earthquake. Elsewhere I have argued that excavating the logics of visibility and invisibility that structure how we "see" and analyze representations of Haitian women and girls is especially crucial in the aftermath of the earthquake.[64] If ethics indeed involves recognition, encounter, and questioning from below as I am arguing, then Norah shows how encounter between people of different classes can lead to a lack of true recognition and so to harmful ethical judgment and neglect. At the same time, in the scenes between Norah and Marylène, we see Norah being re-created in art form and then becoming more deeply aware of her own value and pleasure through their sexual relationship, disclosing the power of the erotic in recognition and subject-making.

Black Feminist Intimacies

The women's intimacy blossoms as they tend to each other with care. "Norah se rapproche de Marylène, dépose sa tête au creux de son épaule, et tournant légèrement son corps vers elle, pose sa jambe repliée en travers de son basin" (Norah gets closer to Marylène, places her head in the hollow of her shoulder, and slightly turning her body towards her, puts her folded leg across her pelvis) (168). The simple gesture communicates warm intimacy between the two women. As the exchange continues, Marylène invariably uses pet names, calling Norah "ma petite chérie" (my little dear) (168), "Ma douce Norah" (my sweet Norah) (168), and "petite Norah coquine" (little adorable Norah) (170). These terms of endearment affirm her desire and display their closeness. Thinking about her past in relation to Norah, Marylène sees it as "tout ce temps passé qui semble irréel dans les bras de Norah" (all that time gone by that seems unreal in Norah's arms) (167).

In addition to their touches and sexual acts, Norah and Marylène's conversations shape their intimacy. When Norah and Marylène have a conversation after making love, their discussion about Alexandre speaks to that closeness. Given her inability to process Alexandre's return with her family, it is especially significant that Marylène tells Norah about her brother's illness and divulges how she feels about it. For most of the novel Marylène shares that information with no one even though all around her the family evaluates and wonders about how she is really reacting.

As Marylène tells her lover, "Norah, ça me fait plaisir que tu me parles d'Alexandre. Tu l'as fait avec simplicité . . . avec curiosité . . . mais sans . . . malice" (Norah, it makes me happy that you talk to me about Alexandre. You asked about him with simplicity . . . with curiosity . . . but without . . . bad intentions) (170). Marylène's decision to share about her brother is even more remarkable when we consider that, earlier in the novel, she discusses her reluctance to talk about Alexandre with her family. As she wonders how her siblings respond to Alexandre's return, Marylène finds herself unable to talk about it with them: "Comment Grégoire et Gabrielle vivent-ils cette sorte de choc? Oui, c'est un choc même si je ne l'admettrai devant personne. Ma vie a été ce qu'elle a été pour beaucoup à cause d'Alexandre, je lui dois mon pire et mon meilleur. Je ne dois pas d'explication à Sylvia ni à personne" (How are Grégoire and Gabrielle experiencing this kind of shock ? Yes, it is a shock even if I will never admit that to anyone. My life has been what it has been because of Alexandre, I owe him my worst and my best. I do not owe an explanation to Sylvia or to anyone) (28). Marylène's interior monologue displays her contemplative awareness about Alexandre's role in her life and her willingness to probe her emotional response. In light of this, her decision to admit her feelings about Alexandre to Norah reveals the strength of the intimacy between them.

The two women take an easy pleasure in one another's bodies. As Lyndon Gill offers, for Marylène and Norah it is "in the touch—the act of making love, the cultivation of pleasure" that we can approach and appreciate their erotic subjectivity:[65] "Marylène se penche sur les lèvres de Norah et le baiser affamé qu'elle lui prend a un goût de délivrance"

(Marylène leans towards Norah's lips and the hungry kiss she takes from her has a taste of deliverance) (170). The word *déliverance* suggests that Marylène achieves freedom as a result of what she experiences with Norah. The novel ends on this liberating note of a new beginning for an intimate, amorous same-sex relationship. It is the story of women-loving-women on the precipice of flourishing. As the scenes described above show, their intimacy is not only about touching and having sex, it is also about looking and talking. Norah says: "Je veux tout savoir de toi. Et c'est moi qui pose les questions maintenant, tu m'en as tant posé depuis qu'on se connaît. Je croyais que tu n'arrêterais jamais" (I want to know everything about you. And it's me who asks the questions now, you have asked me so many since we met. I thought you would never stop) (168). The women's desire to know everything about one another stems from a longing for recognition and fulfillment. The satisfaction of their longing points to a mutually recognized form of erotic subjectivity in which they value and feel the other's desire, pleasure, and joy, fully and acutely.

As an example of the ethical-erotic, the scenes between Marylène and Norah are especially fulfilling and replete with imagery engendering what Audre Lorde describes as the sensual, "those physical, emotional, and psychic expressions of what is deepest and strongest and richest in us."[66] Erotic subjectivity recognizes Black women's social, sexual, and artistic selves and how those operate in relation to one another for the individuated subject. Lorde's original framing of "The Uses of the Erotic: The Erotic as Power" also foregrounds the importance of creativity for forging an erotic self. Digging into her own experiential knowledge, Lorde writes, "Only now, I find more and more women-identified women brave enough to risk sharing the erotic's electrical charge *without having to look away*, and without distorting the enormously powerful nature of that exchange . . . For not only do we touch our most profoundly creative source, but we do that which is female and self-affirming in the face of a racist, patriarchal, and anti-erotic society."[67] A woman free to love another woman does not have to look away, even in the face of a society that requires her to. The steady gaze of the woman who refuses to look away powerfully evokes the intimate look between lovers like Norah and Marylène. As an artist, Marylène maps her own relationship to the erotic, tapping into her creativity and her love for another woman as powerful sources within: the emphasis on both helps to destabilize the centrality of heteronormative family structure in the novel's architecture.

Despite the fact that *Je suis vivant* is not entirely about her, Marylène emblematizes what Rosamond King calls a "fully developed Caribbean character who desires women."[68] By rendering Marylène's sexuality not as a strange or spectacular occurrence but rather as a simple narrative about a woman who finds herself, her artistic praxis, her body, and ultimately herself in the arms of another woman, *Je suis vivant* presents a woman-loving-woman not as exceptional or extraordinary, but as quietly ordinary. The complexity of Black women's sexual lives is rendered with care in *Je suis vivant,* even as it is not always evaluated with care by the other characters in the novel. And yet the particularities of Marylène's sexuality are not the total sum of who she is or how she operates as one of the *Je suis vivant's* protagonists. As a Black upper-middle-class woman who loves another woman and who has traveled the world as an artist, Marylène occupies multiple spheres. That she was born and raised in the upper middle class, has lived in Europe, works as an artist, and is the oldest of the four children in the Bernier family are subject positions that shape her lived experience. To create this sensual portrait of the ethical-erotic, Mars writes Marylène as "a woman knowledgeable of the intimate touch of another, willing to please and be pleasured in return by another" for the first time, despite being in her older years.[69] The union of her creative and sexual selves form the contours of Marylène's erotic subjectivity, in which an ethic of care, intimacy, and freedom characterizes her relationship with Norah. How these women look at, touch, and talk to one another—what I am calling the ethical-erotic—moves beyond the physicality of sex to amplify its spiritual-sensual-political dimensions.

The Undeniable Place of the Erotic

Kettly Mars's corpus notoriously mines the manifold uses of the erotic.[70] Her work has garnered substantial critical attention for its explicit and provocative representations of sex in general, sexual excesses and extremes, and sexual deviance in particular. It would be difficult to analyze the work of Kettly Mars without exploring the role of sex and sexuality in the lives of everyday Haitians, whether they are urban or rurally based, men or women, poor, middle class, or rich, Black or white. For Mars, sex is an essential leitmotif that often signals unequal power dynamics. She has never shied away from writing dangerous and troubling sexual encounters that both compel and repel the audience. The sexual activity represented in her novels is far-ranging in both its form and content. Her characters have sex with women, men, and children. The sex is consensual and nonconsensual, tender and violent, loving and brutal. It is intentional or mindless. For her characters, the pleasures of the flesh are deliciously multilayered: they think about sex, engage in sex, tell stories about sex, and perform sex acts of various kinds, and often, sex serves as a singular motivating force in the lives of her characters. What remains consistent, however, is Mars's probing of sexual ethics and sexual politics to pose larger social and moral questions.

Given this content, it is accurate to say that Kettly Mars's attention to capturing the role of sex in the lives of Haitian people has largely produced a body of work in which violence, exploitation, and deviance, rather than pleasure, play, and the moral imagination, are at the center.

But *Je suis vivant* diverges sharply from this approach, and from her previous novels, due to how quietly and unspectacularly she writes the sex scenes between Norah and Marylène. Describing how she conceptualizes the erotic, Mars tells Nadève Ménard:

> La sensualité est au cœur de nos vies et nos relations. La sensualité est ce que nous sauve de nous-même et des autres . . . La sensualité n'est pas que sexuelle. Elle conduit à la sexualité, mais elle peut prendre des chemins inattendus et surprenants. La sensualité est un langage, un apprentissage . . . Pour explorer le monde tel qu'il est, le monde du racisme, de la violence, des fanatismes, de la brutalité et du désespoir, j'ai trouvé dans la sensualité un médium parfait. La sensualité est l'antichambre de l'érotisme. Nul ne peut nier la place de l'éros dans la vie . . . Je veux donner à la sensualité et à l'éros la place qui leur revient dans la littérature comme dans la vie.[71]

> (Sensuality is at the heart of our lives and our relationships. Sensuality is what saves us from ourselves and from others . . . Sensuality is not only sexual. It leads to sexuality, but it can take unexpected and surprising paths. Sensuality is a language, it is a lesson . . . To explore the world as it is, [a world full of] racism, violence, fanaticism, brutality and despair, I have found sensuality to be a perfect medium. Sensuality is the antechamber of eroticism. No one can deny the place of eros in life . . . I want to give sensuality and eros their rightful place in literature and in life.)

Marylène Bernier's determination to "set about creating something else to be" emerges in her creative praxis and her relationship to the erotic.[72] Here the ethical-erotic operates as a form of becoming that brings the two women closer to themselves as they draw closer to one another. In *Je suis vivant* Kettly Mars presents the relationship between two women as an embodiment of sexual freedom and creativity replete with erotic intimacy, giving the ethical-erotic a space in literature and life. Marylène's plot line in *Je suis vivant* challenges normativity because, through her, Mars destabilizes the portrait of what a bourgeois Haitian family looks like. By clearing fictional space for women who desire women, Mars moves against the grain of many Haitian writers who preceded her and joins with her contemporaries Emmelie Prophète, Évelyne Trouillot, and Yanick Lahens, who have included lesbian characters in their fiction.[73]

Guillaume et Nathalie: Building Sexual Tension

Agency and intimacy operate centrally in Lahens's *Guillaume et Nathalie,* the story of a sociologist and an architect who fall in love shortly before the earthquake of January 2010. Written in poetic language that is rich in metaphor and personification, with a tone that reflects its theme of love, the novel recounts the beginnings of love and its ups and downs for two people in Port-au-Prince's middle class. Thematizing romance, desire, and love as well as the joys and the wounds that accompany them in quotidian life, *Guillaume et Nathalie* is an everyday story.

The couple for whom the novel is named meets in Port-au-Prince in December 2009, one month before the earthquake.[74] My reading emphasizes the novel's significance as a love story that is set before the earthquake and that intentionally ends just prior to the event. Other critics, such as Martin Munro, have argued that, even in not writing about the earthquake, Lahens writes about it: "The very decision not to write about [the earthquake] suggests something of the way in which it necessitates aesthetic, literary, and even ethical choices, the way in which it shadows authors even as they try to escape it."[75]

However, in my view, this kind of reading moves away from the unique power of the novel as a love story. For me, the choice of the romantic genre is rooted in the ethical-erotic. As a love story, *Guillaume et Nathalie* performs a distinct kind of ethical labor that can be interpreted in relation to the question of political/socially relevant writing in the Haitian context. Although some scholars have connected the couple's romance to larger social and communitarian themes, what interests me is what choosing the romance novel as a genre reveals about Lahens's moral imagination.[76] *Guillaume et Nathalie* helps to elaborate how the ethical-erotic functions as a framework that allows erotic subjectivity to flourish, foregrounds intimacy, and pays attention to dialogue and discourse in the development of romantic relationships.

In many ways, Lahens's quiet love story models the "calm and serene" approach she herself extols in women-authored novels of the previous generation.[77] The novel begins with the two protagonists in each other's arms, entering Nathalie's apartment, and about to have sex. From this first chapter, we learn their ages and their occupations but not much else about them, not to mention how they have arrived at this particular location in this particular time.

> Lui, Guillaume, n'a pas particulièrement soigné sa tenue. Il n'a jamais considéré ces attentions de surface comme une nécessité. Et, à l'aube de la cinquantaine, il ne changera pas. Il n'en a plus besoin. Il a déjà fait ses preuves. Dans sa profession et auprès des femmes. La silhouette de Nathalie avoue une trentaine et trois ou quatre années. Pas davantage. Une trentaine épanouie. Ses chaussures de marche à lacets, son jean et son tee-shirt laissent penser qu'elle est une femme de terrain. Guillaume porte une bonne quinzaine d'années de plus qu'elle. Autant dire qu'il a dépassé la première moitié de la vie, alors qu'elle, Nathalie, est de plein-pied dans son épanouissement.

> (He, Guillaume, did not particularly care about his clothes. He never considered these surface details as a necessity. And, at the dawn of his fifties, he will not change. He does not need to anymore. He has already proven himself. In his profession and with women. The silhouette of Nathalie suggests thirty-three or thirty-four years. No more. Thirty blossoming. Her lace-up shoes, jeans and T-shirt suggest that she is a practical woman. Guillaume displays a good fifteen years more than she. Suffice to say that he has passed the first half of life, whereas she, Nathalie, is fully engaged in her blooming.) (11)

The juxtaposition above establishes a contrast between the two protagonists, drawing attention to their age, occupations, and approaches to life. Lahens foreshadows their sexual relationship: "Quelque chose, dans leur façon d'avancer vers la porte d'entrée de l'immeuble, indique que, s'ils ne sont pas encore amants, ils sont sur le point de le devenir. L'imminence d'un tel événement semble inéluctable" (Something, in their way of moving to the front door of the building, indicates that if they are not yet lovers, they are about to become so. The imminence of such an event seems inevitable) (12). As the novel unfolds, the unspoken is just as important as what is spoken for the two lovers, leading up to their embrace of one another. This titillating dynamic increases the tension that pulses through their sexual relationship: "Nathalie et Guillaume sont pour l'instant dans la douceur, l'enchantement, le balbutiement des commencements. Et rien n'enchante davantage que ces balbutiements, ces commencements. Rien. Ces images sont, entre toutes, celles qui retiendront. Après. Longtemps après. Lorsque tout aura été joué" (Nathalie and Guillaume are for the moment in the sweetness, the enchantment, the stuttering of beginnings.

And nothing is more enchanting than those stutterings, those beginnings. Nothing. These images are, among everything else, those that will remain. After. A long time after. When everything will have played out) (12).

In the passage that immediately follows, Nathalie's thoughts are expressed in verse. By writing these sentences like poetry on the page, Lahens endows the erotic with a creative lyricism. The verses present Nathalie in a reverie even as she is clearly an agent of her own desire.

> Elle ferme les yeux. Juste un moment. L'angoisse pourrait la précipiter dans cette grande terre sauvage, abandonné, tout au fond, tout à l'intérieur, et qu'elle redoute encore. Alors, elle respire profondément. Question de rassembler les morceaux épars.
>
> > De faire un nid à l'angoisse.
> > Pour qu'elle sommeille tranquille.
> > Tout au fond.
> > Nathalie veut tenir debout.
> > Debout dans le désir de Guillaume.
>
> (She closes her eyes. Just a moment. Anxiety could precipitate her into this great wild land, abandoned, deep down, all inside, that she still dreads. So, she is breathing deeply. A question of collecting the scattered pieces.
>
> > To make a nest for anxiety.
> > So that she sleeps peacefully.
> > Deep down.
> > Nathalie wants to remain standing.
> > Standing in Guillaume's desire.) (13)

Paying close attention to Nathalie's emotions prior to lovemaking, we see the erotic unfolding through prose that renders the love scene like poem or a song. How the words appear on the page prompts us to contemplate their meaning separately. Written in verse, the passage is a remarkable enunciation of the female subject's desire. It also shows how Nathalie emotionally wrestles in her mind prior to having sex, how she deals with her fears that anxiety will eventually take over. What she wants most is to allow herself to be upright in Guillaume's desire. The word *debout* is an important choice because it means Nathalie is standing, that she is upright and has a foundation of her own. She does not succumb to desire, is not overcome by it, does not fall into desire, but rather stands planted in it. Put differently, Nathalie *rises* in love, recalling Toni Morrison's powerful description of heterosexual romantic love in the novel *Jazz:* "Don't ever think I fell for you, or fell over you. I didn't fall in love, I rose in it."[78] It is noteworthy that Nathalie stands in *his* desire, determining to be upright as a sign of her agency.

The description holds another significance, as we will learn later that Nathalie is a rape survivor; it shows us what erotic agency can look like in the aftermath of sexual violence. Her need for sexual self-determination shapes her understanding of sex, desire, and power. Nathalie is committed to having sex with Guillaume on her own terms, but those terms do not disregard who he is or what his desires are. Furthermore, when we consider that the novel is also narrated by Guillaume, we are reminded that Lahens gives equal weight to both partners in this relationship. References to sex throughout *Guillaume et Nathalie* include explicit details about sexual acts as they occur as well as examples of the protagonists thinking about sex.

The initial love scenes between Guillaume and Nathalie span the first two chapters, in exuberantly sensual in detail. Lahens never obscures the physicality of sex; the various parts of what sex entails for both people involved are rendered in straightforward and unreserved language: "Guillaume s'appuie contre la porte d'entrée de l'appartement, fait pivoter Nathalie et la tient tout contre lui. Il ouvre à peine les lèvres que Nathalie y pose ses doigts et murmure dans un souffle léger qu'elle prolonge à dessein : 'Chuut' Il ne doit pas parler. Pas encore. Pas si vite. Elle veut faire le vide. Faire place nette. La langue qui cherche loin" (Guillaume leans against the door to the apartment, turns Nathalie around and holds her close to him. He barely opens his lips when Nathalie puts her fingers there and whispers in a light breath that she purposely extends: "Shhh" He must not speak. Not yet. Not so fast. She wants to empty herself. Make room. A tongue that searches far) (15). The tongue that searches has a double meaning here; it represents the vigorous kissing that they engage in as well as the edifying conversations that they will have with one another. What it shows is that, as Vanessa Valdés notes in her reading of Audre Lorde, the erotic is "not a question of thinking versus feeling but rather identifying the impetus from which one lives."[79] Living for this pleasurable sensation, Nathalie silences her lover.

Toward the end of the novel the reader learns that Nathalie is a survivor of sexual violence. At eighteen years old, the oldest of three sisters, she was a victim of crime when a group of armed men invaded her home, robbed it, and then raped her, eventually leading her to migrate to the United States. Her disclosure to Guillaume of this event in her past is a sign that their relationship is far more than sexual. Nathalie is exposing a part of herself that had remained hidden from her previous lovers and that had negatively impacted those previous relationships. Similar to what we saw in Marylène and Norah's revelatory conversations about Alexandre, the disclosure operates as a form of intimacy that gives the reader a sign of a deepening relationship between them.

Guillaume and Nathalie's intimacy is marked by a mutual longing for each other's bodies and minds. From the novel's outset, their desire registers with intensity, affection, and emotion: "Lui, Guillaume l'embrasse lèvres ouvertes. Chaleureuses. Charnues. Les yeux noirs et doux. La peau café. La bouche immense. La langue, chercheuse. La langue cherche loin. Nathalie bascule dans ses bras. Lui offre la bouche d'une femme qui veut juste savoir, même pour la cruauté et l'amertume" (He, Guillaume kisses her with open lips. Warm. Fleshy. Eyes black and soft. Coffee skin. A huge mouth. A tongue searching. A that tongue searches far. Nathalie tumbles into his in arms. Offers him the mouth of a woman who just wants to know, even if only to find cruelty and bitterness) (15). The short, staccato phrases here add to the rhythm of the scene as the couple is locked in each other's arms. The pleasure generated by their bodies thrills and excites them. As Nathalie describes her chaotic feelings while thinking about Guillaume, she exemplifies Lorde's observation that "the erotic is a measure between the beginnings of our sense of self and the chaos of our strongest feelings."[80] As we see with Nathalie, these chaotic feelings rebound with pleasure all over her body.

Much of the excitement of Guillaume and Nathalie's budding relationship occurs in how it unfolds temporally. The opening scene stages the first time they make love; then we learn how they meet, and we see how they first interact with one another in less than sexual ways. After the initial scene, it is not until one hundred pages into the novel that their first date takes place. The slow pace at which the story unfolds prolongs the reader's experience since we already know that this couple ends up in bed together. How these two protagonists become lovers is therefore the central drama in the novel.

When they are finally on their first date, it is quietly ordinary and charged with tantalizing energy: "Le rendez-vous entre Nathalie et Guillaume le lendemain fut bien une rencontre galante. De celles qui, en plein midi, par une canicule, entourent même une triste salade ou un café âcre d'une halo festif et insouciant" (The meeting between Nathalie and Guillaume the following day was indeed a date. One of those that, in the middle of the afternoon, during a heat wave, sitting in front of a sad salad or acrid coffee, do so with a festive and carefree halo) (103). From the outset, a special air surrounds them, infusing their interaction with sensual energy. Lahens goes on to describe their attraction in terms of desire. The noise and chaos around them only endow their erotic charge with greater meaning:

> C'est dire qu'autour de Nathalie et de Guillaume tout n'était que vacarme, bruits de couverts, rires et mouvements. Une ronde autour de leur attente. Une farandole autour de leur désir. Tout débordait d'eux pour dire cette attente et ce désir et rejoignait la ferveur qui les enveloppait. Leur désir était *bien trop bavard* et leur impatience, déjà un spectacle.

> (That is to say that around Nathalie and Guillaume everything was only a din, noises of cutlery, laughs and movements. A round around their waiting. A farandole around their desire. Everything overflowed from them to express this expectation and this desire and joined the fervor that surrounded them. Their desire was *far too talkative* and their impatience, already a spectacle.) (104, my emphasis)

Describing them as chatty, Lahens calls attention to the role of conversation, of dialogue and discourse in their courtship. Their fascination with one another is intellectual and physical; it is an attraction energized by their minds. In this moment the couple's desire for one another and attention to each other makes them oblivious to anything else. Their open discussion of their mutual desire reminds us that they are two consenting adults: "Nous sommes là, chère Nathalie, parce que j'ai envie de vous faire l'amour, et plus beau, c'est que vous êtes déjà d'accord. Ma main au feu Nathalie, que nous serons bientôt découverts, dévoilés, dévêtus" (We are here, dear Nathalie, because I want to make love to you, and what is more beautiful is that you already agree. My hand to the fire Nathalie, we will soon be discovered, unveiled, undressed) (104). I call this charged scene an example of the ethical-erotic because it offers a dynamic exchange between characters in which sexual encounters are complex, rich, and fulfilling.

To date, most interpretations of *Guillaume et Nathalie* identify it as a post-earthquake narrative and analyze the novel in relation to Lahens's memoir *Failles,* which immediately precedes and references *Guillaume et Nathalie.* Of course, it is true that to some degree Nathalie and Guillaume's relationship derives its significance from the back story to the novel, which only exists meta-textually in *Failles.* While I find these arguments about the novel as a post-earthquake text compelling, in my view *Guillaume et Nathalie* has much more to offer through its contributions as a story about sex, love, and intimacy between two consenting adults.[81]

As other scholars have pointed out, Lahens's approach to the everyday attempts to create narratives about Haiti that are anchored in reality yet also look for worlds beyond the present circumstances of the characters: "Tout en gardant l'œil sur la réalité de la scène haitienne, l'écrivaine Yanick Lahens veut arpenter les profondeurs de l'abîme, non pour reprendre, une fois de plus, ce que d'autres ont déjà raconté, mais pour *dire l'espoir*" (While keeping an eye on the reality of the Haitian scene, as a writer Yanick Lahens wants to survey the depths of the abyss, not to take up, once again, what others have already told, but to give "hope").[82]

As Nathalie and Guillaume's relationship develops, they display an increased openness to being known by one another, deepening and broadening their intimacy. Recalling the sexologist bill of rights that I made note of at the beginning of this chapter and paying attention to how much they express their thoughts to each other, we find another way to track how their intimacy evolves in relation to pleasure and safety.

> À la première sonnerie du téléphone, ce soir-là, elle sut avant même de répondre qu'elle entendrait la voix de Guillaume. Décembre touchait déjà sa fin et il allait s'envoler vers d'autres cieux. Était-ce à cause de cette inéluctable échéance qu'elle s'abandonna si pleinement à la volupté de la conversation, à ce pincement aigu de chaque mot? (99)

> (At the first ringing of the phone that night, she knew before she even answered that she would hear Guillaume's voice. December was coming to an end and he was going to take off to other skies. Was it because of this inevitable deadline that she surrendered herself so fully to the voluptuousness of the conversation, to that sharp pinch of each word?)

The mutual erotic pleasure that they derive from these "voluptuous" conversations is felt in "the sharp pinch of each word." The couple's discourse seems to mirror their intercourse. Nevertheless, at this point the pull that Nathalie feels towards Guillaume remains unstated: "Mais à Guillaume, elle ne le dit pas. Pas encore. Loin s'en fallait. Elle n'avait aucune envie de lui confier à quel point elle été précipitée dans la force de l'âge, en avance sur le temps" (But, she doesn't say it to Guillaume. Not yet. Far from it. She had no desire to tell him how rushed she was into the prime of life, ahead of time) (100). Increasingly propelled by the intrigue of Guillaume and the possibility of what their relationship may lead to, Nathalie chooses what and what not to disclose to him about her own desire. The thoughts that she does not lay bare become as significant as those she does.

Just as we saw in *Je suis vivant,* disclosure plays an operative role in strengthening the couple's intimacy. Nathalie and Guillaume's conversations include twists and turns in how they speak to and respond to one another, as well as how they privately think about each other: "'Guillaume, je t'emmène chez moi.' La phrase avait été dite avec une telle absence de tours, une telle franchise, que le futur amant fut désarçonné" ("Guillaume, I'm taking you to my place." The sentence had been said with such an absence of tricks, such a frankness, that the future lover was disarmed) (106). In this passage Nathalie's agency and determination to lead the path of their relationship is clear. Her matter-of-fact announcement surprises and titillates Guillaume just as it excites the reader. Lahens's use of sexual tension produces a tale of suspense within the prose of romance.

Their sexual tension is further evinced in the multiple uses of the word "jeu" (game) to describe the dynamic between the protagonists. When Nathalie begins to yield to her attraction to Guillaume, she thinks to herself, "Cet homme me plait. Dieu qu'il me plait" (This man pleases me. God how he pleases me), acknowledging that her desire is beginning to develop (63). Their conversations push their relationship deeper: "Au bas de la pente menant chez Nathalie, Guillaume posa une question pour raviver la douceur et la jubilation. 'A quoi penses-tu Nathalie?–A rien. À nous'" (At the bottom of the slope leading to Nathalie's, Guillaume asked a question to revive their sweetness and jubilation. What are you thinking about Nathalie?–About nothing. About us) (110). Nathalie's honesty reveals a determination to be transparent that is not her first instinct, and she responds truthfully the second time without missing a beat. She corrects her first response to be more honest, showing how she is increasingly open to sharing her mind with Guillaume. Eventually she lets him into her interiority, into the thoughts that she has kept hidden from him for most of the novel. Likewise, Guillaume shares a great deal of his life with Nathalie, going into detail about his personal history, the tensions with his former spouse, and his future hopes for the country.

As their physical intimacy deepens, the emotional and spiritual bonds between Guillaume and Nathalie also intensify. The result is an ethic of care that flows through *Guillaume et Nathalie.* The care with which this love story is written is evidence of Lahens's longstanding affinity for her protagonists, two characters she began writing before the earthquake and to whom she returned afterwards, though not before writing a work of nonfiction about the earthquake. I agree with Darline Alexis's observation about the novel that "grande est l'affection de la créatrice pour ses personnages. Avec tendresse, elle observe la rencontre, elle plante le décor pour la séduction, le ballet des corps, elle décrit les premiers émois de ce couple formé de deux individus qui ont eu leur lot de peines" (great is the affection of the author for her characters. With tenderness, she observes their encounter, she sets the scene for the seduction, the ballet of their bodies, she describes the first emotions of this couple made up of two individuals who have had their share of sorrows).[83] By nurturing these two characters, Lahens performs the labor of care. Her precise attention to their inner lives as well as their material and immaterial worlds radiates from every scene of encounter.

As I have argued throughout this book, ethics is about encounter, relation, recognition, and questioning from below. A Black feminist ethic refracts these elements through an intersectional lens that positions Black women's lived experience as the basis for ethical claims. Watching Nathalie experience a range of feelings, sensations, and emotions as she relates to Guillaume, the reader encounters a woman who is slowly embracing her own erotic freedom.

In *Guillaume et Nathalie* the choice of the romance genre issues a direct challenge to the idea of Haitian literature as one of unequivocal *engagement*. As Lahens explains in *Failles,* she was motivated to set aside the story *Guillaume et Nathalie* after the earthquake in order to reflect on that traumatic event. When she returned to the love story, her devotion to the couple's intimate connection functioned as a new narrative not only because it is a post-earthquake novel but also because it is a love story. Darline Alexis's reading of the novel is again instructive here:

Guillaume et Nathalie c'est une histoire d'amour, celle *qui est à notre portée et que nous nous refusons*. C'est un regard acéré sur nous-mêmes, un récit plein de coups de griffes, mais qui ne dénie pas la tendresse qui a pris place si timidement entre un homme et une femme. C'est l'amour et ce qu'il suppose comme recommencement, possibilité de renaissance. C'est là, le grand charme de ce roman qui embrasse large un pays au bord de l'explosion, sans phagocyter les personnages dans le trop de réalité qui empêche un vécu et une pensée de la fiction.

(*Guillaume and Nathalie* is a love story, one that is within our reach and that we refuse ourselves. It is a sharp look at ourselves, a story full of claws, but does not deny the tenderness that took place so timidly between a man and a woman. It is love and what it implies in terms of starting again, the possibility of rebirth. This is the great charm of this novel that widely embraces a country on the verge of explosion, without cannibalizing the characters in the overwhelming reality that prevents an experience and a thought of fiction.)[84]

The ethical-erotic as crafted by Lahens is anchored in her commitment to her characters' humanity and her desire for Blackness to be envisaged with depth and nuance. Propelled by Black love that offers possibility and rebirth, *Guillaume et Nathalie* is a story about the human need for intimate connection. In her use of a love story to explore an everyday side of Port-au-Prince, Lahens reminds the reader of how depictions of ordinary life are important in challenging more politically or socially charged dominant narratives. Such quotidian depictions also recall Michel-Rolph Trouillot's point from his canonical essay "The Ordinary and Everyday" that I continuously return to because it captures the specificity of why "quiet" matters in the Haitian context. Attending to the mundane, Trouillot argues, becomes a way to emphasize our common humanity. We can look at the use of the romance genre as one of the most ordinary of literary narratives. As individual characters who lead ordinary lives, Guillaume and Nathalie confirm that, "the majority of Haitians live quite ordinary lives. They eat what is for them—and for many others—quite ordinary food." [85] They make love, we might add. While scholars have argued for using the trope of disaster and the event of the earthquake to analyze *Guillaume et Nathalie,* the ethical-erotic helps us to see a beautifully simple human narrative.

During an interview conducted shortly after the novel's publication, Lahens describes the reaction people had to her writing a novel about sexual desire. She pushes back against those who find the idea of an erotic Haitian love story unthinkable. Affirming her commitment to writing about Black love and desire she shares,

> Mais ce n'est pas évident d'écrire l'érotisme quand il s'agit de corps noirs. Beaucoup de projections fantasmatiques y sont associées. Nous-mêmes avons intégré un certain nombre de représentations sur notre propre corps. Comment mettre ce mécanisme du désir, de l'érotisme—qui est quand même une des choses importantes de la vie—en écriture. On m'a aussi demandé: "Pourquoi une histoire d'amour?" Les gens tombent amoureux aussi en Haïti! [86]

> (But it is not obvious to write about eroticism when it's a question of Black bodies . . . So many fantasies are associated with them. We ourselves have incorporated a number of the representations into our own bodies. How does one put this mechanism of desire, of eroticism—which is nevertheless one of the important things in life—in writing? I was also asked, 'Why a love story?' People are falling in love in Haiti too!)

People are indeed falling in love (and making love) in Haiti too. What I read in Lahens's remarks is frustration with how people view Haitians through a reductive frame, so that a single story in which a subject as ordinary as two people falling in love is virtually unthinkable. Her reference to *les corps noirs* signals Lahens's preoccupations with how racial identities influence the erotic, confirming her ethical-erotic standpoint. The ethical-erotic framework asks that we consider what kind of subjectivity, what kind of personhood is made possible and visible through a focus on the erotic. Lahens's awareness of this dynamic informs her decision to write a love story with a Black Haitian couple at the center; the result is a sensual and intimate love story, a narrative of pleasure and play still possible despite the precipice of looming disaster. In fact, the imminence of disaster within the text (which unfolds a month before the earthquake) might make such simple stories even more necessary as they reflect a common humanity that narratives of destruction threaten to obscure.

The Erotic as Freedom: *Rosalie l'infame* and *L'oeil-totem*

Before concluding this chapter, I turn to two examples from Évelyne Trouillot's novels in which the ethical-erotic functions as a force for freedom in the lives of women characters. My first example is Lisette and Vincent; although their relationship is markedly different from the other couples I have previously discussed, in its association with freedom, it also manifests the ethical-erotic. Lisette names the peace she finds in the arms of her lover, describing how Vincent's touch floods her with calm. Their relationship and lovemaking make clear that the erotic gives them a small taste of freedom. "He places his hand on my sex and holds it there soft and still, like a serene, sure comfort": this comfort is one of the few available to her (12). The second example, Marie-Jeanne in *L'œil-totem*, like Marylène in *Je suis vivant*, is an artist with a robust sexual appetite. In many ways Marie-Jeanne typifies M. Jacqui Alexander's point that the body can serve as a "meeting ground for the erotic, the imaginative, and the creative."[87] The erotic subjectivity of both Lisette and Marie-Jeanne calls attention to how the ethical-erotic can be a source of freedom for women, whether they are literally freeing themselves from the horror of slavery or from the expectations of a society that seeks to confine them. Understanding how sexual mores shape Caribbean womanhood, investigating the ethical-erotic requires that we also pay attention to how the overlapping spheres of race, gender, and class inform Haitian women's experiences with sex and sexuality. We can return to Kaiama Glover's *A Regarded Self*, wherein she dexterously argues that a sense of self-worth is a manifestation of freedom for female subjects and that "sexual selfhood" often plays an operative role in allowing women characters to express their individuality.[88]

Sexual selfhood is also a part of how Trouillot accentuates Lisette's humanity as an enslaved person and draws attention to erotic agency and subjectivity. The few scenes in which the couple make love teem with tenderness, touching, freedom, and care. They touch and kiss one another with abandon and passionately cling to each other's bodies, looking for comfort and freedom. After Lisette witnesses another enslaved person being burnt at the stake, she rushes into the woods in search of Vincent: "Suddenly Vincent is standing there, solid and sure, full of the brown, rocky earth in which I bury my tears. Everything comes out: the flames, the screams, the fear, the anguish, the shame, the indignation, the anger and the rage" (10). Her emotions tumble out, setting the stage for their love-making; the emotional connection precedes the physical union that will take place. But as her fingers "reacquaint themselves with his arms—those mysterious lianas, strengthened by every marking and brand on his chest," the reader notices that the imprint of slavery's terror is so deeply marked onto their bodies that it even informs their lovemaking (10). While they have sex as a way to forget, having sex shows them that they can never forget: "Beneath the burns he took of his own volition, I rediscover again the stamp of the inhuman trade, marking much more than his skin. I greet them again. I run my fingers and lips over his skin for a long time, let my tongue find refuge there, seeking tenderness and freedom" (10).

Still, even if there are signs of slavery's terror on their bodies and they can only have sex in hiding, their relationship offers a form of respite from the toll of life on the plantation: "Until those happy moments when we're together again, the violence and horror trouble us deeply" (11). They also share all the details of what deeply troubles them. Vincent describes his concerns related to life on the plantation and in the community of Maroons. He "talks about the recent arrival of slave ships, the new Maroons who have joined his group . . . the loss of three companions" (12). Their touching conversation is as meaningful and as intimate as their lovemaking. They share their minds with each other. Like the lovers art-fully depicted by Toni Morrison in *Beloved,* for whom the choice of lovers is one of the few choices available under the yoke of slavery, they are lov-ers who are friends of each other's minds and "put the pieces of each other back together again": "From that moment on, all of my senses are focused on endlessly multiplying the movement of his hands, the sounds of his desire, the power of his pleasure, the tenderness of his eyes, the tickle of his beard against my chest, the frenzy of his sex against mine" (13). Lisette feels what Vincent feels as well as what she herself feels. As she references "the power of his pleasure," it is clear that her pleasure contains the same kind of power. While they have sex, she sees "the tenderness of his eyes," and it is just as moving as what she feels. The range of feelings expressed here are sensual, physical, emotional, and psychic, situating them on the plane of the erotic conceptualized by Lorde.

A Maroon known as "The Fearless One," Vincent nonetheless has a vulnerability in Lisette's arms that shows us how ordinary he becomes in the context of sex and love. The intimacy between them connects their talking, looking, lovemaking, plotting, and freedom-dreaming in an entangled network of bondage and possibility. When she tenderly says to him, "May your fear be as strong as your anger, my love. You and freedom both relish the rising sun and mother's milk. Your love makes me want to look at the sky," she is expressing what their love makes possible in her worldview (14). That his love makes her "want to look at the sky" can be read in terms of her budding sense of agency that inspires her to look for another world. Their relationship is a soothing balm and safe refuge that demonstrates the freedom to be found in the erotic. When Lisette encounters the violence and the harm of life on the plantation, "only Vincent's warm embrace could possibly make [her] forget" (40). With Lisette and Vincent's sex life, Trouillot renders the humanity of the enslaved people in Saint-Domingue; I identify their story as an example of the ethical-erotic because it asks that we hold the feelings and physical sensations of sex in equal measure, formulates erotic subjectivity, and highlights the importance of looking as an intimate exchange.

Nowhere in the novel is the ethical-erotic more apparent than in the tantalizing and troubling scene I examine below, which unfolds after Vincent loses his leg while fleeing the violence of his former captors. Encountering him after this traumatic injury, Lisette is at once horrified by the pain he must have endured and compelled to make love to him: "I feel human again in Vincent's arms, and our shivering bodies meet. He murmurs words that find refuge in my hair and eyes. I drink our tears, and when we fall on the grass together, I am smothered. Our hands invent words that will never be repeated" (60). She tries repeatedly to touch the stump of his leg, all that remains where the limb used to be. But "in a painful reflex" he pushes her away (60). Refusing to take her hands away, Lisette insists on touching him at the site of the injury. She wants to touch his wound, to embrace it, and to make love to it: "When I finally place my hand on it, I feel the scars, gathered into a bud that conceals the facts of their existence from me. I stroke them with small, hesitant caresses, exposing them, I brush them lightly with my arms, even my breasts, my thighs, my belly, and I am *so filled with desire and rage* I even rub my moist and wild sex savagely against them." (60–61). In frenzied passion, Lisette uses her body as a balm for her lover and for herself, laboring to replace his pain with pleasure and passion. Lisette affirms herself as a desiring subject who is also enraged—that her rage and desire combine points to the manifold uses of the erotic. Her attention to the gruesome stump where his leg once was and the ensuing flood of emotions can be understood as what Tinsley calls "embodied activities—seeing, hearing, moving, feeling, touching—that constitute meaningful human expressions . . . meaningful acts."[89] Her hunger for Vincent also exhibits Kaiama Glover's formulation of a "disorderly sexuality" that brazenly pairs the wound of slavery's violence with unbridled sexual desire.[90] Lisette's sexualized body is activated by the trauma of her lover's wound; it is a wound that she seeks to heal and cover with her desire. After this sexually explicit scene of lovemaking, Vincent shares the graphic tale of how he lost his leg, and, going even further back in his traumatic memories, he recounts "for the first time ever" his experience after being captured, "of the crossing on the ship . . . of his arrival in Cap-Français" (61). The sex unlocks their sharing and arouses their sexual appetites even more. Speaking slides into touching, allowing Vincent to "hold" Lisette with his voice alone: "With his voice Vincent holds me tighter. We find ourselves wrapped around one another, nestled in our clumsy need for tenderness and dignity. Our desperate, feverish caresses are no longer enough, but we can't help ourselves" (61). The erotic expressed through the connection of their bodies and minds amplifies their erotic subjectivity because Lisette is determined to make love on her own terms despite (and even because of) the wound, and Vincent is incited to share about his own personhood as a result of their steamy sexual encounter.

What interests me about this moment is how it contrasts with Lorde's point that the erotic is "firmly rooted in the power of our unexpressed and unrecognized feeling."[91] It is only when Lisette and Vincent unleash their unexpressed and unrecognized feelings that we witness the power of their erotic bond as "those physical, emotional, and psychic expressions of what is deepest and strongest and richest within . . . the passion of love in its deepest meaning."[92] This moment of peaked sexual intensity and activity demonstrates how the ethical-erotic manifests in unexpected ways for the young enslaved woman and makes room for her "embodied freedom."[93] The scene combines intimacy and violence in ways that are unsettling for the reader but absolutely necessary in order to trouble how we conceptualize the ethical-erotic in the context of slavery. The "sexually charged freedom" that Lisette enjoys in the forest as she makes love to Vincent is fleeting, but it manifests a temporary embodied freedom that leads to her decision to flee the plantation and that will ultimately be replicated in her actual freedom.[94] It also tellingly confirms Hortense Spillers's theorization of the body and the flesh in order to distinguish between "captive and liberated subject-positions."[95]

Turning now to Marie-Jeanne, as I discussed in the previous chapter, she makes sense of her sex life and her creativity as an artist in relation to one another. When Marie-Jeanne's mind wanders to her previous lovers, she takes great pleasure in the experience: "ce picotement insolite me rappelle le tourment doux et déchirant d'une bouche sur ma peau" (this unusual tingling reminded me of the sweet and tearing torment of a mouth on my skin). She evaluates her lovers one after another, from her first husband with whom she never experienced the joy of orgasm, to Bernard "qui perdait toute sa timidité devant le plaisir physique" (who lost all of his timidity in the face of sexual pleasure) (74). She refers to him as "Le plus arrogant et le plus humble de mes amants" (the most arrogant and the most humble of my lovers), tellingly linking his personality or character with his behavior in bed (74). Marie-Jeanne's memories of her lovers always center her own pleasure: "Avec lui, c'était si facile d'arriver au vide de la pensée, de n'être que sensations et ondulations, dépendante de deux lèvres et d'une volonté étrangères . . ." (With him it was so easy to come to the void of thought, to be nothing but sensations and waves, dependent on two foreign lips and a will . . .) (74).

The way Marie-Jeanne thinks about and remembers her lovers confirms Tinsley's point that "sexuality and desire are messy, shifting, unstable quantities."[96] While she fondly recalls moments of passion, she also stages conversations in her interior that reveal the challenges of some of those relationships. Imagining an entire conversation with Bernard in her interior monologue, Marie-Jeanne offers a layered perspective on her sexual pleasure from "cette idylle couverte de sensualité d'orgasmes répétés" (this idyll covered with the sensuality of multiple orgasms) to "ongles griffonnaient la peau comme si [elle avait] voulu y peindre une histoire toute nouvelle" (fingernails scrawled across the skin as if [she had] wanted to paint a whole new story on his back) (75).

Through Marie-Jeanne's imagined conversations with previous lovers, we are better able to understand her desire as well as her complex relationship to sex. In point of fact, one of the most telling parts of the reconstructed conversation with Bernard is that Marie-Jeanne shares her entire sexual history with him, including "[ses] expériences de petite fille sage, [ses] masturbations innocentes, [ses] envies de folie, [ses] fantasmes" (her experiences as a good little girl, her innocent masturbations, her cravings, her fantasies) (75). The passage then segues into a longer description of their lovemaking in which Marie-Jeanne imagines her lover's words capturing his reaction to her body in ecstasy.

> Mes doigts ont réinventé ta peau, je t'ai martelé de mon sexe pour te faire crier, crier encore, et tu l'as fait, tu as trouvé tous les mots fous, les couleurs rouge vif, vermeil et plaisir ardent de tes toiles les plus exubérantes, pour toi, pour moi, pour le plaisir de vivre, et tu as joui, encore et encore de cette sensation nouvelle et je te regardais jouir de ta jouissance en m'oubliant, et je ne devenais au bout de tes orgasmes que celui qui t'avait permis de voir un aspect de ton être que tu n'avais jamais entrevu et qui te fascinait. Et j'ai aimé ton émerveillement d'enfant devant ton propre délire, cet éblouissement qui envahissait ton regard.

> (My fingers reinvented your skin, I hammered you with my cock to make you scream, scream again, and you did it, you found all the crazy words, the bright red colors, ruddy and ardent pleasure of your paintings the most exuberant, for you, for me, for the pleasure of living, and you enjoyed, over and over again this new sensation and I watched you enjoy your enjoyment by forgetting me, and I never became at the end of your orgasms anyone but the one who had allowed you to see an aspect of your being that you had never glimpsed and that fascinated you. And I loved your childhood wonder in front of your own delirium, that dazzle that invaded your eyes.) (76)

This descriptive passage reveals that sex is a form of creation and creativity for Marie-Jeanne. Her ability to associate sex and painting reverberate throughout, and she offers intimate detail about what their intimacy felt like to her by offering what it looked like to Bernard. The violence in his words as she imagines them is also telling and leads us to wonder about the details of her relationship with Bernard. Here the point seems to be to foreground the pleasure and the sense of discovery that she derived from their trysts. As she adds more color and precision to the tapestry of pleasure, Marie-Jeanne experiences erotic agency, feeling the contours of her sexual self and her own erotic power. Her reflections on the sexual parts of the life she lived steadfastly move "beyond the sexual as a purely physical relationship to encompass a wider realm of feeling and the sensual."[97]

Recalling my discussion in the previous chapter about Marie-Jeanne's positionality as an elderly woman, we can understand her relationship to her own sexual pleasure in light of Glover's exploration of sexual self-hood. That Marie-Jeanne continues to be "a female protagonist motivated by an open-minded and self-focused sexuality" poses problems for her children but does not diminish her appetite for revisiting her own erotic pleasure.[98] Her erotic agency allows her to lay hold of a wide realm of feelings that are sensual and physical. As an elderly grandmother and a sexually liberated artist, *L'œil-totem*'s Marie-Jeanne expresses and reflects on her sexual encounters with delicious delight devoid of any remorse, despite how others try to make her feel.

The Ethical-Erotic and the Logics of Intimacy

Throughout this chapter I have deployed the term "ethical-erotic" as a summation for how representations of sex can be infused with moral questions linked to intimacy and care. It is also, and perhaps ultimately, a term that asks for sex to be imagined in the context of freedom and possibility. In my discussion of these novels, pleasure, practice, and play function as tropes of intimacy that highlight erotic subjectivity. The intimate sexual and erotic bonds between Marylène and Norah, Nathalie and Guillaume, Lisette and Vincent, and Marie-Jeanne and her lovers show how seeing, touching, and talking are imbued with passion and sensuality. The frame of the ethical-erotic foregrounds their erotic agency and intimacy in order to offer an alternate way of reading sex that clears space for safety and pleasure.[99]

If, as Audre Lorde contends in her landmark essay, "the erotic is a resource within each of us that lies in a deeply female and spiritual plane," then the erotic deserves an esteemed place in our moral imaginations.[100] Using the erotic as a point of departure to elaborate a Black feminist ethic acknowledges its myriad uses and implores that we connect sex to more than to material bodies. Similarly, Gina Athena Ulysse's theory of rasan-blaj points to the erotic as a quotidian reality with spiritual dimensions: "Considering the dailiness of life—living with hunger, illness, bliss and happiness—embodied viscerally in the structural, it invokes Audre Lorde's feminist erotic knowledge in its fullest dimensions, from the personal as political to the sensual and spiritual. It calls upon us to think through Caribbean performance and politics, recognizing the crossroads not as destination—but as a point of encounter to then move beyond."[101] Rasan-blaj implicitly evokes Michel-Rolph Trouillot's concept of the ordinary and everyday, then extends it further by asking that we also account for how sexuality and sensuality function as part of ordinary Haitian lives.

By presenting desiring subjects whose conversations register intimately, *Je suis vivant* and *Guillaume et Nathalie* offer another path for thinking about sex that is equally concerned with the ethical-erotic.

Mars, Lahens, and Trouillot create fully embodied desiring subjects for whom physical and psychological intimacy imbue their sexual relationships. The stories of intimacy in *Je suis vivant* and *Guillaume et Nathalie* register quietly and sensually as exchanges between two adults who move toward one another with mutual desire and who esteem the pleasure of their partner as much as they do their own. In this way, these novels demonstrate the use of an ethical-erotic that focuses first and foremost on relationships of care and intimacy between mutually consensual partners, relationships that can also be understood according to the guidelines established by the sexologist bill of rights that puts safety, pleasure, consent, and care at the center of sexual relations.

In these novels, the narrative construction of identity complicates our perception of the characters' relationships with one another since more is divulged to the reader than between the characters. This is yet another manifestation of the ethical-erotic: it raises questions for the reader who is privy to the stories behind the protagonists' sexual lives. As Hortense Spillers has written, "sexuality is the locus of great drama—perhaps the fundamental one—and, as we know, wherever there are actors there are scripts, scenes, gestures, and reenactments, both enunciated and tacit."[102] These novels stage encounters with sexuality that foreground the erotic subjectivity, the importance of dialogue, and attention to interiority as a way for the readers to engage the scripts, scenes, gestures, and reenactments.

The immediate task of this chapter was to introduce the ethical-erotic as a framework for reading how sex figures in *Je suis vivant, Guillaume et Nathalie, The Infamous Rosalie,* and *L'œil-totem.* As I have shown here, sex is present in the lives of these characters and accompanied by desire, pleasure, and intimacy but is far more than a physical act. These novels present literary examples of what Lyndon Gill sees as, "a symphony of the senses, accompanying provocative conversations about intimacy, sex, and relationships, [serving] only to increase the simmering potential for sexual encounter."[103] The examples of couplings that I have read here foreground intimacy as a way to understand sexual dynamics. More than the act of sex itself, the logic of intimacy functions as a way to make sense of these relationships. Proceeding from an ethical orientation, the logic of intimacy that regulates these sexual relationships points us toward individuated erotic subjectivities and is profoundly rooted in care, connection, and creativity for both partners.

I also understand a Black feminist ethic as an affective project that invites us to explore the emotional registers in representations of sexual intimacy. When Audre Lorde first delineated the "uses of the erotic," to which I have referred throughout this chapter, she issued an explicit challenge to the dichotomy between the sensual and the political: "The dichotomy between the spiritual and the political is . . . false, resulting from an incomplete attention to our erotic knowledge. For the bridge which connects them is formed by the erotic—sensual—those physical, emotional, and psychic expressions of what is deepest and strongest and richest within each of us, being shared: the passion of love in its deepest meanings."[104] The ethical task, then is to imagine how sex intersects with the moral imagination. It is to give space to the ethical-erotic as a framework whose logic affirms intersectional identities and, rooted in safety and pleasure, signals the importance of erotic subjectivity. Ideas about sex are formulated and articulated in many different ways, but too often we short-circuit our analyses by narrowing the scope of what they entail. The framework of the ethical-erotic thus offers a way to reflect on desire, pleasure, sex, love, intimacy, and sensuality as not only physical but also imagined psychologically and expressed through speech acts.

Throughout this chapter I have invoked the logics of intimacy to serve as a guide for analyzing sexual encounters. My interest in intimacy stems from how I understand the function, or, to borrow from Lorde, the use of the erotic in Haitian literature. The erotic is deeply intimate. The erotic is also spiritual. The joy, pleasure, and feeling that it evokes both produces and requires intimacy. A configuration of the ethical-erotic that revolves around intimacies and erotic subjectivity is an important way for us to mine the potentialities of how sex operates in fiction in Haiti and beyond.

Because "sexuality and desire are messy, shifting, unstable quantities," it is important to think about different ways to theorize their presence.[105] Again, when we take into consideration Lahens's point that focusing on love and sex allows us to see the human elements of everyday life, we become aware of how these portrayals point to moral truths. Even more, the idea of the ethical-erotic helps to delineate a Black feminist ethic: in *Je suis vivant, Guillaume et Nathalie, The Infamous Rosalie,* and *L'oeil-totem,* Black women's sexual lives are rendered with care, and their characters are free to imagine and realize their sexual desire with whomever they choose. Mars, Trouillot, and Lahens deftly achieve representations that "address and illuminate Black female sexual desires marked by both agency and empowerment, and pleasure and pain in order to elucidate the ways Black women regulate their sexual lives"; in so doing, they provide a vision of the erotic that is deeply rooted in a Black feminist ethic of care, intimacy, and agency.[106]

I began this chapter with a reference to the popular artist and Haitian music star Rutshelle Guillaume. While Guillaume exemplifies a sonic rendering of the ethical-erotic that privileges intimacy, agency, and freedom for Haitian women, the enthralling work of Haitian artist Tessa Mars contributes a visual example for how to render the body in complex ways that summon the ethical-erotic. As a visual representation that captures this same impulse privileging intimacy, agency and freedom, Tessa Mars's paintings invite the reader to pose ethical questions about how erotic subjectivity circulates in our fields of vision. Mars's paintings exemplify what Chicana feminist Cherríe Moraga calls "theory in the flesh," a quality that scholars have identified as a dominant characteristic of work by feminist artists in the Caribbean.[107] The theory "values the literal space women occupy in critical artistic practices and lived realities," accommodating the political and social realities while privileging experiential knowledge.[108] Theory in the flesh requires the body to occupy a central place in artistic creation. For Caribbean feminist scholars, "the figure of the body, both the epidermal and corporeal, is central to an artist's work, exploring how the body can become a marker within a set of critical frameworks, which at its core yields emancipatory space," meaning that the body serves as a locus of freedom.[109] This visual emphasis on the body captivates, shocks, and inspires. It is also deeply invested in portraying Caribbean bodies that can be seen as what Tinsley suggestively deems "a site in-motion that [Caribbean] women actively, and sometimes contentiously share with other women in their community."[110]

Under Tessa Mars's playful hand, these sites-in-motion are bodies that beckon the viewer to engage ethical questions about how all types of bodies communicate the erotic. Describing her artistic practice in her own words, Mars (who is also the daughter of the author Kettly Mars) explains: "I am always trying to find ways to express my identity as a woman inhabiting this particular body, as a woman from the Caribbean . . . I have renewed interest in history, Haitian history first, but also how it has influenced all of the region all over the Caribbean."[111] Her attention to bodies strikes the viewer of her work. In fact, it seems as though the centrality of the body animates all of her work. Through paintings like the Tessalines series, she assiduously provides fleshy, voluptuous images of a Haitian women. Mars's artwork stages an encounter with the viewer in which we witness what Sheller calls "intimate inter-bodily relations."[112] In *Rèv libète, rev*

Figure 2. *Rèv libète, rèv lanmò (Dream of freedom, dream of death)*, Tessa Mars. (© 2016; used by permission of the artist)

lanmò (Dream of freedom, dream of death) (see fig. 2) the fleshy figure stands proudly displaying her naked body with a knife in between her breasts, asking the viewer to contemplate the relationship between death and freedom. *Beny* (see fig. 3) invokes the spiritual, sensual, and sexual dimensions of the ethical-erotic, displaying a woman who enjoys her own body and associates it with other worlds.

Figure 3. *Beny (Blessed),* Tessa Mars. (© 2021; used by permission of the artist)

Mars's Tessalines appears in a series of self-portraits in which a large woman's body, featured in various positions, stands out next to the bright colors of her surroundings. In *Nan Rara,* for example, she is among a brightly colored group of people celebrating carnival (see fig. 4). What sets her figure apart is her naked body. Mars conjures quotidian scenes

Figure 4. *Nan rara (In rara)*, Tessa Mars. (© 2021; used by permission of the artist)

of Haitian life through the eyes and bodies of the rotund, naked, fleshy woman who can be seen draped in color or situated in a bright rara celebration. Her sexed, gendered, and fluid body luxuriates in different settings that are starkly bright against her shockingly white silhouette.

Tessa Mars's attention to material bodies is a feature of her work that summons the ethical-erotic: what do we see when look at these bodies, and how do they move us? In one image, the precise attention to the contours of women's bodies as they are embraced, backs facing the viewer, both invites and refuses our gaze. There is no question that her subjects move freely in the visual frame and in the world; their nudity signifies freedom especially in the panels where she is surrounded by people who are clothed. Her hat, shaped like that of a general with two bull horns sticking out from it, links her to her namesake and first leader of independent Haiti, the Emperor General Jean-Jacques Dessalines. But though she is linked to this towering historic figure, Tessalines is also the alterego of Tessa Mars herself: "Tessalines, a heroic image of smiling pride and self-determination, reemerges throughout her paintings and drawings: beautiful, bold, defiant, heroic, and mischievous. Tessalines wears the military attire and symbols of the Haitian Revolution and becomes a gender-bended, fictional version of Haiti's national hero Jean-Jacques Dessalines."[113] She is thus playfully and provocatively feminine and masculine, personal and political, historic and intimate. Through Tessalines, Mars has effectively feminized the historic hero, dislodging him from the hetero-patriarchal frame.

Straddling a number of binaries, Tessalines is also a figure bountiful in meaning for the Black feminist critic curious about the ethical-erotic. With each encounter, Tessa Mars invites the viewer to imagine what a Black feminist ethic of the erotic looks like in visual culture, priming our imaginations to embrace Haitian women's embodied erotic freedom. By showing us what erotic subjectivity looks like in visual culture, she allows us to look for *and* to see another world in which the ethical-erotic can flourish. Just as the political-sensual-spiritual triad that Lyndon Gill proposes to conceptualize the erotic "represents a negotiation of the tension between an ideal vision and our lived reality," Tessa Mars's art and the fiction I explored in this chapter make use of the erotic to stimulate our ethical imaginations.[114] In this way, her art is truly visionary, taking into account feminist theorist bell hooks' perspicacious point in *Feminism Is for Everybody* that "To be truly visionary, we have to root our imagination in our concrete reality while simultaneously imagining possibilities beyond that reality."[115] As Mars imagines possibilities beyond our present reality, she invites us to look at the world through an erotic looking glass in which the sensual, spiritual, and political coexist with beauty and ease and to understand that, in the words of Kettly Mars, "nul ne peut nier la place de l'éros dans la vie" (no one can deny the place of eros in life).

4 Geographies of Class Location
Class and Space

> Que savent-ils de la vie dehors? Ils sont toujours enfermés dans leurs voitures, ils vont travailler, vont à la banque, au supermarché, en reviennent, s'installent devant leurs ordinateurs puis devant leurs télés . . . Ils discutent de la vie chère, de la politique, de l'insécurité . . . de leur dernier voyage À Miami ou Montréal . . . Ils ont des passeports étrangers ou des visas valides pour parer à toute éventualité, moi je suis exilée dans ma propre peau.
>
> (What do they know about life outside? They are always locked in their cars, they go to work, go to the bank, to the supermarket, come back, sit in front of their computers then in front of their TVs . . . They discuss the cost of living, politics, insecurity . . . their last trip to Miami or Montreal . . . They have foreign passports or valid visas to deal with any eventuality, but I am exiled in my own skin.)
>
> —Kettly Mars, *Je suis vivant*

IN JULY 2018, the Haitian government announced a 51 percent increase in gas prices, leading to a wave of protests throughout Port-au-Prince. The incident, circulating on social media under the hashtag #gazmonte, resulted in widespread demonstrations in the lower parts of the city as well as in the more affluent Pétionville. The fallout from the rise in prices and the subsequent protests inspired the creation of the Kòt Kob Petrocaribe movement, led to the resignation of several ministers, and would eventually culminate in massive protests and demands for Haitian president Jovenel Moïse to step down.[1] Responding to the chaos during the summer of 2018, Évelyne Trouillot wrote a social media post about the rampant inequality in Port-au-Prince. Her critique is worth citing at length:

> Dans cette grande mouvance de lamentations n'oublions surtout pas les vrais perdants. La situation de violence, de tension qui prévaut dans le pays depuis vendredi provoque toutes sortes de réactions. Citoyens et citoyennes

s'expriment sur les ondes, sur les réseaux sociaux. Les déclarations abondent dans tous les sens: indignation, peur, colère. Certains condamnent, d'autres jugent. Les pertes pour le pays sont énormes. Haïti deviendra encore plus fragile, le manque d'infrastructures se fera plus sentir à tous les niveaux, les prix augmenteront. Port-au-Prince où j'ai pris naissance et où j'ai grandi deviendra encore plus monstrueuse. Delmas où je vis deviendra encore plus chaotique probablement. Il faut déplorer les pertes, pour ceux qui ont investi et ont perdu, surtout pour les petits et moyens commerçants qui ont dû peiner avant de mettre sur pied et de maintenir une entreprise dans des situations difficiles et précaires. Il faut déplorer les pertes pour le pays tout entier car nous allons tous en payer les conséquences. Mais dans cette grande mouvance de lamentations n'oublions surtout pas les vrais perdants. Certains disent qu'il y a eu manipulations, qu'il y a des bras cachés derrière les actions des manifestants. Certes il est clair que certains groupes, certains individus profitent de l'occasion pour s'infiltrer, pour tenter d'orienter et de manipuler mais ramener le mouvement de vendredi après-midi au résultat de manipulations politiques, c'est un déni. Un déni séculaire de l'autre qui souffre, qui a faim, qui ne peut pas envoyer ses enfants à l'école, qui vit dans des habitats insalubres, qui sort de l'école (quand il y va) à demi illettré, qui ne trouve pas d'emploi, qui sait que son avenir est un grand point d'interrogation sans solution, qui voit la vie comme un immense désert où il n'a pas sa place, qui pense que son seul choix c'est de quitter ce pays qui ne lui offre rien, qui devient rempli de frustrations, de colères, de ressentiment, qui fréquente temples et églises, lève le bras vers Dieu, les esprits, la Vierge et ses saints, qui sait que certains endroits lui sont interdits, qui rencontre discriminations et injustices au quotidien, qui ne reconnait pas toujours ses vrais ennemis et attaque parfois avec désespérance, qui apprend à mentir, à voler pour survivre, qui traine dans la rue son désespoir sous des faux sourires ou des yeux farouches, qui meurt car il ne peut se payer ni soins médicaux ni médicaments, qui tombe victime de balles dans une zone de non-droit ou ailleurs, qui mange mal et très peu ou pas du tout, qui court pour monter dans une camionnette déjà bondée, qui transpire sous un soleil de plomb pour arriver à temps à l'usine où elle reçoit un salaire de misère, qui doit se battre contre les attouchements d'un patron pervers, qui se résigne parfois car elle sait que la vie n'est pas de son coté, qui se bat quand même pour rester en vie, qui passe ses journées devant la chaleur des casseroles attendant les acheteurs, qui déambule dans les rues avec son commerce sur la tête pour récolter quelques gourdes, qui rentre fatiguée le soir et ne sait que donner à ses gosses qui l'attendent, qui sait que l'État l'a oubliée, que son sort n'intéresse pas les officiels, que ceux qui ont de l'argent et vivent bien ne la regardent même pas, que sa vie ne changera pas, qui est fatiguée d'entendre les promesses vides

des politiciens, qui . . . qui . . . Celles-là et ceux-là que nous oublions, que le président a une fois de plus oublié dans ses déclarations post-manifestations, n'ont pas besoin d'encouragement pour participer aux pillages. Les frustrations et la colère ne s'achètent pas quand elles sont déjà là.[2]

(In this great movement of lamentations, let's not forget the real losers. The violent and tense situation that prevails in this country since Friday is provoking all sorts of reactions. Citizens express themselves on the airwaves and on social media. Statements run the gamut: indignation, fear, anger. Some condemn. Others judge. The losses for the country are enormous. Haiti will become even more fragile, the lack of infrastructure will be felt at all levels, prices will increase. Port-au-Prince where I was born, where I grew up will become more monstrous. Delmas, where I live, will probably become more chaotic. We must deplore the losses, by those who invested and suffered losses, above all the owners of small and medium-sized businesses, who must have struggled to start up and maintain a business under difficult and precarious conditions. We must regret the losses for the whole country because we are all going to pay the price. But in this great movement of lamenting let us not forget the real losers, above all. Certain people say there were manipulations, self-serving motives behind the protestors' acts. Admittedly, certain groups, certain individuals are taking advantage of the situation to infiltrate the movement to attempt to position themselves, to manipulate, to reduce Friday afternoon's movement to political outcomes. This is to be in denial. A secular denial of the suffering of others who are hungry, who can't send their children to school, who live in unsanitary housing, who leave school (if they even go) half-illiterate, who don't find work, who know their future is a big question mark without a solution, who see life as an immense desert with no place for them, who think that their only choice is to leave this country that offers them nothing, that becomes full of frustrations, anger, resentments, a country of church-goers, arms raised to God, to spirits, to the Holy Virgin and the saints. They know that they are forbidden to go to certain places; they encounter discriminations and injustices on a daily basis, those who don't recognize their real enemies, who sometimes attack out of despair, who learn to lie, to steal to survive, who drag their desperation around with them in the streets, behind false smiles or wild eyes, who die because they cannot afford medical treatment or medicine, who fall victim to bullets in lawless areas or elsewhere, who eat poorly, or little or not at all, who run to board a van that is already packed, who sweat under a blazing sun to arrive on time at a factory where they receive a salary of next to nothing, who must fight off groping by a perverse boss, who give up because they know life is not on their side, who fight all the same to remain alive, who pass their days in front of steaming pots waiting for customers, who wander the streets with their businesses on their heads to collect some gourds, who come home at night, tired, who don't know what to give their kids who are waiting for them, who know that the State has forgotten them, whose fate doesn't interest officials, who know that those who have money don't even pay attention to them, that their life will not change, who are tired of hearing politicians' empty promises, who . . . who . . . who . . . The ones that we forget, whom the president has once again forgotten in his post-protest statements, who don't need any encouragement to participate in pillaging. Frustrations and anger don't need to be bought when they are already there.)

I begin with Trouillot's post and cite it in its entirety because her approach to parsing social inequality and class division identifies an unremitting, omnipresent, and too often neglected social problem. Trouillot's admonishment to "not forget those who have truly lost" issues a warning to Haitians of the middle and upper classes as well as those in the diaspora. The repetition of "qui . . ." suggests that the list of travails could continue in perpetuity because of the unrelenting injustice to which the poor are subject. Trouillot's words distill critical messages about class and also demonstrate what an ethical approach to analyzing class division might resemble. As the post makes clear, for Trouillot, class division is one of the most pressing problems of contemporary life in Port-au-Prince. In addition to its import for thinking through the machinations of class belonging, Trouillot's post is a meditation on how privilege calibrates identity. Like M. Jacqui Alexander, she understands that "one of the habits of privilege is that it spawns superiority, beckoning its owner to don a veil of false protection so that *they never see themselves*" and encourages Haitian people to take a closer look so that they may see themselves more clearly.[3]

Trouillot's personal concern with the everyday lives of people who make up the poor, the working poor, and the poor middle class is reflected in her fiction, in which class division is a social, cultural, political, and ethical problem. Most important for the purposes of this study, Trouillot emphasizes the extent to which the class problem is also an ethical problem. For the contemporary writer then, a concern for literary ethics means using fiction to address class as well as to imagine it differently.

The critical framework that I engage in this chapter is the idea of geographies theorized by Katherine McKittrick as a rethinking of "space, place, and location in their physical materiality and imaginative configurations."[4] Following McKittrick's perceptive argument that there is a need for more Black feminist scholarship that "fill[s] in the conceptual abyss between metaphorical and material space," I find that formulating the idea of class location geographically rather than as a fixed category allows us to see more possibilities in these characters' encounters with socio-economic inequities.[5] In this chapter, I examine how Mars, Trouillot, and Lahens call attention to space and place to negotiate the ethical, cultural, and aesthetic difficulties of representing class division. I argue that Kettly Mars's *Je suis vivant* (2015), Évelyne Trouillot's *Le Rond-point* (2015), and Yanick Lahens's *La Couleur de l'aube* (*The Colour of Dawn*) (2008) and *Dans la maison du père* (2000) highlight the problem of class division through formal choices—narrative voice, plot devices, and interior monologues—that engage the reader in ethical reflection about how and why class divisions persist. McKittrick's formulation of geographies is useful in that it challenges us to see how class is deliberately constructed in ways that attempt to both displace Black women and fix them in space. Here a Black feminist ethic preoccupied with space and narration can offer a critical perspective on how class operates in the lives of individual characters without isolating it from an intersectional framework.

This chapter examines how Mars, Trouillot, and Lahens call attention to space and place to negotiate the ethical, cultural, and aesthetic difficulties of representing class division. I argue that *Je suis vivant, Le Rond-point, Dans la maison du père,* and *The Colour of Dawn* pose ethical questions about the responsibility that people of different classes have toward one another based on their shared humanity and the endless possibilities for encounters. Following the insights in Rolland Murray's argument that class division manifests as "form, ideology, and epistemology" in fiction, I argue that Trouillot, Mars, and Lahens represent class divide as a form of encounter that holds all members of the society, including the elite *and* the government responsible for division.[6] As I explained in chapter 1, the idea of encounter is foundational to my understanding of ethics. Thinking ethically is about encounter because it refers to the internal logic of the text, how characters think about themselves and others, how readers think as a result of the encounters, and what each of these components reveals about the moral universes the authors create.

The intentional way Mars, Trouillot, and Lahens underline the intricacies of class division manifests a Black feminist ethic with care and justice at the center. Care asks that we pay attention, that we look closely, that we see. Justice imagines a world in which all obstacles are removed so that every person can flourish. By amplifying class-based injustice, the authors ask us to imagine what a just world for all might look like. Further, they espouse a Black feminist view of how socioeconomic inequality functions as a site of oppression. Ultimately, *Je suis vivant, Le Rond-point, Dans la maison du père,* and *The Colour of Dawn* exhibit how class tensions animate, hamper, and exacerbate social interactions. How does class inform social relationships? How are daily interactions influenced by class power, access, and privilege? And, in keeping with an intersectional view of identity, how do class and gender oppression intersect?

Class Intersections and Interventions:
Marie Chauvet and Paulette Poujol Oriol

There is no question that the problem of class that Trouillot sensitively dissects in her social media post has a thorny history in Haiti. Many scholars have traced the origins of class division to the colonial system. In *Framing Silence: Revolutionary Novels by Haitian Women,* Myriam Chancy argues that the "rigid caste system instituted under colonial rule affected the ways in which various groups within Haitian society interacted . . . this system, which has grown many tentacles informed by race, gender, color, class, and nationality, is firmly rooted in Haiti."[7] Still, and as other feminist scholars have pointed out, often class is the "neglected component of intersectionality," meaning that, within the race, class, sexuality, and gender constellation, class is given the least attention.[8] This neglect is certainly notable in feminist literary studies. Such so-called "class absences" reflect widespread social discomfort with discussing the issue of class because to speak openly of class location and privilege is still taboo in some circles.

Although little critical attention has been devoted to analyzing the intricacies of class as a marker of identity, it is nonetheless very present as a theme and topic in literature. For their part, Haitian authors have never hesitated to confront the subjects of class and class divisions in their writing. Before turning to the twenty-first-century novels in my corpus, I briefly consider how the vicissitudes of socioeconomic class figure prominently in novels by two twentieth-century feminist authors—Marie Vieux-Chauvet and Paulette Poujol Oriol—to remind us that Lahens, Trouillot, and Mars write within a genealogy of Haitian literature attentive to how intersectionality shapes the lived experience of characters.[9]

Marie Vieux-Chauvet's novels regularly pursued the presence of class differences and divisions in Haitian society. Chauvet, whose work Kaiama Glover describes as consistently representing "the nuances of political affiliation in midcentury Haiti, particularly as regards the ambivalent role played by color in relation to class," can be seen as a template, along with

Poujol Oriol, for what it looks like to represent class from the vantage point of ethics.[10] Chauvet's 1957 novel, *Dance on the Volcano,* is about a poor mixed-race girl who eventually transgresses race and class lines. In his study of Caribbean intellectuals and the public sphere, Raphael Dalleo argues that the novel "consistently foregrounds the discontinuity and possible allegiances between different classes and shades among the island's African-descended population."[11]

Published almost a decade after *Dance on the Volcano,* the triptych *Love, Anger, Madness* delves even more profoundly into the machinations of class, color, and gender. Historian Madison Smartt Bell reads *Love, Anger, Madness* as "a continuum describing the reactions of different classes of people to a generally similar experience of invasion and oppression from without their households, and a suffocating claustrophobia within."[12] Bell goes on to note that Chauvet's text is a powerful example of how "race hatred is understood as a mask for class hatred" in Haiti.[13] Indeed, throughout Chauvet's magnum opus we witness how class, color, and gender oppressions compound and are exacerbated by an overwhelming sense of despair in the context of dictatorship.

Each section of the triptych devotes attention to characters from diverse class backgrounds. The Clamont sisters in *Love* come from a privileged position. In *Anger,* the Normils are a middle-class family whose land ownership is in jeopardy, and the three poets who are the subject of *Madness* are poor, struggling artists living in a dilapidated home. For Dalleo, the novel also evokes a shift signaling "a different set of alliances between segments of the middle and lower classes."[14] But as Carolle Charles points out in her sociological reading of Chauvet, "part of the dynamic of any system of racial and gender inequality is that the social categories that make that domination real are always actively recreated by the human beings they affect."[15] It is insufficient to attend to how characters observe class divisions and dynamics; we must also account for how the text replicates those. In my view, the idea of geographies as spaces and places offers a way to think through the manifold manifestations of class division in these novels. Marie Chauvet's pointed attention to the socioeconomic positioning of her characters has also been poignantly analyzed by Alessandra Benedicty-Kokken, who frames Chauvet's posthumous *Les Rapaces* as "an effort to explore how protagonists representative of social classes other than Chauvet's might experience the oppressions of a despotic regime."[16] Class tension is an omnipresent feature of Chauvet's oeuvre that reflects her refusal to capitulate to socially acceptable themes for a woman writer of her generation. Her lived experience as a woman from the upper class did not prevent her from writing fiction that explored class tensions, transgression, and division. Also, while Chauvet never affiliated herself with the *Ligue féminine d'action sociale,* she was a contemporary of the founders, and her novels delve into many of the subjects these Haitian feminists were invested in at the time. As Glover notes, Chauvet pays attention to "the disenfranchisement of women of every social stratum within the existing sociopolitical structure."[17]

In contrast to Chauvet, Paulette Poujol Oriol was actively engaged in the work of *La Ligue féminine d'action sociale* up until the end of her life. As I discussed in chapter 1, in most of her fiction Poujol Oriol saliently renders class stratification as a problem that is raced, sexed, and gendered.[18] Coralie's precipitous fall in *Vale of Tears* from privileged debutante to homeless beggar exemplifies how class functions intersectionally because it amplifies how class, color, and gender overlap and exacerbate one another.

Long before she wrote *Vale of Tears,* in her first novel, *Le Creuset* (1980), Poujol Oriol focused on the idea of social mobility in a single Haitian family. The novel takes place during the US occupation and relates the story of a boy named Pierre "Roro" Tervil who leaves Haiti and then returns as an adult with a new identity. Roro's grandmother Mansia is known in the neighborhood as a "fam totale . . . fam oraye" (a woman of integrity, a hurricane woman) who shelters several Caco rebels in her home in support of Haitian resistance to the Marines' invasion (8). But the accomplished Mansia was once Hermansia Saintus, a little girl from a peasant family who came to Port-au-Prince as a *restavek* (unpaid and often mistreated domestic worker). Owing to her enterprising nature, guile, and sheer force of will, she eventually starts her own business, which brings her much success in the community and allows her to acquire distance from her humble beginnings, shedding her previous identity, "Ti Sia devenue Manze Sia pour plus de respectabilité" (little Sia became Man Sia for more respectability) (14). After an all-encompassing though short-lived "liaison à la fois tumultueuse et constante" (sexual liaison that was both tumultuous and constant) with a Spanish-speaking lover, Mansia gives birth to her daughter Linda, the mother of *Le Creuset's* protagonist, Roro (18). Although the novel is about Roro's fate as a boy growing up under the thumb of the US occupation and how he eventually escapes, only to return to Haiti as an adult with a new identity, by introducing the story via the incomparable Mansia, Poujol Oriol focuses the reader's attention on the intersections of race, class, sexuality, and gender. Mansia's rise from rural restavek to businesswoman who reigns over the lakou presents a possibility for mobility not commonly associated with class discussions in Haiti. In an essay about the translation of the novel, Carrol Coates observes the role that language plays in designating class: "The play between French and Kreyòl [in the novel] signals a type of class conflict" as the author attempts to tease out and "understand the play of lower- and upper- class discourse."[19] As I mentioned in chapter 1, the themes and topics of Paulette Poujol Oriol's fiction often dovetailed with the mission of *La Ligue féminine d'action sociale,* which encouraged women from the privileged elite to understand class as an ethical problem and called for them to "become conscious of their responsibilities as citizens to the impoverished classes."[20]

As these few examples by Chauvet and Poujol Oriol indicate, the topic of class division is far from novel in Haitian literature in general, and twentieth-century Haitian women writers specifically attest to the long-standing problem of socioeconomic inequities. I am drawn to these novels because they establish a precedent for unflinchingly identifying class differences.

Further, any study examining class in the context of Haitian feminism would be incomplete without a critique of the role that privilege has played within it. It is impossible to raise the topic of class alongside the *Ligue féminine d'action sociale* without attending to how these feminists' elite class privilege influenced their work and legacy. A discussion of how class figures in an intersectional framework must also account for the noticeable gaps in the official history of Haitian feminism as well as some of the drawbacks to a feminist approach in which class "responsibility" takes on a patronizing tone. In a powerfully argued essay about the historiography of Haitian feminism, Natacha Clergé maps what she calls "les invisibilités de l'histoire." (history's invisibilities).[21] Clergé's discerning essay, which appears in *Déjouer le silence,* makes a compelling plea for "une historiographie féministe intersectionnelle et démocratique . . . qui intègre les continuums et les imbrications entre les résistances individuelles, les luttes des Haïtiennes pauvres (cette citoyenneté d'en bas) et les organisations féministes plus institutionnalisées" (an intersectional and democratic feminist historiography . . . that integrates the continuum and overlaps between individual resistance, the struggles of poor Haitian women [citizenship from below] and more institutionalized feminist organizations).[22] I fully agree with Clergé's take that often the failure to be truly intersectional becomes apparent in a neglect of class-based analysis as well as a lack of recognition for how class structures are reproduced in scholarship. Indicting Haitian nineteenth- and twentieth-century feminists for what she calls a "féminisme individuel ou individualiste" (individual or individualist feminism), Clergé forcefully argues that the official histories of the Haitian feminist movement fail to consider the participation of women who are not from the elite classes and entirely erases the feminist contributions of peasant women. Clergé demonstrates that even when Haitian feminist scholars engage class analysis, embedded in their studies are a number of blind spots that fail to account for the agency of women outside of their own social classes. Referring to the work of Madeleine Sylvain-Bouchereau, Clergé writes, "certes, Sylvain-Bouchereau n'est guère aveugle aux hiérarchies de classes qui opposent les Haïtiennes. Néanmoins, elle n'induit pas une redéfinition profonde des rapports de pouvoir entre les différentes couches sociales" (Sylvain-Bouchereau is hardly blind to the class hierarchies that oppose Haitian women. However, it does not induce a profound redefinition of the power relations between the different social layers).[23] Clergé's essay serves as an important counterpoint to official histories of Haitian feminism that lean heavily on the influence of the *Ligue féminine d'action sociale* without interrogating the class absences and erasures resulting from such a focus. Her inquiry also reveals the value of a Black feminist ethic that questions from below—that is to say, asks what and who is missing from ethical inquiry. I introduce her points prior to beginning my analysis of how class figures in twenty-first-century fiction to lay the ground for theorizing class as geography—in relation to space and place rather than as a fixed marker of identity.

In what follows, I show how Mars, Lahens, and Trouillot use narrative polyphony and interiority to reframe the logics of class division, effectively critiquing and reimagining their presence. Scholarly approaches to class in Haiti show how patterns of privilege, power, and domination intersect throughout history, emphasizing that class division is a phenomenon extending and unfolding over time. Further, the idea of class division as a problem requiring ethical engagement and reflection reverberates in the novels I examine. Guided by the undergirding principle of a Black feminist ethic, this chapter considers how class division poses ethical problems that illuminate a discourse of simultaneity and lends itself to thinking class in relation to space.

Sex, Class, and Visibility in *Je suis vivant*

As I noted in my discussion of *Je suis vivant* in the previous chapter, the novel takes place almost entirely within the walls of the Bernier family home, giving it an insular quality. The family drama tells the story of a bourgeois family that must reaccustom themselves to living with the oldest sibling, Alexandre, after he is sent home from a facility for people suffering from mental illness. In addition to narration by characters in the immediate family, several chapters of *Je suis vivant* are narrated by characters who are not family members. As the story unfolds, we encounter first-person narratives by two servants, Livia and Ecclesiaste, who have lived on the Bernier property and served in the home for many years. Then, halfway into the novel, we are introduced to Norah, who becomes the lover of Marylène, the eldest of the Bernier siblings.

As the only character from the outside (she goes in and out of the physical home), Norah observes the Bernier family from a unique perspective and is observed by them. How Norah is seen by the other members of the family, and her awareness of how they see her, provides additional context about how gender and sexuality operate intersectionally in *Je suis vivant*. By definition, intersectionality requires what Françoise Vergès describes as "une analyse multidimensionnelle de l'oppression et refuse de découper race, sexualité et classe en catégories qui s'excluraient mutuellement" (a multidimensional analysis of oppression that refuses to cut race, sexuality, and class intro categories that can mutually exclude one another).[24] How Norah is *seen* by others demonstrates the vicissitudes of class division; one of the first people to express her harsh view of Norah is Livia, the family housekeeper, and her observations are among the most extreme. The novel presents Livia's perspective to us first, which in turn influences how we analyze Norah. When Livia sees Norah for the first time, she is disturbed by her presence in the Bernier home. From her vantage point, not only does Norah not belong in the space, she disrupts it with her presence:

> J'en connais plein de filles comme elle dans mon quartier, dans tous ces bidon-villes aux profondeurs insondables qui ceinturent les résidences des bourgeois. Des filles comme elle qui n'ont que leurs corps pour se forger vite un avenir, avant la misère, avant la fanure de leur chair. Elles ne feront jamais la bonne chez Madame, non, cette génération a des ambitions, elle connaît la luxe, le téléphone portable, la télévision, l'ordinateur.

> (I know many girls like her in my neighborhood, in all those shanty towns in the unfathomable depths that surround the residences of the bourgeois. Girls like her who have only their bodies to forge a future for themselves, before misery, before the fading of their flesh. They will never do well as servants at Madame's, no, this generation has ambitions, it knows luxury, the mobile phone, the television, the computer.) (94)

In a passage that immediately contrasts with how Marylène sees Norah, Livia appraises Norah's physique and her intentions with an objectifying and judgmental gaze. Her comments about Norah's physical features move from her eyes to her breasts in a way that sexualizes the younger woman. Livia also assumes that Norah's sexuality could only operate transactionally; she assumes that Norah is motivated by an appetite for material things and status.

Livia pejoratively assesses Norah as a machann ak machandiz and makes clear that she identifies Norah as a desiring and devouring subject who, if given the opportunity, would swallow Marylène whole. Here the vocabulary of consumption functions differently because, in Livia's eyes, Norah's appetite is only for sex and material objects. Livia cannot see Norah apart from her class identity:

> Norah cherche un seuil. Elle est entrée dans la cour avec l'espoir de trouver un endroit où renaître et jouir sans état d'âme de tout ce que la vie peut donner de bon. Elle a posé le pied dans la cour avec l'espoir de trouver un endroit où renaître et jouir sans état d'âme de tout ce que la vie peut lui donner de bon. Elle a posé le pied dans la cour et j'ai vu son regard, il dévorait tout . . . Elle cherche l'épuisement des nuits. Ce plaisir qu'elle sait apprivoiser et qui lui achète la sérénité des matins où les lits sont douillets et le café chaud et bien sucré.

> (Norah is looking for a threshold. She entered the inner courtyard hoping to find a place to be reborn and enjoy without hesitation all the good things that life can give. She set foot in the yard and I saw her gaze, it devoured everything . . . She seeks the nights' languor. This pleasure that she knows how to tame and that buys her the serenity of the mornings where the beds are cozy and the coffee hot and very sweet.) (95)

But Livia's judgment of Norah also stems from their proximity. She knows girls like Norah from her own quartier; she has a point of reference that the other characters do not. According to Livia, Norah comes to the Bernier household looking for a better life, using Marylène's desire for her as a way to make inroads into the comforts afforded by their wealth. Later on, Livia notices that everyone in the family is curious about Norah; the young woman effectively introduces an appetite *for more* in the entire household. In Livia's mind, Norah's desire to consume becomes a contagion that affects the entire household, inspiring them to devour.

> Depuis qu'elle a mis les pieds dans la cour, quelque chose dans l'air a frémi. *On a tous envie d'en savoir plus d'elle* . . . M. Jules qui causait à sa belle-mère sur la terrasse a failli s'étrangler en buvant son café quand il l'a vue passer. Elle

. portait un pantalon collant mauve, un petit corsage jaune sous lequel on devi-
nait ses seins nus et des sandales aux talons hauts. Mme Éliane l'a regardée de
derrière ses verres épais sans rien dire. Elle voit tout Madame Éliane. Norah a
continué de longer l'allée, vers la maison de Mme Marylène, en laissant derrière
elle une odeur de sexe. Mme Marylène est dans tous ses états. J'ai peur pour
Mme Marylène. Norah va l'accaparer, Norah va l'aimer, Norah va l'obséder
puis la contrôler. Et Mme Marylène qui n'y comprend rien. Et Mme Marylène
qui peint dans son atelier la grande bouche de cette fille sur ses toiles.

(Since she set foot in the yard, something in the air shivered. *We all want to
know more about her* . . . Mr. Jules, who was talking to his mother-in-law
on the terrace, nearly choked on his coffee when he saw her go by. She was
wearing tight purple trousers, a little yellow bodice under which one could
discern her bare breasts and sandals with high heels. Madame Éliane looked
at her from behind her thick glasses without saying anything. She sees everything Madame Éliane. Norah continued along the driveway to Ms. Marylène's
house, leaving behind a smell of sex. Ms. Marylène is in such a state. I am
afraid for Ms. Marylène. Norah will take her over, Norah will love her, Norah
will obsess her then control her. And Mrs. Marylène will understand nothing.
Mrs. Marylène who paints in her studio this girl's big mouth on her canvases.)
(96–97, my emphasis)

By describing Norah as someone who "leaves the odor of sex behind her,"
Livia reductively connects Norah's class to her sexuality. Viewing Norah
as a disruptive presence in the home, Livia pays attention to how her
arrival registers for other characters. Because she does not belong in the
space, Norah is conspicuous to all. Among the more striking narratives
that address class division in the novel, Livia's mercilessly negative view
of Norah shows two people of similar socioeconomic origins unable to
bridge a divide. Their similar class affiliation breeds no affinity; rather, it
is a reason for Livia to have even more contempt for the young woman:

Je l'ai vu tout de suite dans ses yeux. Des yeux affamés, des yeux qui ont déjà
goûté aux certitudes de l'abondance et à l'angoisse de la faim. Des yeux qui
connaissent le pouvoir absolu du vice. Son long corps est un vice, il est beau
et elle le sait trop bien. On ne peut pas avoir des seins durs comme ça, des
fesses rondes comme ça et les porter en plus à la soif des autres comme une
offrande impudique. Elle a des yeux qui ont déjà vécu tant d'histoires dans ce
visage si jeune.

(I saw it right in her eyes right away. Hungry eyes, eyes that have already tasted
the certainty of abundance and the anguish of hunger. Eyes that know the

absolute power of vice. Her long body is a vice, it is beautiful and she knows that only too well. One cannot have hard breasts like that, a round buttocks like that and also present them as a shameless offering to the thirst of others. She has eyes that have already lived so many stories in this face despite being so young.) (94)

Referring to Norah's "devouring eyes," Livia associates the younger woman's body with a desire for consumption. Livia is unable to see Norah for anything other than her socioeconomic status. This connection between class and consumption often relays class division; the poor are seen by the rich as devouring and hungry for more. And Mars does not leave us with only Livia's negative impression of Norah. We will also hear what others in the family think about her, emphasizing how much she is looked down upon and judged before we even encounter her actual voice.

But before long the assumptions that are made about Norah are debunked when we read her perspective. Norah notices how the household members see her, and at the same time observes their house in relation to space and place. From the moment that she enters, Norah observes the Bernier home. She immediately identifies the gap between how and where she lives and how and where the Bernier family lives. She sees their relative wealth and how comfortable they are, and she is especially struck by the insularity, which she notes as a sign of privilege.

Que savent-ils de la vie dehors ? Ils sont toujours enfermés dans leurs voitures, ils vont travailler, vont à la banque, au supermarché, en reviennent, s'installent devant leurs ordinateurs puis devant leurs télés . . . Ils discutent de la vie chère, de la politique, de l'insécurité . . . de leur dernier voyage À Miami ou Montréal. Des bourgeois, voilà ce qu'ils sont, qui pensent tout savoir de la vie dehors. Ils vivent la politique à la télé, mais moi je la vis dans la rue. Ils ont une idée abstraite de la faim, moi je la connais. Ils ont des passeports étrangers ou des visas valides pour parer à toute éventualité, moi je suis éxilée dans ma propre peau.

(What do they know about life outside? They are always locked in their cars, they go to work, go to the bank, to the supermarket, come back, sit in front of their computers then in front of their TVs . . . They discuss the cost of living, politics, insecurity . . . their last trip to Miami or Montreal. Bourgeois, that's what they are, who think they know everything about life outside. They live politics on TV, but I live it in the street. They have an abstract idea of hunger, but I know it. They have foreign passports or valid visas to deal with any eventuality, but I am exiled in my own skin.) (118)

Norah's "reading" of the Berniers' lifestyle immediately sets up a contrast between her experience and theirs. Just by looking around the garden, she sees the marked difference in socioeconomic class and then draws conclusions about the other aspects of their lives.

From her first encounter with the Berniers, Norah situates them in terms of class: "Ce sont des bourgeois. Ils vivent à plusieurs dans un grand jardin. Ils n'ont pas l'air d'être très riches, mais ils doivent bouffer et dormir bien. Teint clair, mais pas beaucoup, une bourgeoisie mulâtre qui s'est basanée avec le temps. Une ancienne bourgeoisie qui s'accroche à ses prérogatives mais que le peuple accule dans ses retranchements" (They are bourgeois. They all live together in a large garden. They don't seem to be very rich, but they clearly eat and sleep well. Fair-skinned, but not by much, a mulatto middle class that has tanned over time. An old bourgeoisie which clings to its prerogatives but in which the people are cornering in their entrenchments) (105).

While Norah scrupulously makes note of the setting, she does not do so with an agenda to acquire, as Livia assumes she does. Through narration, Mars offers Norah's perspective and directs a critical eye toward the Bernier family. The introduction of Norah into the plot further highlights how class and sexuality intersect and prods the reader to ask ethical questions about the family's perception and treatment of her. As Norah looks at them and sees how they look at her, she questions from below, exhibiting the watchfulness that Lorde calls a form of survival for people that society "others." Her evaluations of the Bernier family and their home establishes them in the physical space and place, and also on an ethical conceptual plane that is the foundation for interpreting class division.

Class Division in *Le Rond-point*

Évelyne Trouillot's *Le Rond-point* exposes profound class division and illuminates its cost, inviting the reader to ask ethical questions about how and why such cleavages exist. What does it mean for people of two vastly divergent classes to live side by side yet never interact? How does one make sense of social inequities from an intellectual, material, and moral perspective? How has the creation of different worlds exacerbated social interactions between classes?

In this section I argue that Trouillot's use of narrative devices—such as multiple points of view and lengthy interior monologues—highlight the complex relational dynamics of class in Port-au-Prince. Nowhere is class division more evident in *Le Rond-point* than through the use of three narrators to tell the story; engaging these multiple points of view requires the reader to experience class as encounter and relation. I structure my analysis around the point of view of each protagonist and his/her perception of class location and division in order to highlight how space and place operate in Trouillot's textual world.

Set during the early 2000s, *Le Rond-point* chronicles the lives of Sorel, Titi, and Dominique, three protagonists from different socioeconomic backgrounds. The divide between their disparate worlds is reflected in the narrative structure. Each chapter is narrated by a different protagonist, which has the effect of separating their stories, lives, experiences, and worlds. This material division of one narrator per contained chapter mimics how rigidly class operates in society. It seems to suggest that social mobility is impossible and that class hierarchies are fixed. When examined from the perspective of the protagonists' reflections about class division, the individual chapters contain incisive social commentaries specific to each character's socioeconomic position. Sorel is a young man from an underprivileged background struggling to make ends meet, Titi is an eleven-year-old boy from a modest working-class background uneasy about his place in society, and Dominique is a woman from the elite upper class increasingly ambivalent about what her life has become.

Le Rond-point's paratext initiates the reader into a universe in which social divisions are sacrosanct—but should nevertheless be scrutinized. The novel's second epigraph draws from Victor Hugo's *L'année terrible* (1872) in which Hugo articulates the interdependent relationship among people from different social strata and laments the class-divided conditions of life in nineteenth-century France. The excerpt that Trouillot uses for her epigraph reads, "Hélas! combien de temps faudra-t-il vous redire . . . Qu'il fallait leur donné leur part de la cité; que votre aveuglement produit leur cécité" (Alas! How long will it be necessary to tell you again that they should be given their share of the city . . . that your blindness produces their blindness). The poem's message is categorical: the rich and the poor are mutually dependent, and the rich have an obligation to the poor. And even more, the rich should understand that their lavish lifestyles exacerbate the harms of social inequality. The use of Hugo is noteworthy; no other French author devoted such sweeping and pointed attention to the negative effects of class division. After all, Hugo also famously wrote in *Les Misérables* that the victims of structural inequality are not responsible for their crimes, but, rather, the system is responsible: "cette âme est pleine d'ombre, le péché s'y commet. Le coupable n'est pas celui qui y fait le péché, mais celui qui y a fait l'ombre" (if the soul is full of darkness, sin is committed. The guilty one is not he who commits the sin, but he who has caused the darkness).[25] According to this view, the blame for crimes committed by poor people lies undeniably on the shoulders of the rich. Or, as Évelyne Trouillot expresses in her social media post cited at the beginning of this chapter, these victims of structural inequality are incontestably *les vrais perdants* (the real losers). *Le Rond-point* offers a twenty-first-century example of how considering the perspectives of characters from distinct parts of society and placing them in relation probes social inequality as an ethical problem that is made apparent through encounters, attentive to relationships, and requiring recognition.

Centering the Poor Majority

Class governs social interactions and occupies mental space for each of *Le Rond-point's* three protagonists. In Sorel's case, material concerns restrict his life and drive him to make decisions with negative consequences. Trouillot encourages us to interpret his actions in relation to Hugo's point from the epigraph. As a member of the working poor, Sorel can barely survive on his daily wages: "Comment s'en sortir avec ce salaire minimum? Tu arrives à peine à survivre avec ce que tu gagnes tandis que tes dettes augmentent chez la marchande de fritures, le vendeur de *pate kode*, la gamine qui tient le commerce de bananes de sa mère" (How to get by with this minimum wage? You can barely survive with what you earn while the debts you owe increase—debts to the merchant of fried food, the seller of pate kode, or the girl who looks after her mother's banana trade) (68). Rhetorical in nature, the question is directed to the reader and calls for an answer. It is an ethical question. How can anyone survive on the minimum salary offered to people like Sorel, who make up the poor majority in Port-au-Prince? As a policy-related question, it incriminates the government's maintenance of social inequality.

Despite his difficult material circumstances, Sorel realizes that his situation could be far worse, but he recognizes that his reality is not isolated from the lives of others. The rhetorical use of the French words *les gens* signals his feelings of both belonging and nonbelonging: "Mais *les gens comme toi* doivent compter chaque gourde, chaque centime de leur pitoyable salaire, alors ils n'achètent pas seulement en détail, ils achètent au compte-goutte. La morale de l'histoire c'est que les riches le resteront" (But people like you have to count every gourd, every penny of their pitiful salary, so they do not just buy in detail, they buy per drop. The moral of the story is that the rich will remain rich) (69). *Les gens comme toi. People like you.* There are others. Whenever *les gens* appears in his interior monologue, we see recognition of a difference. There are "these people" and "those people," distinctions that the French grammar makes clear. Distinctions that imply either distance or proximity. In this instance, Sorel's use of *les gens* is also an indication of scale. People *like him* make up the majority, and for them survival is the foremost concern: "Ici, les gens sont tous occupés à survivre, à ne pas augmenter le nombre de cadavres anonymes, morts anodins et multiples dans une ville où la vie humaine passe comme de l'eau claire entre les fentes des orteils" (Here, people are all working at surviving, not increasing the number of anonymous corpses, innocuous and multiple deaths in a city where human life passes like clear water between the toes) (77).

As the novel's moral center, Sorel regularly raises questions about how class operates, asking the reader to contemplate the ethical implications. Sorel represents the poor majority and the centrality of his voice and perspective marks Trouillot's commitment to rendering attentive portraits of the impoverished masses who are more often rendered as faceless. By privileging Sorel's perspective, and by her use of the narrative second person, Trouillot pulls the reader to inhabit Sorel's world more closely, more deeply. The social contemplation that she elucidates parallels efforts by scholars like Michel Acacia, who in *Historicité et structuration sociale en Haïti* concludes: "Voilà un livre qui invite le lecteur à se regarder dans un miroir, par une sorte d'introspection, il s'agit d'un répertoire de détails de la vie quotidienne avec, en filigrane, des raccourcis d'histoires de vie et d'études des cas" (This is a book that invites the reader to look in a mirror, through a kind of introspection. It is a repertoire of details of daily life with implicit life stories and case studies).[26] Acacia uses case studies to illuminate the lived experience of a poor majority and invite introspection; Trouillot accomplishes the same goal through second-person narration.

Sorel's assessment of Port-au-Prince as a universe made up of two worlds articulates one of the basic premises of the novel:

Ce pays c'est pareil. Ce n'est pas un seul pays, ce sont des tas de films différents qui se jouent simultanément. Certains passent dans des endroits incroyablement riches et beaux, tu n'essayes même pas de les reconnaitre. Comme ces jardins bien entretenus que tu aperçois parfois à la sauvette le temps pour un véhicule de franchir le portail avant qu'il ne se referme sur les platebandes de fleurs, le temps pour toi de rester bouche bée et de te retrouver à ta place dans monde brutal et laid. Tu sais que dans ton film à toi, tu ne seras jamais l'acteur principal, celui qui arrive à bout des méchants, le héros qui porte la fille dans ses bras hors d'un immeuble en flammes. Tu voudrais simplement ne pas périr bêtement, comme ces Blacks qui se font régulièrement descendre les quinze premières minutes dans les films de gangsters américains, comme s'il fallait toujours qu'un Noir soit abattu pour que l'action démarre.

(This country is the same. It's not a single country, it's a lot of different movies playing simultaneously. Some go to incredibly rich and beautiful places, you do not even try to recognize them. Like these well-kept gardens that you sometimes see on the sly the time it takes for a vehicle to cross through the gate before it closes on the flower beds, the time for you to be speechless and find yourself where you belong in a brutal and ugly world. You know that in your film, you will never be the main actor, the one who overcomes the bad guys, the hero who carries the girl in his arms out of a building in flames. You just do not want to perish stupidly, like those Blacks who are regularly shot down during the first fifteen minutes in American gangster movies, as if it was always necessary for a Black person to be shot for the action to start.) (70)

The film metaphor offers an apt point of comparison. It exposes the marked difference between the classes, as well as how subject positioning is informed by which social class you belong to. Sharp contrasts capture the difference between the two environments: "des endroits incroyablement riches et beaux" opposes "un monde brutal et laid." The point of view elaborated here, that people of different classes are *worlds apart* and that this chasm has pernicious effects on human interactions, is also reflected in the novel's narrative structure. Sorel's musing in the passage above ends with him noting how inequality unfolds in global terms, explaining that his cousin who migrates to the United States in search of a better life must eventually return with "les yeux éteints et la peur au ventre" (his eyes extinguished and fear in his belly). In this, Sorel effectively debunks the myth that migration is the solution to poverty (70–71). Becoming a part of the diaspora does not put an end to social inequality. Nor does escape provide protection. This concluding anecdote acknowledges social inequalities as a global problem of systemic injustice. Sorel's analysis of how class operates also serves as an example of "questioning from below": he asks himself why the world is so divided even as he realizes that he is powerless to alter it.

Sorel's positionality leads to the development of an intimate awareness, an ability to see with his third eye and to insightfully interpret social dynamics. This practice of looking is akin to Audre Lorde's formulation of watchfulness that I cited throughout chapter 2. Having lived two weeks in Cité Soleil, Sorel understands how the poorest of the urban poor live:

"Et depuis ce jour, malgré toi tu voyais à tous les détours les enfants dans la cité. Le gamin de six ans qui allait à l'aube chercher de l'eau à la fontaine et que la voiture d'un gang en cavale faucha un bon matin . . . La fille de neuf ans violée par un policier. Le bébé séropositif jeté tout nu dans une ravine" (And since that day, in spite of yourself, you saw the children in the poor neighborhoods at every turn. The six-year-old boy who went at dawn to fetch water from the fountain run over by the car of a gang on one fine morning . . . The nine-year-old girl raped by a policeman. The HIV-positive baby thrown naked into a gutter) (72–73). These grim scenes of life inform Sorel's vision of inequality's bleak backdrop. The poor, he reminds us, just as Trouillot's post does, suffer the most as a result of socioeconomic division; they are indeed *les vrais perdants*.

Victimized by class structure, Sorel is in a perpetually precarious economic situation. He repeatedly describes in vivid detail the difficulties of being poor, drawing from his own experiential knowledge: "Un pays où la faim ne s'endort jamais. La faim, tu la connais depuis longtemps que tu dors avec elle, la nuit venue, elle rentre carrément dans tes songes et se moque de toi en t'envoyant des images où tu manges tout à ton soûl. Le matin, elle est encore là et salue ton réveil avec un pincement douloureux" (A country where hunger never sleeps. Hunger, you have known for a long time that you sleep with it, the night comes, it goes straight into your dreams and makes fun of you by sending images where you eat everything until you're stuffed. In the morning, it is still there and greets your awakening with a painful twinge) (158). These searing descriptions contribute to a vibrant story about how one man struggles to survive in a society in which his choices are severely limited.

Narrated in the less frequently used second person, Sorel's story registers as intimately close to the reader, provoking a response that frames our reading in terms of witness. Because it is told from the perspective of an onlooker, second-person narration brings us closer than third person but more distant than first person. Typically, second-person narration is "not defined by who is speaking but by *who is listening*."[27] As a result, second-person narration often rests on dynamics of witnessing as it calls attention to who is listening and who is telling.

This characteristic of witnessing supports the logic of narrative ethics in which scholars define the union of the two terms as such:

> narrative ethicists take the practices of storytelling, listening, and *bearing empathetic, careful witness* to these stories to be central to understanding and

evaluating not just the unique circumstances of particular lives, but the wider moral contexts within which we all exist. In telling stories, they suggest, we both create and reveal who we think we are as moral agents and as persons; in granting these stories uptake—that is, in giving them epistemic credibility—we help to mold and sustain the moral identities of others, as well as our own. Thus, theorists engaged in narratively-based moral scholarship take stories to be foundational for how we view the world and our place in it, arguing that they are the means through which we can make ourselves morally intelligible to ourselves and to others.[28]

The idea of narrative ethics outlined here recalls my discussion in chapters 1 and 2 about the responsibility of the one who listens to (or reads) the story. If stories are the foundation for how we view the world and our place in it, then Sorel's story has something to tell us about class in general and our specific relationship to it far beyond the context of the novel. As readers, we are implicated in this dynamic and called to account for how we accept and uphold class division. In other words, attention to narrative ethics serves as a form of witness.

Trouillot's ethical preoccupation with the situation of the poor and her concern with class division are distinctly informed by how the poor are most often not considered. Her use of second-person narration is effective because it "manifests in narrative technique the notion that someone or something outside of yourself dictates your thoughts and actions . . . the inclusiveness of the you pronoun lumps the readers and the protagonist together."[29] For example, when Sorel explains his decision to join the actions of Ti Kanif's gang, we as readers must put ourselves in his mind, forcing ourselves to imagine what his decision to participate in a kidnapping attack must be like. By following his logic, we notice how easily one can become a part of the life of crime.

Sorel's observations about class division starkly render the extent of the cleavage and reveal how harmfully present it is. In his poignant interior monologue, Sorel wrestles with his life's difficulties and the challenge of his material realities as he travels through Port-au-Prince attempting to make a life for himself (*chache lavi*) and perhaps even more to make sense of his life. His restricted social mobility confines him physically and materially but never intellectually, socially, or emotionally. Continuously aware of the worlds around him beyond his own, his perspective astutely renders the idea of a classed double consciousness—an ethical encounter that we as readers must confront and grapple with.

The Impact of Class Division on the Youth

The perspective of eleven-year-old Titi in *Le Rond-point* exposes the impact of social inequality on the youth of the lower middle classes. Titi, a child from the working poor (or precarious middle-class) goes to a school where he interacts with people from different socioeconomic backgrounds. Rather than serving as an equalizer, school becomes a place where inequality is magnified. Being among children more privileged than he alerts him to what *he does not have,* making him painfully aware of how class division shapes education. The trope of invisibility deployed to describe Titi's feelings is the main lens through which we understand his relationship to social class. For Titi, invisibility occurs in two registers: as an awareness of how he is seen by others and as a learned behavior that becomes a mode of survival: "Graduellement, il avait appris à ne pas se faire voir, à imiter les voix et les gestes, à se glisser parmi eux, à devenir encore plus invisible" (Gradually, he learned not to be seen, to imitate voices and gestures, to slip among them, to become even more invisible) (31). The logic of invisibility also signals deeper truths about how people are classed; different social groups become invisible based on their class status. A potent ocular logic, invisibility is integral to the maintenance of class division. As long as the poor masses are unseen, their humanity remains unrecognized and there will be no moral obligation to them. Trouillot's inclusion of Titi also interests me because it demonstrates how class stratification is experienced by the youth, a topic that has become increasingly relevant in twenty-first-century Haiti. As scholars like Gina Athena Ulysse have discussed, youth and class intersect with social and political ramifications because "the historical neglect of masses by the elite has brought the country to this point where many people and *especially the youth* are so disenfranchised and fed up with the political machine."[30]

In *Le Rond-point* we witness the mounting anger of a young boy whose perception of the world around him, its inequity, and how he figures in it become apparent to him. Titi is effectively experiencing a coming-of-age with regard to how inequality operates around him, and his observations foment feelings of rage in his young mind. Class awareness inspires and exacerbates his anger the more he realizes that he is helpless in the face of it: "Titi s'essuie rageusement le visage tant la colère, le dépit et le chagrin bouillonnent encore en lui. Il déteste ce qu'il éprouve, ne savait pas qu'on pouvait se sentir si mal, au point de vouloir prendre sa propre chair entre ses mains et la frapper pour en faire sortir la douleur" (Titi wipes his face angrily as rage, spite, and sorrow still bubble up in him. He hates what he feels, did not know you could feel so bad, to the point of wanting to take your own flesh into your hands and hit it to release the pain) (58). The frequency with which "colère" and "rage" are associated with the boy powerfully communicates the degree of his frustrations. As we saw with Sorel, the inclusion of a male character reminds us that a Black feminist ethic points to how structures of patriarchy put limits on personhood for all people, regardless of gender.

Titi's understanding of how class functions comes primarily from his family and schoolmates. His cousin Mireille constantly reminds him that he should be thankful to have what he has: "A ton âge, beaucoup de garçons doivent se laisser tripoter tu sais où par de vieux vicieux pour manger à leur faim" (At your age, many boys have to be fondled you know where by dirty old men in order to eat their fill) (136). The sexual implications of her statement remind the reader of how the machinations of inequality are undeniably sexed and gendered. To cite M. Jacqui Alexander, his cousin's chiding makes clear that "the multiple operations of power [are] gendered and sexualized, [and] simultaneously raced and classed."[31]

At school, Titi encounters children of both lesser and greater means. Even in the smallest social interaction with his classmates, he is aware of how they are marked by such class distinctions. For example, as they discuss the need for children to have more play spaces in Haiti, Titi sits back to listen to what his classmates have to say, knowing that they, unlike him, have traveled abroad: "Titi n'a pas dit grand-chose, il a laissé parler les autres qui ont bien plus d'avantages que lui. Curieusement ce sont eux qui ont eu le plus de choses à dire, eux qui tout naturellement se sont retrouvées dans cette école des Frères sans que ce soit suite aux démarches des employeurs de leur mère" (Titi did not say much, he let others, who have more advantages than him, speak. Curiously they were the ones who had the most to say, they who naturally found themselves in this school run by priests without it being because of the intervention of their mother's employers) (137). That he deems it "curious" for the more privileged children to have more responses to this question shows that he does not yet fully understand how class privilege works. But he does understand the difference between him and his classmates; unlike them, Titi is only at the school because of the "intervention of his mother's employers."

Titi's mother's employment as a maid for the wealthy Calvin family also teaches him about the injurious effects of class division and flagrant economic disparities. He regularly thinks about her lived experience as a maid and assumes the people she works for must look down on her. When his mother shares how well she is treated by her employers, he thinks warily to himself, "Comme si les patrons pouvaient bien traité les domestiques!" (As if the bosses could treat the servants well!) (32). Such feelings of resentment are further ignited every time he encounters the Calvins: "A chaque fois que Titi visite les Calvin, il plonge dans un autre monde, comme s'il avait franchi l'écran de la télé pour pénétrer dans une contrée magique" (Whenever Titi visits the Calvins, he plunges into another world, as if he had crossed through the TV screen to enter a magical land) (171). Like Sorel, he notices and names the existence of two disparate worlds. It is also telling that, like Sorel, he immediately associates the affluent world as a magical place that can only make sense in the imagination. Titi's and Sorel's use of the images of film and television to describe the world they do not live in confirms just how distant that world is. Titi also internalizes how he is seen by this wealthy family, feeling othered through their gaze: "le visage outrancièrement maquillé signifia clairement au jeune garçon qu'il n'appartenait pas à leur monde" (the outrageously made-up face clearly signified to the young boy that he did not belong to their world) (182).

The importance of these looks that Titi perceives mirrors what we saw unfolding in *Je suis vivant* when Norah is observed (and aware of how she is observed) by others in the Bernier household. Titi's young age makes sensitivity to a classed lens—the quality of "watchfulness" that Lorde defines as a product of difference—even more striking. I interpret this ability to see oneself through the eyes of others as a form of classed double consciousness that is at work for all of the characters who are not a part of the elite. *Le Rond-point* affirms that those who are not from the upper class are fully aware, even as children, of how people from the upper classes and the elites look (or do not look) at them.

Titi reveals his awareness about the harmful effects of perceived invisibility again when he sums up his interaction with Claude P. Séverin, whom he believes to be his father. In this moment, when Titi sees himself through the eyes of Séverin, his anger reaches a breaking point, radiating from two sources, that his father abandoned him and that in his current state he is invisible to the wealthy man: "Le fait c'est que ce Claude P. Séverin ne l'avait même pas regardé. Il avait aperçu un gosse *n'appartenant pas à son monde* et l'avait tout de suite fourré dans une case : enfant des rues, mendiant en devenir ou petit voyou en herbe" (The fact is that this Claude Séverin had not even looked at him. He had seen a kid not belonging to his world and had immediately stuffed him in a box: street child, beggar in the making or budding little thug) (138). The same language about incongruous worlds that we saw in Sorel's interior monologue returns here. Despite the fact that he has a home, his mother works, and he attends school, to Séverin, Titi is irrevocably invisible. He could be any child from the street; it only matters that he does not present as a child from the elite upper class.

Titi's experience highlights how the logics of visibility and invisibility inform class division. Who is seen? Who is not seen? Who gets to be seen? Who wants to be seen? Visibility operates as a privilege afforded by the few that underscores how class division produces radically unequal worlds. That those who are supposed to be invisible not only notice but also name this problem stands as a demonstrated critique of how social inequities operate. Titi's questioning from below leads to rage and anguish far beyond his eleven years. Class relegates him to a category in which he is invisible to anyone not like him, yet he is able to look out and notice that they do not see him.

The Obsessions of the Rich

These constant references to class difference in each character's interior monologues situate it as hypervisible and invisible; that is to say, class is seldom discussed openly among the characters but regularly contemplated by all, regardless of their social status. From their various subject positions, Sorel, Titi, and Dominique incessantly contemplate the intricacies of class division. When these protagonists comment and reflect on class inequity, their conclusions are unflinching and precise. This is also true of Dominique, whose privileged status does not afford her the luxury of not having to think about it. Much of Dominique's interior monologue is occupied by ruminations on the reality and effects of class division. When analyzed for its ethical implications though, her interior monologue reveals the callousness of her thoughts about people who are different from her. One might expect someone who reflects so regularly on class division and social inequalities to behave differently, but Dominique does not. She is keenly aware of the social inequities that regulate daily life but remains unwilling to do anything about it or to even think differently about those who are not a part of her milieu.

Dominique's lack of self-awareness about how she perpetuates the system she critiques is especially galling because she is so attuned to the problematic habits of her wealthy peers. On a rare occasion in which she discusses the class divisions in Port-au-Prince *with* her friends, Dominique paints a stark picture: "'D'un côté la famine, de l'autre l'opulence. Les expositions d'orchidées et les salons de cadeaux de luxe versus les émeutes de la faim et les hordes d'enfants en guenilles. Les contrastes de ce pays n'en finis-sent pas de me dérouter,' avoue Dominique à ses deux amies" ("On one side famine, on the other, opulence. Exhibitions of orchids and luxury gift salons versus food riots and hordes of ragged children. The contrasts of this country never cease to throw me off guard," admits Dominique to her two friends) (161). Although she claims that the "contrasts of the country" disturb her, she does nothing to challenge these structures or the assumptions that accompany them.

There are times, though, when Dominique mulls over class division with a degree of remorse and culpability, suggesting that she experiences some negative feelings as a result of her privilege. In some moments, she is even demonstratively irked by the conspicuous consumption of those around her: "Combien d'argent un être humain doit-il accumuler avant de s'estimer en sécurité? Mais elle ne formule aucune critique, non pas par acceptation inconditionnelle mais par paresse et besoin de confort mental" (How much money must a human being accumulate before he feels secure? But she makes no criticism, not because of unconditional acceptance but because of laziness and need of mental comfort) (131). But Dominique feels no actual moral obligation to thwart convention or to openly criticize the excesses of her peer group. Her choice to say nothing to her friends conveys the hypocrisy of her thinking and behavior.

The same contrast is clear in how she considers the visibility of the poor people around her. On the one hand, she hates the fact that the socioeco-nomically disadvantaged people have become invisible to people like her, but, on the other hand, she recognizes that she too refuses to see them: "Dominique est consciente qu'en réalité, elle non-plus ne regarde pas les autres, s'y intéresse de très loin" (Dominique is aware that in reality, she does not look at other people, that she is only interested from afar) (151). Though her fraught private thoughts show the reader that Dominique is fully aware of the disparities, she suffers from "the habits of privilege" described by M. Jacqui Alexander, allowing her to "don a false veil of protection" so that she *never sees herself*.[32]

Dominique's position is therefore the opposite of a Black feminist ethical standpoint. The encounter with others who are unlike her does not lead Dominique to question from below, to ask *who are you*, or to move toward recognition. She is fully cognizant of her world as one that is "un monde inégal, où les petits courent sur des pattes trop courtes et ne rattraperont jamais les grands" (an unequal world, where the poor run on paws that are too short and will never catch up to the elite). Her refusal to reconcile her positions about class suggests an ethical failure that is reminiscent of Nadine Magloire's protagonist Claudine in *Le mal de vivre,* perceptively analyzed by Myriam Chancy as an example of upper-class women who are similarly conflicted and contradictory. Chancy explains: "As a middle-upper class woman, Claudine shows little compassion for those less fortunate and, in fact, has contempt for those in poverty . . . Ironically, Claudine also despises her own class, and especially the women within it for their shallowness."[33] Building on Chancy's reading of Claudine, I am interested in how Dominique toggles back and forth between derision and responsibility in her interior monologue but fundamentally lacks the ethical impetus to allow her thoughts to influence her actions.

Dominique's thoughts about class regularly focus on division, the creation of distinct worlds, and the idea of separation: "Ici plus qu'ailleurs, *les gens* semblent évoluer dans des univers différents mais si proches que parfois Dominique pense être en pleine zone fantastique, dans un monde surréaliste et imprévisible" (Here more than elsewhere, people seem to evolve in different worlds but so close that sometimes Dominique thinks she is in the middle of a fantastical zone, in a surreal and unpredictable world) (43). Again, her reference to *les gens* leads us to question to what extent she includes herself among those who contribute to maintaining and perpetuating systems of social inequity. Critical of how those around her live opulently without seeming to even notice the poor that surround them or the enormous chasm between the rich and the poor in Port-au-Prince, Dominique repeatedly questions the actions and the behavior of the rich. During a party she asks herself incredulously, "Dans quel pays vivaient-ils? Ne se rendaient-ils pas compte que la cohabitation y devenait de plus en plus difficile, qu'ils évoluaient telles des fourmis affolées courant chacune après son butin, indifférent au sort des autres?" (In what country did they live? Did they not realize that cohabitation became more and more difficult there, that they evolved like mad ants each running after its own booty, indifferent to the fate of others?) (86). This quotation emblematizes the link between class division and geography: a disconnect from the realities of inequity is tantamount to a misunderstanding of where one actually lives. Dominique's sense of space and place are blindingly shaped by her privilege, and her inner thoughts also expose a glaring paradox: while she thinks about these questions on her own, she never deigns to bring them up to anyone else for discussion. And so, as a result, her admonishment rings hollow when viewed in the context of her own behavior. Overall, Dominique's class identity consolidates around her understanding of what her privilege affords her in terms of comfort, lifestyle, excess, and access.

Given the context of the 2000s, when Port-au-Prince was racked by a series of kidnappings, it is unsurprising that Dominique thinks more deeply about class division because her privileged and protected suburban life appears to be increasingly in jeopardy. Her new awareness emerges as a result of fear: fear for her safety, fear of losing her privilege, fear of losing more friends to the kidnapping crisis, and fear of death. *Le Rond-point* carefully frames kidnapping as a problem born of class division: "Nous sommes en pleine période d'enlèvements. Une atmosphere de peur s'étale sur la ville. Les kidnappings se multiplient, les victims ne se comptent plus" (We are in the middle of kidnappings. An atmosphere of fear pervades the city. Kidnappings are increasing, and the victims are countless). For people like Dominique, kidnappings pose a dangerous and omnipresent threat to their privileged existence. Constant references to kidnapping in Dominique's interior monologue and her conversations with friends reinforce their community's concern.

For example, we learn that "son meilleur ami a été kidnappé l'été dernier" (her best friend was kidnapped last summer), immediately signaling that Dominique is a part of the group for whom kidnapping is an ominous threat touching their lives (40). Her worries about kidnapping soared after this incident in which a close family friend was taken at gunpoint and held for a period of weeks. The occurrence negatively impacts her emotional health: "Je suis traumatisée, je ne sais pas comment Jean-Paul peut endurer la vue de ces rues, de cet espace où il fut agressé" (I am traumatized, I do not know how Jean-Paul can endure the sight of these streets, of this space where he was attacked) (110).

A sense of resignation pervades Dominique's interior monologue. She observes how kidnappings upend the comforts of the upper class and identifies kidnapping as one more in a list of difficult issues that wealthy families must endure when they choose to live in Port-au-Prince. But Dominique ultimately concludes that there is nothing she can do about it: "Il faut accepter ce monde, composer avec l'insalubrité des rues, la corruption administrative, les emmerdes d'un quotidien de plus en plus imprévisible et maintenant les enlèvements" (It is necessary to accept this world to deal with the insalubrity of the streets, administrative corruption, and the annoyances of an increasingly unpredictable daily life, and now the kidnappings) (109). As the linchpin of Dominique's social anxiety, the kidnappings present the paradox of the rich: they are at risk because of their lavish lifestyles, yet they refuse to leave Port-au-Prince because of what these same lifestyles afford them.

Alongside her fear and anxiety about the threat of kidnapping, Dominique relativizes the pain from the poverty that she sees around her. When she muses to herself about the condition of the world, it is merely a way to comfort herself that the injustice in Port-au-Prince is not particular to Haiti; it is a universal problem: "De Gaza à Beyrouth, de Bogotá à Athènes, les hommes s'entretuent, les grands bouffent les petits et l'injustice et la violence règnent" (From Gaza to Beirut, from Bogotá to Athens, men kill each other, the big ones eat up the little ones and injustice and violence reign) (151). By making this global link to other countries, the author reminds us that Haiti does not have a premium on suffering, an important acknowledgment in a novel like *Le Rond-point*. It also locates Haiti in a matrix of power relations that ensnares the Global South and invites the reader to wonder why these countries have in common what they have in common. I interpret Dominique's need to justify the widespread existence of suffering as an attempt to assuage her own culpability in maintaining social inequalities. Furthermore, the fact that she moves so quickly from her own emotions to the suffering of those around her suggests that she is unable to grasp the difference between systemic and structural suffering of the poor and her own concerns as a privileged woman.

Understanding class as geography—that is, space, place, and location—allows us to see how Dominique, Titi, and Sorel are shaped by the social spheres they inhabit. The inner workings of each character's mind: their emotions, judgments, assumptions, fears, and anxieties reveal the effects in their lived experience of the respective "worlds" they inhabit.

When Classes Collide: Encountering the "Other"

Trouillot's attentiveness to the interior lives of these characters emphasizes class divisions as we witness what separates and what unites them and are ultimately brought to see inimical effects that class division has on all members of society. *Le Rond-point*'s turning point and rapid dénouement, in which the worlds of these characters literally collide, suggest a disastrous ending that looms in the future of Haitian class relations.[34] There is an abrupt change of narration in the final chapters, which suddenly include the perspective of each protagonist. Aesthetically, this change in narration mirrors the action of the plot: *Le Rond-point* ends with a high-speed car chase with Dominique and Titi in one car and Sorel and Ti Kanif in another car attempting to carjack her. The imminent crash puts the reader on edge. What will happen as a result of this encounter? Which characters will survive? The suspense increases as the three perspectives alternate, and suddenly the form becomes more condensed because each narrator is present in the chapter, narrating the chase and crash through their own eyes.

The disaster at the novel's ending offers a pessimistic, at best, interpretation of the cost of the different social classes coming in contact with one another. Social stratification makes it such that people can live in the same space without ever interacting. But, the fact is, as *Le Rond-point* forcefully reminds us, that although these characters live in different worlds *metaphorically* they actually live in the same city. Even when they do not see or interact with each other, they coexist. The novel's conclusion highlights a troubling reality but also asks the reader to look far beyond it. Sorel's final act to save Dominique and her family suggests the possibility of an existence beyond class division.

It is telling, in this light, that the title of the novel focuses our attention on this point of encounter. Le Rond-point, the rotary in the middle of downtown Port-au-Prince for which the novel is named, is surrounded by hotels, market vendors, and other small forms of commerce. It is a meeting place for the rich, the middle class, and the poor alike, one where they may encounter one another even if that is not their intention. This technique of encounter recalls Nadève Ménard's point in "The Impact of Fleeting Encounters," in which she contends that Trouillot does not allow class divides to remain undisturbed. Describing several short stories in which there are brief encounters that hold tremendous weight for the characters in question, Ménard writes: "One might be tempted to read these brief texts by Trouillot as commentary on the enduring divide between social classes in Haiti . . . Especially since in popular representations and scholarly discourse on Haiti it is often depicted as a space where separation between classes cannot be breached at all. In these stories, Trouillot reveals that in fact the separations are themselves quite fragile and subject to being flattened at any moment."[35] Ménard's observation that the separations are "quite fragile" is proven in *Le Rond-point* as the reader slowly realizes how Sorel, Titi, and Dominique are connected to one another and come to matter in each other's lives. By giving us characters who eventually *see* each other and who demand interaction across the division dictated by social inequality, Évelyne Trouillot offers another path forward. This final gesture takes us a step beyond critique to imagine otherwise as our Black feminist ethic encourages. It critically represents Trouillot's search for another world in which class is experienced as a produced geography that is far from "secure and unwavering."[36] The novel's prolonged ethical chafing concludes by suggesting an alternative vision, effectively linking the ideas presented throughout the novel with an action.

Trouillot's insistence on portraying the poor, middle class, and upper class *as well as* those in between is telling insofar as her commitment to each one is evident through narrative devices as well as in the elaboration of their agency, interiority, and subjectivity. In general, Évelyne Trouillot's entire corpus is marked by rapt attention to the complexity of human relations in different social, historic, and political contexts. I read her treatment of class in *Le Rond-point* as influenced by her preoccupation with ethics and justice. As she tells us in her own words in a personal and critical essay, her writing stems from an "aesthetic and social vision for a more beautiful and more just world."[37] This vision, which steadfastly foregrounds the intricacies of intersectional dynamics, conveys her ethical commitments as a Black feminist.

Le Rond-point addresses the problem of class division by critiquing the stratification of characters into distinct spheres and highlighting both the material distance and the emotional proximity of characters who live divergent lives. I see this juxtaposition of material distance and emotional proximity as an ethical position because it exposes and questions what lies at the root of these divisions: a refusal to see the self within the other, that is, a denial of shared humanity. If, as Dayan suggests, to be ethical "is to locate oneself in relation to a world adamantly not one's own," then each of the protagonists in *Le Rond-point* fails.[38] The use of three narrators demands rigorous ethical engagement from the reader; through this deep connection we obtain a nuanced perspective about the unique challenges the protagonists face as well as how class shapes their lived experience and is a constant reference point for their moral decisions.

In his essay on how class dynamics operate in African American fiction, literary scholar Rolland Murray posits that "novelists rewrite class division as form, ideology, and epistemology."[39] What he means is that the novelist makes use of textual strategies to convey what class division is as well as what it can be. Form, ideology, and epistemology are all integral to Trouillot's approach to how class operates in the everyday lives of Haitians. The ethical nudge occurs for the reader who must ask, to what end this division and what will it come to? The novel's structure interrogates the construction and maintenance of class division in order to expose the deleterious effects of these cleavages on all members of society. *Le Rond-point*'s conclusion in which the worlds of these characters collide uncovers the disastrous ending that looms in the future of Haitian class relations—but then subtly suggests that individual actions can steer these relations differently, leading the reader to consider what productive possibilities lie beyond class divisions. The end result, and what lies at the heart of Trouillot's ethical project in *Le Rond-point,* is a thoughtful interrogation of humankind that transcends class difference even as it exposes class division.

A Self Divided in *Dans la maison du père*

Whereas *Le Rond-point* calls attention to class division as a quotidian part of life in contemporary Haiti, Yanick Lahens's first published novel, *Dans la maison du père,* highlights how socioeconomic division impacts relationships in one household through the life of a bourgeois family in the first half of the twentieth century. The novel displays how class concerns intersect with race and gender in the experience of protagonist Alice Bienaimé as she looks back over her life. The ways in which socioeconomic inequality surfaces as a problem in Alice's life and for her family present ethical challenges even for those who have the luxury to ignore it.

Dans la maison du père spans a period beginning in the mid-1930s and continuing into the 1950s. Class tensions are interlaced throughout the novel, but the primary optic through which they come to light is that of dance. From a formal perspective, *Dans la maison du père* falls into the genre of the bildungsroman, telling the story of how the adult protagonist became a dancer. As Anne Marty notes in her study of the novel, "Tout au long du récit, l'héroïne cherchera, à travers la danse, à se libérer des tabous de son éducation" (Throughout the story, the heroine seeks, through dance, to break free from the taboos of her upbringing).[40] Dance operates as metonym for class; we observe characters come into dancing as an introduction to different social milieu. Lahens features two forms of dance that are in opposition to one another: the restrained swaying movement to the melodies of the upper class counter the passionate movements inspired by the fomenting beats of Vodou. As a sign of class, dance also encompasses religious practice and belief. Ultimately, *Dans la maison du père* tells the story of a young woman disavowing her class; by choosing a life of dance she rejects her family and the plans they have for her life. This choice is one of mobility but not in the typical direction. Rather than take the path of upward mobility to which she is entitled because of her socioeconomic status, Alice abandons her privileged upbringing and chooses a life of forbidden dance, a move that implicitly links her with the lower classes.

Through a single character—an upper-class woman who abandons the privileges afforded by her class background—*Dans la maison du père* relates the different sides of social hierarchies that characterize life in Port-au-Prince during the mid-twentieth century. But while Alice Bienaimé does ally herself to those from lower classes, she often sees the poor as objects rather than subjects. When she looks, she may see, but she still looks down with a gaze from above and not below. This is clear in how she views the family servant Man Bo and describes her throughout the novel: "Je la regardai et je la trouvai vieille. Sur le coup je ne mesurai pas exactement ce qu'était la vieillesse, cette chair consumée par les jours, cette peau née par les ans sur un squelette qui tentait de livrer seule une dernière bataille" (I looked at her and found her old. At the time, I did not exactly measure what old age was, this flesh consumed by the days, the skin worn by the years on a skeleton that was trying to fight a last battle alone) (38). As I noted in chapter 2, a young person looking at an elderly woman presents an ethical encounter rife with meaning. What would have been the audacity of her look if she was interacting with someone from the upper-class world becomes permissible with Man Bo because she is a servant. Alice often looks at Man Bo in a way that is objectifying and othering. Despite the girl's great affinity for the older woman, her classed look casts Man Bo in a negative light. It is an encounter that irritates the reader as we witness how looking and seeing are not the same practice.

The novel's title and the idea of "the father's house" also symbolize the rigidity and choking respectability that Alice is forced to endure in her life. In my view, the title and the leitmotif of the house in general reflect the "patriarchal architecture" that Imani Perry refers to and deconstructs in *Vexy Thing: On Gender and Liberation*.[41] As an agent of patriarchy, Mr. Bienaimé rules his household with staggering dominion, meting out oppression to his children, his wife, his servants, and sometimes even his friends when they visit his home. Alice's father's house stands not only for the physical house but also for his dominance over the family and the strict ideology that he espouses and forces everyone in the household to live by.

In his study *Architextual Authenticity: Constructing Literature and Literary Identity in the French Caribbean*, Jason Herbeck argues that the figure of the house in francophone Caribbean literature operates as a structure that signals more than just the physical home. Herbeck reads "the Caribbean house as bio-architecture—structures that absorb as well as reflect the historical, political, and cultural realities in which they are constructed and subsequently evolve."[42] Although he is less attentive to the gendered dimensions of these structures and how they might reify or challenge a patriarchal order, Herbeck's study is useful insofar as it concerns "dogmatic structures" and is committed to "probing the structures of pre-determined models."[43] If, as Herbeck argues, "literary houses serve as receptive historical and social repositories of information . . . [that] . . . can furthermore be interpreted, by way of their appearance, purpose, physical preservation (or lack thereof), and (in)occupancy over time, as analogous to the continual search for self-expression and (re)construction of French-Caribbean identity," what might the figure of the physical house itself suggest for the Black female protagonist seeking to free herself from the patriarchal oppression of her childhood home?[44] In my view the "maison du père" refers to the strictures of patriarchy that Alice works to free herself from in the course of her life. Affirming the family home as a generative site for analyzing the complex intersections of race, class, gender, and religion as they unfold over time, *Dans la maison du père* puts pressure on how we evaluate these interimbrications.

Skin color is also invoked throughout *Dans la maison du père* as another element of class distinction. Michel-Rolph Trouillot's *Haiti: State against Nation* makes the point that the long-intertwined history of color and class in Haiti has historic and political roots. Trouillot's landmark study of social relations among Haitian elites presents a nuanced understanding of how class and color function in this context, arguing that "in Haiti conflict between color-cum-social categories does not simply reflect an opposition between social classes, however defined: the dominant classes are not composed of exclusively light-skinned individuals; nor do all such individuals belong to those classes."[45]

Trouillot's investment in deconstructing the notion that color and class are inextricably linked in Haiti also enacts a critique of ideologies that police borders around Haitian identity: "Color divisions do not simply replicate socioeconomic classes, or even income groups."[46] To this end, Trouillot's conceptualization of "social direction," which he describes as "the path that an individual is perceived to be taking up or down the social ladder," can be applied to my analysis of what happens to Alice in *Dans la maison du père* because he concludes that "society judges this continuous movement positively or negatively."[47] This is what we see at play in Alice's life. As we can also recall from my reading of Poujol Oriol's *Vale of Tears* in chapter 1, "social direction" is a fitting descriptor for what happens to Coralie, but with the important difference that in Lahens's novel Alice makes a conscious choice to move down the social ladder.

Alice's class education, her upbringing as a young upper-middle-class girl who must behave according to a fixed set of moral and social codes, also operates in the realm of respectability. For example, while she is out at the parade celebrating the departure of American troops from Haiti, she looks at a woman with interest and curiosity until she recalls her mother's lessons: "ce regard dont ma mère me disait toujours: 'on ne regarde pas ainsi les gens, c'est mal élevé'" (this way of looking about which my mother always said "we do not look at people like this, it is poor upbringing") (20). Alice is aware of what she should and should not do—even if it involves a mere look or an embodied movement. Although the codes of respectability regulating Alice's life cleave to her in every situation, she is a child who sees, looks, and evaluates what unfolds around her.

For example, while observing her mother with a group of women, Alice makes note not only of their behavior but also of their skin color and origins. Alice spends much time looking at other women, learning, absorbing how class operates intersectionally. As she watches them behave in ways that she knows she will be expected to mimic someday, she is discontented with what their lives look like, and her observations inform her will to eventually deviate from her family's social norms and to look for another possibility for her own future.

Watching these women as they interact in her home, Alice notes that their status is permanently yoked to and defined by the men they marry.

Madame Labard . . . D'origine syro-libanaise, elle avait fait descendre quelques marches de l'échelle sociale à Pierre Labard. En l'épousant, celui-ci avait en quelque sorte dérogé son rang, en commettant une faute de goût. Il appartenait à l'une de ces familles de la bourgeoisie mulâtre qui ne ratait jamais l'occasion de rappeler comme une caution ou un label de qualité l'aïeul qui aurait signé l'Acte d'indépendance ou laissé en héritage de vastes étendues de terres. Dans ce salon se retrouvaient, le temps d'une trêve, ceux qui comme nous voulaient échapper à la horde des anciens captifs et ceux qui, à l'instar des Labard, n'appartenaient pas tout à fait aux descendants des conquérants.

(Madame Labard . . . Of Syrian-Lebanese origin, she had caused Pierre Labard to move down the social ladder, by several rungs. By marrying her, he had in a way broken with his rank, by committing an error of taste. He belonged to one of those mixed-race bourgeois families that never missed an opportunity to mention, like a precaution or a label of quality, the ancestor who was said to have signed the Act of Independence or left vast stretches of land to his descendants. In this living room, during a truce, there met those who like us, wanted to escape from the horde of former captives, who like the Labards, were not really descendants of the conquerors.) (22)

Since *Dans la maison du père* is narrated in the first person, every representation of class in the novel is made through Alice's eyes. Even at a young age, she clearly understands the social power enabled by wealth. She also adheres to the spirit of judgment that Michel-Rolph Trouillot names as the evaluation of "social direction." At the same time, Lahens seems to suggest here that history also plays an important role in conferring social power.

As Alice revisits her past and travels further into the recesses of her memory, one of the first scenes she paints is one that ends in shame. One day, after she takes off her shoes and runs into the field to dance in a flagrant disregard of the respectability that she has been raised to abide by, her father slaps her.

> À quelques mètres de moi, il court à toutes jambes, m'attrape et s'abat sur moi comme une torche dans un champ de canne. Il me tient brutalement par les épaules me crie d'arrêter tout de suite cette danse . . . Maudite et me gifle. Je commence par crier très fort. Puis je gémis tout bas en me couvrant le visage des deux mains. Au milieu des pleurs je sens la lente montée de la honte. De la colère aussi. Elles se déversent dans ce qui est déjà ma souffrance la plus lointaine.
>
> (Several meters from me, he ran as fast as he could, caught me and descended on me like a torch setting a sugar cane field ablaze. He held me roughly by the shoulders and shouted at me to stop the dance immediately . . . Cursed and slapped me. I began to scream loudly. Then I moaned softly, covering my face with my two hands. In the middle of my tears I felt shame slowly rising in me. Anger too. They gushed into what was already my deepest suffering.) (11)

This moment becomes a turning point in Alice's life and informs her commitment to leaving the family behind and choosing a life of dance. The imprint of her father's slap is branded onto her soul for the rest of her life: "En avant de cette image il n'y a pas de commencement. L'image est centrale. Elle est le mitan de ma vie. Elle résume l'avant et éclaire déjà l'après . . . je suis née de cette image. Elle m'a mise au monde une seconde fois et je l'ai enfantée à mon tour" (Before this image there is no beginning. The image is central. It is the center of my life. It sums up the before and already sheds light on the after . . . I was born from this image. It gave birth to me a second time and I gave birth to it too) (13). By identifying this moment as the center of her entire her life, Alice sets the stage for how gender, class, dance, and religion will shape her subjectivity. Understanding how this incident definitively marks and forms Alice means reflecting on how the woman she becomes is informed by the nexus of these categories.

While Alice is being reborn and dedicated to dance, the country is in the throes of the historic 1946 revolution. In her analysis of *Dans la maison du père*, Yolaine Parisot has argued that it confronts "la naissance d'une vocation de danseuse avec en arrière-plan la Révolution politique, artistique et littéraire de 1946" (the birth of her vocation as a dancer [combines] with the political, artistic and literary Revolution of 1946 in the background).[48] Parisot correctly highlights the importance of the historic backdrop against which the novel unfolds, an eventful time in Haiti's history. The American occupation, though it ends to the joy of the Haitian people, leaves a disastrous mark on the country: "La première occupation américaine avait laissé un pays blessé" (The first American occupation had left a damaged country) (24). About a decade after the monumental departure of the Marines, another period of unrest ensues in the 1940s when popular uprisings lead to the overthrow of President Élie Lescot in 1946. Those familiar with the history know that the end of Lescot's presidency came about due to a radical movement of activism that had been percolating since the US occupation. Historian Matthew Smith explains that this movement became known as "the five glorious days" and led to the presidency of Dumarsais Estimé.[49] As such, the novel follows a tradition of Haitian women's writing in which the sociopolitical context is of concern, but, as Lahens demonstrates throughout, it is not at the expense of the protagonist's individual story; rather the two unfold simultaneously.

As is often the case in upper-class families, the value of respectability is frequently invoked in Alice's home as well as throughout her childhood. She is instructed how to behave, and the school she attends plays a role in socializing her appropriately: "Tu n'en feras jamais une jeune fille rangée . . . Moi à qui la foule et la rue seraient refusées quelques années plus tard" (You will never be a respectable girl . . . Me, to whom the street and crowds would be denied several years later) (21). Despite her economic privilege as the member of a bourgeois family, as a girl Alice is not afforded much status within her household. From the novel's point of departure above, in which her father disciplines her with violence, it is painfully clear that she has little or no power of her own. She is meant to be unseen and unheard, as girls of her age usually were: "J'étais encore une petite fille qui pouvait impunément s'asseoir sur les genoux de son père sans être contrainte de rejoindre le bavardage des femmes. Je croyais les hommes de cette île vraiment les plus forts" (I was still a little girl who could sit on her father's lap with impunity without being obligated to join in the idle talk of women. I believed that the men of this island were truly the strongest) (24). To be a "jeune fille rangée" is to be a girl without any power in the familial household.

Importantly, Alice's rural vacations at her grandparents' home allow her to observe how gender and power dynamics differ in this context. She sees how, as Myriam Chancy explains, "Haitian women of the rural working classes appear to have some power equity due to the fact that many are market women (handling booths at the market, money, trade) while their male counterparts work the fields," a dynamic that is significantly at odds with the workings of her oppressive household ruled by her father with an iron fist.[50]

When young Alice travels to see her grandparents in Gonaïves, we also witness a completely different part of her life and learn more about her background. Her grandfather's social position provides insight into her father's draconian behavior. For the grandfather, class stability is precarious at best: "Encore paysan par ses mœurs, il vécut dans la méfiance et la solitude son accession au statut de commerçant" (Still a peasant by his manners, he lived in mistrust and loneliness his accession to the status of business man) (66). Refusing to accept the obstinate boundaries of social class, the grandfather embodies Michel-Rolph Trouillot's point about the fluidity of class formation and "social direction."

The stories about class that Alice learns during these visits negate the view of lack of mobility or movement between classes. For example, her father, by going to boarding school in Port-au-Prince, was able to put his rural past behind him. This distancing from his humble origins occurs almost unconsciously: "Sans le savoir sur-le-champ, il se défit de tout ce passé au seuil des portes de cette demeure de la grande ville. Mon père d'abord, oncle Héraclès ensuite y devinrent petit-bourgeois. Ce fut aussi le début d'une distance qui se creusa entre leur père et eux" (Without knowing it on the spot, he got rid of all this past on the doorstep of this school in the big city. My father at first, Uncle Heracles, afterwards became petty bourgeois. It was also the beginning of a distance that grew between their father and them) (67).

The Bienaimé brothers' upward class mobility leads to distance from and disdain for their humble origins. As Alice describes the rift between father and son, she names it is a problem of class division: "L'amour était très fort, couvant sous les silences, mais cette distance de classe pour l'appeler par son nom, les maintient séparés désormais" (The love was very strong, brooding under the silences, but this class distance to call it by its name, kept them separated now) (68). Similarly, her father's upward mobility mirrors (in reverse) Alice's downward mobility. It also explains his anxieties about respectability and efforts to ensure that his family, including his daughter, maintain their class status.

Throughout her childhood, Alice is torn between her allegiance to her parents and to Man Bo, the maid who cares for her, working in their home as well as the surrounding community. The division as she experiences it is between two worlds: the working poor and the rich, the Vodouizan and the Catholics, those who embrace the outdoors and those who are cloistered inside. Although Lahens does not use the same stark language deployed by Trouillot in *Le Rond-point,* we do see in *Dans la maison du père* two universes divided by class affiliation. Due to the reality of domestic servants living in the home, these worlds can even exist in the same household. Alice puts it this way: "la maison des Gonaïves avait elle-aussi son arrière-cour. Man Dia, la sœur de Man Bo y régnait en maîtresse" (Gonaïves house also had its backyard. Man Dia, the sister of Man Bo, reigned supreme) (69). The "arrière-cour" to which she refers has two meanings: it is those who live outside of the home in the yard, as well as those who occupy a kind of eighteenth-century-style court with its own politics of belonging and behaving.

Alice's interactions with a boy her age is an encounter that peels back yet another layer of her class education. Unlike Alice, Elie, who lives in Gonaïves with her grandparents, is haunted by remorse and hopelessness about the future: "Il jouait avec dans les yeux un regard grand large, le regard de celui qui ne veut plus laver les parquets, porter les seaux, et cirer les chaussures des autres, sans espoir aucun. Lui ne chantait déjà plus les hommes d'ici" (He was playing with a wide-eyed look in his eyes, the eyes of those who no longer want to wash the floors, carry the buckets, and wax the shoes of others, without any hope. He was no longer singing about the men from here) (30). Just as she notices how her mother and the group of women around her are socialized to behave according to the dictates of class, Alice sees how Elie is restricted in his space and place as a poor boy. In this rare moment she sees him and is attentive to how he sees the world.

In the first part of the novel, Vodou exists only as a shadow, or a hidden trace. There are rumors about who serves the spirits, but they are mentioned only in hushed tones. Regarding Man Dia, Alice explains, "Et puis il y avait ses absences, comme on disait dans la famille. On croyait qu'elle conversait avec les esprits" (And there were absences, as people in the family called them. They believed that she conversed with the spirits) (71). But as the novel progresses, Vodou become one of the most important images used to convey prevailing class divisions. When Alice's

214 Looking for Other Worlds

grandmother is dying and others in the community observe the family's last rites for her, they make note of their spiritual praxis: "'Ils ont comme tout le monde laissé en secret un anneau en gage chez l'orfèvre' une façon de dire que malgré nos airs de chrétiens civilisés, nous fréquentions les prêtres vaudous comme les gens d'en bas" (They have, like everyone else, secretly left a ring as a pledge at the silversmith's, a way to say that, in spite of our civilized Christian airs, we frequented Vodou priests like the people below) (57). The reference to *les gens d'en bas* recalls Trouillot's use of *gens* to connote class-based belonging and difference. Alice's rural education also allows her to observe how gender and power dynamics differ in this context.

Alice's keen understanding of her body stems from her passion for dance, but it is also the subjugated knowledge of a girl who knows how bodies are policed due to gender and class. When she begins dancing, she learns that "le corps pouvait parler si fort et si haut" (the body can speak so powerfully and so loudly) and eventually decides to trust the calling of her body to become a dancer and to relocate to New York. I read how Alice relates to her body as an expression of geographies because it connects her to spiritual and material realities that agitate her sense of space and place. As Marty affirms for Alice, "les manifestations du corps sont révélatrices d'un contexte moral et socio-économique en errance, elles représentent aussi un indéniable force vitale" (manifestations of the body are indicative of a wandering moral and socioeconomic context, they also represent an undeniable vital force).[51] Alice's body is marked as a site through which she can not only embrace the spiritual call of embodied movement in her life but also contest the patriarchal order of her home.

The relationship between dance and class is of course routed through the Haitian religion of Vodou as Lahens draws on both to explore how the percolations of class division and the reality of social direction manifest in the life of the protagonist. Just as we saw in chapter 2, and as feminist scholars of Vodou continually demonstrate, religion operates intersectionally. In *Dans la maison du père,* dance serves as an index of class, religion, and space. There is, on the one hand, the music and dance of the Bienaimé home and, on the other hand, the music and dance of the rural life she is privy to on vacation.

That Alice prevails over the rigidly controlled categories she is confined to because of being female can be attributed to her own self-determination and what Kaiama Glover credits as an "ethic of self-regard" that enables her to choose herself over a suffocating class affiliation. Once she makes the decision to live her life for dance and follow the beat of the drum,

Alice inhabits a profound sense of selfhood. Out from underneath her father's yoke, she blossoms and claims her space in another world. To resist patriarchy, to refuse respectability, to embrace Vodou, to dance, to be free: these are the desires of Alice's heart, each of which confirms a resolutely Black feminist ethic at work in *Dans la maison du père*.

La Couleur de l'aube: Geographies of Class Location

Unlike *Le Rond-point* and *Dans la maison du père*, there are no narrators from the upper classes in Yanick Lahens's *La Couleur de l'aube*. However, like *L'œil-totem, Je suis vivant*, and *Le Rond-point, La Couleur de l'aube* has more than one narrator: sisters Angélique and Joyeuse Méracin, whose voices alternate in thirty short chapters. The novel begins with the mysterious disappearance of their brother, Fignolé Méracin. Set during Jean-Bertrand Aristide's second rule in the 2000s, the novel explores the harmful effects of that government on a socioeconomically disadvantaged family based in Port-au-Prince. Regarding class dynamics, the story is anchored in an egregious irony: the very people that President Aristide purported to represent are those who suffer most from his rule.

In this section I argue that Lahens's use of space in *The Colour of Dawn* foregrounds the vicissitudes of class belonging and the multiple manifestations of class division. Space, as I read it here, refers to the textual space of narration, the geographical space of Haiti's capital, and the different material and immaterial spaces present in the novel. My analysis of space returns to McKittrick's critical framework of geographies in *Demonic Grounds: Black Women and the Cartographies of Struggle*, in which she argues that "geography is not . . . secure and unwavering; we produce space, we produce its meanings."[52] Although class is a space that reflects a social reality, the production of class(ed) spaces is nonetheless influenced by individual subjects. Furthermore, how Black women characters move in and interact with the class(ed) spaces they inhabit reflects an ability to see beyond the reality of their socioeconomic and social status as well as an awareness of how they themselves are seen. What McKittrick refers to as "the spatialization of the racial-sexual subject" helps to "reveal how social categorization is also a contested geographic project."[53]

From this perspective, while the social production of space in *The Colour of Dawn* is shaped by class divisions, understanding those spaces as geographies opens possibilities for interpreting the function of class in order to see beyond their divisions. Indeed, class determines who gets to circulate where, how, and when. My interest in the *geographies of class* acknowledges that class functions as a location that is constitutive of identity but that must not be overdetermined. Put differently, and to cite McKittrick: "space and place give Black lives meaning in a world that has, for the most part, incorrectly deemed Black populations and their geographies as 'ungeographic.'"[54]

Haiti can be situated within this framework particularly well when we consider that it has routinely been epistemologically rendered as a place of (un)inhabitability.[55] What Joyeuse and Angélique's lives attest to is how the idea of (un)inhabitability impacts Black female consciousness in a way that begs for constant class analysis. The novel casts a wider net about class division that is not specific to Haiti but rather illuminates how forms of inequality relate to and exacerbate one another.

As early as the first few lines of the novel, in which Angélique walks out the front door to the family home and contemplates her surroundings, *The Colour of Dawn* calls our attention to concrete and discrete spaces: "Stealing a march on the dawn, I have opened the door onto the night. Not without first going down on my knees and praying to God—how could I not pray to God on this island, where the devil has such a hold and must be rubbing his hands with glee? In this house, where he has stealthily established himself as each day passes" (11).

Multiple spaces show up in these opening sentences. There is, first, the natural space of the environment outside of the house, beyond the door while dawn is breaking. Second, Angélique notes a divided spiritual space in which both God and the devil are equally present. Finally, she explicitly names the island (*cette île*) and then the house and the neighborhood (*ces quartiers*) where she lives. The variety of these locations introduce the reader to how Angélique interacts with spatial realities. As a deeply religious woman, her worldview is first and foremost spiritual. But she is also painfully aware of the struggles in the material space of her home, her community, and her entire country. Space as she inhabits it is fraught; it is always contested, and often for women this means having to fight for and claim the space to be seen. Only after establishing these distinct spaces in her mind does Angélique move on to a preoccupation that will take center stage in the novel: her brother Fignolé did not return home the previous night. Angélique and Joyeuse will spend the day wondering and worrying what has happened to him. They suspect that his disappearance is related to his resistance to the Aristide government. Even as this element of the plot dominates the novel, it is only present through the eyes of the sisters—and largely in the quiet thoughts they have to themselves—privileging the interior lives of these Black women.

As we saw in *Le Rond-point,* the choice of interior monologues and the dual narrative structure summon the ethical imagination to interrogate and reimagine socioeconomic disparities. In Lahens's novel, the formal use of space reflects the problem of class as it relates to individual experiences because the two sisters from the same household and background experience this aspect of their identity differently. The differences in the sisters' experiences, reactions, and approaches to the divisions around them foreground the problem of class as a vexed moral issue. Lahens's narrative devices play a role in illuminating and reflecting the construction of social class. She uses the divergence in perspective between the sisters to anchor this meditation on how class functions for two socially disadvantaged women caught in the power networks that structure their lives. How these women understand class and approach its reality informs their individual relationships to space and place—to class as geography.

For the Méracin sisters, class is a prevalent aspect of their lived experience at home in the family, at work in their professional spaces, and in what they do outside of those environments. One of the more abstract spaces we see delineated in the novel is the intimate one of the of family, which is conveyed through the sisters' tenuous relationships to each other. How they live in relation to one another, yet separately, materializes in the book's structure; similar to the structure of *Le Rond-point,* the relegation of each narrator to her own chapter emphasizes the division between them. Because we are privy to their interior monologues, we know how they think about each other, even if they never express those thoughts aloud.

Angélique and Joyeuse's sibling relationship is hardly affable; from the outset, their dynamic is fraught with tension and shaded with misunderstanding. The sisters' names, Joyeuse and Angélique, trumpet their personalities for the reader; these names reflect their approaches to life as well as the noteworthy character differences between them. At twenty-seven years old, Angélique is the more serious, devoted to her work at the hospital, her Protestant faith, and raising her young son, Gabriel. Twenty-three-year-old Joyeuse, on the other hand, is the younger, winsome, carefree sister who moves through life with curiosity and sensuality. If Joyeuse is full of life and joy, then Angélique is filled with regret, ambivalence, and caution. But, as Joyeuse notes, Angélique was not always so severe. During their childhood, well into adulthood and prior to having Gabriel, Angélique was full of life and joy herself. But in the present, Angélique is unhappy, and even her aesthetic choices reveal an ambivalence toward the joy that her sister embodies. Noticing this, Joyeuse describes her older sister's hairstyle: "She keeps all her happiness tightly bound in a severe bun at the nape of her neck" (21).

Angélique also sees the contrast in their approaches to life, calling her youngest sibling "my sister Joyeuse, my sister Joyeuse, so free, so free" (27). But is Angélique's comment about her sister intended to suggest that freedom should be looked down on, or does she long to have the same kind of freedom? What if Angélique, like her sister, longs to be free but feels confined by the world locking her in? When we read Angélique's evaluation as longing, we see how the older sister's sense of self has developed in opposition to ideas like choice and freedom. If she is unable to live as freely as her sister does, it is because of her lived experience and the burden that weighs on her as the older sister and as a single mother.

Angélique and Joyeuse's respective relationships to their brother, Fignolé, further complicate how the family space functions for them. Angélique describes him in terms of suffering and desperation: "he wears despair like a second skin," she thinks to herself (51). Joyeuse's description of him is more tender, which speaks to the more intimate relationship between them: "Recalcitrant, rebellious Fignolé, inhabited by poetry, crazy about music. Fignolé has no place on this island where disaster has broken spirits" (29). A tormented artist in his own right, Fignolé's turn to politics puts his life in jeopardy. The space that Fignolé occupies in the novel is despite his absence, or one could say his space is emphasized by his absence. Making an explicit reference to his place, which I read here as taking up space, Joyeuse thinks to herself about her brother: "You alone, Fignolé, have the power to take the place of my whole childhood. You alone were able to extinguish before time the pleasures of my childhood" (92). As a presence that looms over her entire childhood, Joyeuse's older brother is imposing and all-consuming. In contrast to his sisters, as a man Fignolé is allowed the freedom to take up space. At the same time, Joyeuse has learned a lot from him. It is telling, for example, that she attributes her development of class consciousness to her brother's radical politics: "Fignolé told me on one of his talkative days that something was there turning the world against us and those like us. That life was an absurd lottery where those who won have everything and those who lost, nothing. Absolutely nothing" (95). The "absurd lottery" that Fignolé warns his sister about is the architecture of a society in which there are haves and have-nots, winners and losers, rich and poor. It is a binaristic view that he entreats his sister to understand as part of her social education. Elsewhere, in *Failles*, Lahens has similarly described the lacunae dividing the "haves" and "have-nots."

Commenting on the creation of camps for displaced people in the after-math of the earthquake, she calls it a "new spatial distribution of the haves and have-nots." Lahens observes that before the earthquake "the have-nots were more or less hidden, either behind houses of the haves, or in the shanty-towns that surround their neighborhoods. Today a large part of the have-nots are in front of the houses of the haves, or in what remains of the public squares in the city and its outskirts."[56]

The marked difference in how the sisters interact with their brother becomes central to the plot, explaining their mismatched approaches to Fignolé's disappearance. Who is willing to act and who is not, as well as how they choose to do so further underscores the dissimilarities between Angélique and Joyeuse. As sisters, they are particularly well-suited to demonstrate that "women's subjectivity is contradictorily experienced."[57] Though these two women could not be more unalike in their approaches to life, each one has something to tell us about the way class and gender mark how Haitian women move through space.

Sisters in Suffering

Angélique and Joyeuse are held together by their common awareness of suffering; it operates as a constant point of reference for them. They suffer, they notice each other's suffering, and they notice the suffering of others. Evaluating her sister, for example, Joyeuse thinks, "I even suspect she uses her profession to distance herself from the sufferings of us mortals, and uses prayer to measure the extent to which she can resist earthly pleasures" (22). The sisters also notice how their mother perpetually suf-fers. Observing her mother after Fignolé's disappearance, Joyeuse notes: "Mother's suffering is obvious. She suffers in silence. Something has been torn from her. She submits totally to this void, this great empty space, sub-merged in suffering and the waiting for Fignolé, but she won't talk about it. Mother must have faltered by her son's bed and invoked her *loas* as if grasping a pair of crutches. Mother falters but never falls. While Mother lives, the end of the world will never arrive" (24). The chronic suffering is another by-product of disparities in socioeconomic class that invades both material and psychological spaces, and it is always there, even when it is not directly acknowledged. While the suffering she notices is first and foremost of a personal nature, she identifies it as a quotidian part of life for many in the city, and, from her perspective, the island at large. We can thus easily situate the sisters' suffering because of Fignolé's disappearance in a much larger context. At the same time, the breakdown that it leads to in the relationships among the women confirms how this moment of political crisis is deeply personal and unfolds within the confines of their home: "We yell all the same. We yell because we cannot talk of the only thing that would relieve us, the only thing that would ever restore our humanity. Our sufferings began a long time ago and those we would wish them on are too far away . . . We are cruel by default. Wicked by obligation" (24).

Suffering is more than material, physical, or psychological, it can produce an ethic that causes relationships, familial and social, to disintegrate and devolve. Here again I see Lahens explicitly in relation to Marie Chauvet's *Love, Anger, Madness,* in which the protagonist of *Love* laments how communal suffering results in a breakdown of social bonds. Chauvet also writes, "we have been practicing at cutting each other's throats since independence," a move that Edwidge Danticat explains as her suggestion that Haiti "has continued to fail to reach its full potential, in part because of foreign interference, but also because of internal strife and cruelty."[58]

Suffering also functions as a leitmotif for injustice in the eyes and experiences of both Joyeuse and Angélique. When Joyeuse sees Angélique punish her son Gabriel and the family's *restavek* Ti Louze, it leads to a long reflection on the nature of their suffering: "Ti Louze and Gabriel must think that the world is an unfair place, and they're not wrong. Gabriel will get used to it, sooner than he may think. For Ti Louze the game has already been played out, in full. Ti Louze whose braids are no longer than finger-bones; a true African's head with no future on this island—Ti Louze, so Black she is invisible" (25). Joyeuse's interpretation of Ti Louze is raced, classed, and gendered. The underlying implication is that suffering is Ti Louze's only lot in life.

As we saw with Évelyne Trouillot, Lahens carefully distinguishes the conditions of suffering from the circumstances that create them, highlighting structural inequalities and its ingrained effects. Joyeuse muses, "I understood in that day that there is no wrong in turning malicious when you are enslaved. When there is no point to your life, not to the lives of all those like you since the beginning of the world, and one day a moment will come when a man will show you the way out" (38). For all the characters in the novel, suffering is unremitting even in the face of joy and laughter: "It is hard to hear these voices and this laughter without thinking of the pain which hides behind the eyes, beneath the chest, in the small of the back and along calves weary from running towards nothing. These voices and this laughter also explain why misfortune always finds as much space as it needs on this island to spread its wings slowly, but not enough space to be alone" (42). A wave of despair emanates from Joy-euse's thoughts about her community, her city, and her country. Despite her name and the *joie de vivre* that characterizes her nature, she cannot process joy without also accounting for pain.

Black Feminist Watchfulness

As we saw in *Le Rond-point,* the protagonists' acute awareness of class dynamics regularly interrupts their reveries, pulling them back into their lived experience in the present. Both Joyeuse and Angélique reflect on their status and relative lack of privilege in relation to others. From a young age, they are attentive to how class operates as a formative part of who they are and how they think. Describing herself as a child, Joyeuse notes, "I also experienced the discomfort, the unease of having a place in that school among girls who were strangers to me. Mother was jubilant at the idea of her daughter's unexpected advance towards that world of stucco, lace and frills, but never imagined the violence it would imply for her, never" (31). Joyeuse is sharply aware of her positionality, of how she is seen by people from the upper classes. Like Titi and Sorel, she demonstrates an awareness about her position vis à vis Port-au-Prince's privileged elite. In a passage describing her interactions with her wealthy employer, Madame Herbruch, she discloses how she is rendered invisible:

> I will never forget the day when Madame Herbruch asked me to help her with a large banquet she was preparing in her luxurious residence. When I crossed the living room to the beautiful toilet with its blue ceramics beneath the stairs, I felt the eyes of prestigious guests burn into me, reducing me to the mere idea of a being. To these bourgeois mulattoes with their fair skin I was not a bud-ding young woman but merely a Black female of a breed with simple, distinc-tive equipment: two breasts and a vagina. A breed doomed to the shanties, to domestic service, or to breed. (84)

That Joyeuse "feels the eyes of prestigious guests" burning into her addresses the power of a look. Again, looking relationships are exacer-bated when people look (but refuse to see) across class locations. Noticing that these men want only to "reduce" her "to the mere idea of a being," Joyeuse demonstrates her awareness of how looking is sexualized, classed, gendered, and raced. Of equal importance is her ability to name the harm in these unequal looking relations, her ability to conceptually challenge what bell hooks calls "a way of looking and seeing the world that negates her value."[59] This experience marks Joyeuse for life, becoming one of the definitive points of her class education: "It is events like this that penetrate a life like a violent torrent that slashes through dry, hard earth" (84). By referring to negatively charged class encounters as a form of violence, Joyeuse identifies the oppressive force of social inequality.

Describing the difference between her character and that of her mother and sister, Joyeuse understands their lot through an intersectional lens: "Like many women, Angélique hoped for everything and, when it never came, lost it at a single stroke. Waiting for what you cannot have and realizing too late that you will never have it makes for a life led in a narrow grind of sadness, the life of the defeated. Mother is exhausted but not defeated: 'Exhaustion bends your spine but defeat is ugly.' From the day when I first understood that something made the world turn against me and all those like me, I chose to become precisely the opposite of defeated, the opposite of exhausted" (101–2). Joyeuse's determination to interact with others beyond the choking limits of her class location is expressed in geographic terms. By willing herself to never become a *vaincue* (defeated woman), Joyeuse creates a space and a place for herself where society tells her there is none. As McKittrick reminds us, "acts of expressing and saying place are central to understanding what kinds of geographies are available to Black women. Because Black women's geographies are bound up with practices of spatial domination, saying space and place is understood as one of the more crucial ways geography can work for Black women."[60] Naming her place in the society, Joyeuse becomes an example of McKittrick's geographic mapping and refusing to be relegated to the spaces that her socioeconomic class prescribes.

In the passage below, Joyeuse describes her experience at school, articulating again for the reader her understanding of how class operates as well as how she fits into it: "I was not afraid when I arrived at the Sisters' up town. They would not admit to their school a little girl born out of wedlock, those whose intake was limited to the daughters of the middle classes, those from the middle classes, those from the good districts. A little bastard who had usurped the name of my Uncle Antoine, I broke my way into this world that was not mine" (102). By "breaking her way into a world" that is not hers, Joyeuse defies the codes dictated to her and circumvents her geographic placement. She shows what it looks like to refuse the confines of class as a fixed location. Lahens thus picks up where Trouillot leaves off with *Le Rond-point* and extends what she began to pursue in *Dans la maison du père*. An understanding of class as geography rather than architecture offers a more expansive point of entry that defies the strictures of class stratification. This practice brings into greater relief that even if, as McKittrick puts it, "more humanly workable geographies are not always readily available," Black feminist authors deploy fiction to imagine them.[61]

Comparing *The Colour of Dawn* to novels written under the first US occupation of 1915, Marie-José Nzengou-Tayo comments on Joyeuse's refusal to submit to the *vaincue* label. As Nzengou-Tayo sees it, the subjectivity of "des jeunes femmes qui divisent le monde entre vainqueurs et vaincues" (young girls who divide the world into conquerors and conquered) is about calculation and survival: "Lahens tout comme d'autres auteur-e-s proposent une nouvelle image de la femme haïtienne: quelquefois romantique certes, mais lucide, voire cynique" (Like other authors Lahens proposes a new image of the Haitian woman, at times romantic, but lucid and even cynical).[62] Refusing to be a *vaincue,* Joyeuse offers another version of what Glover terms "an ethic of self-regard" because she refuses to allow others to define and contain her.

A reflection on how space functions in the novel reveals the extent to which *The Colour of Dawn* is about Port-au-Prince under Aristide in the early twenty-first century. An urban landscape impregnated with fear owing to government unrest is palpable throughout the novel. Lahens renders the sociopolitical context through a charged lens, describing Haiti as an island under duress and rife with trouble: "this island where the Devil has such a hold and must be rubbing his hands in glee" (11). That view, one so often peddled in the popular media outside of Haiti, smacks of the external gaze that refuses to see Haiti in its complexity and nuance. Another signal of the fraught time that the protagonists live in is how Lahens refers to the Haitian government of the early 2000s. When Aristide is referred to in the novel, it is as "the Prophet-President, the head of the Démunis" (27). The word démunis translates into "deprived" again emphasizing lack.

This historical moment in which the novel is set is also characterized by a breakdown in how people relate to one another. In the following passage Joyeuse thinks through her brother's lack of trust when responding to her questions and reframes his behavior in relation to the political and historic realities: "He replied to my questions without apparent distrust, but I knew that, deep inside, he was distrustful. As we all are. On this island, we are made that way. It is a game to which we devote the brightest of our days, a result of living within reach of those whom we have good reason to distrust" (68–69).

Joyeuse's interior monologue is a conversation she has with herself in which she questions how social division structures society. She pays attention to the effects of socioeconomic inequality and notices how it impacts daily life. Her questioning from below cues the reader to notice the ethical complexity of the current moment. The dialogic nature of her interior narrative recalls Mae Gwendolyn Henderson's point that "what is at once characteristic and suggestive about Black women's writing is its interlocutory, or dialogic, character, reflecting not only a relationship with the 'other(s),' but an internal dialogue with the plural aspects of self that constitute the matrix of Black female subjectivity."[63] Joyeuse's interior is a landscape of astute commentaries and observations about class politics in which she constantly articulates the plural aspects of herself. In addition to "constituting the matrix of Black female subjectivity," her interior dialogue advances a Black feminist ethic of encounter, relation, and questioning from below that reveals profound self-knowledge.

One of the many merits of Lahens's novel is that it allows us to appreciate how much the fraught context of the 2000s under Aristide requires feminist analysis. In her study of political organizing in Haiti during this period, Myriam Merlet writes, "Poverty, inequality, the permanence of antidemocratic structures, totalitarian temptations, and state violence are among the many motifs that push feminist thought to question the exercise of citizenship in this country, which, for the moment, receives a great deal of media coverage but remains nevertheless poorly understood."[64] I see Lahens's novel as a literary example of how feminist thought brings to light this period of Haitian history through a different lens. The degraded and desolate environment that the Méracin family lives in cannot be separated from the political situation. Describing the troubles that plague the novel's characters, literary scholar Marie-Agnès Sourieau characterizes their suffering as endemic and unspoken.

> Les personnages principaux du roman sont confrontés à une telle abjection que la plupart du temps ils ne peuvent l'évoquer à travers un discours cohérent; leurs souffrances résistent à la parole. Ils se servent alors des succédanées, tels que plaintes, gestes, regards, silences, voix étouffées, cris. Plongés dans le gouffre collectif nauséabond de la jungle port-au-princienne, nombre d'entre eux se déshumanisent, se transformant en bêtes sauvages, devenant même invisibles quand l'excès du dire des 'autorités' prend la relève pour anéantir leur volonté de lutte.[65]

> (The main characters of the novel are confronted with such abjection that most of the time they cannot express it through coherent speech; their sufferings resist the word. They then use substitutes, such as complaints, gestures, looks, silences, muffled voices, and shouts. Immersed in the foul-smelling collective

abyss of the Port-au-Princienne jungle, many of them dehumanize themselves, turning into wild beasts, even becoming invisible when the excess of talking by the authorities takes over to destroy their will to fight.)

According to Sourieau, this atmosphere of degradation and decay that surrounds the characters plays out in their personalities and their inability to interact with one another in functional ways. Dispossession and struggle become the identifying markers of daily life. Drawing from McKittrick's conceptualization of how geography functions for Black women in relation to space, I want to suggest that Lahens's descriptions be read not as symbols of the degraded environment in which the women live but rather as a recognition that they can nonetheless live otherwise. When we read their active interiority as examples of questioning from below, we notice how Joyeuse and Angélique look for different ways to live their lives. These descriptions reflect their interiority and show how paying attention is essential to their subjectivity. As McKittrick explains, examining the "spatial practices that Black women employ across and beyond domination" brings into relief how spaces that might be read as sites of captivity can be transformed into locations of possibility.[66] The Méracin sisters' spatial practice displays how geographies throughout the city are classed. It also demonstrates how these women choose to operate within and beyond those parameters. They are not only confined to the spaces in which the live and work, they also move about and throughout the city. These movements through space coupled with Joyeuse and Angélique's awareness as they engage the world, evince a Black feminist ethic linking experience and ideas. Furthermore, that Joyeuse and Angélique—like all of the characters I explore in this study—live in Haiti and never express a desire to live elsewhere is an important iteration of Alessandra Benedicty-Kokken's point that "choosing to live somewhere that others perceive . . . as hopelessly dispossessed is to repossess that place, to make it one's own."[67] This repossession associates the sisters with a stubborn volition to inhabit; they claim space.

Throughout the novel, references to marginalized neighborhoods anchor the reader in a geographic space and place, highlighting society's physical demarcations. There are distinctions to be made between, for example, where the Méracin family lives and where they visit Tante Sylvanie: "Aunt Sylvanie's neighborhood is on the edge of an even poorer area—*on this island, poverty has no limits*. The deeper you dig, the more you will find poverty even greater than your own. And so, between Sylvanie and that which doesn't yet have a name there is merely a small area of trapped water, full of silt and mud, enough to turn your stomach" (44). In the original French, the repeated use of definite articles further underscores the present moment and inscribes the novel into its historic context of the Aristide government. There is the neighborhood in which the family lives described as a place where girls and women must "fight with your claws out to stay alive" (40). There is the city of Port-au-Prince, "this voracious city" (41), and its surrounding neighborhoods populated by marginalized people. The politically motivated targeting of people from those marginalized and peripheral neighborhoods empha-sizes the injustice of social inequality, and frames suffering in relation to a larger system of power.

The phrase *cette île* recurs throughout the course of the novel; track-ing its iterations reveals that it addresses a wide range of subjects, each time returning to the geographic space of Haiti. For example, describing relationships between men and women: "in any case, all the men on this island are just passing through. Those who stay longer are just a little more permanent, that's all. On this island there are only mothers and sons" (43). Or, with regards to the necessity of being hard and tough of character in order to survive: "On this island, in this city, you have to be a stone. I am a stone" (56). At one point Angelique even refers to Haiti as "cette terre reculée" (a backwards land) (212). Lahens is careful to associate this depiction of Haiti with the political context and the reign of Aristide that in the early 2000s plummeted from an atmosphere of hope to one of despair. Overall, the multiple references to cette île reinforce a feeling of insularity that is suspended from reality, unmooring Haiti as a specific place and presenting the universal. Here Haiti becomes a place that is not named but that is repeatedly described in relation to dispos-session. In a similar way, descriptions of Port-au-Prince regularly invoke struggle and challenge: "The city, pregnant with a hideous beast, fought an insidious war" (45).

Again, space as I analyze it here includes overlapping spheres that are geographic, psychological, and material. Each time, for every use of space, we notice how it is impacted by class division and influenced by encounter. The material physicality of the Méracin sisters' ordinary and everyday lives locate them in spaces and places that they occupy and negotiate dif-ferently. In a long reflection about her childhood, Joyeuse describes the house they grew up in and the conditions under which they lived: "Aunt Sylvanie helped us to move into a single room, damp and dark, at the end of the passage. We three children slept on a mattress on the floor behind a curtain cut from a coarse cloth. It may have been only a room, but Mother wanted wherever she lived to be her own; she would not be accountable to anyone" (93). This clear-eyed description of the meager surroundings accentuates the Méracin family's challenging material reality. The materiality of the space is underscored by the mother's desire to make it her own, a need to claim a personal space that we eventually come to understand not only as repossession, but also as a way to survive.

Later on, as an adult, when Joyeuse enlists the help of her wealthy uncle to assist in the search for her brother, she notices that the space in which he receives her is determined by her class:

> Black-skinned and from a poor background, Uncle Antoine used this despised colour and low origins as an incontestable argument for robbing the State and committing one wrong deed after another . . . I'm always nervous . . . talking to this uncle who would receive us, the poor, between the backyard and the kitchen. The wealth of Antoine Neriscat was always a source of wonder for those of us whom poverty sought to entrap. Antoine Nériscat thought deep down that all those who were poor were only like that because they were unable to manage the range of tricks and schemes that were actually within reach. Or because they had got bogged down in those useless, endless considerations, justice and injustice, the master and the slave, as if they imagined that these things could have any weight in the reality of the world. (128)

Antoine's caustic and condescending treatment of the poor does not spare his own relatives. Even among relatives, the reception of guests in a family home links domestic space to socioeconomic status. It does not matter that Joyeuse is his niece, the differential in their class power deems her unworthy to be received within the home. The passage thus suggests that class divisions can exist within a single family and create distances that are spatially marked. Ultimately, even familial ties are not as significant as the ties that yoke a person to her respective class.

The Tap Tap: A Mobile Space of Class Division

Another sign of geographic and material space marking class division is public transportation. The tap tap that Joyeuse uses daily operates as an enclosed space where people of the same class status interact; in fact, their presence on it is enough to announce which class they belong to. These colorful vans represent how the majority of the population navigates the city. As a communal space, the tap tap offers a source of fleeting joy: "packed into the tap-tap, véritable disco on wheels, we finally make our way, half deaf, to the city centre" (65).

For Joyeuse the material space of the tap tap, a place that links under-privileged people in their common existence, is also a signifier of life's daily indignities. Examining the tap tap as its own distinct space, small and mundane yet conspicuously reflecting social realities, helps to demonstrate how Lahens's attention to geographic space takes many shapes in the novel. There are, among others, the "quartier," the family's neighborhood, their places of employment (the store for Joyeuse and the hospital for Angélique), and the clubs and bars, like Groove Night Club where Joyeuse spends time with her friends. As the characters navigate these locations, they observe what is around them, often questioning from below how and why these spaces exist in the way they do. As Angélique looks "from the other side," her class awareness is marked by material space: "From the other side of the bank I often look across at this world like someone who, in the midst of battle, just escaped by means of a well-sharpened machete blade or a hail of bullets from a submachine gun, and is now unable to believe their luck. Anyone who once sets foot in that district will from that moment know why the streets sometimes spread their legs for the highest bidder or shed blood with the calendars. It's impossible not to know, impossible!" (45). In this passage Angélique's quiet awareness of how the city operates unfolds in class terms.[68] Cognizant of how Port-au-Prince is divided into different spaces, she and Joyeuse characterize their geographic locations with socioeconomic indicators referring to different "parts." Noting her presence in "that part of the city where thousands of bodies mill about in a mix of bustle and lethargy between the pavements and the road," Angélique indicates that she sees how space is classed based on how many bodies are present; her geographic view of the city tellingly associates more bodies with poverty, underscoring the idea of the body and multiple bodies as indicators of socioeconomic disparities (46).

On her rides in the tap tap, Joyeuse is often accompanied by her best friend, Lolo, described by Joyeuse as "sister," "accomplice," and "vixen" (40). This young woman offers a compelling point of analysis as an example of someone for whom the desire to move beyond her own class position is pronounced. For Lolo, the possibility of accessing money and financial status is available only through the men she dates. Her appetite for nice things is nourished by her relationships with older men. References to material objects that are also markers of socioeconomic status highlight that Lolo gains access through her sexual relationships, reinforcing the machinations of class and sex. When she tells Joyeuse that they must make their way out of their own class status using whatever tools are available to them, she shows that she is what Carolle Charles calls machann ak machandiz, a woman aware of her positionality as someone who is simultaneously a seller and someone to be sold: "You know full well that misery and I just don't get on. I'm not like all those people we're surrounded by who wait for God, Notre-Dame du Perpétue Secours, Sainte Thérèse, Agoué, their boss, the government or the revolution to come to their aid. No-one's going to come and save us Joyeuse, no-one," Lolo tells Joyeuse (57). Here her critique of religious affiliation—whether for Catholics, Protestants, or Vodouizan—stems from a belief that only her sexuality can change the material conditions of her life. Lolo's aware-ness of how class limits her, coupled with her refusal to remain poor, underscores how greatly social class is sexed and gendered.

Lolo's explanation of her actions does not condemn her but rather casts her as an enterprising young woman determined to move beyond the place that society has set for her. Charles's concept of a machann ak machandiz is fitting because it is rooted in a contradiction and "reflects a paradox, which . . . in many ways characterizes gender relations in Haitian so-ciety."[69] As Charles sees it, "Haitian women have been in a subordinate position in all fields of gendered, racialized, and classist relations of power within Haitian society, yet at the same time they have been able to act as agents defining and negotiating these same relations of power."[70]

Beyond the material spaces of their environments, the psychological space of the mind is presented through the sisters' interior monologues. Their interiority, a space in which Joyeuse and Angélique refer to the effects that their emotions have on them, dominates the flow of the novel. For example, filled with anxious thoughts about her brother, Joyeuse is exhausted by worry: "The anxiety gives me an empty feeling and I no longer know what to think or who to think about" (52). By naming the ability of anxiety to empty her, she calls attention to a bereft psychological and emotional space. Shortly after this observation she looks up at the sky, becoming more aware of her natural surroundings:

> It's been so long since I looked up at the sky. Since I took notice of days drenched with light, flowing towards a languid twilight of mauve and orange. Since I gave myself up to this obstinate, avid city, because of its overflowing energy, because of its strength that can eat me, swallow me whole. Because of the uniformed school children who set it ablaze at mid-day. Because of its excesses of flesh and images. Because of the mountains which seem to come forward to engulf it. Because there is always too much. Because of the way it has of taking me and not letting go. Because of its incendiary men and women. Because . . . because . . . (53)

In this mediation ending with a repetitive chorus, Joyeuse reflects on her disconnection from the land, yet ends up reinforcing that very connection. Contemplating her mental space leads her to think about the geographic and specifically the environmental space that she occupies. Up until this moment, for her the island is always about what Haiti has come to represent sociopolitically under Aristide rather than what the ecology of the island itself suggests. As the move from the mind to the landscape connects her to the land, Joyeuse becomes firmly planted in the environmental space. Then another moment takes over, pulling her back into the realities of class division: "When an old woman with rough skin, bent back and vacant gums raises her face to mine as she stands by my side, to tell me in a conspirational whisper: 'Mademoiselle, these are difficult times. You know in my day . . .' I remain unmoved. Because that face and that voice could trap me. Compassion is a luxury I can't afford. And so, I consciously raise a wall between the old woman and myself, topped with barbed wire, broken glass, and a 'Beware of dog sign in large red letters" (54). Joyeuse's determination to erect a wall between herself and the woman who is more disadvantaged than she reveals that her true self is one that would have compassion on this woman. The wall between them is not physical but psychological. Joyeuse sees it as necessary in order to protect her own mental space. Although she recognizes the woman's humanity, in order to survive, she must refuse to see the other woman and disregard her humanity, recognizing this psychological wall as necessary in order to protect her own mental space. For Joyeuse, negotiating the space that she inhabits requires emotional labor that constrains her. She concludes her reflection with an explanation of what it feels like to always be guarded: "This city has taught me a lesson, only one: to never give up on yourself. Never let a single sentiment soften your spirit. In place of my heart a lump of hard, crude matter has settled inside of my chest, right between my breasts. I recognize my little grey stone. And I breathe heavily as I know with certainty that it will remain firmly fixed in place. On this island, in this city, you have to be a stone. I am a stone" (56). Joyeuse's lingering thoughts about her interaction with the woman provide insight into how she has learned to negotiate the space she occupies in order to move beyond place. Aware of her own positionality and the space she is supposed to occupy (or the space she is supposed not to take up), her interior life divulges how she equips herself to inhabit the world she lives in.

Overall, the Méracin sisters are examples of how the cruelties of class intersect with race and gender for Black women in Port-au-Prince. The novel enacts Myriam Merlet's feminist maxim about looking "through the eyes of Haitian women . . . conscious of the roles, limitations, and stereotypes imposed on us."[71] But while the sisters' lives illuminate these problems, they also suggest a way forward, and although the class and gender hierarchies that regulate their lives relegate them to the margins, Lahens places their voices at the center. This gesture is significant especially in the context of and potential reasons for their brother's absence, which puts him, although missing from the narrative, in a prominent (but empty) space in the plot.

Challenging the Single Story of Poverty

One final and stirring example of how *The Colour of Dawn* confronts social inequalities from a perspective that is both local and global and raises questions about space and belonging comes through the character of John, who enters the plot after befriending Fignolé: "John, [is] a young American journalist, [who] had followed Fignolé over all the blazing barricades he had raised in order to shout out his hatred of the men in uniform and demand the return of the leader of the Démunis whom they had driven from power" (49). While the first sentences introducing John are innocuous, the subsequent descriptions of him devolve into a caricature of a guileless symbol of baser white US attitudes toward Haiti. John's portrayal is at once an amusing, ironic, and a cringeworthy example that conveys a pointed critique of the problematic neoimperial relationship between the United States and Haiti. As a character whose interactions with the Haitians in the novel raise ethical questions, John is an example of how a Black feminist lens can trouble what some might see as the naive curiosity of a white journalist in Haiti.

Situating him in the context of the United States military's second occupation of Haiti, Lahens describes John as having "arrived ten years ago with a contingent of American soldiers during the second occupation of an island where there has since been no-one but subjects returning with tails between their legs or losers leaving on their knees" (60). Lahens's choice of journalism as John's profession is far from innocent because Haiti has long been a sensationalized hotspot for journalists whose reporting reveals "much about the messiness of race, class, and gender, and show[s] us yet again how much Haiti is popularly misperceived."[72] Alternately portrayed as eager, naive, and ignorant, John epitomizes the stereotype of an intrusive American looking to consume Haiti. To him, Haiti is an exotic and impoverished land in need of his love and attention.

John embraces, and even delights in, the "poverty trope" as a primary lens through which he can interact with Haitian people; Haiti is fixed in a singular narrative of poverty that he is deeply invested in: "John put his backpack down beside his chair and began by saying: 'I love this country, I love the poor.' He made his declaration in the way that others would say I'm a doctor, a plumber or a lawyer" (49–50). Angélique immediately sees through what John perceives as his noble position, judging his ignorance on her own terms. She thinks to herself, "'I'll talk to you about hunger one day, John, about the kind of deprivation that bends backs, that opens thighs, about the arrogance of conquerors and the humiliations of the defeated. I'll tell you what goes on inside the head, the stomach, and genitals of a woman who is hungry. Of a woman who has nothing to give her children'" (52).

Evaluating his crass assumptions about poverty, Angélique evaluates John from the perspective of a daughter and a mother who has experienced the suffering of hunger. As in *Le Rond-point*, we can understand this reference to hunger as metaphorical and literal. It is the hunger of the Méracin family as experienced by the children growing up poor. It is also John's metaphorical hunger evinced through his desire to consume Haiti and Haitian lives. Here the notion of consumption operates in reverse of that in *Je suis vivant* when Livia accuses Norah of wanting to consume the Bernier family's wealth. John's interest is in consuming the Haitian poverty trope, using it to nourish his own cannibalistic fantasies. Sensitive to his voyeuristic and othering gaze masquerading as humanitarian work, Angélique is uncomfortable with how John observes the family: "I didn't particularly like this constant attention to our slightest movement. I got the impression that we were like those urine or blood samples that specialists examine in hospital laboratories for microbes, to confirm or tackle infections" (63).

Angélique's analysis of John's interactions with the family openly names the troubling dynamic in which outsiders from the Global North (especially the United States and European countries) take advantage of Haiti and Haitians. In fact, her language and tone remind me of the words used by a group of thirty-six Haitian women journalists and researchers responding to US American reporter Mac McClelland's story in *Mother Jones* about an encounter with a Haitian woman who had been gang-raped. The group letter stated unequivocally that "the way [McClelland] uses Haiti as a backdrop for this narrative is sensationalist and irresponsible."[73] By interacting with the Méracin family as though they are native informants on subjects like poverty rather than as people with individuated selves, John emblematizes the disturbing dynamic sometimes found among white journalists and academics who work in Haiti. Angélique goes so far as to say that John even imagines them as more socioeconomically disadvantaged than they actually are in order to fuel his fantasy: "And to make himself love us even more, John imagined us even poorer than we were" (63). John's occupation as a journalist carries with it a stinging indictment of how the US-based media portrays the second independent republic in the Western hemisphere. In the passage below, Angélique perspicaciously summarizes how this narrative works for people like John:

> The dream has already died where he comes from, on the streets of Seattle and New York, on the receiving end of a baton and a few clouds of tear gas, so he wants to revive it here, whatever the cost. Even at the cost of renouncing himself, even at the cost of sacrificing our lives. He twists and retwists events to make his reports look good and to populate that sham paradise he has invented in his head. In any case, John is risking nothing here, John is losing nothing. He's not at home. (65)

John's relationship to Haiti troubles the reader; it can be seen as sensationalist and irresponsible as he searches for the comfort of poverty to shore up his own moral positioning. The "false paradise he has invented in his head" was selfishly created to serve his own ambition and ego.

Recalling my point that ethics depends on recognition and relation, John serves multiple purposes for those committed to viewing class through a Black feminist ethic. First, he embodies the white savior stereotype. John has fixed Haiti into a single story of poverty. He places himself at the center of an equation in which he must rescue Haitian people from their misery. His insertion into the novel mirrors contemporary neoimperial scripts about Haitian and US relations that were amplified in the aftermath of the 2010 earthquake, but that have always existed. Second, his presence underscores the global machinations at work under Aristide during a time that was referred to as the second occupation of Haiti. Lastly, he provides another way to think through the ideas of space, place, and belonging that we see at play throughout the novel. John is out of place in Haiti but does not see himself as such. Unlike the two Black women protagonists who regularly feel out of place, unstable in space, unable to claim their space, and even foreign in their own country, he circulates with the freedom and presumptuousness of someone who has never been refused entry into any place. He feels ownership over Haiti and Haitians to the extent that he attempts to define Haiti for the Haitians he encounters. This practice is one that the novel is deeply critical of, as we see clearly when Fignolé ends their friendship: "Fignolé did not hesitate to shout his anger at John, to tell him what he thought of him, an aristocrat from the well-to-do neighborhoods of Philadelphia come to warm up his soul in the tropics. Come to dispel his rich kid's boredom by sowing chaos among the poor whom he admired like exotic animals walking around on their hind legs" (73).

By ending the relationship between John and the Méracin family on this sour note, Lahens issues a sharp critique of tourist ideologies that regulate how foreigners interact with Haiti and Haitians. Fignolé's deduction that John is nothing more than a bored "rich kid," reminds the reader that class difference and division reverberates in ways that have local, transnational, and global consequences. The relationship ends on the Méracins' terms rather than John's. Together, and without John in their lives, they reclaim their place and inhabit the space that belongs to them. Following Benedicty-Kokken's penetrating arguments about possession, I read Angélique's critique of John as a way to reclaim her space. As Benedicty-Kokken argues, "material dispossession's counterpart— becomes a means of reclaiming one's space. Possession is ultimately a path to *self-possession,* to relocate and reassert one's home, one's sense of home, one's body, and more generally, one's sense of being in a world."[74] Or, in the language that I have been using throughout this study, it is to look for a world beyond the one that is in front of you, to look for another world.

At the same time, the ethical problems that arise from the confluence of race, class, and gender are about more than interactions between different races and nationalities highlighted by the example of John. From Angélique's point of view, one of the pernicious outcomes of class division is a society in which people turn on each other and are charged with negative emotions such as rage, wariness of their fellow human beings, and a general indifference toward others. When Angélique expresses this connection between the emotional and material worlds, she ponders the affective responses to class division: "The present-day mistrust creeps through their veins like a seeping liquid, thicker than that of the mistrust there has always been—the mistrust that older people always obliged us to maintain towards those who resemble us like peas in a pod. Together with misfortune, mistrust is the only inheritance to which we, the defeated, are truly entitled" (33). Angélique's observation mourns the breakdown of human relations brought about by class division and the tensions that make the novel's protagonists unrecognizable to themselves. *The Colour of Dawn* offers a thought-provoking perspective on class division, representing a breakdown in society that is deeply human.

Beyond Class Division and toward the Human

To understand the implications of reading a novel that draws painstaking lines around class division and goes so far as to replicate those categories through formal choices is to question why these divisions exist. Effectively planted in disparate geographies, *Le Rond-point, Dans la maison du père, Je suis vivant,* and *The Colour of Dawn* are novels that work through the complex dynamics of class division using narrative techniques that inspire such ethical questions. Most especially, both Trouillot and Lahens foreground the jarring ways that class division, though omnipresent and experienced by all, is rarely spoken about publicly. Formal devices such as the use of the narrative voice, a focus on interiority, and the separation of chapters make the depth of these cleavages visible and legible.

There is a striking search for social equity implicit in each of these novels. For Trouillot, this manifests itself in giving equal narrative space, weight, and autonomy to the characters of different social classes. For Lahens in *Dans la maison du père,* it is through the use of embodied movement to signify and transgress class divides and realize a childhood dream. In *The Colour of Dawn,* it is through the use of space and how two economically disadvantaged Black women protagonists negotiate the multiple geographies they inhabit. And by choosing multiple narrators from different classes, each of whom reflects on the effects of socioeconomic inequalities, *Le Rond-point* and *Je suis vivant* offer a rendering of class that refuses to be reduced to simplicities. In taking on the problem of class division in Haiti, these authors perform a sign of address that calls attention to inequality in a way that implicates the reader and poses pressing questions to a contemporary audience, people who must be reminded that the plight of the poor and working poor is not only a political and social question but also an ethical problem.

Lamenting the deep cleavages of class in Haiti, the author Lyonel Trouillot observes that we should reframe the problem in terms of humanity and of citizenship. He writes, "En Haïti, quelque chose de caché et de pas si caché que ça, des préjugés et des structures toujours au travail, refuse le principe de la citoyenneté à l'ensemble, et le droit de la citoyenneté à certains" (In Haiti, something hidden and not so hidden is that prejudices and structures are still at work, that refuse the principle of citizenship to the whole, and the right of citizenship to some).[75] As the gap between the rich and the poor widens all over the world, class polarization is increasingly a hidden and not so hidden problem. This reality unsettles Lyonel

Trouillot because it means that "les gens ne sont jamais des individus ou des individualités, mais les représentants de catégories fixés une fois pour toutes" (people are never individuals, but rather always representatives of categories that are forever fixed for all).[76]

Indeed, one of the greatest concerns about representations of class divides is that the characters ascribed to a particular socioeconomic status will be mere caricatures, denied of their fully fleshed-out humanity. *Je suis vivant, Le Rond-point, Dans la maison du père,* and *The Colour of Dawn* uncover and wrestle with this aspect of class division in both form and in content. By delving into the interiority of characters from each of the "fixed categories," Mars, Lahens and Trouillot add depth, texture, and nuance that make it possible for us to look at the characters as more than representatives of their respective class locations.

These novels also remind us that examining class as a location of identity requires paying attention to its locally rooted meanings and contexts because "class has functioned as a critical category when it has a degree of cultural relevance or when overly rigid assumptions of class consciousness have left it open to deconstruction. The rejection of class essentialism has yielded a version of class not as a stable material fact, but as a polymorphous, constructed, and contradictory cultural arena."[77] This view recalls McKittrick's charge to *think geographically* because in doing so we redraw the maps that seek to contain and dispossess. Redrawing the cartographies of class with a Black feminist ethic in mind allows us to grapple with class division intersectionally in order to imagine a future that is more just. *Je suis vivant, Le Rond-point, Dans maison du père,* and *The Colour of Dawn* present class division as constructed and imagined as much as it is lived and experienced. By attending to space as constructed and by using narrative techniques that interrogate their construction, Mars, Trouillot, and Lahens advance a Black feminist ethic of encounter, relation, and recognition that highlights and challenges how class functions in Haitian society.

5   An Environmental Ethic

Land and Sea

Je suis d'ici, mon sang coule dans chacun de ces arbres, ma chair est
pétrie de la boue de ces mornes. Je suis l'eau enfermée dans ces roches,
mes yeux sont bourgeons de soleil.

(I am from this place, my blood runs in each of these trees, my flesh is
kneaded from the dirt of these hills. I am the water enclosed in these
rocks, my eyes are buds of the sun.)

—Kettly Mars, *Kasalé*

IN A series of paintings titled *When the Island Keeps All the
Secrets*, Mafalda Mondestin's visual art represents the bond between humans and nature. Each painting features figures interacting with their
natural environment in varying degrees of intimacy. One image foregrounds the silhouette of a person, presumably a woman, who stands
in the middle of a field of tall, thick grass and leaves that rise well above
her shoulders (see fig. 5). The silhouette's Black body is entirely covered
with small, short brushstrokes of multicolored lines in orange, pink, and
red. Her hand is perched on her belly, and she wears a crown whose
bright yellow is muted in the middle of the shades of green on the field.
The color palette of deep reds and bright royal blues implicitly evoke the
Haitian flag. The sky is neither bright blue as in the daytime nor dark blue
black as at nighttime, marking the temporal frame with ambiguity. It is
as though she is suspended in time. The entirely white backdrop causes
the other parts of the scene—the bright green landscape in which the
woman stands, her dark body—to leap off the canvas. The grass in the
background is punctuated by the occasional black leaf, which stands in
stark contrast to the vibrant greens, blues, and reds.

With her hand on her belly, she projects the image of a woman who
may be newly pregnant but is not yet showing. Is she the one who gives
birth *in* the land or *to* the land? Is she Mother Nature taking a stroll
through her land and deciding what to birth next? Is she a queen of the
environment? Understanding how spirit and nature operate as one in

Figure 5. *When the Island Keeps All the Secrets, Part I*, Mafalda Mondestin. (© 2015; used by permission of the artist)

the Haitian cosmology of Vodou, she might even be Madan Ayizan, a spirit connected to the mysteries and medicine of the forest. Or perhaps, when we consider Maya Deren's point that Vodou is "a religion of creation and life. It is the worship of the sun, the water and other natural forces," the figure might be simply worshipping the elements around her.[1]

Another painting in the series draws the eyes upwards to eight pairs of dangling legs belonging to several more silhouettes set against a brilliant

Figure 6. *When the Island Keeps All the Secrets, Part II*, Mafalda Mondestin. (© 2015; used by permission of the artist)

fuchsia sky (see fig. 6). The legs hover above what resembles tall stalks of sugar cane. The hanging legs in the context of cane fields conjure histories of violence, from the eighteenth-century sugar plantations that led to France's financial dominance in the world to the twenty-first-century *bateyes* (sugar mill settlements) in the Dominican Republic where human rights abuses against migrant workers of Haitian descent tragically occur on a daily basis. After all, as Omi'seke Natasha Tinsley notes, the cane field is "a site of sexual violence and exploited labor, a Caribbean landscape that was never a natural topos but one constructed for colonial purposes."[2] The idea conveyed by the title of Mondestin's series, that the land holds secrets it does not disclose, is significant in that it positions the environment as an element that carries the weight of history. An environmental witness to history, the land holds secrets, trauma, violence, and so much more. Mondestin's work reminds us that the juxtaposition of land and people is fertile ground for staging examinations of history and investigating how nature and culture influence each other. The paintings in *When the Island Keeps All the Secrets* burst with meaning, inviting the viewer to consider various configurations of nonhuman and human interaction. They also stage intimate relationships between humans and nature and remind us of how Black geographies can be reclaimed and resignified, evoking M. Jacqui Alexander's discerning comment that "the land holds memory."[3]

As these images show us, the land figures prominently in twenty-first-century Haitian cultural production, as it has for centuries. The long-standing significance of the environment in Haitian history, literature, and popular culture goes as far back as the inception of the nation and is embodied in the name of the nation itself: "Haiti" is a Taino word meaning "mountainous land." This indigenous name, chosen after the French colonizers were vanquished in the Haitian Revolution, identifies the island with its ecology as well as with the native population. Nature and culture fuse together as one. The symbolism of the name reconnects the land to its past prior to slavery, to before the land was a place of suffering for Africans who were brought there to be enslaved.[4]

Haiti is a strikingly beautiful landscape of breathtaking mountains surrounded by sparkling oceans, a typical Caribbean topography. The preeminence of mountains on the Haitian landscape means that if we are to take seriously the words of Evelyne O'Callaghan that "Caribbean landscapes are texts in their own right, huge canvasses on which history has certainly painted very different pictures over time which can be read in different ways," these resplendent mountains have something to tell us about history, about culture, about Haiti.[5] Following the logic of the proverb "Deye mòn gen mòn" (behind mountains there are more mountains), and dislodging it from a meaning that points exclusively to suffering, means pondering the possibilities of interpretation offered by the mountains.[6] Mountains figure prominently in Caribbean writing, but they are far from alone in the robust metonymy they offer to Haitian authors. The thickness of the forest, the lushness of the mangroves, the lavish flora and fauna of tropical landscapes, the pungent odors of the soil, the flow of great rivers, the crashing waves of the Atlantic Ocean and the Caribbean Sea, and the broad expanse of the plateau—all make the natural world an exigent site of Caribbean cultural production overall, and more specifically, in Haitian fiction.

In the Haitian context, the concept of the land is inextricable from the spiritual realm. Religion scholar Leslie Desmangles explains that "If Catholicism is identified with heaven, Vodou is associated with the earth. And if Haitian writers say that the *lwas* 'have to do with the earth' hence cannot be uprooted from Haitian life, it is because Vodou fulfills important functions in Haitian society."[7] What I turn my attention to in this chapter is how Desmangles's point that "Vodou is associated with the earth" manifests in these novels, all of which are deeply embedded in their natural environments and reveal a Vodou ethic in which the physical and spiritual worlds are united. The connection between the land and the gods, or nature and the spirits, reminds us that Vodou—the national religion—is regulated by its own ethic. Following Kantara Souffrant's compelling argument that "if Vodou can be understood as a trope capable of shaping Haitian cultural, social, and philosophical thoughts and relations, then we must also consider Vodou as a hermeneutic," my reading of how the environment figures in these novels rests on the coupling of spirit and nature.[8]

I argue that the relationship between human activity and the natural environment communicates ethical concerns in the novels *Rosalie l'infâme* (*The Infamous Rosalie*) (2003), *Kasalé* (2007), and *Bain de Lune* (*Moonbath*) (2014), which highlight Black women's intimate relationships to nature according to a Vodou ethic. By focusing on these authors' inscription of a Black feminist ethic that has spiritual dimensions, I attend to the variety of contexts in which that ethic is articulated. How Black women interact with the land, how they pay careful attention to its needs (and secrets) when others are not willing to, displays parallels between gender and nature and underscores the role of spirituality in subject formation. I deem this approach to the environment consistent with a Black feminist ethic because it questions relationships "from below" and foregrounds the lived experience of Black women. My readings of how these characters relate to the land privileges both/and, sees the natural and supernatural worlds as fully integrated, locates individual selves in relation to community, links experience and ideas, and is built on an intersectional analysis of identity.

I am especially interested in how these authors reconfigure relationships between nature and humans to subvert a hierarchy in which humans are in control. They emphasize instead nature's importance to individual people, whether it is because of religion as in *Kasalé*, because of genealogy across generations as in *Moonbath*, or because of resistance to slavery as in *The Infamous Rosalie*. By highlighting these women's relationships to the land through embodied movement, spiritual connection, and familial bonds, these novels develop a distinct environmental ethic that is resolutely Black feminist and rooted in Haitian religion, history, and culture.

My investigation of the environmental ethic at work in these novels draws from theories of ecocriticism, ecofeminism, and Caribbean studies. Close-reading these novels from an ecofeminist perspective shows how Trouillot, Mars, and Lahens intertwine gender, spirit, and nature to observe and critique social hierarchies in ways suggested by feminist scholar Greta Gaard's insight that ecofeminism allows us to "challenge the culturally produced links among gender/race/sexuality/nation/nature."[9] By observing how Lisette, Antoinette, and Cétoute—the protagonists I examine here—relate to the environment, we can discern a difference that sets them apart from the other characters in their textual worlds. These female characters often have a relationship to nature that is specific to their own subjugated knowledge—Lisette, Antoinette, and Cétoute often associate themselves and their identities with nature as a point of comparison to highlight unique positionalities.

Intimate relationships to the environment register in my analyses in three ways: contradictory, caring, and contentious. Intimacy with the environment surfaces in myriad ways but in each configuration calls attention to ethical questions: How can we account for the magnificent beauty of nature alongside all the stories of suffering it holds? What responsibility do the elderly have to the land? How does one remain faithful to a land that refuses to produce generation after generation? Thus, the robust engagement with the environment in these novels affirms the landscape's function as much more than mere backdrop.[10] Overall, in each of the novels under consideration, the environment is rhetorically, symbolically, and materially represented in ways that point to an ethical framework of divine care and justice. Further, as examples of "how the biophysical environment is represented in relation to the human . . . [and] reconsiders what it means to be human," these novels attest to how a Black feminist ethic intersects with environmental visions.[11] As I have argued throughout this book, the ethic at work in these novels is a mode of encounter and relation that leads to questioning and reframing the world through a Black feminist lens.

The Infamous Rosalie, *Kasalé*, and *Moonbath* are stunning examples of how novels can simultaneously convey and even privilege two different kinds of landscapes, interior and exterior.[12] What interests me is a both/and approach that immediately acknowledges how *both* the exterior and the interior are present *together*, following the logic of Vodou guided by a Black feminist perspective. Furthermore, the Vodou cosmology that regulates encounters with the land is rooted in the union of the interior and exterior landscape, reflecting a dynamic that scholars of Vodou and the environment have insisted on: "in Vodou spiritual maturity rests on the understanding of the necessary balance between cosmic forces and the natural world."[13] As described by Claudine Michel, it is the nonhierarchical nature of Vodou that is especially striking for the scholar of Black feminism: "Le Vodou n'est pas un système imposé d'en haut; c'est une religion essentiellement démocratique et fonctionnelle, inscrite dans les vicissitudes de l'existence quotidienne de ses fidèles et dans leur lutte pour faire de leur vie une entité bien balancé" (Vodou is not a system imposed from above; it is an essentially democratic and functional religion, inscribed in the vicissitudes of the daily existence of its faithful and in their struggle to make their lives well-balanced).[14] In fact, as Michel further outlines, a Vodou ethic hinges on the unity of the exterior and the interior: "la vie religieuse de ceux qui servent les esprits tournent autour d'une forme d'auto-conscience où l'être intérieur et le monde extérieur convergent pour former une orientation éthique" (the religious life of those who serve the spirits revolves around a form of self-conscience in which the interior selves and the exterior world converge to form an ethical orientation).[15]

Again, it is important to note that while the use of ecocriticism as a lens for analyzing Haitian literature is somewhat recent, the centrality of the environment within Haitian texts is far from new, and, of course, the unique relationship between Vodou and nature has always been essential.[16] From the nineteenth century onwards, Haitian literature has insisted on foregrounding the presence of the natural environment. In Haiti as well as in the Caribbean in general, the significance of the environment takes into account the legacies and influences of slavery, colonial (and imperial) invasions, and tourist fetishization.[17] Emphasizing this, Chris Campbell and Michael Niblett in *The Caribbean: Aesthetics, World-Ecology, Politics* propose that "a concern for the environment and an emphasis on colonial-capitalist exploitation of labour and the domination and degradation of the landscapes has long been a preoccupation of Caribbean writers and artists."[18]

For Caribbean writers, environmental aesthetics extend far beyond depictions of gorgeous tropical landscapes. Much of the history that has unfolded on Caribbean islands has had direct effects on the land, and, because Caribbean landscapes are texts in their own right, thoughtful explorations of how nature is represented take into account the ground—literal and figurative—upon which representations of the landscape occur.[19] For example, the first US occupation of Haiti from 1915 to 1934 was the beginning of massive deforestation that has resulted in aggravating the effects of every flood on the island. Indeed, and as Elizabeth DeLoughrey rightly observes, "there is probably no other region in the world that has been more radically altered in terms of human and botanic migration, transplantation, and settlement than the Caribbean."[20]

Numerous scholars have noted that when Caribbean landscapes occupy space in literature it is often to evoke an ongoing conflicted relationship. For example, when thinkers such as Edouard Glissant acknowledge the union of history and land in the context of the Caribbean, it is also to recognize how the creation of the plantation economy irrevocably altered the landscape and had environmentally devastating consequences. According to this history, "the Caribbean sugar plantation grew at the expense of the dense and moist tropical forests that needed to be cleared to make way for the new profitable crop. This rapid deforestation led to forest depletion, landslides, erosion, and climatic changes."[21] Elucidating the relationship between ecocriticism and Caribbean studies, Elaine Savory offers: "Ecocriticism reads texts through a politically engaged lens for their representation of ecology, past, present, and looking forward to the future," whereas scholars focused on the Caribbean note "the long historical entanglement between landscape production highlighting the mutually constitutive relationship between nature and violence."[22]

Going beyond the significant contributions of environmentalist thought in the Caribbean context, my Black feminist intervention pairs ecofeminism and Caribbean ecocriticism in the Haitian context. My analysis also relies on an understanding that Vodou, the national religion, depends on appreciation of and a relationship to nature, and I lean on the extensive work of scholars such as Claudine Michel, Colin Dayan, and Alessandra Benedicty-Kokken, whose work on Vodou has been particularly sensitive to gender and nature.

From a feminist perspective, it is necessary to problematize how the use of nature in Haitian literature occurs in gendered terms, as does Dayan, for example, when she argues that everything depends on a triad relationship: "Land, women, and gods.[23] The creation of a national identity in Haiti has depended on the working ensemble of this metaphoric accretion."[24] Her insights in *Haiti, History, and the Gods* emerge in the context of her commitment to thinking through how Haitian religion and history demand gendered analysis. Following Dayan, in her essay, "'All Misfortune Comes from the Cut Trees': Marie Chauvet's Environmental Imagination," ecocritic Lizabeth Paravisini-Gebert calls attention to environmental crisis as a trope of Haitian literature that emphasizes nature and human interaction: "Understanding full well the import of Haiti's environmental situations, both as a historical reality and as a metaphor for addressing this history in literature, Haitian writers have made it a cornerstone of the development of the national novel and drama."[25] By acknowledging a "decades-long tradition of Haitian environmental writing," Paravisini-Gebert lays the groundwork for analyzing how nature figures in Haitian literary works.[26] In canonical novels like Roumain's *Masters of the Dew,* Alexis's *General Sun, My Brother,* and Chauvet's *Fonds-des-nègres,* the land is present through personification, operates as central to the plot, and indicates supernatural forces at work. But again, what I am more interested in here is how attention to the environmental dimensions of Haitian literature intersect with Black feminist concerns about the environment—in particular, how is a Black feminist ethic invested in care, environmental justice, and reflecting spiritual truths conveyed in these novels?

What sets these novels apart is that they also offer suggestions for how people *should* interact with the land, based on the experience of several Black women characters in communion with nature. Furthermore, these novels show that figurations of the environment and inclusion of environmental themes create space to explore ethical questions about how humans, spirits, and nature interact. Throughout this chapter I pay close attention to how the natural and spiritual worlds (land and gods, to use Dayan's lexicon) coalesce to demand a more ethical relationship to the environment. In my view, a Black feminist ethical relationship to nature demands intimacy between humans and nature in ways that refuse preconceived hierarchies and binaries. Whether that relationship is contradictory, as we see in *The Infamous Rosalie,* caring as we see in *Kasalé,* or contentious as we see in *Moonbath,* familiarity with the land and an understanding of its inner workings shape the ethical discourse in these novels.

The Infamous Rosalie: Strange Fruit in Saint-Domingue

If, as Greta Gaard argues, "ecofeminism's challenge of social domination extends beyond sex to social domination of all kinds, because the domination of sex, race and class, and the domination of nature are mutually reinforcing," then the lens of ecofeminism offers a useful point of departure for analyzing the racial terror and violent power relations of the colonial plantation.[27] Évelyne Trouillot's *The Infamous Rosalie* displays how the natural environment functions as a space of possibility and entrapment in the context of slavery. Set in colonial Saint-Domingue several decades before the Haitian Revolution, *The Infamous Rosalie* is one of the few Haitian novels that unfolds during the eighteenth century but does not have the Revolution as its main focal point, or even as an event that occurs in the text. Instead, the novel concentrates on the lived reality of enslaved people as it displays the unremitting violence and indignities of daily life alongside small pleasures, passion, friendship, and romance, each of which amplifies their humanity.[28]

Trouillot's novel is a coming-of-age story about the Creole protagonist Lisette, who goes from being a privileged young domestic enslaved girl to a spy for the Maroons as a young woman and eventually a Maroon herself.[29] *The Infamous Rosalie* also relates the story of three generations of women who came before Lisette and who knew life prior to the plantation and the Middle Passage. Women occupy the center of Trouillot's narrative; their experience with slavery confirms Saidiya Hartman's point that "the ultimate *nègre*, the exemplary slave, is the Black female; she is the everything and the nothing that constitutes our modernity. She is the belly of the world, the factory, the crop, the implement of future increase, and the captive maternal that nurtures the world."[30] As I discussed in chapter 2, the generational perspective informs the protagonist's radicalization and development of consciousness because it is the elder women sharing their stories about the baracoons and the Middle Passage with Lisette that leads to her putting into action her dreams of freedom.

Lisette is different from other protagonists in this chapter in that she does not explicitly serve the spirits. Although she is not a Vodou practitioner per se, there are many spiritual dimensions that inform her consciousness, including her ongoing recognition of her ancestors' presence and her investment in sacred objects. I read Lisette's "divine accompaniment" by her foremothers in *The Infamous Rosalie* through the lens nou mache ansanm described by Lamothe, Chapman, and Durban-Albrecht to capture how "the spirits walk with devotees and vision each person's ancestral legacies walking with them."[31] As Lisette walks, and often runs through the landscape she inhabits, her ancestral foremothers act as a spiritual covering.

Explaining the destruction of the Haitian landscape as a result of the plantocracy, Lizabeth Paravisini-Gebert stresses multiple stages of deforestation that killed the forests as they were prior to colonial invasion: "By far the greatest damage to the forests . . . was done by the development of the plantation economy. Throughout the Caribbean, coastal mahogany forests were completely cleared to make room for sugarcane plantations. In Haiti, coffee plantations were created on previously forested territories."[32] What Paravisini-Gebert refers to as the "assault on the forests" means that what became the plantation was once the forest. The enslaved people experience the torturous labor of the sugarcane fields, and the lush forests are where the Maroons can hide and be free. Given the ways that this aspect of the natural landscape facilitates flight, "it is fitting, then, for the forest to have become a powerful site and symbol for marronage" as well as the sacred grove of Vodou initiation.[33]

Postcolonial ecocritics have previously identified "the recuperative role of place" as a way to theorize Caribbean landscapes.[34] How can a land that is not only the locus but also the motivation for enslavement be recuperated? When place signifies the terror of enslavement and the violence of colonialism, how do authors attempt to recuperate that place? My reading of *The Infamous Rosalie* posits that recuperation takes place when we pay attention to how the enslaved people interact with the physical landscape and use it to their advantage so that it is not only about the degradation of slavery but also about the possibility to imagine life otherwise.[35] I associate this conceptual duality with a Black feminist ethic because it attends to the both/and possibility born from the land and essential to the development of the female protagonist's coming into awareness; and also because it unites *le monde intérieur et le monde extérieur* as the locus of that ethic. In this context, the Maroons emblematize how land can be reimagined and recuperated through acts of flight and resistance. In the words of visual artist Mafalda Mondestin, the land has secrets that it allows the Maroons to keep. In fact, "Maroon communities of runaway slaves emerged throughout the Americas in rugged and marginal territories surrounding zones of colonial slave plantations," a pan-Caribbean form of resistance to slavery.[36]

In her examination of Caribbean plantation landscapes, literary scholar Melanie Otto returns to the original definition of the word *landscape* "in its most basic definition, landscape means 'shaped land.' Cultural landscapes create a sense of history and belonging; they express narratives of culture and regional identity."[37] In Haiti, as in many parts of the African diaspora, huge tracts of the land were shaped by the hands of the enslaved whose labor was exploited to create it, as well as by the colonizers who determined the size and shape of the plantations. As McKittrick notes in her Black feminist ruminations on the function of geography, transatlantic slavery "provides a striking example of how the physical landscape and geographic knowledges, together, suppressed, imprisoned, and spatialized the Black population."[38] And yet, in a telling intervention, Black feminist authors reimagine the land so that it functions as more than a site of abjection and death. Put differently, they foreground the land as a place of what Kevin Quashie calls "aliveness."[39] The landscape in *The Infamous Rosalie* reveals the duality of an island that holds the scourge of bondage but also the promise of liberation.

Prompted by Trouillot's rendering of a land that both oppresses and frees, I want to think through the possibilities offered by the natural environment. The height of the mountains, the preponderance of the hills, and the density of the forests work together to create the possibility of another future for those who escape into it. Overall, Trouillot's novel evinces an environmental imagination that is caught in the tension of the potential promise of the land and its function as a prison that destroys those forced to work it. It helps to map the kind of geography that McKittrick asks us to imagine as possible. Lisette's ability to imagine (and eventually realize) the possibility of freedom from slavery is inspired by the environment she inhabits. This is not different from Ulysse's articulation of rasanblaj because, though Lisette's is an individual act, as I explained in chapter 2, she carries the words and memories of her elders with her—the ancestral legacies carry her. Her pursuit of freedom is informed by those who came before her as much as by her Maroon lover. When Vincent finally shares parts of his story with her, she connects his narrative to the stories passed on by her grandmother and godmother.

Each time Lisette furtively runs into the forest to meet Vincent, we are reminded of how the Maroon presence affirms a natural environment that facilitates the opportunity for flight. Without the thick forests and steep mountains for the runaways to take refuge in, the possibility of flight would not exist. In keeping with this idea, the depiction of nature that Trouillot offers in *The Infamous Rosalie* includes the use of natural metaphors to describe freedom, calling attention to the landscape as more than geography. The environmental impact of the plantation economy haunts Lisette. As she observes the natural beauty of the land, she can only do so by also recognizing that it is first and foremost a site of terror: "I fall asleep amid the beauty of this land that seems to bear the mark of our pain—Creoles, Aradas, Congos, Nagos, Ibos, newly arrived Negroes, forever bossales, confronting our chains. In my sleep, I struggle against miasmas and stagnant waters, barracoons and the steerage of ships, the growl of dogs, bodies too hot and damp, the sound of bludgeons" (12). Lisette's description of Saint-Domingue and her reference to "the beauty of this land that seems to bear the mark of our pain" identifies the paradoxical nature of a land that is physically captivating while it holds unremitting violence and produces unrelenting pain. Her experience is also a reminder that, as McKittrick notes, "it is important to begin to address some of the key ways Black geographies can be recognized, and are produced, in landscapes of domination."[40] When we recognize that "Black women are negotiating a geographic landscape that is upheld by a legacy of exploration, exploitation, and conquest," we begin to understand how land shapes the lived experience of Black women from history through the present day.[41] Viewed in this context, Lisette's daily encounters with the land maintain a significance beyond the material. Through her encounters with the trees, Lisette begins to map a different relationship to the landscape that contains her, revealing that even as an enslaved Black woman, her relationship to the land she inhabits is not fixed and will change as she changes.

As many Caribbean scholars of the environment have noted, trees and forests populate the Caribbean literary imagination in myriad ways, and we cannot help but note "their centrality to any discussion of environmental colonialism in the region."[42] Or, as M. Jacqui Alexander summarizes, for Caribbean people "the call of the forest is in our DNA."[43] Trouillot shows us through the eyes of her enslaved characters what the land looks like, how the trees move, how the plants feel, and what the mountains beyond inspire. This description of the land by Haitian historian Jean Fouchard highlights its natural fecundity:

C'était une île avec beaucoup de richesses naturelles. Les planteurs sont arrivés et ont commencé les plantations de café et de canne à sucre. Mais il fallait que les planteurs aient des esclaves pour travailler dans les champs. Donc, les bateaux nègres amenaient les esclaves qui viennent d'Afrique . . . Et bientôt, elle, avec l'aide des esclaves, est devenue la plus importante colonie de la France, qui s'est appelée Saint-Domingue.

(It was an island with much natural wealth. The planters arrived and started the coffee and sugar cane plantations. But planters had to have slaves to work in the fields. So, the boats brought slaves from Africa . . . And soon, the island, with the help of slaves, became the most important colony of France, which was called Santo Domingo.)[44]

The natural environment of *La perle des Antilles*—the Pearl of the Antilles—made it the most productive of the French colonies. Haiti's topography set the stage for the plantation labor and helped to inspire the creation of the Code Noir in 1685, a royal edict issued by Louis XIV concerning "the discipline and commerce of Blacks and slaves."[45] The legal discourse of the Code Noir inaugurated a new, even more brutal phase of colonial life, effectively institutionalizing and normalizing violent practices such as burnings at the stake.[46]

As the main source of France's wealth and world dominance, the plantation system generated significant revenue that was instrumental in maintaining the power of the monarchy. Without the land, France would not have prospered. Without the land, the enslaved people might not have been uprooted from the African continent, packed into ships, and forced onto plantations. That the beauty, richness, and fecundity of the colony was also a mechanism of entrapment, violence, and death is not lost on young Lisette, whose embodied movements further illuminate a vexed relationship to the land. Whether she is running, hiding, or searching, she observes how the Caribbean landscape is a fraught space.

Possibility is present in the plot of *The Infamous Rosalie* through the forbidden practice of marronage because the Maroons make an alternative relationship to the land possible. As one of the earliest examples of resistance on the plantation, described by Neil Roberts as the concept of perpetual flight,[47] marronage is an act and a state of being that demonstrates the enslaved people's ability to imagine their lives "otherwise."[48] Lisette's experience emblematizes how Maroons cogently exemplify how freedom is reimagined in the context of New World slavery. Maryse Condé also highlights the well-established relationship between the Maroons and their natural environment, explaining that "the hills were the refuge where the Maroons had escaped the sufferings of the plantation, the trees the silent witnesses of an eternal exploitation."[49] These formerly enslaved runaways founded communities on the edges of the plantation under the cover of the trees and in the caverns of the mountains. They are, "un peuple d'ombres fuyantes qui d'un pas souvent mutilé, monte à la lumière. . . D'étapes en étapes, par des chemins difficiles, poursuivis par la Maréchaussée, ils s'en vont à l'Espagnol ou s'enfoncent dans les bois. . . . Ils changent souvent de quartier pour brouiller les pistes" (a people of fleeting shadows, who with a an often mutilated step, rise to the light . . . Stage by stage, by difficult paths, pursued by the Maréchaussée, they go to the Spaniard or sink into the woods . . . They often change neighborhoods to cover their tracks).[50]

Explaining the Maroon acts of rebellion further, Fouchard writes that "la rébellion du marron ne peut prouver en effet qu'une indivisible et active protestation, une évidente et commune hostilité aux conditions de l'esclavage, à la mesure, certes, des circonstances, des possibilités, du courage ou du tempérament de chaque marron. . . . la recherche par l'esclave d'un souffle de liberté ou de la liberté elle-même" (the rebellion of the Maroon can prove indeed only an indivisible and active protest, an obvious and common hostility to the conditions of slavery, to the extent, certainly, of circumstances, possibilities, courage or temperament of each Maroon . . . the slave's search for a breath of freedom or freedom itself).[51]

Universally recognized figures of resistance in the Caribbean, Maroons symbolize flight, fugitivity, and freedom.[52] Those familiar with the history of Haiti know that the community of Maroons played a crucial role in the initial phases of the Haitian Revolution when it began in 1791. Through representations of this population, Trouillot gestures toward the imminent revolution without deploying its central tropes. Throughout the Americas, Maroon communities stood out as "a heroic challenge to white authority, as the living proof of the existence of a slave consciousness that refused to be limited by the whites' conception or manipulation of it. It is no accident that throughout the Caribbean today, the historical Maroon— often mythologized into a larger-than-life figure—has become a touchstone of identity for the region's writers, artists, and intellectuals, the ultimate symbol of resistance and the fight for freedom."[53] Trouillot's intervention asks us to think intersectionally about the trope of marronage. Lisette's trajectory from an enslaved domestic to a spy to a Maroon determined to birth her daughter in freedom wrests the concept of marronage from the domain of masculinity.

"The Call of the Forest"

M. Jacqui Alexander names the power of the forest as a force that is spiritually, culturally, and historically relevant in the Caribbean: "it's the call of the forest. That's our spiritual DNA. The forest. Land, with a capital L. She is a living, breathing entity. We know Her by that name. Communities, nations live in the forest even in the face of massive defor-estation. We escaped and went to the forest as captive peoples; we called it *marronage*."[54] In their conversation about rasanblaj, Alexander refers to the call of the forest as a quintessentially Caribbean tradition. Trees are essential to the machinations of survival for both the enslaved and the Maroons. The trees offer shelter, provide medicine, allow fugitives to see better, and serve as hiding places. In the section that follows, I pay attention to the uses and the mention of trees to argue that they serve as the ultimate leitmotif for the contradictory nature of the landscape. Trees become a necessary part of the lived environment that facilitate both death and life. At times, it seems as though they take on the characteris-tics of what happens around them; the unmitigated atrocities of slavery result in the land and the bodies of enslaved people seemingly becoming one. As Alexander reminds us, the forest is sacred and foundational in the subject formation of Caribbean people: "That's where we developed our sensibilities; how to read, how to read tracks, markings on the ground;

how to develop respectful relationship with animals. That's where we learned about plants. That's how we knew what was 'poisonous' and what was not 'poisonous.' That's how we developed the cure and the antidote. That's how we came to know that it resided in the same place. That in the forest, the poisonous plant and its antidote lived next to each other." The trees that make up the forest serve several purposes: they are hiding places for people and things, they allow for gatherings and meetings that lead to insurrection, they contain the secrets of healing remedies and antidotes.[55]

Even the scent of the forest carries with it evidence of the enslaved people who are attempting to escape, and the dogs sent in by their colonizers to find them. When Lisette is in the forest, she inhales the "smell of droppings from men and animals that clings to the trees" (9). Holding the scent of the people who are oppressed and the dogs that pursue them alters the composition of the tree, which now bears the grisly history of slavery. Just as human activity shapes the natural environment, the violence of slavery fashions the land, leaving indelible marks.

Lisette's use of the tree to hide her talisman, and herself, relates to another important use of trees, as hiding places for people in need of protection. Here again, the fecundity of the natural landscape is advantageous in small acts of resistance to slavery further associating the ecology of Saint-Domingue with liberation. Referring to her Maroon lover Vincent, who has a sophisticated ability to disappear in nature, Lisette says, "I almost always look over my shoulders at the last mountain slope where the hills hide him from me completely, as if once again he's disappeared into the bark of a tree or the bend of a stone wall." (13). Vincent shows how enslaved people become masters of disappearance as they discern the natural environment and make it work in their favor.

Talismans are forbidden under the regulations of the Code Noir, so Lisette hides hers in a tree to protect herself from punishment. It is a sacred object that she refuses to discard because it also connects her to her ancestral heritage: "I removed my talisman made of rooster feathers, sand from an hourglass, and leather and went to place my treasure at the very top of the mango tree, behind the shacks, deep in a hollow I'd discovered long ago. I couldn't bring myself to destroy them. I already felt too vulnerable, as if an important part of me had been torn away." (11). That she discovers this hollow "long ago" suggests intimacy with the land; she is adept in searching it to extract what she needs. Her survival depends on this tree, which hides the object whose possession could lead to severe punishment.[56] At several different points in the novel she goes to the tree where she keeps these precious objects: "Nestled among the leaves of the tree, I take the talismans out from their hiding place" (23). Holding the hidden talisman, the mango tree, which exemplifies Mafalda Mondestin's image of a land that keeps secrets, faithfully keeps Lisette's secret. It thus becomes an example of how Lisette relates to nature as an invaluable resource in her daily life.

Also, when Lisette says, "I'm worried about Fontilus, my friend from our days of running around butt-naked. When we were children, we used to hide sometimes in the tree where I stashed my valuables," we learn that even as young children, Lisette and her friends have a relationship to the trees (23). But Fontilus and Lisette's childhood game of hiding in the trees was a form of play, not a form of survival. The description of their childhood game achieves Trouillot's objective to render the humanity of enslaved people for whom too often history denies the significance of their subjugated knowledge. It points to the duality of a land that functions as a resource providing some kind of respite for the enslaved, all the while being profoundly linked to oppression. That Fontilus and Lisette played in the trees as children evokes the pleasures of childhood, despite the fact that slavery robs them of childhood joys. Now that they are older, they have developed a more complex (and intimate) relationship to the same trees, which they now recognize can serve them in other ways.

In the following scene, which I analyzed in chapter 3, Lisette and Vincent have sex under a tree: "We're asleep under the shade of *a large poisonwood tree,* from which Vincent can survey the surrounding area. He places his hand on my sex and holds it there soft and still, like a serene, sure comfort" (12). For the Maroons, the utility of the poisonwood tree is in its size and large branches. Because the tree is so tall, Vincent can use it to "survey the surrounding area." Even more than a hiding place for the Maroon population, the trees help them to strategize and plan. As a site where Maroons assemble, the forest (*bwa*) recalls one of the most important gatherings in the Haitian history, that of Bwa Kayiman, which was where a Vodou ceremony took place on August 14, 1791, prior to the beginning of the Haitian Revolution.[57] Bwa Kayiman represents "that primal moment of Vodou revolutionary impulse," as Omi'seke Natasha Tinsley describes the ceremony in *Ezili's Mirrors.*[58]

Lisette's lover Vincent—or, as she refers to him, "my love from the endless hills"—is a Maroon who reinforces the connection between that community and the natural environment (22). Vincent is rarely present without the mention of a tree alongside him in some form. He hides in the trees, leans against the trees, climbs the trees, and uses trees as his guides.

He seems to be one with the trees, evoking the trope of the Vodou spirit of the forest Gran Bwa [Grand Bois]. Half human and half tree, Gran Bwa is deeply rooted in the forest. His heart-shaped head might have a double signification as we consider how Lisette falls in love with Vincent. By extension of that attachment, she falls in love with the forest and falls in love with freedom. As the example of Bwa Kayiman confirms, freedom dreams can be born in the forest and successfully take root as they did in the Haitian Revolution. When Vincent speaks to Lisette, it is in the language and the land, as in the final words she remembers him saying to her: "My Lisette . . . we mustn't forget that this island has its own four ends of the earth. Ants take their time to cross the road, but one day they reach the other side" (90).

In his study on the urban forest in Haiti, anthropologist Gregory Beckett asks, "what does a tree mean?" To this he receives the following response from a local Haitian environmental activist: "'Every tree in Haiti has medicine. There is medicine in every tree.' This is science, yes. But Haitians, we know all of this."[59] Although Beckett's study is situated in Port-au-Prince under Aristide in 2003, the acknowledgment of the trees' many functions and deeply embedded roots is useful for my purposes because in *The Infamous Rosalie* the medicinal qualities of the trees in Saint-Domingue provide a healing balm for the enslaved. This is the case for the character of Tante Brigitte, the Arada midwife who knows the secrets of the leaves. As a midwife, Tante Brigitte assists women with birth, and she is also a healer with sacred knowledge of the trees. If nature is an active agent in the lives of the enslaved, it is because they can use it for their purposes, and their adherence to the spirit world thrives on the balance between spirit and nature.

Along with Tante Brigitte, who is a healer with knowledge of the plants, Vincent represents a connection to nature that surpasses the realm of reality and becomes almost spiritual. Seeing Vincent standing against a tree, Lisette experiences a wave of calm: "When I see Vincent standing against the tree, my muscles relax, and I suddenly inhale the sweetness of the mountain" (59). As I discussed in chapter 3 on the ethical-erotic, their sexual relationship is lovingly sensual. Seeing Vincent brings peace and pleasure to Lisette. It also allows her to notice the beauty of the landscape. Besides the ubiquitous pairing of the mountains and the trees, in this case the mountains are described in relation to pleasure.

There are many different kinds of trees that Trouillot names and describes in *The Infamous Rosalie:* the mapou, poisonwood, mango, and lemon trees, among others. References to trees in the novel vary, but they are most often present in terms of protection: "Here I am back in my *favorite refuge* for when I want to be alone without being too far from the plantation. Hidden again among the branches of the tree where I bury my treasures, I gently stroke my talisman. Can it protect me from the unease taking root in me? I caress my great-aunt Brigitte's cord, as if to beg her to tell me its secret" (73–74). As Lisette's *favorite refuge,* the tree provides temporary respite from her life of terror on the plantation. The safety that people experience when they hide in the trees exists because of the vegetation. Trees provide constant cover for the Maroons and the enslaved people about to be rescued: "Michaud leads me to the rear of the old shack, where he lives along with the other discarded people, on this small piece of land where, with old Désirée and the other survivors, he's planted a few fruit trees. Scattered under the shade of the orange trees, away from inquisitive glances, are gathered about twenty slaves" (100). The recurrent examples of trees that provide cover and offer healing for enslaved people in *The Infamous Rosalie* exhibit how the natural environment can operate in service of the people who are also oppressed within it.

As Lisette's earlier reflection on "the beauty of the land that holds so much pain" eloquently expresses, the plantation landscape is one of startling contradiction. While the trees are examples of how enslaved people were able to use the natural environment to their advantage, they are also symbols of violence, pain, and cruelty: "In the foggy darkness of the shack, my imagination fueled by the *sound of tree branches* hitting the boards, I would see terrible beings, cruel and menacing things" (40). The sound of the tree branches leads Lisette's mind down a path of imagined terror.

The Infamous Rosalie communicates the bitter irony of the land's beauty. The idea of blood as part of the vegetation owing to the murder of the enslaved people reminds the reader of an intimate and nefarious connection between material bodies and natural elements:

> Standing next to me, Florville holds me back to keep me from seeing the body. A few slaves had already gathered around the corpse. Pierrot the coachman and Charlemagne, a bossale who took care of the horses on the plantation, were holding Gentilus up. Fontilus's father was no longer crying, but he had shrunk so much that we could only see the top of his coarse, gray hair. They had laid Fontilus's body on the ground, but no one thought of taking down the rope that was still swinging between the tree branches with its grotesque, pitiful knot. (106)

This scene extends the connections between the violence of slavery and the physical environment. Here the branches seem to have conspired with the rope that Fontilus uses to die by suicide. His suicide asks the reader to link the violence of the plantocracy with the natural environment.

In her thoughtful study *The Properties of Lynching,* which puts representations of lynching in dialogue with history, Sandy Alexandre argues for the practice of reading the natural landscape for signs of slavery. Her theorizing of African American iconography and portrayals of the built environment acknowledges that "no interrogation of Blacks and their relation to nature, the outdoors, or the pastoral ideal would be complete without considering what we might term the politics of nature."[60] By connecting Trouillot's novel to a study on the literary representations of slavery's violence in the American South, my goal is to signal *The Infamous Rosalie*'s belonging in a larger network of African diasporic literary representations that portray how the land is implicated in the terror of slavery. Other literary scholars like Renée Larrier have noted that *The Infamous Rosalie* can be read through the theoretical frameworks elaborated by scholars of slavery in the context of the United States. According to Larrier, "*The Infamous Rosalie,* a novel set in the mid-eighteenth century colonial Saint-Domingue could be read in the context of [Saidiya] Hartman's historical analysis of the American south . . . Examining the various forms of domination in daily life, a phenomenon she calls the 'terror of the mundane and quotidian' Hartman focuses in particular on covert performances."[61] As Larrier's comparison makes explicit, the system of chattel slavery in the Americas merits comparative examination, and studies such as Alexandre's and Hartman's are instructive insofar as they offer critical frameworks for analyzing representations of slavery throughout the diaspora. Still, it should be noted that, as Sharpe demonstrates in *In the Wake,* the afterlives of slavery recur across regions throughout the Americas, although the specificities may differ. Despite the geographical differences between Haiti and the United States, the differences in colonial identities, and the differences of African heritage among the enslaved, there is the remarkable consistency of slavery as a violent apparatus of terror and dehumanization.

What Hartman calls "the terror of the mundane and quotidian" defines the Black feminist ethic unfolding in Trouillot's novel. Shortly after the passage describing Fontilus's dead body, Lisette returns to the tree as a source of comfort:

> I feel as if I no longer have any tears to shed. From Samuel to Grandma Charlotte, from Gracieuse to Fontilus, from Vincent to Makandal, from start to finish my sorrows have taken on the shape of an abyss that makes jumping

into it so tempting. I've gotten into the habit of going to sit in the branches of the sapota tree after working in the big house and getting Michaud's messages, even though my whole body cries out for rest. It's as if the branches of the sapota still hold the imprint of my friend's neck, as if the wind rustling the leaves is the same one that last caressed his cheek. (107)

Becoming a refuge for her once again, the tree operates differently from how it did in earlier passages, reminding us that the responsibility for the violence of slavery is in the hands of the perpetrators who use nature to create terror. Nature itself (in this case the tree) is not to blame for this violence. It has been manipulated to achieve the slaveholder's ends.

Describing the house and the land that surrounds it, Lisette notices "the patios filled with flowers, the clipped hedges that were my hiding place and refuge since Grandma Charlotte's time, the broad roads, the fields of sugarcane, the bare-chested Negroes in short britches, the workrooms, the Negroes' gardens that extended all the way to the mountains—all the way to the hills that surround us, so close, so far" (7). That the hills are "so close" and at the same time "so far" mirrors the contradiction between freedom and enslavement that I have highlighted throughout this section. The promise of the ecology is the possibility contained in the mountains; the hills are where the Maroons find refuge. Lisette's reference to her childhood, when she would hide in the bushes for refuge, prefigures how nature will accommodate her future flight. When she finally makes the decision to flee, she looks toward these same mountains: "It's my turn now to walk with my daughter, who will be born, like me, from this land of waves and mountains and whose fate is anchored in the four corners of this island" (128–29). The novel concludes with Lisette looking toward the mountains, both literally and figuratively, underscoring the role of the mountains in her future and her freedom. As a sign of the future and of nature, the mountains relate the significance of the environment for all kinds of enslaved people—from those who are forced to work the land to those who flee from bondage. By concluding her story with Lisette looking toward the mountains, Trouillot signals freedom and futurity together in one stroke. The figure of the Maroon is already future-facing because, as Bajan poet Kamau Braithwaite posits, Haiti is "the greatest and most successful Maroon polity of them all."[62] Lisette's concluding gesture and declaration to her unborn daughter reminds the reader of the potential for freedom that the nature makes possible; it also ends on a note of agency, with a young Black woman planning for a different future for her child.

By asking that we contemplate the paradox of the landscape in colonial Saint-Domingue, *The Infamous Rosalie* exposes the contradiction of a lived environment in which enslavement, freedom, terror, and safety can coexist in complex ways. In some ways, this understanding of how Caribbean landscapes are necessarily embedded in history is not innovative. After all, as the editors of *Caribbean Literature and the Environment: Between Nature and Culture* note, "Caribbean writers have had to recover a sense of historicity."[63] What strikes me about *The Infamous Rosalie* is how the encounter with nature leads to a sense of self in the protagonist that motivates her to pursue liberation. When her lived experience as an enslaved woman combines with an encounter with the natural world's powers, she is able to catapult herself and her unborn daughter into another world that is different and, most important, free.

Kasalé: Where Nature Is Spirit and Spirit Is Nature

The Haitian environment is endowed with a spiritual significance formed and informed by the Vodou religion. As I discussed in chapter 2, Vodou is an immutable force in Kettly Mars's *Kasalé,* one that we also experience as deeply gendered. I return to the novel now to show how Mars's mapping of the physical landscape is inextricable from the spiritual world and daily practice of Vodou, underscoring Paravasini's point that "the bond between [woman] and [her] natural environment [is] the most crucial relationship in African-derived religions."[64] By attending to terrestrial relationships that are unequivocally spiritual, the novel accentuates the intimate connection between Vodou and the physical landscape. It offers a portrait of the land as a rich, fertile, and lush environment that is wholly dependent on the connection between the spirit and natural worlds. In doing so, *Kasalé* adheres closely to Dayan's sacred trinity of "women, gods and land."

Following my argument that the trope of the land raises ethical questions about how the human and nonhuman environment relate, I am interested in how the intimacy between nature and women evinced throughout *Kasalé* depends entirely upon Vodou. These relationships point out a Vodou ethic made up of "syncretism, materialism, holism, and communalism."[65] First elaborated by Claudine Michel in her rigorous study *Aspects éducatifs et moraux et du Vodou haïtien,* the idea of a Vodou ethic "ties together the visible and the invisible, material and spiritual, secular and sacred."[66] Vodou is a fully integrated and balanced system that informs all aspects of life on earth, as well as the afterlife. As Michel indicates, "la religion Vodou est omniprésente, pénétrante, puissante et remplit d'importantes fonctions dans tous les aspects de la vie sociale d'Haïti" (the Vodou religion is omnipresent, penetrating, powerful, and fulfills important functions in every aspect of social life in Haiti).[67]

What Michel outlines in her work is precisely the type of Vodou ethic that animates Gran'n's intimacy with the land throughout *Kasalé;* even the most basic of her quotidian interactions with nature is informed by Vodou.[68] Describing Haiti's national religion, Leslie Desmangles explains, "Vodou in Haiti is a religion that, through a complex system of myths and rituals, relates the life of the devotee to the deities who govern that life. Like many religions of the world, Vodou is a system of beliefs and practices that gives meaning to life: it uplifts the downtrodden who experience life's misfortunes, instills in its devotees a need for solace and self-examination, and relates the profane world of humans to that of incommensurable mythological divine entities, called *lwas,* who govern the cosmos."[69] Desmangles's description of Vodou helps us to make sense of how serving the spirits gives meaning to Antoinette's entire life. As a woman in her late nineties, her intimacy with nature pivots on her relationship to the lwa and the ancestors, a position especially relevant as she draws nearer to becoming an ancestor herself.[70]

Kasalé, tells the story of a small village outside Port-au-Prince on the main road to the south of Haiti. The two main protagonists, Antoinette/ Gran'n and Sophonie share a spiritual bond surpassing familial ties. Set during the 1970s, the novel introduces the reader to a lakou where there are several houses set up around the cachiman tree. That this particular lakou was once the Salé plantation further imbues it with a historical significance linked to enslavement. Mars's use of the lakou sets the stage for the social and spiritual story that is about to unfold. The importance of the lakou setting and the multiple significations of what that space implies cannot be understated. As scholars of Haitian religion have pointed out, the lakou is a sacred, secular, and social space: "Contemporary lakou(s) remain important and multifaceted centers for family and community life. As the headquarters of the extended-family economic activities, they are commercial centers; as dwellings for the *lwas* [Haitian gods] and the ancestors (who partake in rituals held for them there), they are religious and ancestral centers; and finally, as locations for daily interaction between neighbors and for organizational meetings, they are important community centers."[71] The lakou functions as far more than a physical location. As Haitianist scholar Charlene Désir writes, "the lakou is more than a community; it is a theoretical and social framework and an integral part of the social fabric of Haiti. Within the community, there is a poto-mitan—the center post—that brings strength to all parts of the surroundings, including all aspects of family and community life."[72] Taking Désir's invitation to read the lakou as a theoretical and social framework, my analysis of *Kasalé* explores how intimate relationships between people in the lakou are marked by the presence of the spirits and the land together. Encounter, relation, and recognition play an operative role in this analysis. What *Kasalé* shows us is how encounters with nature bring people into the realm of the spirits and ancestors.

The prominent role of nature in *Kasalé* begins with the cachiman tree at the center of the lakou. As I discussed in chapter 2, the cachiman serves as a religious symbol and as a sign that shapes the story. As a community, the people of the lakou are aware of and able to read the natural environment for signs that have a significance in the spiritual world. When the cachiman tree falls, the entire community identifies with the event, regardless of whether or not they adhere to the Vodou belief system: "Le cachiman est tombé, hier au soir" (The cachiman fell last night), we learn shortly after the novel opens (14). The cachiman tree is important as a Vodou symbol and portent that triggers a series of events with spiritual significance: "Cette histoire du cachiman et d'Antoinette, la famille et les anciens de la cour la connaissaient. Elle était *une sorte de légende, un mythe auquel plus personne ne croyait,* sauf quelques d'antan qui savaient que le commerce des esprits continuait dans la cour, malgré leur mutisme, malgré le temps, l'oubli des hommes" (This story of the cachiman tree and Antoinette, the family and the elders of the community were all aware of it. It was a *sort of legend, a myth that no one believed,* except a few from yesteryear who knew that the business of spirits continued in the community, despite their silence, despite the time, the forgetfulness of men) (14). Referring to the story of the cachiman as "a legend or myth that no one believed" implicitly invalidates the Vodou worldview. Many members of the lakou community espouse this prejudicial attitude toward the national religion. Stereotypical renderings of Vodou are in no small part to blame for how certain members of the lakou distance themselves from what many consider the only truly Haitian religion.[73] The invalidation of the spirit world also has gendered connotations because, in this lakou, to deny a natural sign of spiritual significance is to also minimize Antoinette.

Through the figure of Antoinette, *Kasalé* exemplifies LeGrace Benson's point that "Vodou prepares its practitioner to understand human life as ecologically embedded."[74] Informed by this dynamic, *Kasalé* charts the webs of affiliation between spirit and nature and terrestrial relationships between humans and nature, revealing the spiritual underpinnings of natural events.[75] But even if most people from the community deny this heritage and choose not to serve the spirits, they cannot deny the link between Vodou and the environment.

As the only Vodouizan in her community, Antoinette's understanding of ecological embedding guides her path in life as well as her awareness of her imminent death. With nature and spirit as intertwined forces of her life, Antoinette lives according to a logic that privileges both. As we saw in *The Infamous Rosalie,* it is not simply that these characters have intimate relationships with the trees; the trees symbolize the people themselves. Similarly, there are at least three links between Antoinette and the cachiman: she is the center of the novel, she is an upright pillar (poto-mitan) in the lakou to be revered, and she represents the transcendent nature of life through her serving of the spirits. This view aligns with Mars's stated intention to pay homage to Vodou in *Kasalé* that I also noted in chapter 2: "Je voulais représenter le côté humain du vaudou, une religion qui est un miroir pour le peuple haïtien" (I wanted to represent the human side of vaudou, a religion that is a mirror of the Haitian people).[76] The mirror of the Haitian people held up in *Kasalé* reveals a Vodou ethic in which nature is spirit, and spirit is nature. For Antoinette, serving the spirits is a way of life rather than just a religious practice that can be isolated from other parts of her identity. She is thus an example of what scholar Kyrah Daniels thoughtfully designates as "the respectful, creative approaches that the living take to communicate with the invisible world, which for Vodouizan remains eternally present, and to pay ritual tribute to the ancestors, whom they will eventually become."[77]

A Vodou ethic understands that nature and spirit are one and the same and that the physical and metaphysical worlds overlap. When the tree falls, the members of the community quickly recognize that there is a larger spiritual significance, whether or not they actually believe it should influence them in the present. The action of the plot is set in motion by the falling of the cachiman, which in turn leads to Antoinette's determination to construct the *kay-mistè,* a sacred family shrine devoted to the ancestors.[78] An enormous tree that sits in the middle of the rural community, the tree also symbolizes the centrality of the poto-mitan in her lakou. Since Antoinette is the *doyenne,* a role that invests her with authority, she is also the guardian of the documents and keeper of memory. That Antoinette dies at the end of the novel suggests that we frame *Kasalé* around the fall of two trees, one that is literal and one that is figurative. Ending with

Antoinette's death, the structure of *Kasalé* further compels us to associate the fall of the cachiman and the death of the *doyenne de la cour*.

As I discussed in chapter 1, *Kasalé* chronicles the transmission of Vodou knowledge from one generation to the next, which manifests in the intimate relationship between Antoinette and Sophonie. When Antoinette and Sophonie make the arduous pilgrimage to Terre-Rouge, the older woman's connection to the land guides them with each step. Antoinette recognizes the route by its environmental signs; following cues in nature, she knows exactly where to go. Along the path Antoinette experiences a form of communion with nature and returns to what she identifies as her natural self:

> Cette promenade la ramenait *au temps de sa vérité*. Au temps de ses convictions. Quand les hommes et les femmes savaient qui ils étaient. Quand ils pouvaient regarder leur destin en face, frapper leur poitrine en disant, je suis d'ici, mon sang coule dans chacun de ces arbres, ma chair est pétrie de la boue de ces mornes. Je suis l'eau enfermée dans ces roches, mes yeux ses bourgeons de soleil.

> (This journey brought her back to the time of her truth. To the time when people lived by their convictions. When men and women knew who they were. When they could look their destiny in the face, hitting their breasts and saying, I am from here, my blood flows in each of these trees, my flesh is kneaded with the mud of these hills. I am the water locked in these rocks, my eyes its sun buds.) (111)

On this pilgrimage to build the *kay-mistè*, Antoinette connects more deeply to "the time of her truth." She returns to an original and authentic part of herself. Walking up the mountain, Antoinette is reminded of who she is and longs for a previous time when the entire community esteemed the traditional religion. This passage affirming Antoinette's connection to the land also recalls Jacques Roumain's *Masters of the Dew*, a celebrated *roman paysan* (peasant novel) in which the protagonist declares that *he* is the land ("Je suis ça, je suis cette terre là" [I am this, I am this land right here]). Antoinette's reflection takes Manuel's point even further as Mars endows the land/body connection with more specificity and texture. Antoinette is the land, in the sense of both being and becoming. Her blood flows in the trees, her flesh is in the mud, she is the water in the rocks, and her eyes are part of the sun. As a devoted Vodou practitioner, Antoinette's intimate kinship with the land functions as ceremony and communion. Realizing that her death is near, Antoinette tells Sophonie:

Mon enfant, depuis le devant-jour, j'avance avec un pied sur la terre et l'autre sur la route du pays sans chapeau. Mon heure approche. Le cachiman est tombé, il va sombrer dans peu de temps, emporté par le courant, l'eau qui descend, descend sans jamais remonter. Je . . . je ne peux nier la peur qui me noue les tripes, car *l'arbre et moi partageons le même destin*. Cependant, le poids de mes certitudes l'emporte sur celui de mon angoisse.

(My child, from dawn, I advance with one foot on the soil and the other on the road to the afterlife. My hour is approaching. The cachiman has fallen, it will disappear in a short time, swept away by the current, the water descending, descending without ever rising again. I . . . I cannot deny the fear that binds my guts, because *the tree and I share the same destiny*. However, the weight of my certainties prevails over that of my anguish.) (37)

As she makes explicitly clear here, Antoinette and the tree share the same destiny. This speech emblematizes Antoinette's thoughts about and relationship to both nature and to death. She recognizes death as imminent and inevitable, but she fears it nonetheless. Antoinette's fear thwarts the image of her as a courageous model of resilience boldly staring death in the eye. She is not a singularly drawn brave woman who laughs in the face of death. Even her devotion to the spirits does not mitigate her fear of death. A devoted Vodouizan, her body's slow deterioration means that she will soon join the ancestors and the sprits that she serves. The prospect of entry into the community of ancestral spirits is the only comfort to her in the face of her anguish about death. The certainty of her imminent death, which the cachiman portends, influences her perspective on what comes at the end of old age. As she relates to the land, Gran'n achieves greater peace about her condition. The pilgrimage to build the *kay-mistè* is a ceremony that she must perform; it also fortifies her and helps to prepare her for death.

The physical description of Kasalé depicts the natural environment that surrounds it as verdant and hilly. As we saw in *The Infamous Rosalie*, Haiti's topography as a mountainous land is omnipresent in the novel: the hills are in constant view for the people of Kasalé and contribute to the community's isolation. In Kasalé, the privileged role of nature further distinguishes the community from city life. Early in the novel, Mars paints a physical description of the geographic location that suggests how her environmental vision might subsequently unfold:

Kasalé, vu de la route, est un relais de *verdure*, l'un des derniers poumons de la périphérie sud de la capitale. On ne croirait pas qu'au cœur de ces *mornes* vivent depuis les décennies des *lakous* aux histoires silencieuses. Au fur et à mesure de la montée, la fraicheur, le calme du lieu exercent un effet lénifiant sur celui qui laisse l'effervescence de l'autoroute. *La rivière, maîtresse des lieux,* rappelle aux visiteurs d'abandonner derrière lui la ville et ses incohérences. Ici règnent les grands arbres, l'eau, la terre, les esprits et les pierres.

(Kasalé, seen from the road, is a stretch of greenery, one of the last gasps of the southern periphery of the capital. One would not imagine that in the heart of these melancholy hills lakous with silent stories have been living for decades. As the climb progresses, the freshness and calm of the place exerts a soothing effect on someone who leaves the effervescence of the motorway. The river, mistress of the place, reminds visitors to leave behind the city and its inconsistencies. Here reign the great trees, the water, the earth, the spirits and the stones.) (16)

Kasalé is a special, sacred place where nature reigns. The great trees, the lapping water, the pungent earth, the hovering spirits, and the rough stones all operate together in a singular ecosystem that sets Kasalé apart from the city. Consider how Mars's combination of the natural and the spiritual appears here in a list that places the spirits alongside elements of nature: trees, river, water, and stones, signaling an environmental vision in which the nature and spirit assert their presence together.

Set in a rural environment that is just outside of the city, the novel juxtaposes rural and urban spaces: "À Kasalé, comme dans tous les *lakous* du pays, il n'existe aucune notion d'urbanisme. . . . Le hameau comprenait plusieurs pâtés de maisons avec au centre de chacun les cases des parents les plus proches. Au fur et à mesure des alliances, des naissances, de la poussée démographique, d'autres s'élevèrent, plus en retrait, rappelant un peu les cercles formés autour du point de chute d'une pierre dans l'eau" (In Kasalé, as in all the lakous of the country, there is no notion of town planning . . . The hamlet consisted of several blocks with the boxes of the nearest relatives in the center of each one. Keeping pace with marriages, births, population growth, others were built, further back, somewhat reminiscent of the circles that form around a stone dropped in the water) (7). The portrayal of the community of Kasalé collapses the divide between the people that inhabit it and its physical geography in a manner that I interpret as further evidence of what should be a desirable intimacy between people and nature.

Part of the challenge in *Kasalé* is that the community, with the exception of Antoinette, has strayed so far from this true identity of serving the spirits. Their isolation from the national religion amounts to an alienation from their identity. Often the people of Kasalé operate like a unified mass, with one person indistinguishable from the other. When the town rises to find that the cachiman tree has fallen, the shock that it has fallen registers as a collective response: "Kasalé, étonnée, rompue par la violence de l'orage nocturne" (Kasalé, shocked and broken by the violence of the night time storm) (7). By giving Kasalé human characteristics, Mars highlights that a lakou is made up of people rooted in place; she also personifies the environment in ways consistent with nature writing. At times the references to the physical properties of Kasalé call attention to distinct natural elements, as we see in this passage after the storm in which the omniscient narrator notes the insalubrious quality that settles over the village: "Kasalé gorgée d'eau fraiche exhalait un mélange de sève, de zèbaklou, de bonbonyen, de caca mouillé de cabri. Le lakou coiffant l'une des berges surélevées de la Rivière-Froide semblait rajeuni" (Kasalé, full of fresh water, exhaled a mixture of sap, zebaklou, bonbonyen, wet goat's poop. The lakou capping one of the raised banks of the Rivière-Froide seemed rejuvenated) (11). Connecting land and breath, Mars amplifies the sacred nature of this landscape. Here the description of the lakou engages multiple senses and acknowledges how the range of its vegetation, the effects of the storm, and the presence of the animals come together to create a unique ecosystem. Even though the smells described here are unpleasant for those who breathe its air, Kasalé exhales and appears rejuvenated.

Almost every time she speaks, Antoinette refers to nature. She is attentive to how the wind blows, how the rain falls, and how the plants feel. As one who "perceives the relationships in nature" with acuity, Antoinette's daily encounters with nature are spiritually rooted. Describing her affinity for Kasalé, she uses environmental language:

Puis, se disait-elle, je ne quitterai jamais Kasalé tout à fait. Même quand je déambulerai dans ces lieux où l'enveloppe du corps ne m'embrasse plus, je sais au fond de mon cœur que je reviendrai ici. Je reviendrai avec le souffle frais du vent annonçant la pluie. Je serai le sang du flamboyant dont les grappes de fleurs écarlates cascadent dans les mornes dès le mois de mai. Je m'élancerai dans le ciel, libre et orgueilleuse comme la flèche du palmiste.

(Then, she said to herself, I will never leave Kasalé altogether. Even when I wander in those places where the body's envelope embraces me no more, I know deep in my heart that I will come back here. I will come back with the fresh breath of the wind announcing the rain. I will be the blood of the flamboyant whose clusters of scarlet flowers cascade in the hills from the month of May. I will leap into the sky, free and proud as the arrow of the palm kernel.) (141)

Antoinette explains that she will not only be one with the land after death but she will in fact return in different elements of nature. Her reference to the forms she will take after her death is clearly "ecologically embedded."[79] This intimate relationship to the land that preserves life by returning it as a spirit in nature. In *Kasalé,* the boundaries between the human and natural worlds are mediated through the spirit world; when she joins the land of the spirits, Antoinette's formerly physical self will join spirits and nature.

Landscape Is a Character

Few Caribbean scholars have theorized the landscape more intricately than Edouard Glissant, whose view of how nature, history, and culture are combined also reveals an environmental ethic operative in literary texts. Maryse Condé explains his influence by writing that "Glissant is also responsible for the reintroduction of nature and the environment in the West Indian novel."[80] For Glissant, a relationship to landscape should be dynamic, inclusive of movement and metamorphosis. In *Poétique de la Relation (The Poetics of Relation),* Glissant insists on the relationship between history and the environment, exploring the manifold configurations of Caribbean landscapes in both critical and creative work. In Glissantian terms, "describing the landscape is not enough. The individual, the community, the land are inextricable in the process of creating history. Landscape is a character in this process."[81] Glissant consistently argued for the preeminence of the environment, cautioning that there is far more at stake in Caribbean representations of the land than the appreciation of flora and fauna. His work actively "foregrounds humanity's relationship with 'the land' as 'one that is even more threatened because the community is alienated from that land.'"[82]

Part of the challenge in *Kasalé* is that the community, with the exception of Antoinette, has strayed so far from this true identity of serving the spirits. Their isolation from the national religion amounts to an alienation from their identity. Thus, in Kasalé, culture is threatened by a refusal to recognize nature. The community's renouncement of Vodou results in their alienation from the land. A rejection of the spirits is the same as a rejection of the land because nature and spirit are one. According to Glissant, that alienation from the land has moral consequences:

> La signification (l'histoire) du paysage ou de la Nature, c'est la clarté révélée du processus par quoi une communauté coupée de ses liens ou de ses racines

(et peut-être même au départ, de toutes possibilités d'enracinement) peu à peu souffre le paysage, mérite sa Nature, connaît son pays. . . . Approfondir la signification, c'est porter cette clarté *à la conscience. L'effort ardu vers la terre est un effort vers l'histoire.*[83]

(The meaning (story) of the landscape or Nature reveals the lucidity of the process through which a community, cut off from its ties or roots (and perhaps even at the beginning, from all possibility of putting down roots) little by little accepts the landscape, deserves its Nature, knows its country. . . . To delve deeper into the meaning is to bring that lucidity to the conscious mind. The arduous task of [connecting with] the earth is an effort toward [connecting with] history.)

With the exception of Antoinette and Sophonie, who honor and abide by a Vodou ethic, the people of Kasalé are alienated from nature, culture, and the national religion. But as the quotation above suggests, the alienation from the land need not be binding. It is possible for the individual to develop a more dynamic and intimate relationship in which the land becomes more than backdrop, an environmental and spiritual balance becomes possible, and the relationship between humans and nature shows care and attention. In *Kasalé* this kind of relationship is made possible only by Vodou. Explaining her ethnographic methodology for *Mama Lola,* Karen McCarthy Brown writes that she "chose to follow the feminist maxim that when gender is taken as a primary category of analysis it reveals levels of meaning otherwise unsuspected. I discovered a woman's history and a parallel kinship structure buried beneath the official versions."[84] As a Vodouizan, Antoinette relates to nature on spiritual terms; serving the spirits requires understanding nature, which in turn leads to an intimate relationship to the environment. Together, Gran'n and Sophonie are an example of the feminist kinship structure Brown mentions. In contrast to the other characters of *Kasalé,* Gran'n and Sophonie share an intimacy with nature and each other that consolidates around their practice of Vodou. Moreover, their sacred bond as practitioners of Vodou, as a mentor and a mentee, as sisters in the spirit helps us to read beneath layers of meaning that Mars inserts into her novel.

Moonbath: Of Gods, Land, and Sea

Unlike *Kasalé,* in which the relationship to nature is one of care and intimacy, in Yanick Lahens's *Moonbath* the characters are in a constant struggle with land and sea. My analysis of the latter rests on the idea of a vexed relationship to the land captured through the spiritual lens of Vodou. Karen McCarthy Brown articulates a similar understanding of Vodou in relation to suffering, writing that "life, in the Vodou view of things, is characterized by alternating cycles of suffering and the transient relief from suffering that is called 'having luck' [*chans*]."[85] She goes on to explain that "*chans* is not entirely a matter of chance" because it involves quotidian attention to "maintaining and enhancing good luck, and, when necessary, fending off and removing bad luck are forms of labor necessary to life."[86] Taking into account Brown's description of these cycles as central to the Vodou worldview, I am interested in how land and sea also figure within this constellation of suffering.

Moonbath presents a moral vision in which humans are held accountable for neglecting nature: ethical challenges related to the environment regularly indict how people operate in relation to place. Following my argument that Lahens espouses an ethics of form, I focus on how the tensions between people, nature, and spirits probe the reader's moral imagination, inviting us to ask questions about who takes care of the land, how, and why. The Black feminist ethic also expressed in this novel helps us to better understand Cétoute, the dying Black woman protagonist and narrator whose encounter with the land places her at odds with the other characters in the novel.

Throughout *Moonbath*, the importance of the environment to the community of Anse Bleue is established through the description of ecological forces at work, including the hurricane, the presence of the sea and mountains (often juxtaposed), and the people's daily dependence on the land because of the demands of rural life. This lyrically written saga of a peasant family living in the seaside Haitian village unfolds over four generations. For each generation, the presence of Vodou, the influence of politics, struggles with the land, and economic suffering connect them to one another across time. The constant suffering of the people in *Moonbath* suggests that, as Brown's specifies, "it is not exaggeration to state that Haitians believe that living and suffering are inseparable."[87] But if suffering is inevitable, it does not occur in isolation. The communal suffering that we see in Anse Bleue is therefore also consistent with Brown's argument that, "in the Vodou understanding of personhood, the individual is given identity, solidity, and safety in a precarious world by a thick weave of relationships with other human beings as well as with spirits and ancestors. That the world is precarious is the core of the Vodou philosophy of life."[88] The precarious world inhabited by *Moonbath*'s characters is one in which they are submissive to the whims of nature, threatened by whichever political order is unfolding, and vulnerable to the will of people more dominant and powerful than they. That precarious nature of life is one of the most consistent features in Anse Bleue across the four generations we meet in the novel.

By experimenting with narration, Lahens negotiates the ethics of telling—how can we trust the dying woman's story? Who gets to tell their story, and how many stories do we need to know in order to understand the history of Anse Bleue? *Moonbath* opens with the main narrator, Cétoute Thérèse Florival, washed up on the shore.[89] As the first character and narrator the reader encounters, and the *only* first-person singular narrator, the initially unnamed protagonist's fusion with nature is noteworthy. The mystery behind her body commingled with nature, awash with seawater and covered in grains of sand, is critical to the structure and the development of the novel. In my view that fusion is far from what Marie-José Nzengou-Tayo refers to as the troubling "fusion/confusion between nature and women."[90] Rather it is a thoughtfully rendered representation of how a woman's embodied connection to the land can be both life-giving and death-inducing. As we learn later in *Moonbath*, Cétoute has a profound connection to and love for the sea, the very place where she meets her death; the novel refuses to equate intimacy with ease.

Through Cétoute, Lahens shifts our understanding of what the relationship between humans and nature looks like in Anse Bleue. The opening scene of Cétoute's body regurgitated by the sea is suspended in time and precedes all other events in the novel. The description of the woman's body that washes up on the shore situates her as entirely one with nature. Spat up from the ocean and covered in sand, she is described as "an apparition that emerged from the belly of the sea" as though she herself is a sea creature rather than a human being (158). When Cétoute begins to speak, her words are marked by uncertainty. She knows neither what happened to her nor where she is: "Something happened at dusk on the first day of the storm. Something that I still can't explain. Something that broke me. Even though my eyes are closed, nearly shut, and my left cheek is pushed right up against the wet sand, I still manage, and this gives me some relief, to look over this village built like Anse Bleue. The same narrow huts. All the doors and all the windows shut. The same leprous walls. On both sides of the same muddy road leading to the sea" (7). In this passage that introduces the narrator, we are immediately struck by her lack of awareness about her condition and circumstances. This ambiguity is highlighted by the repetition of "something," emphasizing the gravity of what has taken place. The sea serves as her only comfort in this ambiguity. Just as the feeling of the sand against her cheek connects her to the land of Anse Bleue, her sense of place stabilizes her in the midst of uncertainty.

Even her inability to convey a coherent message is framed by the effects of natural elements on her body: "I ramble like an old woman. I rant like a mad woman. My voice breaks at the back of my throat. It is because of the wind, the salt, the water" (9). Cétoute's confusion about what happened to her is a sign to the reader, a thread we must pursue that unravels as the novel progresses. Only toward the very end of *Moonbath* does the reader come to fully understand how this woman landed on the shore.[91] In the process, we encounter the people of Anse Bleue, a community made up of many characters whose relationships to nature and spirit inform how they interact with one another. When we consider "the narrative dimensions of ethics and the ethical dimensions of narrative," the fact that the first-person, female narrator's words always appear in italics within chapters that are distinct from the other stories in the book further privileges her voice and point of view.[92]

As readers, we align with her in our uncertainty about where she is, how she got there, and why she is there. She is a disturbing example of how humans are powerless before nature, wholly incapable of controlling their interactions with an environment that seems to challenge them at every turn. Cétoute illustrates the point that, as scholars of the environment have noted, "Caribbean writers refuse to depict the natural world in terms that erase the relationship between landscape and power."[93]

Locating the novel in the geographic setting of Anse Bleue allows Lahens to endow the land with physical properties that provide additional context for each character. Nature in *Moonbath* is in representations of the sea, the sand, the mountains, and the hurricane. As I have argued throughout this chapter, because spirit is nature, for each of these, Vodou operates as a constant point of reference. Vodou regulates how humans interact with the natural environment confirming scholarship that rightly emphasizes how religious practice is woven into almost every aspect of quotidian life. As Claudine Michel affirms, "Dans le Vodou, comme dans d'autres traditions africaines et non-occidentales, il y a une complète unité de la religion et de la vie de tous les jours, chaque aspect de l'existence d'une personne étant sacré" (In Vodou, as in other African and non-Western traditions, there is a complete balance between religion and daily life, with every aspect of a person's life being sacred).[94] What this means—and it should pique the interest of a Black feminist scholar—is that Vodou effectively dissolves binaries between the spiritual and the secular to embrace a spiritual logic that is always both/and.

Moonbath is about four generations of two feuding rural families—the Lafleurs and the Mésidors—who represent the haves, or the conquerors (*les vainqueurs*), and the have-nots, or the conquered (*les vaincus*). The family line is routed through Cétoute's grandmother, Olmène, who at fifteen years old is forced to marry Tertulien Mésidor. The novel tells the story of how their fates intertwine over the course of several decades from the period of the US occupation of Haiti (1915–34) to the present day in the early 2000s. Narrated in the voice of a female protagonist and a "nous collectif," *Moonbath* recounts the daily lives of a cast of characters from the fictional seaside village of Anse Bleue, located in the northern Artibonite region of Haiti, where devotion to Vodou, a need for the land, the machinations of political history, and the presence of the sea shape their lived experience.

A study of how the natural environment figures in *Moonbath* conveys a challenging and contentious relationship between people and nature in which nature usually triumphs, if not only because it is controlled by the spirits. For the people of Anse Bleue, what should be the "symbiotic relationship between man, nature, and the gods" is out of balance, upsetting the workings of the Vodou ethic.[95] Nature is an essential part of life for this town that is routinely subject to the whims of the environment. The name of the village itself is charged with a natural significance; translated into English as a cove, *anse bleue* is a name that conjures the physical properties of its geographic location. As a rural community, the people of Anse Bleue have a communal relationship with the natural world. Throughout the novel, the story of four generations of two rural families centers the land as an enduring and formidable enemy. In *Moonbath*, the land serves a function that is familial and viewed through the prism of legacy and heritage. But in every generation the land is also situated as a site of conflict and contention.

The Eye of the Caribbean Storm

Moonbath begins with a tropical storm that all but destroys Anse Bleue. From the outset, we notice the impact of natural disasters on the land and the people: "What a storm! What a tumult! Throughout this story, it will be important to pay attention to the wind, the salt, the water, not just the men and women. The sand was turned around and upside-down in the greatest disorder. Like land waiting to be sowed. Loko blew three days in a row and swallowed the sun. Three long days. The sky finally turned a lighter and lighter gray. Milky in places" (9). This description, which likens nature to a person invading the landscape, foreshadows nature's role in the novel. As a calamitous force, the hurricane tears apart both the land and the people. It is a reminder of St. Lucian poet Derek Walcott's invitation to "find the storm's swirling core, and understand."[96] Understanding the hurricane will give the people of Anse Bleue insight into what is happening to their community.

The hurricane is a recurrent literary motif that reflects environmental realities for all of the Caribbean region. Analysis of how hurricanes figure in Caribbean literature bring this dynamic into greater relief: "Since the ur-text of *The Tempest,* imagery of tropical storms has reverberated throughout representations of the Caribbean, not merely as thematic content and setting, but as plot, trope, noise, rhythm, syntax, diction, structure and geopoetics. If storms served throughout the imperialist imaginary as an intertextual, transhistorical metaphorics for rebellion, mutiny, and colonial insurgency, then in the post-colonial imaginary tempests, cyclones, hurricane and typhoons have been linked to insurrection, slave rebellions, labour unrest, general strikes, anticolonial liberation movements, nationalist movements, and socialist revolution. In real life, hurricanes disrupt space and time of the human everyday."[97] The disruption of space and time at work in *Moonbath* reinforces the dynamic in which the hurricane has multiple significations. Because the storm opens the novel at the same time that we discover the mystery of Cétoute's bruised and bloody body on the beach, we wonder how much of her condition is because of the storm. Hurricanes very often have disastrous outcomes that lead to flooding, loss of property, and death. As a metaphor for disaster, the hurricane confirms the powerlessness of people to conquer nature, which Lahens highlights in the passage above, using (in the original French) words of devastation like "tumulte" and "grand désordre." Living in a hurricane zone means having to pay steadfast attention to all of the elements of nature—the wind, the water, the salt, the ocean.

If the trees are the most central element of nature in *The Infamous Rosalie,* then in *Moonbath,* it is hurricanes that occupy this role, influencing the lives of the novel's characters at every turn. As metonym, the use of the hurricane reifies the charged relationship between humans and nature: "We were in July, the month when the heat announces the hurricanes. The first drops of rain, slow, thin, spaced out, tolled with regularity, like bare steps, and blended with the rattle of the snakes in the straw. Darkness had fallen and submerged us in its secrets, its strange creatures, its spells" (51). As the hurricane surges, the inhabitants of Anse Bleue feel incapable of facing its force: "The next day, the storm didn't let up. It rained three days in a row, as though it was a wall of water pushed by the mountains that imprisons us. Confinement in a vast liquid country" (52). Here the reference to "the mountains that imprison" facilitates a view of nature as the enemy of the people. Their "confinement" suggests that they are unable to escape from the land. Contrary to what we saw in *The Infamous Rosalie* where the mountains were signifiers of freedom's possibility, in *Moonbath,* they trap and contain the community, cutting the people off from the rest of the world.

In a passage narrated by Cétoute, her observation of the hurricane's power suggests that it can penetrate her entire body, reinforcing the idea of the helplessness of human beings in the face of relentless nature: "I'm in pain and I am exhausted. The dawn slowly dissolves the heavy clouds, somber and dark like mourning, which flooded the sky nearly three days ago. A very soft light finally veils the world. Reflections of pinkish mother-of-pearl, almost orange in places, brush my lacerated skin, my open wounds, and sink into me, to the bone" (116). The hurricanes repeatedly devastate the land, and their negative effects are felt far more harshly by people from the rural countryside. Those familiar with the Caribbean know already that July marks the beginning of a transition into the high hurricane season. The region of l'Artibonite where Anse Bleue is located was pummeled by a series of storms in the early 2000s. Most notably, in September 2004 thousands of people died in Gonaïves after the flooding that resulted from Hurricane Jeanne.[98] Hurricane season is reasonably marked by fear and ambiguity that underscores the precarity of Caribbean islands: "The country has entered a long season of mourning. For the political catastrophe embodied by the rise of the man in the Black hat with thick glasses, combined with the ravages of Flora, a devastating hurricane if ever there was one, which left us bled dry. I didn't stop thinking of my brothers and my sisters that this disaster touched: the peasants and the left-behind of cities. And to top it all off, now our vigilance must extend to beyond our borders, since the Yankees invaded the Dominican Republic" (119). By adding concerns about the environment to the challenging political situation—connecting political and environmental disasters—this passage invites the reader to consider the two jointly. Also, depicting the force of hurricanes as life-altering realities, Lahens shows the impact of the Caribbean climate on people who are most disenfranchised.

Nature and Power

Often this imagining of the land leads to what I am describing here as a contentious dialectic in which the land seems to be unremittingly against the people. Yet while for the people of Anse Bleue the land has an incredible influence on their daily lives and the larger directions they take, we also see that people can influence the land in small ways by appealing to the power of the spirits. Only by recognizing the spirits can they understand and have an effect on nature.

Networks of power, especially those in which the powerful dominate the powerless, calibrate the relationships that unfold in *Moonbath* and provide a fascinating parallel when viewed in relation to the environment. In one of the novel's first scenes, the tempestuous Tertulien Mésidor arrives in Anse Bleue and decides that he wants to claim fifteen-year-old Olmène for himself. From the outset, Tertulien Mésidor is an example of someone with power and class privilege who lords it over others in order to manipulate and oppress. The discrepancy between the power he possesses and the people he oppresses is immediately apparent to the community of Anse Bleue: "He belonged to the others—the victors, the rich, the conquerors—not to the conquered, the defeated, like her. Like us. Poor like salt, *maléré*, ill-fated" (12).

Noting these dialectics of power, the narrator describes them as a game. The Lafleurs are mere pawns of the dominant order ruled by more powerful families like the Mésidors: "A game that chained us all to the Mésidors and that shackled them to us despite themselves. A game that we, victors and captives, had mastered long ago. Very long ago. An ancient story entangled the Mésidors, the wind, the earth, the water, and us" (14). Yet, while Tertulien has a vicelike hold over the community based on his power and privilege, as the novel continues, we learn that nature can upend these power dynamics, and that, by appealing to the gods, the people can configure new ways of being in the communities they live in. This suggests in turn that the domination of people by human forces is not in fact eternal.

In *Moonbath*, the challenging relationship between humans and nature has a long history that dates back to refusal to serve the spirits. After all, and as Claudine Michel makes clear in her study on the educational and ethical aspects of Vodou: "La moralité pour ceux qui servent les loas représente donc un effort constant pour maintenir la cohésion sociale, l'harmonie et l'équilibre" (For those who serve the spirits morality is thus a constant effort to maintain social cohesion, harmony and balance).[99]

The tale of a land that obdurately betrays the people by not allowing them to live off of it takes shape in the lives of multiple characters across the generations. It is this dynamic we see at work when Léosthène returns from his life in diaspora and the community gathers to tell him what has occurred in his absence: "In front of Orvil and Ermancia's hut, each came to tell their story of the last fifteen years in just a few minutes. Births, deaths, and departures. The earth emptied of its blood, its flesh, brought to its knees, the stingy sea, the eradication of pigs, the death of crafts-men, the disease of the coffee, palms, and lemon trees, the clothes from elsewhere" (130). This parade of problems features several environmental crises that reflect a deeply rooted disconnect between humans and nature. The land's refusal to give, to be productive for the people of Anse Bleue is a problem that plagues the community.

By the time we reach Cétoute's generation, the final one described in *Moonbath,* her brother Abner concludes that they must make different choices about how to interact with the land: "You have to do something else, since the earth does not give as much, nor does the sea" (138). Abner's perspective is remarkable and evinces an environmental ethic that cherishes the land. It acknowledges the importance of the land as some-thing that is there to serve the people but also for them to care for. Like Cétoute's, Abner's relationship to the land reflects care, intimacy, and responsibility.

Difficulties with the land are also linked to departures for the people of Anse Bleue. When the land stops giving, characters like Orvil and his son Léosthène decide to leave. Their departures are marked by a desire to no longer be subject to nature's dominance. For Orvil that departure is inextricably linked to the spirit world: "He no longer had the strength to call the gods. Of this he was certain. He wanted to join them. Where they were. Be by their side. Fall asleep at their feet. Feel their hands on his wounds. Return to Guinée. To the early days of the sea. To the lights, the ones you can see in the *devant-jour,* those that you can't see in the storms at night, those in the hearts of the trees and plants, the pristine and intact light of the *bon ange,* the same, always, only" (142). Orvil's inability to compete with nature informs his decision to depart through death. Rather than by taking a journey to Port-au-Prince, he ventures to Ginen. It is important to note the sharp contrast between his attitude and that of Léosthène, who makes numerous attempts to leave. When he leaves for a second time, Léosthène realizes that he must first honor the spirits: "He told himself that it really was time for him to leave, but before doing so, he would honor all the spirits and the dead of the lakou" (137).

276 Looking for Other Worlds

Léosthène's choice to honor the ancestors and the spirits leads to a deep communion with the natural landscape. Alongside his mother and cousin, he performs a series of Vodou rituals.

> Cilianise, Ermancia, and Léosthène made salutations to the four directions, and gently moved their lips, eyes closed, candles in hand, to evoke the protective gods the Disappeared, and all the Invisibles of the family. It didn't take long for tears to trickle down our cheeks . . . A light fresh breeze worked through all of his pores, and his flesh and the earth became one. This wind that tormented the branches told us that they, like us, had resisted everything. Exposed to the dust of the seasons, to the corrosion of salt, to the passing of hurricanes, to the slow fermentation of vegetables, to the fury of men, to torrential rains. They had resisted everything. (138)

This moment when Léosthène honors his spiritual heritage by serving the spirits recalls Brown's point that in Vodou "the spirits and the ancestors—neither properly referred to as gods—. . . handle day to day problems and . . . if necessary mediate between the living and God."[100] The passage evokes a triad relationship among nature, people, and the gods in which the gods become facilitators for the human relationships to nature; that is, the spirits act as mediators between the people and the land.

What interests me here is that Léosthène only decides to serve the spirits *because* he is leaving Anse Bleue. As Kyrah Daniels has smartly observed, there is a connection between departure and a return to Vodou that results from ritual anxiety produced by migration. According to Daniels, "as the process of urbanization continues to increase, Haitian families' ritual anxiety grows as to whether the spirits will be well-taken care of in the busy new rhythm of town—whether the ancestors will be remembered in the fast-moving city. Indeed, as M. Jacqui Alexander has stated, 'the result of moving away from . . . [the spiritual] center is imbalance.'"[101] When people leave the rural areas for urban centers, they fear losing the protection of their ancestors and the practice of their faith. This is because, as we saw in Kasalé, Vodou is firmly anchored in place. It is, as Leslie Desmangles notes, "about the earth." Léosthène's experience as he again leaves Anse Bleue further establishes his connection to the land. Looking back, he sees his hometown clearly: "It was a beautiful day. Léosthène, taking in the view of his childhood, turned his back for a moment to the wounds of the earth, to its deep scars, and looked at Anse Bleue bathed in liquid light, the sky and the water spreading as far as the eye could see. Each wave that was sinking, frothing on the sand, would die in a shining net of water. The birds brushed against the crests of the waves, came out of the sea, and took flight over the weary sky" (139). Léosthène appreciates the land in its beauty even though he blames it as the reason he must depart, suggesting the same kind of duality that we saw at work in *The Infamous Rosalie*. He is grateful for the land but recognizes his impotence in the face of its dominance. Although a supernatural experience precedes this moment of appreciation, he nonetheless chooses the path of urban migration.

Lahens's environmental vision in *Moonbath* resonates with ecocritics who urge literary scholars not to "reinforce the impression that attentive representation of environmental detail is of minor importance even in writing where the environment figures importantly as an issue."[102] In its attentive representation of environmental detail, *Moonbath* persists in revealing a Vodou ethic in which every aspect of nature has a spiritual significance. The characters' relationship to the national religion divulges how Vodou operates as an ethic; in fact, the environmental ethic at work *is* a Vodou ethic. According to these principles, "the appearance of the gods depends upon their involvement in a social world: the spirits respond to the demands of quite specific sociopolitical situations."[103] Thus relationships with nature become an omnipresent and paramount force in the lives of *Moonbath's* characters. Nature dictates their comings and goings, as we saw with Léosthène. The nonhuman environment shapes the patterns of their lives, as we saw with Cétoute. And nature even determines how and when they die, as we saw with Orvil.

"Water Is the First Thing in My Memory . . ."

In *A Map to the Door of No Return*, Dionne Brand writes, "Water is the first thing in my imagination . . . Water is the first thing in my memory. The sea sounded like a thousand secrets, all whispered at the same time."[104] The same can be said of *Moonbath's* Cétoute, the only first-person narrator in the novel, whose relationship to nature is of particular relevance to my analyses. Cétoute relates to the land as an active listener and a woman prepared to hear the secrets the island wants to share with her. Her unfolding story also demonstrates the influence of the lwa on the land, underscoring how religion and oral tradition relate to the environment. Initially present as an unnamed narrator, Cétoute continually connects her body and nature, using natural elements as her points of reference: "No matter what, in this story, you have to pay attention to the wind, its saline breath on our lips, the moon, the sea, Olmène absent . . . The earth that doesn't give anymore. The stingy sea" (32).

Cétoute's intimacy with the ocean begins long before she is trapped in it and dies. In the passage below, she explains that the bond begins from an early age during her childhood:

> With Altagrâce, my sister, Éliphète, my brother, this fondness for water began very early. Between the work in the house and the work in the fields, we try to swim by imitating the frantic movements of dogs treading in the water. We knead the sand in our hands to make gray bread, mud huts. Even when our fingers are numb and we chatter our teeth, we still demand the spectacles of sparks and mirrors from the sea. Often, we lay out on the sand, the sea licks our feet and we laugh with rainbows in our eyes and large birds perched on our hands. In the evening, we fall asleep, body, face, and hands frosted with salt. (152)

Cétoute delights in the ocean. She is like the woman Dionne Brand describes in *A Map to the Door of No Return* quoted above, for whom "water is the first thing in [her] memory. The sea sounded like a thousand secrets, all whispered at the same time."[105] Explaining her affinity for the sea, Cétoute relates it to her mother's example: she is captivated by the ocean because it is what she learned from her, and her relationship to it is one of particular intimacy and proximity. From her careful descriptions of what it looks like ("The sea shines. Each wave like so many mirrors shaking softly under the moon") to her invocation of what the sea means to her, to a connection between the sea and her maternal heritage, what we see at work here is a longstanding and robust rapport (113). The ocean is energetic and active in this passage: it moves, licks, and holds. The novel's title, *Moonbath* (*Bain de lune*), is an explicit reference to intimate walks under the moon, often with her brother Abner, when they would watch the ocean bask in the moon's light: "Abner is much bigger than any of us. He is the only one to accompany me in the night. To take these moon baths with me. To taste the wild beauty, the violent mystery of the night" (152). Cétoute's intimate communion with the ocean recalls Omi'seke Natasha Tinsley's gracefully rendered analysis in her essay "Black Atlantic, Queer Atlantic," a shining example of ingenious Caribbean ecocriticism. Tinsley writes that "literary texts turn to ocean waters themselves as an archive, an ever-present, ever-reformulating record of the unimaginable."[106] For Cétoute the water is an archive that holds her mother's memory, as well as a site of freedom that eventually leads, ironically and tragically, to her death. Her relationship to the ocean is spiritually evocative and affirms M. Jacqui Alexander's point that "Water overflows with memory . . . Emotional memory. Bodily memory. Sacred memory."[107]

Holding her body, her memories, and her sacred communing with her ancestor Olmène, the water laps over and around Cétoute. Of course, following the logic of the relationship to nature that most people in Anse Bleue have, it is unsurprising that even what was once a safe natural space for her eventually leads to her death.

Mache ansanm in Anse Bleue

To even begin to understand Anse Bleue and the four generations of families whose stories it tells, we must first understand the landscape, the physical properties of a land that is as much a part of the community as the member of their own families. For every character in *Moonbath,* the relationship to the land is mediated by the spirit world; the land and gods operate in union in a mutually interdependent relationship, thus endowing the landscape with spiritual qualities. As Philomène's father tells him, "There up high in the *dokos* where the spirit of the *Ancêtres marrons* still blew. 'The land, my son, it's your blood, your flesh, your bones, you hear me!'" (16). Their characters' relationships to the spirits exemplify how "Haitian subjectivities are consistently enlarged and relational as the *lwa mache avek nou* (spirits walk with us/you all)," as Mario Lamothe, Erin Durban-Albrecht, and Dasha Chapman point out in their performance-studies-based readings of Vodou.[108]

In *Moonbath,* the intimacy with the land is specifically named and amplified because of Vodou. The Vodou cosmology that relies on the land as its foundation is present in actual ceremonies that occur in the community, as well as in passing references to the spirits as a part of daily life. Taken together, the dual importance of Vodou and the land dismantles any false dichotomy between the natural and spiritual worlds in the same way we observed in *Kasalé,* although with a more fraught backdrop. Whereas in *Kasalé* Antoinette is able to achieve that sacred balance, the characters in *Moonbath* never do, and so in a real sense the network of relationships places spirit and nature above humanity.

The abiding knowledge of how the spirits are relevant to their daily lives is explained in the following terms by Cétoute's father Dieudonné when he is still a child and becomes a new initiate to Vodou: "he knew that the Invisibles, the *lwas,* are greater than life, but not different from life. And that's because they live out their own dramas, they are so close to us. They are thirsty and hungry, even more than we are, and we have to feed them. They are the mirror to the present and the star to guide us toward our future" (126). Dieudonné's newfound sacred knowledge provides him with an understanding of how humans and spirits interact. His observation also exalts a Vodou ethic of interdependence and mutuality that resonates with how Black feminists understand the importance of other forms of knowledge that influence daily life.

Only in the final paragraphs of the novel do we see that there might be a more hopeful future for the Lafleurs, and this is because Cétoute transitions to be with the spirits: "When, after forty days, they take me out of the water, I shall at last turn my eyes toward the light, and it will be, for my people, the beginning of a companionship with them. My death will no longer be a torment. I will bandage their wounds. I will sweeten the bitterness. I will intercede with the lwas, the Invisibles" (190). Disclosing her intention to walk with the generations to come, Cétoute conveys another sense of nou mache ansanm which, according to Chapman, Lamothe, and Durban-Albrecht also serves as a form of protection in the spiritual realm: "*Mache ansanm* can also be interpreted as a practical strategy for protection, collectively claiming and occupying space."[109] Determined to intercede with the lwas, Cétoute plans to walk with the people of Anse Bleue after her death. She will become a part of the ancestral legacies guiding her descendants. Even as she dies, Cétoute is concerned with those she is leaving behind, displaying a sense of collective responsibility for her people. *Moonbath* thus ends on a final note of possibility—by joining the spirits, Cétoute will ensure a better future for the generations to follow.

Le nous collectif

Lahens's use of distinct narrative voices, one of which is present only in italics, can be analyzed through the lens of literary ethics because through each narrator she stages a different kind of encounter with the reader. Each of these encounters then invites the reader to ask a different set of questions about how Vodou and the environment figure in the novel. The novel presents a third-person narrator who recounts most of the story, a first-person plural *nous* that surfaces throughout the novel, and finally our first-person narrator, Cétoute, the granddaughter of Olmène and Tertulien, who bears her grandmother's name and regrets never having met her while she was alive.

Robert Sapp has argued that Lahens deploys these different voices to highlight the cyclical nature of Haitian history. He contends that the "narrative voices and the formal division between *je* and *nous* within the novel call into question conventional wisdom on the narrative capacity of the recently departed but also, and perhaps more importantly, illustrate the novel's active engagement with the past, as *Moonbath* undermines traditional distinctions of past, present, and future."[110] Sapp goes on to argue that these voices "offer a historical matrix that allows the novel to uncover Haiti's history in a way that challenges traditional historiographical practices."[111]

To this I add that, in its insistence on this recently dead woman's voice, *Moonbath* takes a Black feminist position vis-à-vis history. The story begins with gendered violence as its point of departure—when the mutilated body of Cétoute Florival washes up on the shores of the village. In my view, the purpose of these dual narrative voices has to do with an ethical narrative style that is tethered to the land. That is to say, every time the characters speak of, invoke, or describe the land, an environmental ethic emerges that holds it in higher esteem than they hold one another. Some read *Moonbath* as a novel in which Yanick Lahens "shifts away from Haiti's role in a larger world to examine the importance of history for individual Haitians," but it should be noted that this is a gendered and feminist history that decries violence against Black women and amplifies the perspectives and position of its female protagonists, beginning with Olmène and ending with Cétoute.[112]

Reading the novel from an ecocritical perspective reveals how the ancestral spirits govern nature, which in turn has longstanding effects on the community, generation after generation. As Lahens engages "the enduring capacity of literature to grapple with the complicated and ever-evolving relationships between humans and the nonhuman environment," she does so with a Vodou ethic at the center.[113] What *Moonbath* seems also to suggest is that, when nature is not compliant with human aspirations, individuals are forced to question their relationship to the environment with greater care. The people of Anse Bleue are eternally subject to the whims of nature. Being forced to live one's life according to nature's capricious ebbs and flows also serves as a reminder of the enormity of the spiritual world and humankind's inability to overpower it.

When the lwa Gédé appears to deliver a revelatory message about life, he reinforces truths about Vodou philosophy that are intended to give the people a renewed perspective on their lived experience: "As though to remind us that between life and death everything happens very fast. Very fast. Pleasures faster than misfortunes, but everything passes. And that we need to take everything, pleasure and dread, suffering and bliss. The joys and the sorrows. All of it. Because life and death hold hands. Because death and pleasure are sisters" (69). Gédé reminds the people of Anse Bleue that there is a time for everything. Joy, suffering, pleasure, and pain are all parts of life for them to accept. Gédé's intervention articulates Brown's salient point that "Vodou spirits are larger than life *but not other than life*. Virtue for both the lwa and those who serve them is less an inherent character trait than a dynamic state of being that demands ongoing attention and care. Virtue is achieved by maintaining responsible relationships, relations characterized by appropriate gifts of tangibles and intangibles . . . Moral persons are those who give what they should, as defined by who they are."[114] Another manifestation of this intimate relationship between the land, humans, and gods is how an understanding of their relatedness transfers from one generation to the next. Before she leaves Anse Bleue for good, Olmène spends the night with her parents, and her mother passes down vital information to her daughter: "Ermancia reminded her of all the lessons of life, men, women, of the earth, of the gods" (96). The litany of lessons emphasizes the fusion of land, gods, and human life.

Who Will Fight for the Land?

In concluding this section on *Moonbath,* I want to consider the question posed by Père Bonin, the local Catholic priest in Anse Bleue, about who has responsibility to care for the land. When he asks ominously, "And the land, tell me, who is going to fight for her?" his question is a powerful indictment (98). The idea that the land requires an advocate espouses an environmental ethic holding human beings responsible for what happens to it. The directive is not only to take care of the land but to fight for it, to stand up for it. Père Bonin goes on to curse the people because of what he perceives as their lackadaisical and often reckless relationship to the land: "So, I am going to tell you, I am, what will happen to you: the night will no longer give way to day, the plants will soon become stones, that's right. The fish will only be memories in your dry nets. And your animals will no longer reproduce. That will be the will of God" (100). The priest articulates his curse in terms of nature, especially as it relates to people's needs for survival, and, in this, his Catholic worldview contrasts with how Vodou encourages communion between nature and humans in service of the spirits. In Vodou, what appears to be the land's contempt for the people should not diminish their desire to cultivate it; rather they must seek balance. As Lizabeth Paravisini-Gebert points out, Vodou epistemologies frame spiritual maturity in relation to the natural world, "the belief in Vodou that spiritual maturity rests on the understanding of the necessary balance between cosmic forces and the natural world."[115] This daily balanced interaction with the physical landscape is transformative, formative, and spiritual even while it is profoundly challenging and often contentious.

After *Bain de lune* won the prestigious Prix Fémina in 2012, the Haitian newspaper *Le Nouvelliste* featured an essay describing Lahens's authorial presence in moral terms: "[Yanick Lahens] est là-dedans au cœur des faits non-pas comme une ingénue encore moins une moraliste. Elle y vit. Yanick Lahens est comme ce témoin vérace qui ne met pas la puce à l'oreille. Elle vit dans tous les compartiments du roman, partage la joie et le chagrin de ses personnages. Comprend aussi les difficultés auxquelles ils se heurtent" (Yanick Lahens is there in the heart of the facts not as an innocent, and even less as a moralist. She lives there. Yanick Lahens is like this veracious witness who does not shy away from anything. She lives in every segment of the novel, shares the joy and sorrow of her characters. She also understands the difficulties they face).[116]

In her depictions of the land, Lahens calls attention to structural power dynamics, the forces of religion, and the vicissitudes of community for how they shape and are shaped by the environment. What emerges is an environmental ethic attentive to the environment's impact on individual lives and the emotional and spiritual choices people make as a result. By endowing the land with a metaphysical significance informed by serving the spirits, Lahens urges the reader to contemplate the inner workings of nature in a much broader context that is deeply rooted in a Vodou ethic.

The Environment as Text

The Infamous Rosalie, *Kasalé*, and *Moonbath*, lend themselves to ecocritical readings because of how they showcase the environment and the characters' relationships to the environment in ways that probe our own ethical imaginations. My readings of how the environment figures in these novels unpack how the landscape operates as a text in three discreet time periods. History is central to the stories elaborated in each novel, although it does not always take center stage. The recurring thread in Mars's, Lahens's, and Trouillot's representations of the environment is that nature influences human activity in intimate and intricate ways that have direct consequences in the lived experience of female characters. In each of these novels, a sense of place leads to variegated relationships to nature. Whether it is for the enslaved woman who becomes a Maroon and flees into the forest, the aging *Vodouizan* who understands that her life will soon end because the great cachiman tree has fallen, or the murdered woman who washes up on the shores covered in sand and ocean water and reflects on her life while dying, the protagonists in these novels understand their relationship to the place they belong to in environmental terms of proximity and intimacy. *The Infamous Rosalie, Moonbath,* and *Kasalé* espouse an environmental ethic that is deeply planted in the local and anchored in Vodou.

Examining the role of the environment in these novels amplifies our understanding of place as Black women experience and inhabit it. In her study *Oshun's Daughters: The Search for Womanhood in the Americas,* Vanessa Valdés argues that African diasporic religions offer "alternative models of womanhood that differ substantially from those found in dominant Western patriarchal culture."[117] The Black feminist ethic I track in these novels is articulated by Lisette, Antoinette, and Cétoute, Black women heroines who relate to the environment as sacred ground for them to attend to and be tended by. Their specific articulation that spirit is nature and nature is spirit can be identified as an environmental ethic embracing Vodou and Black feminism. The Black feminist ethic at work in these renderings of Haitian landscapes and seascapes emphasizes the spiritual role of the environment in the ethical imagination. A Black feminist ethic that privileges Vodou also affirms the connection between the individual and the collective and understands that religion functions as a crucial location of identity.

When we see the environment as central rather than marginal, the intimacy that informs how humans interact with nature and nature with humans comes sharply into focus. Trouillot, Mars, and Lahens develop environmental poetics that insist on the proximity of humans and nature, highlighting their interdependence. Their novels illumine how people interact with land and sea in ways that are ethically diverse and that challenge the reader to look more deeply into how we understand the relationship between humans and the natural environment by accounting for how that rapport is influenced by history, religion, and genealogy. In *The Infamous Rosalie, Kasalé,* and *Moonbath* the authors delineate an environmental ethic in which care of nature, attention to its history, and a destabilization of the hierarchies between humans and nature are increasingly possible. Here the environment situates the characters in space even while it suggests the possibility of a different relationship to nature and a destabilization of the hierarchies between humans and nature; thus, they reimagine ethics in relation to the environment, creating an ecoethical poetics and politics.

In my attempt to investigate how these authors elaborate an environmental vision that is rooted in a Black feminist ethic, I have also outlined their distinct ecoethics, which foreground care of the environment. Care of the environment means honoring it, tending to it, and understanding that the role of humans is not simply to dominate it. It is the search for balance lovingly articulated in Vodou. If ethics does indeed represent "continual questioning from below," as I posited in chapter 1, then an environmental ethic must question relationships and encounters between people, nature, and spirits in order to generate new ways of knowing and looking for other worlds.[118] I began this chapter with the work of Mafalda Mondestin, whose series of paintings *When the Island Keeps All the Secrets* foregrounds a relationship between humans and nature that is complicated by history and informed by culture. Mars, Lahens, and Trouillot depict the environment in highly visual terms that resonate with Mondestin's project. Replete with the stories and secrets of history that artists probe in order to facilitate ethical encounters, the environment provokes, reifies, and inspires. Whether those encounters occur for protagonists, minor characters, readers, or the artist themselves, they call for ethical attention to a landscape that seeks recognition, respect, and proper naming.

Coda

A More Just and More Beautiful World

Considérant que le féminisme est un art de vivre, qui accorde donc énormément d'importance au cheminement, les féministes continuent à s'engager, à renforcer leurs organisations, à se concerter à investiguer les moyens de gagner une masse critique à la cause défendue par ce mouvement d'émancipation pour l'avancement de toute la société.

(Considering that feminism is an art of life, which therefore attaches a great deal of importance to progress, feminists continue to commit themselves, to strengthen their organizations, to work together to investigate the means of gaining a critical mass for the cause defended by this emancipation movement for the advancement of all of society.)

—Danièle Magloire

Black women certainly are at the center of my stories. I think part of this is from my personal experience of growing up with women who are very powerful—to me—but very vulnerable in their society . . .

—Edwidge Danticat

I believe in Black feminist futures.

—Fania Noel

IN A rousing essay about the global power dynamics driving translation, Évelyne Trouillot eloquently captures the essence of what I have referred to throughout this book as the Black feminist impulse to "look for other worlds." Trouillot writes, "And my writings, stemming from my lived experience and my aesthetic and *social vision for a more beautiful and just world,* are presented to readers who are not always acquainted with my reality."[1] There are three parts to her statement that relate to my arguments here. First, her writings stem from her *lived experience.* A hallmark of Black feminist thought, the idea that Black women's lived experience deserves to be centered as a point of departure for cultural expression highlights positionality. Recalling that "womanist ethics" seek to derive ethical claims from the lived experience of Black women represented in literary texts, we can also infer that when Trouillot cites positionality she is connecting it to the ethical imagination. Second, her writings also stem from her aesthetic *and* social vision for a more beautiful and just world. This vision, articulated in both form and content, conveys the principle of Black feminism as an action-oriented social justice project invested in acts of the imagination. Third, Trouillot's vision for a "more beautiful" and "more just" world is accompanied by a sense of the responsibility she carries as an author who inevitably will also communicate with those to whom her world is unfamiliar. This final point foregrounds an ethical stance that excogitates what encounters with her writing will yield for others. It also speaks to the act of writing as a form of encounter for the author, her characters, and her readers. If I am drawn to Trouillot's words to conclude this book, it is because throughout this study I have turned to "encounter" and "responsibility" as key words in the elaboration of a Black feminist ethic, and I believe that these encounters, this acquired knowledge, should ultimately lead to action.

I began this book with a question: What if we were to reorient our study of Haitian literature toward ethics, and what if those ethics were anchored in Black feminism? Guided by what I discerned as "a Black feminist ethic" in the works of Yanick Lahens, Kettly Mars, and Évelyne Trouillot, my readings were informed by a methodology inspired by literary ethics, informed by Haitian culture, and ingrained in Black feminist criticism. I argued that "a Black feminist ethic" is created by forging a conceptual connection among encounter, relation, recognition, and reframing all through an intersectional lens. Each writer asks us to summon our own imaginations and open our minds to pose ethical questions about how the lived experience of ordinary Haitian people is shaped by race, class, gender, sexuality, religion, and more.

By reading these novels intersectionally, I have also recognized a vision that attends to the interimbrications of multiple oppressions while also imagining a world in which more justice and more beauty are indeed possible. By "looking for other worlds," the authors challenge us as readers to view their works through the ethical lens of Black feminist principles precisely because, as Farah Jasmine Griffin emphatically notes, "Black feminism has never been only about Black women . . . It's always been about a more just world."[2] Literary ethicists have argued convincingly that "by learning a story we are introduced to another world"; in this light, the worlds that Mars, Lahens, and Trouillot create ask their readers to look for other worlds in much the same way as their characters are doing.[3] As I conclude this book, I am ever more convinced of the directive to look, to look again, to look elsewhere, to look for more, and to look otherwise, because it is what I have learned from these authors and because it is only by looking that we can begin the transformation of building a better world.

The goal of my inquiry was to reconceptualize, rethink, and reframe rather than to offer conclusive tautologies or taxonomies because these would be antithetical to the dynamic framework of Black feminism, which tells us to resist totalizing portraits of womanhood and gender identity. Thus, I have paid attention to the multiple ways that ethics, Black feminism, and Haitian literature intersect with and illuminate one another. Along the way, I discovered that, like the polyphonic voices that characterize its aesthetic, a Black feminist ethic has multiple manifestations. It is an ethic of survival that rises in the life of an enslaved woman determined that her child "be born free or not at all." It is an ethic of self-determination that allows an elderly woman to refuse to capitulate to the will of others and instead to claim her own geography, or a dying woman's capacity to envision how her ritual practice will live beyond her. It is an ethic of refusal that rejects a rich man's desire to objectify and ensnare a young woman with far less privilege than he. It is an ethic of the erotic in which a rape survivor rediscovers pleasure, play, and agency in sex. It is an ethic of self-making that leads a young woman to imagine a future in which her social position does not determine her fate. It is an environmental ethic that embraces water as memory and answers the call of the forest. It is an ethic of encounter that causes people of different classes to collide in order to recognize one another's humanity. Ultimately, it is an ethic of possibility because of which the world and Black women's social configurations can be imagined otherwise—more beautiful and more just. The idea of possibility affirms that if a Black feminist ethic is the framework of this book, it is certainly a dynamic and open system that asks for engagement.

A final instructive—if contradictory—example surfaces in Kettly Mars's novel *Aux frontières de la soif* (2013), a provocative depiction of post-earthquake Haiti. Frankly, I was ambivalent about including this novel in these pages because it troubled me more than I thought my critical lens could accommodate. I am not the first literary critic to find a novel by Kettly Mars disturbing. In fact, the author's provocative protagonists and unresolved conclusions have regularly frustrated scholars of Haitian literature. Engagement in Mars's oeuvre forces the reader to confront thorny questions about the intersections of sex, power, and ethics. To me, Fito Belmar, the protagonist of *Aux frontières de la soif,* is a particularly repugnant manifestation of Mars's problematic protagonists.[4] It was my disdain for Fito that almost drove me away from *Aux frontières de la soif.* The novel tells the story of Belmar, who was once a best-selling and award-winning author. But Fito now suffers from extreme writer's block and has not written in five years. He is also an older man who preys on young girls, and the loss of his libido is disturbingly associated with his sexual predation and pedophilia.[5] Fito's internal angst and constant interrogation of why his sexual proclivities exist are on display especially because they connect to his craft. His inability to write, which he refers to as a writing "blocus" mirrors a sexual "blocus." Fito is unable to be sexually aroused by women; he is only attracted to girls. As the novel progresses, these sexual dynamics become increasingly intense and insidious; Fito processes his downward spiral, and the reader must suffer through his sexual predation.

My investment in a Black feminist ethic of care initially led me away from *Aux frontières de la soif.* Something about the novel unsettled me; it seemed to contradict the ethic that I also wanted to model and champion in my critical praxis. In my view, this novel was nothing more than a grisly tale demonstrating a complete lack of regard for and care of the most vulnerable Haitians in the aftermath of the earthquake—poor Black girls living in tent cities. But when I returned to my central question about what kind of ethic emerges from this text, and how a Black feminist ethic might help us to make sense of it, I began to read the novel through a lens of reframing, relation, encounter, and questioning from below. I realized that if a Black feminist ethic is to function as a method and a framework, then it should accommodate the diversity of African diasporic expressive culture.

We can see how the context of post-earthquake Haiti evokes myriad ethical tensions. By creating a protagonist who is a perpetrator and a producer of post-earthquake fiction, Kettly Mars adds new kinds of predators to the cadre of post-earthquake NGOs, aid workers, and UN soldiers who descended upon Port-au-Prince (too often to the city's detriment) in the aftermath of the earthquake. Many of these representations jettison the real first responders of the crisis who were local—Haitian neighbors simply helping one another. Like the NGO workers who frequent the bars, restaurants, and clubs in Pétion-Ville after the earthquake, Fito consumes Haiti for his pleasure, then mines it for his productivity (and eventual prosperity). The novel also tells of the camps where he rapes six little girls. This results in a glaring ethical failure: the protagonist's appetite for underage girls paired with his soul-searching as a central aspect of the plot.

An analysis of the title puts Fito's desire for young girls at the center. *Aux frontières de la soif:* On the borders of thirst. Fito's unquenchable thirst sucks life out of young Haitian girls, who, living in camps for the displaced and exploited into becoming sex workers, are already pushed to the margins. His meanderings around the city after the earthquake are primarily motivated by his pedophilic desire for these little girls. An insatiable sexual predator who experiences sexual dysfunction unless he is sleeping with girls, Fito repeatedly blurs ethical lines and makes harmful decisions that impact those who are most vulnerable in the society. A consideration of ethics alone vexes the thoughtful reader of *Aux frontières de la soif.* But a Black feminist ethic asks that we consider how and why Mars purposefully unsettles the reader. Better still, why does *Aux frontières de la soif* frustrate the Black feminist reader? My questioning from below led me to ask about the girls, to look for what they say and what they see. Espousing a Black feminist ethic means grappling with the novel's ethical challenges and attempting to see otherwise.

Note, for example, that *Aux frontières de la soif* is dedicated to survivors of the earthquake.[6] While many authors of post-earthquake texts have used the space of dedication to honor those who died, Mars purposefully chooses to *honor the living.* Naming the critical role that writers play in processing natural disaster, she writes: "January 12th taught me once again about the power of the written word. Haitian authors and intellectuals were the first ones, before the government, to express themselves after the earthquake."[7] At the same time, Mars has also publicly noted her reluctance to pen a "post-earthquake" novel. Explaining her ambivalence, she expressed that "following the earthquake, she had vowed to herself that she would not write a novel about the earthquake, because that is what was expected of all writers."[8] This perspective shifted after seeing Camp Canaan (in Kreyòl Camp Kanaran), which inspired her to write *Aux frontières de la soif.* But "her interest in the novel . . . is not the facts and figures of the disaster, nor even the dead, but the *lives of those who live* with the disaster, across divides of class, color, and gender."[9] The reference to class, color, and gender is significant—*Aux frontières de la soif* insists on an intersectional approach to exploring post-earthquake problems. The novel is influenced and complicated by the multiplicative experiences of race, class, and gender in the lives of her characters.

For much of the novel, the stories of Haitian girls figure marginally in the textual space. Girls are present physically, conceptually, and figuratively throughout, but it is ultimately Fito's story, and the girls' voices, perspectives, and stories are far less present than his. As Alessandra Benedicty-Kokken sees it, "the other voices [in the novel] serve as subportraits that frame, reframe, and recast the principal male character."[10] In my view these other voices are essential to the novel's plot, even though they are mostly absent from its development. But *the girls are there* nonetheless. Their presence recalls the Haitian proverb that Edwidge Danticat uses in an essay—and translates as the title—describing the conditions of disadvantaged Haitian women: "nou lèd, nou la."[11] We are ugly, but we are here. Explaining the title further, Danticat writes, "Watching the news reports, it is often hard to tell whether there are real living and breathing women in conflict-stricken places like Haiti. The evening news broadcasts only allow us a brief glimpse of presidential coups, rejected boat people, and sabotaged elections. The women's stories never manage to make the front page. However, they do exist."[12] Reading *Aux frontières de la soif* solely from Fito's perspective, one wonders whether the girls he uses are in fact living and breathing. Even scholars analyzing the novel focus exclusively on Fito, just barely considering the young Haitian girls who are the victims of his sexual offenses, confirming that readings placing Black girls at the center are few.[13] What I pondered in my rereading of *Aux frontières de la soif* was how, if at all, does Mars account for the girls as more than the objects of Fito's pedophilia or signs of his deviance? I went looking for the girls and located a Black feminist ethic of encounter, reframing, and relation that I had not noticed before.

Each of the girls in *Aux frontières de la soif* exists at the margins of society (and of the novel). These girls are victims of the same unjust system that *Le Rond-point's* Dominique describes, "an unequal world, where the poor run on legs that are too short and will never catch up to the elite." (152). They are young girls forced into prostitution by the conditions of post-earthquake life. As impoverished girls living in IDP camps, they are vulnerable and unprotected. They are victims first of poverty, then of the earthquake, then again of sexual exploitation.

When the novel begins, we notice immediately that Fito exploits the girls' vulnerability. The first girl is introduced through a description in which her youth and her fear are palpable: "Elle portait un shorts en jeans à l'ourlet effiloché, et un tee-shirt rose sans manches. A la place des seins, deux bourgeons se devinaient, durs, tendus de peur" (She was wearing jean shorts that were frayed at the hem, and a sleeveless pink T-shirt. Instead of breasts, two buds could be seen, hard and tensed with fear) (20). The child's fear is unmistakably embodied in her prepubescent body.

Mars repeatedly notes the youth of each girl: "Ketia avait douze ans mais en paraissait moins. Elle n'allait plus à l'école depuis le séisme" (Ketia was twelve years old but looked younger. She no longer went to school since the earthquake) (114). Although the girls are initially written into the novel from Fito's perspective, eventually we begin to hear their voices and become privy to their interiority. As I have noted throughout this study, interiority is essential to understanding how Haitian women and girls look for other worlds. The chapters narrated by the girls are always short, fleeting even, but haunting in their presence. While the girls' narratives appear to be marginal to the elaboration of the novel, assembling the traces of their stories unveils much about who they are as a collective.

Mars purposefully names the girls as individuals—Louloune, Ketia, Fabiola, Medjine, Esther, Rosemé, and Mirline. Each one has a story, told from *her* perspective, about how she arrives at Canaan. When the girls are present through narration, they often speak in the first person. Take, for example how Mirline fearfully anticipates being sent into the tent:

Ce soir, ils vont m'envoyer sous la tente, je le sais, je le sens. Ma tante ne m'a rien dit mais je l'ai vue parler au monsieur qu'on appelle Golème . . . Yasmine, qui habite de l'autre côté du camp . . . elle est allée sous la tente l'autre soir, pour la première fois. Elle ne veut pas m'en parler elle pleurait en cachette vers les latrines. Je sais qu'elle avait mal. *Nous les filles, on a toutes peur d'aller sous la tente.*

(Tonight, they'll send me to the tent, I know it, I feel it. My aunt did not tell me anything, but I saw her talking to the man called Golème . . . Yasmine, who lives on the other side of the camp . . . she went to the tent the other night, for the first time. She does not want to tell me about it, she was crying secretly near the latrine. I know she was in pain. *We girls, we are all afraid to go to the tent.*) (86, my emphasis)

The last sentence in this passage—"We girls, we are all afraid to go to the tent"—calls attention to the girls' unanimity. They are all afraid, yet powerless in the face of their fear. By devoting some part of her novel to these girls' perspectives, Mars asks the reader to imagine their precarious situation and their vulnerability on their own terms. The short chapters interspersed throughout *Aux frontières de la soif* show that these young girls share a story of victimization, violation, and vulnerability. They are legible only as vulnerable victims of violation until a point about ten pages from the end of the book, when we meet Medjine, whose story throws into question the narrative of victimization and asks us to see these girls *otherwise.* The last girl we encounter, Medjine, reveals her self-awareness in several ways. For one thing, she lies to Golème about her age, realizing that pretending to be younger will be advantageous: "Medjine had lied to Golème because in this month of January 2011, she was fourteen years old as opposed to twelve years which she pretended to be. Golème was her only chance. He was looking for young girls and did not want anyone older than twelve" (151). Here the transactional nature of their relationship is brought into stark relief for the reader who had not imagined how the girls participate in these circumstances. Finally, at the end of her chapter, when we learn that Medjine works with Golème so that she can help to provide for her nephew and that she aspires to become a midwife, there is a shift to the kind of life that she imagines possible for herself. Despite what surrounds her, she dreams of a different future. Medjine cultivates possibility in her imagination. She is looking for another world despite her present predicament.

My analysis of *Aux frontières de la soif* is invested in a reading practice whereby even the most marginalized Haitian girls emerge as focal points, through which they occupy their own space. It is a reading that also demands what Black feminist scholar Jasmine Johnson calls a practice of *complicated care,* because these girls are surrounded by desolation.[14] What does it mean for these girls to not have visibility? To whom are they visible? How do we unwittingly perpetuate invisibility in our criticism?[15] *Aux frontières de la soif* leaves readers with difficult and unresolved questions that Mars purposefully leaves unanswered as part of her ethical project. Benedicty-Kokken generously posits that "Mars's narratives force the reader to accompany the characters in their trajectories, without judging them," but as a reader I myself was less compelled to follow that path.[16] Through my lens of complicated care, what appeared upon first reading to be a graphic and gratuitous portrayal of the excesses of a pedophilic protagonist, in fact, exists alongside a story of Haitian girls' precarity and vulnerability in post-earthquake tent cities. Focusing on the girls does not erase Fito from the story or obscure his predation; rather, it asks that the reader reflect on what we pay attention to and why.

As one of the epigraphs of this chapter, I cited a quotation by Edwidge Danticat because it conveys the dynamic that I have attended to throughout this book—a Black feminist sensibility that is specifically Haitian. When asked by theorist Nadège Clitandre how Black women and girls feature in her work, Danticat responded, "Black women certainly are at the center of my stories. I think part of this is from my personal experience of growing up with women who are very powerful—to me—but very vulnerable in their society."[17] As a Haitian American author, Danticat's both/and appreciation of Black women's power and vulnerability resonates with me and the goals of this book. What she does not say is that her intimacy with Black women and girls required "complicated care" in writing these stories. In each of the novels that I have analyzed here, the logics of intimacy are central to how ethics function. Whether it is the intimate relationship between two women stemming from Vodou, the ironically intimate relationship between strangers whose lives overlap but never touch, the intimacy of a grandmother sharing family history with her grandson, or the intimacy of a woman's relationship to the women in her family who came before her—intimacy animates how these characters interact with one another. When we define intimacy as "close familiarity" or "closeness of knowledge," it reinforces a dialectic of encounter, connection, proximity, and relation. At a time when Haitian studies is theorized according to and through polarities—glory and devastation, poverty and elitism, crisis and romance—care, intimacy, and proximity generate opportunities to look for new articulations of how race, gender, class, religion, and sexuality operate in Haitian fiction.

Reflecting on the role that literature plays in society, Évelyne Trouillot frames writing as a process of discovery: "Je crois que la littérature permet de rendre une société vivante et vraie. Je ne prétends pas montrer toute la diversité et la complexité du pays. D'ailleurs, lorsque j'écris, j'essaie de mieux comprendre cette complexité . . . de créer des personnages qui montrent l'humanité qui est en eux" (I believe that literature allows a society to be vibrant and true. I do not claim to show all the diversity and complexity of the country. Indeed, when I write, I try to better understand this complexity . . . to create characters who will show all of their humanity).[18] I read Trouillot's faithfulness to complexity as an ethical commitment. Similarly, in an interview with Alessandra Benedicty-Kokken, Kettly Mars expresses her desire to use literature as a space for truth and reconciliation: "As Mars herself has acknowledged, after the François and Jean-Claude Duvalier and Raoul Cédras dictatorships, as well as the multiple Jean-Bertrand Aristide presidencies, there has never been a formal apparatus set up for transitional justice. She sees her work, in a sense, as offering up a forum—albeit fictional, and rather private—through which Haitians may work through an unofficial and intimate sort of truth commission."[19]

The convictions that undergird these novels demonstrate that, for each author, ethics is bound to a larger project. For Kettly Mars, it is a commitment to contradiction that provokes the reader. The Black feminist ethic that emerges from the work of Évelyne Trouillot issues an ethical challenge of responsibility. Yanick Lahens's Black feminist ethic embraces a communal vision of what it means to be human—a perspective from which the collective is seen to inform the development of the individual. My mapping of a Black feminist ethic is rooted in an intersectional analysis of identity, but it points toward the possibility of moving against the multiple oppressions experienced by Black women as well as against the singular analyses that offer only oppression as a way to view their experiences. With the goal in mind of expanding our study of Haitian literature by pushing it in a distinctly Black feminist direction, in this book I have analyzed how representations of aging, sex, class, and the environment reveal a Black feminist ethic that is dynamic, relational, and concerned with care. In doing so, I aspire to demonstrate that the notion of a Black feminist ethic is one of the reasons why contemporary writers write today, and why we need them to continue doing so.

There is indeed urgency.

Denouncing the death of twenty-year-old Évelyne Sincère in 2020, Edwidge Danticat writes, "We long for a day when Haiti will have conscious feminist female politicians who will understand all that has led to a young woman ending up on the side of the road on a pile of trash. And leaders who are willing to do something to stop it. We long for a day, when, if she had lived, Évelyne Sincère could have looked forward to a safe and promising future in her country."[20] Until this day we long for comes, feminist organizations are leading the way. In September of 2020 a group of Haitian feminist organizations banded together to denounce the attempts by government officials to silence their work. As they wrote in their statement, "Despite pernicious attacks, feminists resolutely intend to continue to fight against gender-based and sexual violence, to counter toxic masculinity and to stand in solidarity with abused women. Breaking with denial of male violence, remains essential in the fight for respect for the dignity of women."[21] In June of 2021 the radio broadcaster and outspoken feminist human rights activist Antoinette Duclair was assassinated by killers who have yet to be captured. Events such as these remind us of the urgency.

Throughout this book I have turned to extraliterary texts—a photograph, a painting, a blog post, and a song—to complement and complicate my readings of how Black feminist concerns circulate in Haiti and the diaspora. My inclusion of these other forms draws on a deeply rooted Black feminist commitment "to do theorizing—that is to analyze a set of narratives in relation to one another—in conversation with many unconventional ways of knowledge production."[22] With this in mind, I offer the final words of *Looking for Other Worlds* to a Haitian feminist organization that is relatively new (especially as compared to the *Ligue féminine d'action sociale*). I choose to end on this note of highlighting the work of an activist organization because activism has always been central to Black feminism. As the example of Paulette Poujol Oriol shows us, in the Haitian context, feminist activism and writing are often intertwined and can mutually influence each other. The ethical paradigm that I elaborate is first and foremost a Black feminist project that asks us to examine the world differently and carries with it a mandate to change the world and our futures. Imagining the world differently also leads to working to create change. My understanding that activism and advocacy are necessary to carry out this vision is why I choose to end with Nègès Mawon, a feminist organization founded in 2015.[23]

Nègès Mawon. The choice of name is telling. The Kreyòl phrase translates as "Black Women Maroons." It conjures the flight, fugitivity, and freedom of the Maroons for whom upending the power structures of the plantocracy required radical action. As feminist practices, flight, fugitivity, and freedom represent a triad commitment to not only look for other worlds but stolidly create them. It embraces the spirit of possibility that was born centuries ago and is determined to live on today. It situates Haitian women in terms of Blackness and freedom. For the past several years the Nègès Mawon festival has issued a call for a new generation of feminists to make their voices heard in the Haitian public sphere. Describing their work and the genesis of the festival, they write:

Aujourd'hui, le combat des féministes n'est pas encore perçu comme un combat pour les droits humains. C'est toujours un mouvement méconnu, mal compris et dénaturé par ses détracteurs. L'idée de ce festival répond à la nécessité de regarder avec une perspective féministe la production culturelle et artistique, mais aussi d'expérimenter une nouvelle façon de comprendre et de renouveler les enjeux de la militance féministe en utilisant l'art en général, pour tenter de redynamiser le mouvement féministe haïtien, lui donner un nouveau leadership et une nouvelle image, impliquer de nouvelles actrices et de nouveaux acteurs—les artistes par exemple—dans la lutte, explorer de nouvelles stratégies de militance et de transmission des valeurs du féminisme. Ce Festival est aussi une étape fondamentale pour commencer à créer un public, en particulier les jeunes, qui sera sensibilisé, informé, formé, et on l'espère, engagé dans le combat pour les droits des femmes et l'équité de genre.

(Today, the feminist fight is not yet seen as a fight for human rights. It is still a little-known movement, misunderstood and distorted by its detractors. The idea of this festival responds to the need to look at cultural and artistic production from a feminist perspective, but also to experiment with new way of understanding and renewing the challenges of feminist militancy by using art in general, to try to revitalize the Haitian feminist movement, give it a new leadership and a new image, involve new actresses and new actors—artists for example—in the struggle, explore new strategies of militancy and transmission of feminist values. This Festival is also a fundamental step towards starting to create an audience, especially young people, who will be sensitized, informed, trained, and hopefully, engaged in the fight for women's rights and gender equity.)

The founders and organizers of Nègès Mawon unabashedly identify their intention to bring Haitian feminism into the public sphere and amplify its popular relevance. Their creation of a festival is a gesture of collaboration and celebration that is locally anchored. Their commitment to a new generation of artists and leaders reframing feminist debates and engagement gives us another vision of what it looks like to publicly look for other worlds. Nègès Mawon affirms the Black feminist principles of change and evolution, dynamism and intervention, while demonstrating the importance of contributions that extend far beyond the academy. Espousing a worldview in which feminism is a human rights struggle, their work evokes the Black feminist ethic of looking for other worlds that embraces a vision for a more just and more beautiful world, and works to build it.[24]

Notes

Introduction

1. With the exception of a special issue of the *Journal of Haitian Studies* honoring Poujol Oriol after her death, there is very little scholarship on her.

2. Verna and Poujol Oriol, "Ligue Feminine," 246.

3. Augustin, "Décès de Paulette Poujol Oriol." A word about translation in my study: throughout this book all translations are my own unless otherwise noted. I have used official translations wherever possible, and when using my own translations, I always include the original French. Three of the primary texts in my corpus have published English translations—*Rosalie l'infâme* (trans. *The Infamous Rosalie*), *Bain de lune* (trans. *Moonbath*), and *La couleur de l'aube* (trans. *The Colour of Dawn*)—and for each of these I only include English citations.

4. I am referring to the six distinguishing features outlined by Patricia Hill Collins in *Black Feminist Thought: Knowledge, Consciousness, and the Politics of Empowerment*. To paraphrase, the distinguishing features of that Black feminism are 1) intersectional, 2) links between experience and ideas, 3) activist, 4) intellectual, 5) dynamic, changing, and evolving, 6) social justice project-oriented.

5. Gumbs, "Ceremony."

6. Wright, "Feminism," 88.

7. Gumbs, "Ceremony."

8. Boyce Davies, *Migrations of the Subject*, 55.

9. Anim-Addo, *Framing the Word*, xi.

10. Haynes, "Interrogating Approaches to Caribbean Feminist Thought," 29.

11. Ulysse, "Why Rasanblaj," 69.

12. Alexander, "Groundings on Rasanblaj."

13. Alexander, *Pedagogies of Crossing*, 186.

14. Trouillot, "Respecting the Diversity of Creativity."

15. Merlet, "More People Dream," 219.

16. Christian, "Race for Theory," 12. Here I am thinking of the full quotation: "For people of color have always theorized (and I intentionally use the verb

rather than the noun). And I am inclined to say that our theorizing is often in narrative forms, in the stories we create, in riddles and proverbs, in the play with language, since dynamic rather than fixed ideas seem more to our liking."

17. hooks, *Black Looks,* 115.

18. Ulysse, "Why Rasanblaj," 70.

19. Spivak, *Aesthetic Education,* 32.

20. Spivak, *Spivak Reader,* 13.

21. Nash, *Black Feminism Reimagined,* 78.

22. Sharpe, *In the Wake,* 5.

23. Here I am thinking about Min Song's thought-provoking discussion of deep reading in *The Children of 1965:* "much can be learned by such attentiveness, or what night more descriptively be called *deep reading.* This involves reading every word and image, lingering over details, savoring the many permutations of meaning that a piece of reading offers, and allowing oneself to consider how these meanings are formed in relation to concerns outside the text."

24. Bernard, "*L'œil-totem.*"

25. My use of "the otherwise" comes from Ashon Crawley's call for "otherwise" as modes of alternative existence. Crawley writes, "It is the gift, the concept, the inhabitation of and living into otherwise possibilities. Otherwise, as word—otherwise possibilities, as phrase—announces the fact of infinite alternatives to what is." Crawley, *Blackpentecostalbreath,* 2.

26. Lionnet, *Postcolonial Representations,* 1.

27. Henderson, "Speaking in Tongues," 349.

28. Spiller, "Time and Crisis," 30.

29. Dash, "Neither Magical Nor Exceptional," 24.

30. Benedicty, "Safe Place."

1. Haitian Women's Studies, Black Feminism, and Literary Ethics

1. Bernard, "*L'œil-totem.*"

2. Lamour, Côté, and Alexis, *Déjouer le silence,* 15.

3. Lamour, Côté, and Alexis, 16.

4. Lamour, Côté, and Alexis, 16.

5. The authors cite Évelyne Trouillot's intervention at the colloquium as the genesis of the phrase "Déjouer le silence."

6. Lamour, Côté, and Alexis, *Déjouer le silence,* 15.

7. Collins, *Black Feminist Thought,* 24.

8. Poujoul Oriol, "La femme haïtienne dans la littérature haïtienne," 80.

9. Sylvain-Bouchereau, *Haiti et ses femmes,* 87.

10. Clark, "Developing Diaspora Literacy and Marasa Consciousness," 10.

11. Condé, *La parole des femmes,* 3.

12. Condé, 80–82.

13. Condé, 83.

14. Gardiner, *Visages de femmes,* 5.

15. Gardiner, 6.
16. Gardiner, 6.
17. Parisot, *Regards littéraires haitiens,* 246.
18. Alexander, *Pedagogies of Crossing,* 283.
19. Alexis, *Déjouer le silence,* 67.
20. Joseph-Gabriel, "Tant de silence à briser," 84.
21. Lahens, "L'apport de quatre romancières," 88.
22. In fact, Black feminist writers have been especially adept in uniting the personal and the political in the creation of fiction that reflects and critiques social realties.
23. Kevin Quashie's *The Sovereignty of Quiet* eloquently analyzes interiority.
24. Harris, *Gifts of Virtue,* 11.
25. Spillers, "Time and Crisis," 25.
26. Sanders, *La Voix des femmes.*
27. Ménard, "Cléante Valcin."
28. Chancy, "Feminist Movement."
29. Sylvain-Bouchereau, *Haiti et ses femmes,* 82.
30. Magloire, "L'antiféminisme en Haiti," 200.
31. Magloire, 200.
32. Glover, "'Black' Radicalism in Haiti," 10.
33. Ménard, "Cléante Valcin."
34. Chancy, *Framing Silence,* 26.
35. Ulysse, "Papa, Patriarchy," 27.
36. It is also important to note that while this is widely recognized as the "official history" of Haitian feminism, as I discuss in chapter 3, scholars like Natacha Clergé and others have begun the work of contesting this genealogy because of the ways it only focuses on the voices of elite and privileged Haitian women.
37. Magloire, "L'antiféminisme en Haïti," 203.
38. Magloire, 203.
39. Magloire, 203.
40. Chancy, "Feminist Movement."
41. Lahens, *Littérature haïtienne,* 67.
42. Nash, *Black Feminism Reimagined,* 13.
43. Ulysse, *Haiti Needs New Narratives,* 51.
44. I am referring to literary analyses of fiction by Haitian women. Jasmine Claude Narcisse's *Memoires de femmes* (1997) is an overview of Haitian women's contributions to society that spans literature, culture, and politics. *Féminines traversées* by Marie Alice Bélisaire is also a collection that includes many different figures throughout history.
45. Chancy, *Framing Silence,* 26.
46. Chancy, 44.
47. Chancy, 52.
48. Chancy, 27.

49. Charles, "Reflections on Being a Machann ak Machandiz," 119.

50. McCarthy Brown, *Mama Lola,* 156.

51. Christian, "Race for Theory," 68.

52. Ulysse, "Why Rasanblaj," 58.

53. Alexander, "Groundings on Rasanblaj."

54. Ulysse, "Why Rasanblaj," 49.

55. Zimra, "Haitian Literature After Duvalier," 85.

56. Chapman, Durban-Albrecht, and Lamothe, "Nou Mache Ansam," 145.

57. Verna and Paulette Poujol Oriol, "Ligue Feminine d'Action Sociale," 248.

58. Davis et al., "Introduction: Art as Caribbean Feminist Practice," 34.

59. In her essay, "Between Plot and Plantation, Trespass and Transgression," Curdella Forbes elaborates "an ethic of disobedience" as a "fascinating space of ethical contradiction."

60. Collins, *Black Feminist Thought,* xi

61. Taylor, *How We Get Free,* 44.

62. Collins, "Social Construction of Black Feminist Thought," 770. See also Alain Badiou "Ethics: An Essay on the Understanding of Evil."

63. "Carol Gilligan."

64. The ethical imagination as I conceive of it throughout this book registers in three ways. It is present in how these authors 1) deploy narrative strategies to engage ethical arguments, 2) present protagonists for whom ethical dilemmas are among their main preoccupations, and 3) pose ethical questions of the reader.

65. Here I am reminded of Chielozona Eze's point that "Feminism as ethics is different from feminist ethics because the latter seeks to rethink traditional ethics to the extent that it deprecates or devalues women's moral experience." *Ethics and Human Rights,* 41.

66. While Kimberlé Crenshaw first coined the term "intersectionality" in her 1989 essay, "Demarginalizing the Intersection of Race and Sex: A Black Feminist Critique of Antidiscrimination Doctrine, Feminist Theory and Antiracist Politics," in recent years amid the "intersectionality wars" in the US, she has refined and simplified the definition: "It's basically a lens, a prism, for seeing the way in which various forms of inequality often operate together and exacerbate each other. We tend to talk about race inequality as separate from inequality based on gender, class, sexuality or immigrant status. What's often missing is how some people are subject to all of these, and the experience is not just the sum of its parts."

67. Alexander, *Pedagogies of Crossing,* 5.

68. My use of world-making is an explicit invocation of how Adom Getachew defines it along the lines of "self-determination." Getachew, *Worldmaking.*

69. Walker, *In Search of Our Mothers' Gardens,* i.

70. Eze, *Ethics and Human Rights,* 9.

71. Harris, *Gifts of Virtue,* 10.

72. Harris, xi.

73. Harris, 11.

74. Sanders, "Womanist Ethics," 301.

75. Combahee River Collective, "A Black Feminist Statement," qtd. in Taylor, *How We Get Free*.

76. Chancy, *Framing Silence*, 41.

77. Boyce Davies, *Black Women, Writing, and Identity*, 48.

78. Boyce Davies, 56.

79. Lambert, *Comrade Sister*, 8.

80. Lahens, *Littérature haïtienne*, 66.

81. Valdés, *Oshun's Daughters*, 2.

82. Michel, *Aspects éducatifs et moraux du Vodou haitïen*, 35–36.

83. Marty, *La littérature haïtienne dans la modernité*, 84.

84. "Entretien de Anne Bocandé avec Yanick Lahens."

85. Griffin, *Read Until You Understand*, 91.

86. Griffin, 176.

87. Cited in Meretoja, *Ethics of Storytelling*, 14.

88. Eze, *Ethics and Human Rights*, 3.

89. Eze, 3.

90. See McNulty, "Literary Ethics, Revisited."

91. See Gikandi "Theory, Literature, and Moral Considerations," and Nussbaum, "Exactly and Responsibly."

92. Hale, "Fiction as Restriction," 188.

93. Goldman, "Introduction: Literature, Imagination, Ethic," 560.

94. Banita, *Plotting Justice*, 17.

95. Palladino, *Ethics and Aesthetics*, 74.

96. Hagberg, *Fictional Characters, Real Problems*, 11.

97. Nussbaum, "Exactly and Responsibly."

98. Christian, "Race for Theory," 77.

99. Eze relies on Terry Eagleton to make this argument: "For [Eagleton] feminism has been the paradigm of classical morality in our own time largely because it 'insists in its own way on the inter-wovenness of the moral and political, power and the personal.' It is in this tradition above all that the precious heritage of Aristotle and Marx has been deepened and renewed." *Ethics and Human Rights*, 144.

100. Eze, *Ethics and Human Rights*, 3.

101. Eagleton cited in Eze, *Ethics and Human Rights*.

102. Campbell, "Narcissism as Ethical Practice?" 34.

103. Eze, *Ethics and Human Rights*, 4.

104. These categories are inspired by the book *Mapping the Ethical Turn*.

105. Lahens, *L'exil*, 65.

106. Lahens, 50.

107. Ménard, *Écrits d'Haïti*, 274.

108. Trouillot, "Respecting the Diversity of Creativity."

109. "Inauguration du Centre culturel Anne-Marie Morisset," *Le Nouvelliste*. Accessed July 2017. https://lenouvelliste.com/public/index.php/article/95899/inauguration-du-centre-culturel-anne-marie-morisset.

110. Danticat, "Évelyne Trouillot," 52.

111. See for example, Trouillot, "Jovenel Moïse: An Instigator, A Victim, and Haiti's Descent into Violence," https://www.politico.com/news/magazine/2021/12/27/2021-obituary-jovenel-moise-520597.

112. Vitiello, "Douceurs et violences," 369.

113. "Biographie."

114. "Biographie."

115. Vitiello, "Douceurs et violences," 369.

116. Charles, "Gender and Politics in Contemporary Haiti," 136.

117. Clitandre, *Edwidge Danticat,* 72.

118. I am referring to *Saisons Sauvages* and *La Mémoire aux abois.*

119. "Kettly Mars et Melissa Belarus au Centre Anne Marie Morisset," *Le National*. Accessed October 2017. http://www.lenational.org/kettly-mars-melissa-beralus-centre-anne-marie-morisset/.

120. Ménard, *Écrits d'Haiti,* 272.

121. Ménard, 273.

122. "Entretien de Anne Bocandé avec Yanick Lahens."

123. The novels that I examine in this book are *Le Passage* (trans. *Vale of Tears*) by Paulette Poujol Oriol; *Bain de lune* (trans. *Moonbath*), *La couleur de l'aube* (trans. *The Colour of Dawn*), *Dans la maison du père*, and *Guillaume et Nathalie* by Yanick Lahens ; *L'œil-totem, Rosalie l'infâme* (trans. *The Infamous Rosalie*), and *Le Rond-point* by Évelyne Trouillot; and *Kasalé, Je suis vivant*, and *Aux frontières de la soif* by Kettly Mars.

124. Hale, "Fiction as Restriction," 189.

125. Harpham, "Ethics," 394–95.

126. Washington, "Darkened Eye Restored," 35.

127. Parisot, "L'écrivaine haïtienne en son miroir," 313.

128. Alexander, *Pedagogies of Crossing,* 275.

129. Taylor, *How We Get Free,* 45.

130. Davis, *Freedom Is a Constant Struggle,* 3.

131. Tinsley, *Ezili's Mirrors,* 17.

132. Nash, *Black Feminism Reimagined,* 116.

133. McKittrick, *Demonic Ground,* xii.

134. A *madan sara* is a woman who buys, sells, and trades in the Haitian markets. These extraordinary and ordinary women are pillars of the Haitian economy. As the filmmaker Etant Dupain explains in reference to his documentary about Madan Sara, "To talk about Madan Sara is to talk about Haiti." See Jean-Charles, "Madan Sara."

135. Nash, *Black Feminism Reimagined,* 115.

136. Spivak, *Spivak Reader,* 5.

137. Freadman, "Ethics, Autobiography," 18.

138. Text references are to Poujol Oriol, *Le Passage,* translated by Dolores Schaefer as *Vale of Tears.*

139. In the novel's foreword, Edwidge Danticat writes, "as the dual narrative strands are woven together, we watch Coralie's fall become more and more humiliating" (5).

140. Spear, "Paulette Poujol Oriol's Tragicomedies," 17.

141. Quashie, *Sovereignty of Quiet,* 48.

142. I am grateful to my friend Richard Paul, who made this observation after reading an early draft of my chapter.

143. Ulysse, *Why Haiti Needs New Narratives,* ix.

144. Ulysse, 97.

145. Nevertheless, it should be noted that the idea of new narratives grows out of the need for resistance to a dominant narrative, or what Chimamanda Adichie calls a "single story," that circulates primarily outside of Haiti. In many ways, the authors that I study here are less concerned with writing against this dominant narrative, or to purposefully disrupting it, because they occupy a reality that is local and contemporary even as it speaks globally and historically.

146. In his essay "The Odd and the Ordinary," Michel-Rolph Trouillot writes, "Haiti is not that weird, it is the fiction of Haitian exceptionalism that is weird." Trouillot, "Odd and the Ordinary," 11.

147. Boyce Davies, *Black Women, Writing, and Identity,* 56.

148. I am purposefully echoing the words of bell hooks, who refers to the need for images that are invested in "shifting paradigms, changing perspectives, and ways of looking." hooks, *Black Looks,* 4.

2. *Gran moun se moun*

1. Romain, "Ayiti."

2. As Kyrah Daniels points out, "Ginen signifies a mecca and cosmic homeland not simply for African ancestors and descendants living in the African Diaspora, but also for those of various ethnic backgrounds who have become initiated to Haiti's national religion of Vodou." See Daniels, "Mirror Mausoleums, Mortuary Arts, and Haitian Religious Un-exceptionalism."

3. Campt, "Black Visuality."

4. Campt.

5. Campt, *Listening to Images,* 8.

6. Children are often taught not to look adults in the eyes as a sign of deference to their age and authority.

7. Turnbull, *Hidden Meanings of Haitian Proverbs,* 39.

8. While the film scholar Cécile Accilien suggests that the proverb has sexual connotations, I am interested in what it connotes about age.

9. Woodward, *Figuring Age,* 42.

10. O'Neil and Zamorana, *Aesthetics of Aging,* 61.

11. Haitian literature is rife with examples of elderly characters. Manuel's parents in *Masters of the Dew,* Grann Zo in Danny Lafferière's novels, the grandfather in Chauvet's *Colère* are but a few to name here.

12. Woodward, *Figuring Age,* 50.

13. Lorde, "Age, Race, Class, and Sex," 114.

14. Lorde, 114.

15. Lorde, 115.

16. Of the novels written by the authors whose work I examine, elderly characters are featured in eight: *Je suis vivant* and *Kasalé* by Kettly Mars. *L'œil totem, Rosalie l'Infâme, La mémoire aux abois,* and *Absences sans frontières* by Évelyne Trouillot.

17. A Kreyòl phrase often used in the imperative meaning "respect your elders."

18. Woodward, *Figuring Age,* x.

19. The extent to which being a mother *does not* figure as an important part of these women's stories and interior lives also displaces the centrality of motherhood tropes in these novels.

20. See Jean-Charles, "Getting around the *Poto-Mitan.*"

21. Glover, *Regarded Self,* 13.

22. Segal, *Out of Time,* 72.

23. Woodward, *Figuring Age,* xi.

24. Sanchez-Eppler, *Dependent States, xxv.*

25. Woodward, *Figuring Age,* xiii–xvii.

26. Woodward, xii.

27. Spivak, *Spivak Reader,* 269–70.

28. See Dovey, "What Old Age Is Really Like."

29. Glover, *Regarded Self,* 2.

30. Glover, 2.

31. Ahmed, *Willful Subjects,* 3.

32. Glover, *Regarded Self,* 3.

33. Glover, 27.

34. The name Marie-Jeanne was also appropriated under Duvalier to refer to members of the all-female police force, also known as the *fillette-lalo.*

35. Claude-Narcisse, "Marie-Jeanne."

36. Trouillot, "Infamy Revisited," 56.

37. Glover, "'Black' Radicalism in Haiti," 7.

38. hooks, *Feminism Is for Everybody,* 103.

39. Glover, *Regarded Self,* 5.

40. Bernard, "*L'œil-totem.*"

41. Bernard.

42. Destinvil, "Mireille Neptune Anglade."

43. Glover, *Regarded Self,* 17.

44. Ahmed, *Living a Feminist Life,* 66.

45. Walker, *In Search of our Mothers' Gardens.*
46. Cristofovici, *Touching Surfaces,* 18.
47. Quashie, *Sovereignty of Quiet,* 21.
48. Quashie, 48.
49. Quashie, 48.
50. Cristofovici, *Touching Surfaces,* 2
51. Cristofovici, 18.
52. Magloire, "L'antiféminisme en Haïti," 199.
53. Magloire, 199.
54. "The occupation years were a period of intense encounters throughout Haiti, including armed skirmishes between US Marines and Haitian Cacos . . . a time of urban renewal, financial uncertainty, and social conflicts" (*Duke Haiti Reader,* 178). In her study of literature of the occupation, *The Occupied Novel.* Nadève Ménard describes how this period took hold of literary imagination, arguing that "Haitian occupied novels suggest that France becomes less dominant as a foreign reference in the Haitian imagination during the occupation period and tends to be replaced by the United States. In these narratives, Haitians continually assert themselves in opposition to the American invaders. The US occupation changed the Haitian identity from something automatically acquired at birth to something to be earned through patriotic acts of resistance." See also Ménard, *Occupied Novel.*
55. Alexander, *Pedagogies of Crossing,* 16.
56. This generational transmission is similar to what Trouillot creates in *The Infamous Rosalie,* albeit in the extremely different context of slavery in which families were torn apart.
57. Calasanti and Slevin, *Gender, Social Inequalities, and Aging,* 198.
58. Glover, *Regarded Self,* 13.
59. Glover, 54.
60. Sheller, *Citizenship from Below,* 10.
61. Bernard, "L'œil-totem."
62. Dovey, "What Old Age Is Really Like."
63. Alexander, *Pedagogies of Crossing,* 285.
64. Washington, "The Darkened Eye Restored," 38.
65. In Chapter 5 I examine environmental ethics and discuss how the land functions as another character in the novel.
66. Benedicty-Kokken, *Spirit Possession,* 77.
67. Benedicty-Kokken, 77.
68. Alexander, *Pedagogies of Crossing,* 290.
69. Désir, "Diasporic Lakou," 282.
70. Désir, 282.
71. Lamour, Côté, and Alexis, *Déjouer le silence,* 18.
72. Valdés, *Oshun's Daughters,* 7.
73. N'Zengou-Tayo, "Fanm se Poto-Mitan," 134.

74. Alexis, *Déjouer,* 46.

75. Similarly, in the film *Madan Sara,* Étant Dupain shows how Haitian women operate together in the informal economy, sustaining, supporting, and collaborating with one another to feed the nation. Whereas N'Zengou-Tayo relies on the notion of resilience to portray Haitian womanhood, Dupain emphasizes belonging: "Madan Sara is Haiti, Madan Sara is ours." See Jean-Charles, "Madan Sara."

76. Valdés, *Oshun's Daughters,* 2.

77. Vansteenkiste and Schuller, "Gendered Space," 148.

78. Lamour, Côté, and Alexis, *Déjouer le silence,* 18.

79. Vitiello, "Douceurs et violences dans l'écriture de Kettly Mars," 370.

80. Benedicty-Kokken, *Spirit Possession,* 233.

81. Quashie, *Sovereignty of Quiet,* 119.

82. Valdés, *Oshun's Daughters,* 7.

83. Lahens, *Littérature haïtienne,* 66.

84. Alexander, *Pedagogies of Crossing,* 320.

85. Ulysse, "Papa, Patriarchy," 35.

86. Tinsley, *Ezili's Mirrors,* 72.

87. Glover, *Regarded Self,* 23.

88. See Jean-Charles, "Getting around the Poto-Mitan."

89. Dalembert and Trouillot, *Haiti,* 66–67.

90. While the examples noted here are exclusively Haitian, it should be noted that the poto-mitan is a figure that circulates in all of the French speaking Caribbean. For example, Gaël Octavia bases her novel, *La Bonne histoire de Madeleine Démétrius,* published in 2020, on the poto-mitan trope for Martinican women.

91. Lamour, Côté, and Alexis, *Déjouer le silence.*

92. See Jean-Charles, "Getting around the Poto-Mitan."

93. Danticat, "'Haitians Are Very Resilient.'"

94. Michel, *Aspects éducatifs et moraux du Vodou haitien,* 25.

95. Vitiello, "Douceurs et violences dans l'écriture de Kettly Mars," 371.

96. Herbeck, "Intertexts of the Ecological," 82.

97. Munro, *Writing on the Fault Line,* 69.

98. Daniels, "Mirror Mausoleums, Mortuary Arts, and Haitian Religious Unexceptionalism," 957.

99. Brown, *Mama Lola,* 220.

100. Alexander, *Pedagogies of Crossing,* 283.

101. Alexander, 297.

102. Alexander, 322.

103. Deren, *Divine Horsemen,* 33.

104. Sharpe, *In the Wake,* 10.

105. Sharpe, 10.

106. Sharpe, 51.

107. Ulysse, "Why I Am Marching."

108. Alexander, *Pedagogies of Crossing,* 328.
109. Larrier, "In[her]itance," 137.
110. It is important to note here that the ship gets its description of "infamy" from the slaves. As Renée Larrier points out, it is called *"Rosalie l'infâme* by the captives to reflect its perverted mission, this site of rupture, dispossession, and indignity has an oxymoronic nickname that juxtaposes rose—a beautiful flower, color, and the Christian name Lisette's mother Ayouba refuses—with *infâme,* an adjective used to describe a loathsome occupation, unspeakable act or disgusting odor, all of which are entirely appropriate in this context." Larrier, "In[her]itance," 140.
111. Hartman, *Scenes of Subjection,* 51.
112. Palladino, *Ethics and Aesthetics in Toni Morrison's Fiction,* 29
113. Daniels, "Haitian Divine Nine."
114. Sheller, *Citizenship from Below,* 26.
115. Sheller, *Citizenship from Below,* 23.
116. Ulysse, "Introduction."
117. Alexander, "Groundings on Rasanblaj."
118. Banita, *Plotting Justice,* 17.

3. The Ethical-Erotic

1. "Ten Haitian Female Artists You Should Be Listening To," Kreyolicious, https://wapkonnjojanko.com/for-international-womens-day-rutshelle-takes-n8k8d-photos-with-another-girl-awww-very-cute-couple-photo/. Accessed May 6, 2017.
2. Sheller, *Citizenship from Below,* 240.
3. Guillaume, *Emotions.*
4. As Barbara Christian writes in "The Race for Theory," "our theorizing . . . is often in narrative forms, in the stories we create, in riddles and proverbs, in the play with language, since dynamic rather than fixed ideas seem more to our liking" (12).
5. Gill, *Erotic Islands,* 216.
6. Plenary Session: Decolonizing and Reshaping Sexual Diversity and LGBTI Discourses in the Caribbean. Caribbean Studies Association, Thursday, June 7, 2018.
7. As such, scenes of sexual violence are the opposite of what interest me in this chapter. Having written a monograph on representations of sexual violence in literal and cultural studies, I have done extensive work on cultural productions that feature rape scenes. See Jean-Charles, *Conflict Bodies.*
8. Dayan, *With Dogs at the Edge of Life,* xvi.
9. See Jean-Charles, *Conflict Bodies.*
10. Washington, "Darkened Eye Restored," 38.
11. Dayan, *Haiti, History, and the Gods,* 48.

12. Gill, "Situating Black, Situating Queer," 35–36.

13. Gill, cited in Sheller, *Citizenship from Below,* 20.

14. Zylinska, *Ethics of Cultural Studies,* xii.

15. Francis, *Fictions of Feminist Citizenship,* 3.

16. Lorde, "Uses of the Erotic," 89.

17. Valdés, *Oshun's Daughters,* 53.

18. Tinsley, *Thiefing Sugar,* 106.

19. Tinsley, 106.

20. Tinsley, *Ezili's Mirrors,* 4.

21. Accilien, *Haitian Hollywood,* 185.

22. Tinsley, *Ezili's Mirrors,* 4.

23. Sheller, *Citizenship from Below,* 242.

24. Bocandé, "Interview."

25. King, *Island Bodies,* 1.

26. See Cléante Desgraves, *Cruelle destinée.*

27. Poujol Oriol, "La femme haïtienne dans la littérature," 83.

28. See Lafférière, *Vers le sud* (2006) and *Comment faire l'amour avec un nègre sans se fatiguer* (1985).

29. Lahens, "L'apport de quatre romancières au roman moderne haïtien."

30. Tinsley, *Thiefing Sugar,* 7.

31. I want to be clear that the way I understand ethics to operate is not based on a dominant or monolithic value system but rather one that is curious about the feminist imagination.

32. Sheller, *Citizenship from Below,* 16.

33. Sheller, 47.

34. In this the novel reads well with Gessica Généus's powerful documentary film *Douvan jou ka leve* (2018), in which a daughter explores her mother's mental illness in a reflective and personal journey.

35. In fact, *Je suis vivant* engages almost every area of focus in this book: Éliane is an elderly protagonist, and the question of class encounter occurs through Norah's arrival in the Bernier home.

36. Ellis, "Out and Bad," 9.

37. Alexander, *Pedagogies of Crossing,* 260.

38. Alexander, *Pedagogies of Crossing,* 22.

39. Gumbs, *M Archive,* ix.

40. I am nonetheless interested in, and invested in what Nadia Ellis describes as the utility of queer in the context of the Caribbean and agree with her that, "if queer began as critical term within a European American–oriented academic sphere, it has since expanded its limits, staying true to its roots as a term of unstable and shifting signification, and has been deployed by scholars of varied backgrounds, theoretical orientations, and fields." Ellis, "Out and Bad," 11.

41. kouraj.org.

42. Migraine-George, "From Masisi to Activists," 9.

43. Muñoz, *Cruising Utopia,* 1.

44. Bailey, "Homolatent Masculinity," 187.

45. Accilien, *Haitian Hollywood,* 179.

46. Agard-Jones, "Le Jeu de Qui?" 189.

47. Tinsley, *Thiefing Sugar,* 67.

48. In *Conflict Bodies: The Politics of Rape Representation in the Francophone Imaginary,* I analyze the confluence of sex, violence, and politics in Mars's 2010 novel *Saisons sauvages.*

49. King, *Island Bodies,* 93.

50. King, 8.

51. King, 9.

52. Valdés, *Oshun's Daughters,* 109.

53. Allen, "Blackness, Sexuality, and Transnational Desire," 83.

54. Lorde, "Uses of the Erotic," 54.

55. Mars, "La Sensualité au coeur de la vie," 233.

56. King, *Island Bodies,* 77.

57. Miguel, *Review of Island Bodies,* 1186.

58. Perry, *Vexy Thing,* 9.

59. Gill, *Erotic Islands,* 11.

60. Vitiello, "Douceurs et violences dans l'écriture de Kettly Mars," 370.

61. King, *Island Bodies,* 8.

62. Tinsley, *Thiefing Sugar,* 152.

63. Ulysse, *Why Haiti Needs New Narratives,* 53.

64. See Jean-Charles, "*Nou pa gen vizibilite.*"

65. Gill, *Erotic Islands,* 201.

66. Lorde, "Uses of the Erotic," 56.

67. Lorde, 59.

68. King, *Island Bodies,* 103,

69. Gill, *Erotic Islands,* 201.

70. See Scott, "Selling Sex, Suppressing Sexuality."

71. Mars, "La Sensualité au cœur de la vie," 233.

72. Ferguson, *Aberrations in Black,* 52.

73. In Évelyne Trouillot's *Absences sans frontières,* the sister Cynthia Tante Za'a same sex relationships are intended to be kept secret, but everyone is aware of them.

74. Many scholars have analyzed the role of the earthquake in the novel, especially in relation to *Failles,* Lahens's book about the earthquake and her attempts to write after it.

75. Munro, "New Pastoralism?"

76. Walsh describes *Guillaume et Nathalie:* "A love story set just before the earthquake, the text depicts two Haitians who struggle to reconcile their pasts at

the same time they work on a community project designed to improve the future of Haiti." Walsh, "Global Frame of Haiti," 300.

77. Lahens, "L'apport de quatre romancières," 88.
78. Morrison, *Jazz,* 135.
79. Valdés, *Oshun's Daughters,* 110.
80. Lorde, "Uses of the Erotic," 88.
81. See Martin Munro's *Writing on the Fault Line;* John Walsh, *Migration and Refuge;* Kasia Mika, *Disasters, Vulnerability, and Narratives.*
82. Adamson, "Yanick Lahens romancière," 107.
83. Alexis, Review of *Guillaume et Nathalie,* 294.
84. Alexis, 295.
85. Trouillot, "Odd and the Ordinary," 13.
86. Bocandé, "Interview."
87. Bocandé.
88. Glover, *Regarded Self,* 61.
89. Tinsley, *Thiefing Sugar,* 51.
90. Glover, *Regarded Self,* 42.
91. Lorde, "Uses of the Erotic," 87.
92. Lorde, 89.
93. Sheller, *Citizenship from Below,* 67.
94. Glover, *Regarded Self,* 48.
95. Spillers, "Mama's Baby, Papa's Maybe," 67.
96. Tinsley, *Thiefing Sugar,* 77.
97. Sheller, *Citizenship from Below,* 244.
98. Glover, *Regarded Self,* 52.
99. Halberstam, Muñoz, and Eng, "What's Queer about Queer Studies Now?" 11.
100. Lorde, "Uses of the Erotic," 87.
101. Ulysse, "Why *Rasanblaj,* Why Now?" 70.
102. Spillers, "Interstices," 74.
103. Gill, *Erotic Islands,* 184.
104. Lorde, "Uses of the Erotic," 89.
105. Tinsley, *Thiefing Sugar,* 77.
106. Melancon and Braxton, *Black Female Sexualities,* 4.
107. Davis et al., "Introduction," 35.
108. Davis et al., 35.
109. Davis et al., 36.
110. Tinsley, *Thiefing Sugar,* 51.
111. "Tessa Mars."
112. Sheller, *Citizenship from Below,* 243.
113. Fronahpfel, "Tessa Mars."
114. Gill, *Erotic Islands,* 10.
115. hooks, Feminism is for Everybody, 110.

4. Geographies of Class Location

1. The question "Kote Kòb Petwo Karibe'a?" (where is the Petrocaribe money?) became wildly popular and led to an anticorruption movement when Haitian writer and filmmaker Gilbert Mirambeau posted a video on social media asking the whereabouts of the funds from Haiti's participation in the oil-sharing program created by Venezuelan oil company Petrocaribe.

2. Évelyne Trouillot, Facebook post.

3. Alexander, *Pedagogies of Crossing*, 2. My emphasis.

4. McKittrick, *Demonic Grounds*, 8.

5. McKittrick, x.

6. Murray, "Time of Breach," 16.

7. Chancy, *Framing Silence*, 82.

8. "Gender, race, and class compose the holy trinity of feminist studies." Boris, "Class Returns," 74.

9. Though I focus on Chauvet and Poujol Oriol, earlier writers like Cléanthe Desgraves Valcin and Annie Desroy also used fiction to articulate and interrogate the machinations of class and power in the lives of women. As Chancy highlights in *Framing Silence,* "For Valcin . . . racial consciousness leads to destructiveness because it disallows the crossing of racial lines and hence class lines as well. Desroy, on the other hand, champions women of the underclass and seeks to expose the violent treatment Haitians faced during the occupation. Race is not as much of an issue here as is the meeting of class and gender" (71).

10. Glover, *Regarded Self*, 113.

11. Dalleo, *Caribbean Literature and the Public Sphere*, 130.

12. Bell, "Permanent Exile."

13. Bell.

14. Dalleo, *Caribbean Literature and the Public Sphere*, 136.

15. Charles, "Sociological Counter-reading," 68.

16. Benedicty-Kokken and Glover, "Revisiting Marie Vieux Chauvet," 57.

17. Glover, *Regarded Self*, 114.

18. Poujol Oriol's short stories also take on these themes; for example, in "Lucette," a young *restavek* is abused by her privileged captors.

19. Coates, "Paulette Poujol Oriol, *Le Creuset* and Other Works," 56.

20. Chancy, *Framing Silence*, 41.

21. Clergé, "Pour en finir avec une historiographie héroïsante," 224.

22. Clergé, 234.

23. Clergé, 229.

24. Vergès, *Un féminisme décolonial*, 34.

25. Hugo, *Les Misérables*, 30.

26. Acacia, *Historicité et structuration sociale en Haiti*, 91.

27. DelConte, "Why *You* Can't Speak," 204.

28. Gotlib, "Feminist Ethics."

29. DelConte, "Why *You* Can't Speak," 205.
30. Ulysse, *Why Haiti Needs New Narratives*, 39.
31. Alexander, *Pedagogies of Crossing*, 4.
32. Alexander, 2.
33. Chancy, *Framing Silence*, 110.
34. With regard to the plot, toward the end of the novel, more of the connections become clear when we learn that Magda works for Gabrielle, who is Dominique's cousin (165).
35. Ménard, "Lasting Impact," 11.
36. McKittrick, *Demonic Grounds*, xi.
37. Trouillot, "Respecting the Diversity of Creativity."
38. Dayan, *With Dogs at the Edge of Life*, xvi.
39. Murray, "Time of Breach," 16.
40. Marty, *La littérature haïtienne dans la modernité*, 88.
41. Perry, *Vexy Thing*, 11.
42. Herbeck, *Architextual Authenticity*, 29–30.
43. Herbeck, 8.
44. Herbeck, 30.
45. Trouillot, *Haiti*, 109.
46. Trouillot, 120.
47. Trouillot, 121.
48. Parisot, "L'écrivaine haïtienne en son miroir," 319.
49. Smith, *Red and Black in Haiti*, 71.
50. Chancy, *Framing Silence*, 126.
51. Marty, *La littérature haïtienne dans la modernité*, 89.
52. McKittrick, *Demonic Grounds*, xi.
53. McKittrick, xvi.
54. McKittrick, xiiii.
55. See Benedicty-Kokken, "Male Protagonists."
56. Lahens cited in Dubois et al., *Haiti Reader*, 470.
57. Barnes, "Reluctant Matriarch," 137.
58. Danticat, *Create Dangerously*, 67.
59. hooks, *Black Looks*, 3.
60. McKittrick, *Demonic Grounds*, xxiii.
61. McKittrick, 145.
62. Nzengou-Tayo, "Impact de l'occupation américaine sur la représentation des femmes," 65.
63. Henderson, "Speaking in Tongues," 349.
64. Merlet, "More People Dream," 217.
65. Sourieau, "La couleur de l'aube de Yanick Lahens," 52.
66. McKittrick, *Demonic Grounds*, xvii.
67. Benedicty-Kokken, *Spirit Possession*, 5.

68. Here I am purposefully invoking quiet in the context of awareness the same way that Kevin Quashie analyzes its function in *The Sovereignty of Quiet: Beyond Resistance in Black Culture.*

69. Charles, "Reflections on Being a Machann ak Machandiz," 119.

70. Charles, 119.

71. Merlet, "More People Dream," 219.

72. Ulysse, *Why Haiti Needs New Narratives,* 82.

73. Ulysse, 83.

74. Benedicty-Kokken, *Spirit Possession,* 16.

75. Lyonel Trouillot, qtd. in Acacia, *Historicité et social structuration en Haïti,* 92.

76. Lyonel Trouillot, qtd. in Acacia, 92

77. Jones, "Poverty and the Limits of Literary Criticism," 768.

5. An Environmental Ethic

1. Deren, *Divine Horsemen,* 113.

2. Tinsley, *Thiefing Sugar,* 3.

3. Alexander, *Pedagogies of Crossing,* 284.

4. With regards to the environment, the Haitian Revolution can be seen as a simultaneous destruction and reclaiming of the land. One of the main acts of resistance was the burning of plantations. Thus, in order to take hold of the land, the landscape had to be destroyed.

5. O'Callaghan, "Gardening in the Tropics."

6. Negative connotations of this proverb arose especially after the earthquake when it was used in relation to the manifold problems that proliferated in its wake.

7. Desmangles, *Faces of the Gods,* 178.

8. Souffrant, "Circling Dantò's Daughter," 231.

9. Gaard, "New Directions for Eco-feminism," 68–69.

10. Just as Lawrence Buell points out, even the term *setting* used to describe the role of the environment in fiction is problematic: "It deprecates what it denotes, implying that the physical environment serves for artistic purposes merely as backdrop, ancillary to the main event." Lawrence Buell, "Representing the Environment," in Glotfelty and Fromm, *Ecocriticism,* 98.

11. Travis, "Introduction to Postcolonial Ecocriticism," 4–5.

12. Lopez, *Crossing Open Ground,* 97 (my emphasis).

13. Paravisni-Gebert, "'He of the Trees,'" 182.

14. Michel, *Aspects éducatifs et moraux du Vodou haïtien,* 24.

15. Michel, 34.

16. As critics of Haitian literature pay increasing attention to ecocriticism as a theoretical lens for reading fiction, the themes of disaster and apocalypse have been central to their analyses. My goal is to move away from the tropes of

disaster and catastrophe to explore the duality of harmony and enmity between people and land that we can observe in these novels. I am especially interested in how women's relationships to the land evoke futurity, intimacy, and care in each of the novels under considerations here.

17. See, for example, Lizabeth Paravisini-Gebert, Martin Munro, John Walsh, Kasia Mika, Jason Herbeck.

18. Campbell and Niblett, *The Caribbean: Aesthetics, World-Ecology, Politics,* 2.

19. See Jean-Charles, "'Perceiving the Relationships in Nature.'" As early as in the nineteenth century, Haitian authors from diverse perspectives have devoted their attention to the land. Some examples include Cléante Desgraves of Cercle Fémina, along with Ida Faubert's poetry in the early twentieth century, Jacques Roumain's canonical *Gouverneurs de la rosée* (1944), and Marie Chauvet in *La Légende des fleurs* (1947) and *Fonds des nègres* (1961) are among those who in earlier centuries highlighted the significance of the Haitian ecosystem in literature. These authors also draw from the natural world for inspiration for the creation of entire literary universes, as is clear in Chauvet's first play, *La Légende des fleurs.*

20. DeLoughrey and Handley, *Postcolonial Ecologies,* 11.

21. Paravisini-Gebert, "'He of the Trees,'" 184.

22. Savory, "Toward a Caribbean Ecopoetics," 80–81.

23. In *Conflict Bodies,* I examine the "woman as land metaphor" from a Black feminist perspective.

24. Dayan, *Haiti, History, and the Gods,* 124.

25. Paravisini-Gebert, "All Creation Is Cut Trees," 76.

26. Other scholars working on Haitian literature who have espoused ecocritical approaches are following this impulse include contemporary literary scholars such as Carine Mardorossian, Charles Forsdick, Jason Herbeck, and John Walsh.

27. Gaard, "Ecofeminism Revisited," 31.

28. Elsewhere I have written about *The Infamous Rosalie's* singular position as a novel set well before the Haitian Revolution; see Jean-Charles, "Memwa se paswa."

29. In fact, the name *Maroon* in and of itself is linked to the ecology of the mountains. They were first called *cimas* because they fled to the mountains (tops of the mountain); see Gonzalez, *Maroon Nation.*

30. Hartman, "Extended Notes on the Riot."

31. Chapman, Durban-Albrecht, and Lamothe, "Nous Mache Ansanm," 144.

32. Paravisini-Gebert, "Deforestation and the Yearning," 102.

33. Fawaz, "(Up)rooted Identities," 40.

34. DeLoughrey and Handley, *Postcolonial Ecologies,* xii.

35. As Ashon Crawley explains in *Blackpentecostal Breath: The Aesthetics of Possibility,* imagining "otherwise" is the imperative of the African diaspora thought. "Otherwise" possibilities, relations, and meanings activate our imaginations in alternative ways.

36. Gonzalez, *Maroon Nation*, 8.

37. Otto, "Reading the Plantation Landscape," 25.

38. McKittrick, *Demonic Grounds*, 9.

39. See Quashie, *Black Aliveness*.

40. McKittrick, 10.

41. McKittrick, xiv.

42. Paravasini-Gebert, "Deforestation and the Yearning," 3.

43. Alexander, "Groundings on *Rasanblaj*."

44. Fouchard, *Les marrons de la liberté*. See also *Les marrons du syllabaire*.

45. "Dans cette perspective, l'objectif fundamental du Code noir est d'instaurer un mode de relations entre les proptiétaires. Et leurs esclaves qui garantisse la rentabilité des 'Isles', c'est-à-dire qui évite à tout prix les désordres ou, pire, une soulèvement de la population servile" (From this perspective, the fundamental goal of the Black Code is to establish a mode of relationship between the owners and their slaves who guarantee the profitability of the 'Isles', that is, that avoids at all costs the disorders or, worse, an uprising of the servile population). *Le Code Noir*, 13.

46. See, for example, Malick Ghachem's *The Old Regime and the Haitian Revolution*.

47. Roberts, *Freedom as Marronage*, 98.

48. See Roberts.

49. Condé, "Order, Disorder," 154.

50. Fouchard, *Les Marrons de la liberté*, 390–91.

51. Fouchard, 380.

52. Allewaert, "Super Fly."

53. "Maroons in the Americas." *International Encyclopedia of the Social & Behavioral Sciences*, 2nd edition, Vol. 14, 591, http://dx.doi.org/10.1016/B978-0-08-097086-8.12106-3.

54. Alexander, "Groundings on *Rasanblaj*." See "IV. The Return to Land."

55. It is also worth noting that the Kreyòl word for tree is *pye bwa*, which translates literally into "foot of the forest" or "foot of wood."

56. The Code Noir forbade enslaved people to have any amulets of any kind. As Gran'n Charlotte warns Lisette about her forbidden talisman: "Burn it, hide it from here, throw it in the river, but don't have it on you. They hang people for less than that."

57. Gerdès Fleurant describes Bois-Caiman/Bwa Kayiman as the "ceremony of August 1791, a starting point in the struggle which led to the independence of Haiti in 1804." Fleurant, "Vodun, Music, and Society in Haiti," 53.

58. Tinsley, *Ezili's Mirrors*, 11.

59. Beckett, *There Is No Haiti*, 23.

60. Alexandre, *Properties of Violence*, 17.

61. Larrier, "Évelyne, Scenes, and Rosalie," 4.

62. Braithwaite cited in Gonzalez, *Maroon Nation*, 12.

63. Deloughrey, Gosson, and Handley, *Caribbean Literature and the Environment*, 12.

64. Paravisni-Gebert, "'He of the Trees,'" 183.

65. Mocombe, "Vodou Ethic and the Spirit of Communism," 91.

66. Bellegarde-Smith and Michel, *Haitian Vodou*, 33–34.

67. Michel, *Aspects éducatifs et moraux du Vodou haïtien*, 33.

68. Describing the *Kasalé* for the *Journal of Haitian Studies,* Leslie Péan writes, "*Kasalé* peint le monde haitien dans ses contradictions, ses splendeurs, ses mesquineries inextricables. Tout y est passions, rivalités, déchirements, malentendus, manipulations, retrouvailles, et surtout énigmes. Ils traversent et animent à souhait le nœud des relations familiales et/ou sociales qui unissent les personnages du *lakou*, dans un espace compris en gros dans les hauteurs de la Rivière Froide et au cours d'une période qui est celle de la dictature des Duvalier" (Kasalé paints the Haitian world in its contradictions, its splendors, its inextricable pettiness. Everything is passion, rivalries, rifts, misunderstandings, manipulations, reunions, and especially enigmas. They cross and animate at will the knot of family and/or social relations that unite the characters of the lakou, in a space roughly in the heights of the La Saline River and during a period that is that of the dictatorship of the Duvalier).

69. Desmangles, *Faces of the Gods*, 2–3.

70. In *Ezili's Mirrors: Imagining Black Queer Genders,* Omi'seke Natasha Tinsley's writes about vodou as epistemology by positing the only feminine lwa as epistemology and theory. Her acknowledgment of Ezili as a trope of Haitian cultural production is important, but her argument fails to account for how contemporary Haitian writers in Haiti approach (or do not approach) Vodou epistemologies in their work.

71. Smith, *When the Hands Are Many.*

72. Désir, "Diasporic Lakou," 282.

73. Gerdes Fleurant describes Vodou as the "one true religion of the Haitian people." Fleurant, "Vodun, Music, and Society in Haiti," 57.

74. Benson, "Religious and Material Aspects."

75. Benson.

76. Munro, *Writing on the Fault Line*, 69.

77. Daniels, "Mirrors, Mausoleums," 978.

78. Mars defines kay-mistè [*sic*] as a temple in the glossary of *Kasalé,* whereas Bellegarde-Smith and Michel describe it as a small family altar in *Haitian Vodou: Spirit, Myth, Reality.*

79. Edouard Glissant cited in DeLoughrey, Gosson, and Handley, *Caribbean Literature and the Environment*, 27.

80. Condé, "Order, Disorder," 158.

81. Glissant, *Caribbean Discourse*, 2.

82. Glissant, 105–6.

83. Glissant, *L'intention poétique*, 190.

84. Brown, *Mama Lola,* 17.
85. Brown, 345
86. Brown, 345.
87. Brown, 10.
88. Brown, 345.
89. See Herbeck, "Intertexts of the Ecological," 85.
90. N'Zengou-Tayo, "Fanm se Poto-Mitan," 135.
91. It takes thirty chapters for the character's identity to be revealed. We learn the protagonist's name at the beginning of chapter 31, which is twelve chapters before the final chapter of the book. "Quelqu'un m'a tuée avant de s'échapper vers *les bayahondes au loin sur la colline.* Je suis Cétoute Olmène Thérèse, la benjamine de Philomène Florival et Dieudonné Dorival" (Someone killed me before escaping to the bayahond trees far away on the hill. I am Cétoute Olmène Thérèse, the youngest daughter of Philomènne Florival and Dieudonné Dorival) (207).
92. Gronstad, *Film and the Ethical Imagination,* 32.
93. DeLoughrey, Gosson, and Handley, *Caribbean Literature and the Environment,* 4.
94. Michel, *Aspects éducatifs et moraux du Vodou haïtien,* 24.
95. Paravasini-Gebert, "'He of the Trees,'" 182.
96. Walcott, "Sea is History," 69.
97. Deckard, "Political Ecology of Storms," 27.
98. This flooding in Gonaïves was a critical moment of artists gathering and sounding the alarm. The bilingual poetry collection *24 Poèmes pour Gonaïves* was published shortly afterwards to honor the dead and raise funds to address the damage from the storm. Trouillot, Lahens, and Mars have poems in the collection.
99. Michel, *Aspects éducatifs et moraux du Vodou haïtien,* 35.
100. Brown, *Mama Lola,* 6.
101. Daniels, "We Who Are Vulnerable."
102. Buell, *Environmental Imagination,* 98.
103. Dayan, "France Reads Haiti," 160.
104. Brand, *Map to the Door to No Return,* 10.
105. Brand, 10.
106. Tinsley, "Black Atlantic, Queer Atlantic," 194.
107. Alexander, *Pedagogies of Crossing,* 290.
108. Chapman, Durban-Albrecht, and Lamothe, "Nou Mache Ansanm," 144.
109. Chapman, Durban-Albrecht, and Lamothe, 144.
110. Sapp, "Talking Dead," 119.
111. Sapp, 120.
112. Sapp, 121.
113. Herbeck, "Intertexts of the Ecological," 82.
114. Brown, *Mama Lola,* 6.
115. Paravasini-Gebert, "'He of the Trees,'" 182.
116. "Anse bleue et ses histoires," *Le Nouvelliste.* Accessed May 2017.

117. Valdés, *Oshun's Daughters*, 2.

118. Spivak, *Aesthetic Education*, 18.

Coda

1. Trouillot, "Respecting the Diversity of Creativity."

2. Hobson, "Farah Jasmine Griffin on the Legacy of Black Feminism."

3. Palladino, *Ethics and Aesthetics*, 29.

4. Others include Rico, the protagonist of *L'heure hybride*, who rapes another man at the end of the novel, and Raoul Vincent in *Saisons sauvages*.

5. Fito's concupiscence is not unique among Mars's characters; those familiar with her work are aware of the extent to which sex and in particular sexual deviance figures prominently in her oeuvre.

6. Mars dedicates her novel with the phrase "Aux survivants du séisme du 12 janvier."

7. Vignoli, "Des secrets sous les décombres."

8. Munro, "Kettly Mars's *Aux frontières de la soif*," 3.

9. Munro, 4.

10. Benedicty-Kokken, *Spirit Possession*, 342.

11. Danticat, "We Are Ugly, But We Are Here."

12. Danticat.

13. See Munro "Kettly Mars's *Aux frontières de la soif* and the Haitian Post-Earthquake Novel," and Walsh, *Migration and Refuge,* neither of whom mentions the young girls that Fito preys on.

14. Johnson, "Politics of Tenderness," 21.

15. Or, as Toni Morrison puts it in her discussion of Ralph Ellison's *Invisible Man,* "And the question for me was, Invisible to whom? Not to me." Morrison qtd in Als, "Toni Morrison and the Ghosts in the House."

16. Benedicty-Kokken, *Spirit Possession*, 343.

17. Clitandre, *Edwidge Danticat*, 15.

18. Joseph-Gabriel, "Tant de silence," xiii.

19. Benedicty, "Safe Place."

20. Danticat, "Évelyne Sincère Is Haiti."

21. http://kayfanm.org/wp-content/uploads/2020/09/2020.09.14-Feminist-position-on-Minister-Culture-attacks-English.pdf.

22. Tinsley, *Thiefing Sugar,* 33.

23. Noel, "Unrelenting."

24. Hobson, "Farah Jasmine Griffin on the Legacy of Black Feminism."

Bibliography

Primary Texts

Lahens, Yanick. *Bain de lune*. Paris: Sabine Wespeiser, 2014.

———. *The Colour of Dawn*. Translated by Alison Layland. Bridgeland, Wales: Seren Books, 2013.

———. *Dans la maison du père*. Paris: Le Serpent à plumes, 2000.

———. *Guillaume et Nathalie*. Paris: Sabine Wespeiser, 2013.

———. *La couleur de l'aube*. Port-au-Prince: Presses Nationales d'Haïti, 2008.

———. *Moonbath*. Translated by Emily Gogolak. New York: Deep Vellum, 2017.

Mars, Kettly. *Aux frontières de la soif*. Paris: Vents d'ailleurs, 2013.

———. *Fado*. Paris: Marcure de France, 2008.

———. *Je suis vivant*. Paris: Vents d'ailleurs, 2017.

———. *Kasalé*. Port-au-Prince: Imprimeur II, 2003; La Roque d'Anthéron, France: Vents d'Ailleurs, 2007.

———. *L'heure hybride*. La Roque d'Anthéron, France: Vents d'Ailleurs, 2005.

———. *Saisons sauvages*. Paris: Mercure de France, 2010.

Octavia, Gaël. *La Bonne histoire de Madeleine Démétrius*. Paris: Gallimard, 2020.

———. *La fleur rouge*. Port-au-Prince: Le Natal, 1992.

———. *Le Creuset*. Port-au-Prince: H. Deschamps, 1980.

———. *Le Passage*. Port-au-Prince: Le Natal, 1996; nouvelle édition revue par l'auteure, Port-au-Prince: Deschamps, 2008.

———. *Le Passage (Vale of Tears)*. Translated by Carrol Coates. Bethesda, MD: Ibex Publishers, 2005.

Roumain, Jacques. *Gouverneurs de la rosée*. Pompano Beach, FL: EducaVision, 1999.

Trouillot, Évelyne. *Absences sans frontières*. Montpellier: Chèvre Feuille Étoilée, 2013.

———. *The Infamous Rosalie*. Translated by M. A. Salvadon. Introduction by Edwidge Danticat. Lincoln: University of Nebraska Press, 2013.

————. *La mémoire aux abois.* Paris: Hoëbeke, 2010.

————. *Le Rond-point.* Port-au-Prince: L'Imprimeur, 2015.

————. *L'oeil totem.* Port-au-Prince: Presses Nationales d'Haïti, 2006.

————. *Rosalie l'Infâme.* Paris: Éditions Dapper, 2003.

Secondary Texts

Acacia, Michel. *Historicité et social structuration en Haïti.* Port-au-Prince: L'imprimeur II, 2006.

Accilien, Cécile. *Haitian Hollywood.* New York: SUNY Press, 2022.

Adamson, Ginette. "Yanick Lahens romancière: Pour une autre voix/voie haïtienne." In *Elles écrivent des Antilles: Haïti, Guadeloupe, Martinique,* edited by Susan Rinne and Joëlle Vitiello, 109–17. Paris : L'Harmattan, 1997.

Agard-Jones, Vanessa. "Le Jeu de Qui? Sexual Politics at Play in the French Caribbean." In *Sex and the Citizen,* edited by Faith Smith, 181–98. Charlottesville: University of Virginia Press, 2011.

Agiletti, Jessica, and Évelyne Trouillot. "Entretien, 107." *Francofonia,* no. 52 (Primavera 2007): 105–114.

Ahmed, Sara. *Living a Feminist Life.* Durham: Duke University Press, 2017.

————. *Willful Subjects.* Durham: Duke University Press, 2014.

Alexander, M. Jacqui. "Groundings on *Rasanblaj.*" *E-misférica* 12, no. 1 (2015).

————. *Pedagogies of Crossing.* Durham: Duke University Press, 2005.

————, and Chandra Talpade Mohanty. *Feminist Genealogies, Colonial Legacies, Democratic Futures.* New York: Routledge, 1997.

Alexandre, Sandy. *The Properties of Violence: Claims to Ownership in Representations of Lynching.* Jackson: University Mississippi Press, 2012.

Alexis, Darline. *Déjouer le silence: Contre-discours sur les femmes haïtiennes,* edited by Sabine Lamour, Denyse Côté, and Darline Alexis. Montréal: Éditions remue-ménage, 2018.

————. Review of *Guillaume et Nathalie. Journal Haitian Studies* 19, no. 1 (2013): 293–95.

Allen, Jafari. "Blackness, Sexuality, and Transnational Desire: Initial Notes toward a New Research Agenda." In *Black Sexualities: Probing Powers, Passions, Practices, and Policies,* edited by Juan Battle and Sandra Barnes, 82–96. Newark: Rutgers University Press, 2010.

Allewaert, Monique. *Ariel's Ecology: Plantations, Personhood, and Colonialism in the American Tropics.* Minneapolis: University of Minnesota Press, 2013.

————. "Super Fly: François Makandal's Colonial Semiotics." *American Literature* 91. 3 (2019): 459–90.

Als, Hilton. "Toni Morrison and the Ghosts in the House." *The New Yorker* 19 October 2003.

Anglade-Neptune, Miriam. *L'autre moitié du développement: À propos du travail des femmes en Haïti.* Paris: Karthala, 1986.

Anim-Addo, Joan. *Framing the Word: Gender and Genre in Caribbean Women's Writing*. London: Whiting and Birch, 1996.

"Anse-bleue et ses histoires." *Le Nouvelliste*. https://lenouvelliste.com/article /137981/anse-bleue-et-ses-histoires#:~:text=Elle%20y%20vit.,difficult%C3 %A9s%20auxquelles%20ils%20se%20heurtent.

Augustin, Chenald. "Décès de l'écrivain et femme de théâtre Paulette Poujol Oriol." *Le Nouvelliste*, Mar. 14, 2011. lenouvelliste.com/article/90136/deces -de-lecrivain-et-femme-de-theatre-paulette-poujol-oriol.

Babin, Céline, Marcia Brown, and Pedro A. Sandin-Fremaint, ed. *Le roman féminin d'Haïti: Forme et structure,* présentation de Maximilien Laroche, Sainte-Foy (Québec), GRELCA, 1985.

Badiou, Alain. *Ethics: An Essay on the Understanding of Evil*. London: Verson, 2001.

Bailey, Marlon, and L. H. Stallings. "Sexuality." In *Keywords for African American Studies,* edited by Erica Edwards, Roderick Ferguson, and Jeff Ogbar, 196– 200. New York: New York University Press, 2018.

Bailey, Moya. "Homolatent Masculinty." *Palimpsest: A Journal on Women, Gender, and the Black International* 2, no. 2 (2013): 187–99.

Banita, Georgiana. *Plotting Justice: Narrative Ethics and Literary Culture After 9/11*. Lincoln: University of Nebraska Press, 2012.

Barnes, Natasha. *Cultural Conundrums: Gender, Race, Nation, and the Making of Caribbean Cultural Politics*. Ann Arbor: University of Michigan Press, 2006.

———. "Reluctant Matriarch: Sylvia Wynter and the Problematics of Caribbean Feminism." *Small Axe* 5, (March 1999): 34–47.

Beckett, Gregory. *There is No Haiti: Between Life and Death in Port-au-Prince*. Los Angeles: University of California Press, 2019.

Bell, Madison Smartt. "Permanent Exile: On Marie Vieux Chauvet." *The Nation* 14 January 2010.

Bellegarde-Smith, Patrick, and Claudine Michel, eds. *Haitian Vodou: Myth, Spirit, and Reality*. Bloomington: Indiana University Press, 2006.

Benedicty, Alessandra. "A Safe Place: A Conversation with Kettly Mars." *SX Salon* 18, February 2015. smallaxe.net/sxsalon/discussions/safe-place.

Benedicty-Kokken, Alessandra. "Male Protagonists and Haitian (Un)inhabitability in Kettly Mars's *L'Heure hybride* and *Aux frontières de la soif*." *Francosphères* (2015): 105–20.

———. *Spirit Possession in French, Haitian, and Vodou Thought*. Lexington: Lexington Books, 2014.

———, and Kaiama Glover. "Revisiting Marie Vieux-Chauvet." *Yale French Studies* 128 (2015).

———, Jhon Picard Byron, Kaiama L. Glover, and Mark Schuller. *The Haiti Exception: Anthropology and the Predicament of Narrative*. Liverpool: Liverpool University Press, 2016.

324   *Bibliography*

Benson, LeGrace. "Religious and Material Aspects for Creative Education and Expression," Caribbean Studies Association Conference panel, Cuba. Friday, June 8, 2018.

Bernard, Robenson. "*L'oeil-totem* un roman entrainant d'Évelyne Trouillot," *Le Nouvelliste,* July 27, 2006. lenouvelliste.com/article/32324/loeil-totem-un -roman-entrainant-develyne-trouilot.

Berrou, Raphaël, and Pradel Pompilus. *Histoire de la littérature haïtienne.* Port-au-Prince: Éditons Caraïbes, 1975.

Berrouït-Oriol, Robert. "Hommage à Paulette Poujol Oriol: Décès d'une grande dame des letter haïtiennes." *Journal of Haitian Studies* 17, no. 1 (Spring 2011): 9–11.

"Biographie." Kettly Mars, 2021, kettlymars.com/biographie/.

Bocandé, Anne. "Interview of Anne Bocandé with Yanick Lahens." *Africultures,* February 2, 2014. africultures.com/je-ne-peux-pas-mempecher-decrire-a-partir -de-ma-situation-de-femmeaussi-12055/#prettyPhoto.

Boris, Eileen. "Class Returns." *Journal of Women's History* 25, no. 4 (2013): 74–88.

Boyce Davies, Carole. *Black Women, Writing, and Identity: Migrations of the Subject.* New York: Routledge, 1994.

Brand, Dionne. *A Map to the Door of No Return: Notes to Belonging.* New York: Penguin Press, 2002.

Brodziak, Sylvie. *Haïti enjeux d'écriture.* France: Presses Universitaires de Vincennes, 2013.

Brown, Karen McCarthy. *Mama Lola: A Vodou Priestess in Brooklyn.* Berkeley: University of California Press, 1991.

Buell, Lawrence. "Ecocriticism: Some Emerging Trends." *Qui Parle: Critical Humanities and Social Sciences* 19, no. 2 (2011): 87–115.

———. *The Environmental Imagination: Thoreau, Nature Writing, and the Formation of American Culture.* Cambridge: Harvard University Press, 1995.

———. *The Future of Environmental Criticism: Environmental Crisis and Literary Imagination.* Malden, MA: Wiley-Blackwell, 2005.

———. "What We Talk about When We Talk about Ethics." In *The Turn to Ethics,* edited by Marjorie Garber, Beatrice Hanssen, and Rebecca L. Walkowitz, 1–14. New York: Routledge, 2000.

Butler, Judith. *Giving an Account of Oneself.* New York: Fordham University Press, 2005.

———. *The Psychic Life of Power: Theories in Subjection.* Stanford: Stanford University Press, 1997.

———. *Undoing Gender.* New York: Routledge, 2004.

Calasanti, Toni M., and Kathleen Slevin, eds. *Gender, Social Inequalities, and Aging.* Walnut Creek, CA: AltaMira Press, 2001.

Caminero-Santangelo, Byron. *Different Shades of Green: African Literature, Environmental Justice, and Political Ecology.* Charlottesville: University of Virginia Press, 2014.

Campbell, Chris, and Michael Niblett, eds. *The Caribbean: Aesthetics, World Ecology, Politics.* Liverpool: Liverpool University Press, 2016.

Campbell, Chris, and Erin Sommerville. *What is Earthly Paradise? Eco-critical Responses to the Caribbean.* Newcastle, UK: Cambridge Scholars Publishing, 2007.

Campbell, Elaine. "Narcissism an Ethical Practice?: Foucault, Aksesis and an Ethics of Becoming." *Cultural Sociology* 4, no. 1 (March 2010): 23–44.

Campt, Tina. "Black Visuality and the Practice of Refusal." *Women & Performance,* February 25, 2019, womenandperformance.org/ampersand/29–1/campt.

———. *Listening to Images.* Durham: Duke University Press, 2017.

"Carol Gilligan: Interview on June 21st, 2011." *Ethics of Care,* July 16, 2011, ethicsofcare.org/carol-gilligan/.

Cavarero, Adriana. *Relating Narratives: Storytelling and Selfhood.* Translated by Paul A. Kottman. London: Routledge, 2000.

Chancy, Myriam. "Ayiti çé ter glissé: L'occupation américaine en Haïti et l'émergence de voix féminines en littérature." In *Elles écrivent des Antilles: Haiti, Guadeloupe, Martinique,* edited by Suzanne Rinne and Joëlle Vitiello, 17–37. Paris: L'Harmattan, 1997.

———. "The Feminist Movement." *Haiti: Island Luminous,* IX. 1935 to 1956. islandluminous.fiu.edu/. Accessed June 15, 2020.

———. *Framing Silence: Revolutionary Novels by Haitian Women.* New Brunswick, NJ: Rutgers University Press, 1997.

———. *From Sugar to Revolution: Women's Visions of Haiti, Cuba and the Dominican Republic.* Waterloo, Ontario: Wilfirs Laurrier University Press, 2012.

Chapman, Dasha A., Erin L. Durban-Albrecht, and Mario Lamothe. "Nou Mache Ansanm (We Walk Together): Queer Haitian Performance and Affiliation." *Women & Performance: A Journal of Feminist Theory* 27, no. 2 (2017): 143–59.

Charles, Carolle. "Gender and Politics in Contemporary Haiti: The Duvalierist State and the Emergence of a New Feminism." *Feminist Studies* 21, no. 1 (1995): 135–64.

———. "Reflections on Being a Machann ak Machandiz." *Meridians: Feminism, Race, Transnationalism* 11 (2011): 118–23.

———. "A Sociological Counter-reading of Marie Chauvet as an 'Outsider-Within': Paradoxes in the Construction of Haitian Women in *Love, Anger, Madness.*" *Journal of Haitian Studies* 20, no. 2 (Fall 2014): 66–89.

Chemla, Yves. *La question de l'autre dans le roman haïtien contemporain,* préface d'Émile Ollivier. Paris: Ibis Rouge, 2003.

Christian, Barbara. "The Race for Theory." *Cultural Critique* 6 (Spring 1987): 51–63.

Ciurria, Michelle. *An Intersectional Feminist Theory of Moral Responsibility.* New York: Routledge, 2020.

Clark, Timothy. *The Cambridge Introduction to Literature and the Environment.* Cambridge: Cambridge University Press, 2011.

Clark, Vèvè. "Developing Diaspora Literacy and Marasa Consciousness." *Theatre Survey* 50, no. 1 (May 2009): 9–18.

Claude-Narcisse, Jasmine. "Marie-Jeanne." *Haiti Culture,* 2005, haiticulture .ch/Marie-Jeanne.html. Previously published in Jasmine Claude-Narcisse, *Mémoire de femmes.* Port-au-Prince: UNICEF-Haiti, 1997.

"Cléanthe Desgraves Valcin." *Prabook,* 2021, prabook.com/web/cleanthe _desgraves.valcin/1120474.

Clergé, Natacha. "Pour en finir avec une historiographie héroïsante: Critique de l'historiographie féministe traditionnelle." In *Déjouer le silence: Contre-discours sur les femmes haïtiennes,* edited by Sabine Lamour, Denyse Côté, and Darline Alexis, 224–35. Montreal: Les Éditions remue-ménage, 2018.

Cless, Downing. *Ecology and Environment in European Drama.* London: Routledge, 2010.

Clitandre, Nadège. *Edwidge Danticat: The Haitian Diasporic Imaginary.* Charlottesville: University of Virginia Press, 2018.

Coates, Carrol. "Paulette Poujol Orion, *Le Creuset* and Other Works: Problems of Translation from Kreyòl to English." *Journal of Haitian Studies* 17, no. 1 (2011): 53–70.

Collins, Patricia Hill. *Black Feminist Thought: Knowledge, Consciousness, and the Politics of Empowerment.* London: Routledge, 2008.

———. *Intersectionality as Critical Social Theory.* Durham: Duke University Press, 2019.

———. "The Social Construction of Black Feminist Thought." *Signs* 14, no. 4 (1989): 745–73. http://www.jstor.org/stable/3174683.

Condé, Maryse. *La parole des femmes: Essai sur des romancières des Antilles de langue française.* Paris: Harmattan, 1979.

———. "Order, Disorder, Freedom, and the West Indian Writer." 50 Years of Yale French Studies: A Commemorative Anthology. Part 2: 1980–1998, *Yale French Studies* 97 (2000): 151–65.

Crawley, Ashon. *Blackpentecostalbreath: The Aesthetics of Possibility.* New York: Fordham University Press, 2016.

Crenshaw, Kimberlé. "Mapping the Margins: Intersectionality, Identity Politics, and Violence Against Women." *Stanford Law Review* 43, no. 6 (1991): 1241–99.

———. "What Intersectionality Means Today." *Time,* February 2, 2020.

Cristofovici, Anca. *Touching Surfaces: Photographic Aesthetics, Temporality, Aging.* Amsterdam: Rodopi, 2008.

Dalembert, Louis-Philippe, and Lyonel Trouillot. *Haïti: Une traversée littéraire.* Port-au-Prince: Presses nationales d'Haïti, 2010.

Dalleo, Raphael. *Caribbean Literature and the Public Sphere: From the Plantation to the Postcolonial.* Charlottesville: University of Virginia Press, 2011.

Daniels, Kyrah. "The Haitian Divine Nine: Initiations in Vodou's Sacred Arts." In *Africana Religious Women,* edited by Rachel Panton and Funlayo Wood-Menzies. Jackson: University of Mississippi Press, forthcoming.

———. "Mirror Mausoleums, Mortuary Arts, and Haitian Religious Unexceptionalism." *Journal of the American Academy of Religion* 85, no. 4 (December 2017): 957–84.

———. "We Who Are Vulnerable Are Also Powerful: Motherhood, Birth, and Religious Healing in the Black Atlantic." Yale University Lecture, April 1, 2019.

Danticat, Edwidge. *Create Dangerously: The Immigrant Artist at Work.* Princeton: Princeton University Press, 2011.

———. "Évelyne Sincère Is Haiti, She Is Also All of Us," *Woy Magazine,* November 6, 2020. woymagazine.com/2020/11/06/evelyne-sincere-is-haiti-she-is-also-all-of-us/.

———. "Évelyne Trouillot." *Bomb Magazine* 90 (Winter 2004/05): 48–53.

———. "Novelist Edwidge Danticat: 'Haitians Are Very Resilient, But It Doesn't Mean They Can Suffer More Than Other People.'" *Democracy Now,* January 12, 2011, democracynow.org/2011/1/12/novelist_edwidge_danticat_haitians_are_very.

———. "We Are Ugly, but We Are Here." *The Caribbean Writer* 10 (1996).

Dash, Michael. *Literature and Ideology in Haiti, 1915–1961.* Totowa, NJ: Barnes and Noble Books, 1981.

———. "Neither Magical nor Exceptional: The Idea of the Ordinary in Caribbean Studies." *Journal of Haitian Studies* (Fall 2013): 24–32.

Davis, Analee, Joscelyn Gardner, Erica Moriah James, and Jerry Philogène. "Introduction: Art as Caribbean Feminist Practice," *Small Axe* 52, no. 3 (2017): 34–42.

Davis, Angela. *Freedom Is a Constant Struggle: Ferguson, Palestine, and the Foundations of a Movement.* New York: Haymarket Books, 2016.

———. *Women, Race, and Class.* New York: Vintage Books, 1981.

Davis, Todd F., and Kenneth Womack. *Mapping the Ethical Turn: A Reader in Ethics, Culture, and Literary Theory.* Charlottesville: University of Virginia Press, 2001.

Dayan, Colin (Joan). "France Reads Haiti: René Depestre's *Hadriana dans tous mes rêves.*" In "Post/Colonial Conditions: Exiles, Migrations, and Nomadisms," special issue, *Yale French Studies* 2, no. 83 (1993): 154–75.

———. *Haiti, History, and the Gods.* Berkeley: University of California Press, 1998.

———. *With Dogs at the Edge of Life.* New York: Columbia University Press, 2015.

De Caires Narain, Denise. "Naming Same-Sex Desire in Caribbean Women's Texts: Toward a Creolizing Hermeneutics." *Contemporary Women's Writing* 6, no. 3 (November 2012): 94–212.

———. "Writing 'Home': Mediating Between 'The Local' and 'The Literary' in a Selection of Postcolonial Women's Texts." *Third World Quarterly* 26, no. 3, Connecting Cultures (2005): 497–508.

Deckard, Sharae. "The Political Ecology of Storms in Caribbean Literature." In *The Caribbean: World-Ecology, Aesthetics, Politics,* edited by Chris Campbell and Michael Niblett, 25–45. Liverpool: Liverpool University Press, 2016.

De Ferrari, Guillermina. *Vulnerable States: Bodies of Memory in Contemporary Caribbean Fiction.* Charlottesville: University of Virginia Press, 2007.

DeLoughrey, Elizabeth, Renée K. Gosson, and George B. Handley, eds. *Caribbean Literature and the Environment: Between Nature and Culture.* Charlottesville: University of Virginia Press, 2005.

DeLoughrey, Elizabeth, Jill Didur, and Anthony Carrigan, eds. *Global Ecologies and the Environmental Humanities: Postcolonial Approaches.* New York: Routledge, 2015.

DeLoughrey, Elizabeth, and George Handley, eds. *Postcolonial Ecologies: Literatures of the Environment.* Oxford: Oxford University Press, 2011.

DelConte, Matt. "Why *You* Can't Speak: Second-Person Narration, Voice, and a New Model for Understanding Narrative." *Style* 37, no. 2 (Summer 2003): 204–19.

Deren, Maya. *Divine Horsemen.* New Paltz, NY: McPherson, 1983.

Désir, Charlene. "Diasporic Lakou: A Haitian Academic Explores Her Roots in Post-Earthquake Haiti." *Harvard Educational Review* 81, no.2 (Summer 2011): 278–95.

Desmangles, Leslie. *Faces of the Gods: Vodou and Roman Catholicism in Haiti.* Chapel Hill: University of North Carolina Press, 1992.

Des Rosiers, Joël. *Théories Caraïbes: Poétique du déracinement.* Montréal: Tryptique, 1996.

Destinvil, Jeff. "Mireille Neptune Anglade, économiste (1944–2010)." *Éditions science et bien commun,* scienceetbiencommun.pressbooks.pub/haitiennes/chapter/mireille-neptune-anglade-economiste-1944–2010/.

Dolan, Josephine, and Estella Tincknell, eds. *Aging Femininities: Troubling Representations.* Newcastle, UK: Cambridge Scholars, 2012.

Donnell, Alison. *Twentieth-Century Caribbean Literature: Critical Moments in Anglophone Literary History.* London: Routledge, 2006.

Douyon, Frantz. *Démocratie et éthique vaudoue en Haiti.* Paris: Harmattan, 2018.

Dovey, Ceridwen. "What Old Age Is Really Like." *New Yorker,* October 1, 2015, newyorker.com/culture/cultural-comment/what-old-age-is-really-like.

Dubois, Laurent. *Avengers of the New World: The Story of the Haitian Revolution.* New York: Belknap Press, 2005.

————, Kaiama Glover, Nadève Ménard, Millery Polyné, and Chantalle Verna, eds. *The Haiti Reader*. Durham: Duke University Press, 2020.

Durocher, Évelyne, et al. "Ethical Questions Identified in a Study of Local and Expatriate Responders' Perspectives of Vulnerability in the 2010 Haiti Earthquake." *Journal of Medical Ethics* 43, no. 9 (2017): 613.

Edmondson, Belinda. *Making Men: Gender, Literary Authority, and Women's Writing in Caribbean Narrative*. Durham: Duke University Press, 1999.

Ellis, Nadia. "Out and Bad: Towards a Queer Performance Hermeneutic in Jamaican Dancehall." *Small Axe 15, no. 2* (July 2011): 7–23.

"Entretien de Anne Bocandé avec Yanick Lahens." *Africultures,* February 2, 2014, http://africultures.com/je-ne-peux-pas-mempecher-decrire-a-partir-de-ma-situation-de-femmeaussi-12055/.

Etienne, Gérard. *La femme noire dans le discours littéraire haïtien*. Montreal: Balzac-Le Griot éditeur, 1998.

Eze, Chielozona. *Ethics and Human Rights in Anglophone African Women's Literature: Feminist Empathy*. New York: Palgrave MacMillan, 2016.

Fawaz, Yasmina. "(Up)rooted Identities: Caribbean Environmental and Cultural Interplay in Glissant's Mahogany." *Symposium: A Quarterly Journal in Modern Literatures* 70, no. 1 (2016): 36–45.

Ferguson, Roderick. *Aberrations in Black: Toward a Queer of Color Critique*. Minneapolis: University of Minnesota Press, 2003.

Fleurant, Gerdes. "Vodun, Music, and Society in Haiti: Affirmation and Identity." In *Haitian Vodou: Spirit, Myth and Reality,* edited by Michel and Bellegarde-Smith, 45–57. Bloomington: Indiana University Press, 2006.

Forbes, Curdella. "Between Plot and Plantation, Trespass and Transgression: Caribbean Migratory Disobedience in Fiction and Internet Traffic." *Small Axe* 16, no. 2 (2012): 23–42.

Forsdick, Charles, "Haïti et les études postcoloniales: Dimensions théoriques, dimensions littéraires." In *Perspectives européennes des études littéraires francophones,* edited by Claude Coste and Daniel Lançon, 155–66. Paris: Honoré Champion, 2014.

Fouchard, Jean. *Les marrons de la liberté*. Paris: L'école, 1972.

————. *Les marrons du syllabaire*. Port-au-Prince: Henri Deschamps, 1988.

Francis, Donette. *Fictions of Feminine Citizenship: Sexuality and the Nation in Contemporary Caribbean Literature*. New York: Palgrave Macmillan, 2010.

Freadman, Richard. "Ethics, Autobiography and the Will: Stephen Spender's *World Within World*." In *The Ethics in Literature,* edited by Andrew Hadfield, Dominic Rainsford, and Tim Woods, 17–37. London: Palgrave MacMillan, 1999.

Frohnapfel, David. "Tessa Mars." *Berlin Biennale,* bb10.berlinbiennale.de/artists/T/tessa-mars.

Fumagalli, Maria Cristina, Hulme Peter, Robinson Owen, and Wylie Lesley, eds. *Surveying the American Tropics: Literary Geography from New York to Rio*. Liverpool: Liverpool University Press, 2013.

Gaard, Greta. "Ecofeminism Revisited: Rejecting Essentialism and Re-Placing Species in a Material Feminist Environmentalism." *Feminist Formations* 23, no. 2 (2011): 26–53.

———. "New Directions for Ecofeminism: Toward a More Feminist Ecocriticism." *Interdisciplinary Studies in Literature and Environment* 17, no. 4 (2010): 643–65.

Gardiner, Madeleine. *Visages de femmes, portraits d'écrivains.* Port-au-Prince: Henri Deschamps, 1981.

Gertz, Charlotte. "Growing Old with Dignity: Women in Francophone Literature of the Caribbean." PhD diss., City University of New York, 2009.

Getachew, Adom. *Worldmaking after Empire: The Rise and Fall of Self-Determination.* Princeton: Princeton University Press, 2020.

Ghachem, Malick. *The Old Regime and the Haitian Revolution.* Cambridge: Cambridge University Press, 2012.

Gikandi, Simon. "Theory, Literature, and Moral Considerations." *Research in African Literatures* 32, no. 4 (Winter 2001): 1–18.

Gill, Lyndon. *Erotic Islands: Art and Activism in the Queer Caribbean.* Durham: Duke University Press, 2019.

———. "Situating Black, Situating Queer: Black Queer Diaspora Studies and the Art of Embodied Listening." *Transforming Anthropology* 20.1 (2012): 32–44.

Glissant, Edouard. *Caribbean Discourse: Selected Essays.* Translated by Michael Dash. Charlottesville: University of Virginia Press, 1989.

———. *Le discours antillais.* Paris: Seuil, 1981.

———. *L'intention poétique.* Paris: Gallimard, 1997.

Glotfelty, Cheryl, and Harold Fromm, eds. *The Ecocriticism Reader: Landmarks in Literary Ecology.* Athens: University of Georgia Press, 1996.

Glover, Kaiama. "'Black' Radicalism in Haiti and the Disorderly Feminine: The Case of Marie Vieux Chauvet." *Small Axe* 17, no. 1 (2013): 7–21.

———. *A Regarded Self: Caribbean Womanhood and the Ethics of Disorderly Being.* Durham: Duke University Press, 2021.

———. "A Woman's Place Is In . . . : The Unhomely as Social Critique in Marie Chauvet's *Fille d'Haïti.*" *Yale French Studies* 128 (2015).

Goldman, Marlene. "Introduction: Literature, Imagination, Ethics." *University of Toronto Quarterly* 76, no. 3 (2007): 809–20.

Gonzalez, Johnhenry. *Maroon Nation: A History of Revolutionary Haiti.* New Haven: Yale University Press, 2019.

Gotlib, Anna. "Feminist Ethics and Narrative Ethics." *Internet Encyclopedia of Philosophy,* iep.utm.edu/fem-e-n/.

Gouraige, Ghislain. *Histoire de la littérature haïtienne: De l'indépendance à nos jours.* Geneva: Slatkin Reprints, 2003.

Griffin, Farah Jasmine. *Read Until You Understand: The Profound Wisdom of Black Life and Literature.* New York: Norton, 2021.

Gronstad, Asbjorn. "The Return of Ethics in Literary Studies." *Film and the Ethical Imagination,* 31–43. Bergen, Norway: Palgrave MacMillan, 2016.

Guillaume, Rutshelle. *Emotions.* Ayiti Deploge, 2014.

Gumbs, Alexis Pauline. "Ceremony." May 15, 2020. *Writing Home: American Voices from the Caribbean,* podcast, interview with Kaiama Glover and Tami Navarro, season 1, episode 2, https://www.writingho.me/2020/05/15/episode-02-ceremony/.

———. *Dub: Finding Ceremony.* Duke University Press, 2020.

———. *M Archive.* Durham: Duke University Press, 2018.

———. *Spill.* Durham: Duke University Press, 2016.

Hagberg, Garry L. *Fictional Characters, Real Problems.* Oxford: Oxford University Press, 2016.

Halberstam, Jack, José Esteban Muñoz, and David L. Eng, eds. "What's Queer about Queer Studies Now," *Social Text* 84–85, vol. 23, nos. 3–4 (Fall–Winter 2005).

Hale, Dorothy J. "Aesthetics and the New Ethics: Theorizing the Novel in the Twenty-First Century." *PMLA* 124, no. 3 (2009): 869–905.

———. "Fiction as Restriction: Self-Binding in New Ethical Theories of the Novel." *Narrative* 15, no. 2 (2007): 187–206. http://www.jstor.org/stable/30219250.

Harpham, Geoffrey Galt. "Ethics." In *Critical Terms for Literary Study,* edited by Frank Lenttrichia and Thomas McLaughlin, 394–5. Chicago: University of Chicago Press, 1995.

Harris, Melanie. *Gifts of Virtue, Alice Walker, and Womanist Ethics.* New York: Palgrave MacMillan, 2013.

Harris, Wilson. *The Guyana Quartet.* Boston: Faber and Faber, 1985.

Hartman, Saidiya. "Extended Notes on the Riot." *e-flux Journal* 105 (2019). https://www.e-flux.com/journal/105/302565/extended-notes-on-the-riot/.

———. *Scenes of Subjection: Slavery, Terror, and Self-Making in Nineteenth Century America.* Oxford: Oxford University Press, 1997.

Haynes, Tonya. "Interrogating Approaches to Caribbean Feminist Thought." *Journal of Eastern Caribbean Studies* 42, no. 3 (December 2017): 26–58.

Henderson, Mae Gwendolyn. "Speaking in Tongues: Dialogics and Dialectics and The Black Woman Writer's Literary Tradition," In *African American Literary Theory: A Reader,* edited by Winston Napier, 348–68. New York: New York University Press, 2000.

Herbeck, Jason. *Architextual Authenticity: Constructing Literature and Literary Identity in the French Caribbean.* Liverpool: Liverpool University Press, 2017.

———. "Entretien avec Évelyne Trouillot." *The French Review* 82, no. 4 (March 2009): 822–29.

———. "Intertexts of the Ecological: Literary Space Revisited in Yanick Lahens's *Bain de lune." Journal of Haitian Studies* 23, no. 2 (Fall 2017). ·

———. "Review of *Le Rond-point* by Évelyne Trouillo*t*." *Journal of Haitian Studies 22,* no. 1 (2016): 190–94.

Hobson, Janell. "Farah Jasmine Griffin on the Legacy of Black Feminism—and the Black, Feminist Future." *Ms. Magazine,* 2 February 2020. https://msmagazine.com/2020/02/20/farah-jasmine-griffin-on-the-legacy-of-black-feminism-and-the-black-feminist-future/.

Holland, Sharon. "Beached Whale." *GLQ: A Journal of Gay and Lesbian Studies* 17, no. 1 (2011): 89–95.

hooks, bell. *Black Looks: Race and Representation.* Cambridge: South End Press, 1992.

———. *Feminism Is for Everybody.* Cambridge: South End Press, 2000.

Houlden, Kate. *Sexuality, Gender and Nationalism in Caribbean Literature.* New York: Routledge, 2016.

Hugo, Victor. *Les Misérables.* Paris: Gallimard, 1862. Reprint, 1999.

Jean-Charles, Régine Michelle. *Conflict Bodies: The Politics of Rape Representation in the Francophone Imaginary.* Columbus: Ohio State University Press, 2014.

———. "Getting around the Poto-Mitan." In *Teaching Haiti: Strategies for Creating New Narratives,* edited by Cécile Accilien and Valerie Orlando, 15–33. Gainesville: University Press of Florida, 2021.

———. "Madan Sara tells the Story of Haitian Women Who Are Both Ordinary and Extraordinary." *Ms. Magazine,* March 1, 2021, https://msmagazine.com/2021/02/28/madan-sara-review-haitian-women-haiti/.

———. "Memwa se paswa: Sifting the Slave Past in Haiti." In *The Psychic Hold of Slavery: Legacies in American Expressive Culture,* edited by Soyica Diggs Colbert, Robert J. Patterson, and Aida Hussen-Levy, 86–106. New Brunswick: Rutgers University Press, 2016.

———. "*Nou pa gen vizibilite:* Haitian Girlhood and the Logics of (In)Visibility." *The Black Scholar* 50, no. 4 (October/November 2020): 43–53.

———. "'Perceiving the Relationships in Nature': An Eco-critical Reading of *La Légende des fleurs.*" In *Marie Chauvet's Theaters of Revolt: Action, Aesthetics and Adaptation,* edited by Christian Flaugh and Lena Taub, 13–30. Amsterdam: Brill, 2019.

Johnson, Jasmine. "A Politics of Tenderness: Camille Brown and Dance's Black Girl," *The Black Scholar* 49, no. 4 (2018): 20–34.

Jonassaint, Jean. *Des romans de tradition haïtienne: Sur un récit tragique.* Paris: L'Harmattan, 2002.

Jones, Gavin Rogers. "Poverty and the Limits of Literary Criticism." *American Literary History* 25, no. 4 (Winter 2003): 765–92.

Joseph-Gabriel, Annette. "Tant de silence à briser: Entretien avec Évelyne Trouillot." *Nouvelles Études Francophones* 32.1 (2017): 82–94.

Kempadoo, Kamala. *Sexing the Caribbean: Race, Gender and Sexual Labor.* New York: Routledge, 2004.

King, Rosamond. *Island Bodies: Transgressive Sexualities in the Caribbean.* Gainesville: University Press of Florida, 2014.

———. "Sex and Sexuality in English Caribbean Novels—A Survey from 1950." *Journal of West Indian Literature* 11, no. 1 (November 2002): 24–38.

Lahens, Yanick. "L'apport de quatre romancières au roman modern haitien." *The Journal of Haitian Studies* 3/4 (1997–1998): 87–95.

———. *L'exil: Entre l'ancrage et la fuite, l'écrivain haïtien.* Port-au-Prince: Editions Deschamps, 1990.

———. *Littérature haïtienne: Urgence(s) d'écrire, rêve(s) d'habiter.* Paris: Fayard, 2019.

———. "Littératures caribéennes au présent: Histoire(s) en Relation, nouveaux partages éc(h)opoétiques." Author Round Table, Amphithéâtre Michel Louis: Université des Antilles, Schoelcher. June 2017.

Lambert, Laurie. *Comrade Sister: Caribbean Feminist Revisions of the Grenada Revolution.* Charlottesville: University of Virginia Press, 2020.

Lamour, Sabine, Denyse Côté, and Darline Alexis, eds. *Déjouer le silence: Contre-discours sur les femmes haïtiennes.* Montreal: Éditions remue-ménage, 2018.

Laroche, Maximilien, *La littérature haïtienne: Identité, langue, réalité,* Montreal, Leméac, coll. Les Classiques de la francophonie, 1981.

———. *Littérature haïtienne comparée.* Quebec : GRELCA, 2007.

Larrier, Réné. "Évelyne, Scenes, and Rosalie." *Palimpsest* 8, no. 1 (2019): 3–5, 40.

———. "In[her]itance: Legacies and Lifelines in Évelyne Trouillot's *Rosalie L'Infâme.*" *Dalhousie French Studies* 88 (Fall 2009): 135–45.

Latortue, Régine. "Haitian Women Underground: Revising Literary Traditions and Societies." *Journal of Haitian Studies* 5/6 (1999–2000): 80–93.

———. "Le discours de la nature: La femme noire dans la littérature haïtienne," *Notre Librairie* 73 (January–March 1984): 65–69.

Legler, Gretchen T. "Ecofeminist Literary Criticism." In *Women, Nature, Culture,* edited by Karen Warren, 227–38. Bloomington: Indiana University Press, 1997.

Lewis, Linden. *The Culture of Gender and Sexuality in the Caribbean.* Gainesville: University Press of Florida, 2003.

Lionnet, Françoise. "Critical Conventions, Literary Landscapes, and Postcolonial Ecocriticisms." In *French Global: A New Approach to Literary History,* edited by Christie McDonald and Susan Rubin Suleiman, 127–44. New York: Columbia University Press, 2010.

———. "A Politics of the 'We'?: Autobiography, Race, and Nation." *American Literary History* 13, no. 2 (2001): 376–92.

———. *Postcolonial Representations: Women, Literature, Identity.* Ithaca: Cornell University Press, 2013.

Logan, Rayford W. "Review of: *Historiographie d'Haïti* by Catts Pressoir, Ernst Trouillot and Henock Trouillot." *The Hispanic American Historical Review* 35, no. 1 (February 1955): 132–33.

Lopez, Gary Holstun. *Crossing Open Ground.* New York: Vintage, 1989.

Lorde, Audre. "Age, Race, Class, and Sex: Women Redefining Difference." In *Sister Outsider: Essays and Speeches,* pp. 114–23. 1984. Reprint, New York: Crossings Press, 2007.

——. "Uses of the Erotic: The Erotic as Power." In *Sister Outsider: Essays and Speeches,* pp. 53–59. 1984. Reprint, New York: Crossings Press, 2007.

Louis, Martina Carla. "Expressions of gender and sexual non-normativity in Haiti: Preliminary research." African & African Diaspora Studies Program Graduate Student Scholarly Presentations, 2013, digitalcommons.fiu.edu/africana_student_pres/15.

Magloire, Danièle. "L'antiféminisme en Haïti." In *Déjouer le silence: Contre-discours sur les femmes haïtiennes,* edited by Sabine Lamour, Denyse Côté, and Darline Alexis, pp. 99–211. Montreal: Les Éditions du remue-ménage, 2018.

——. "La recherche féministe pour l'action sociale," *Nouvelles Questions Féministes* 22, no. 1 (2003): 31–47.

Mardorossian, Carine. "Nature-Function in Caryl Phillips' Cambridge." *ARIEL: A Review of International English Literature* 48, no. 3–4 (July–Oct. 2017): 187–207.

——. "Poetics of Landscape: Édouard Glissant's Creolized Ecologies" *Callaloo* 36, no. 4 (Fall 2013): 983–94.

"Maroons in the Americas." *International Encyclopedia of the Social and Behavioral Sciences,* 2nd ed., vol. 14, http://dx.doi.org/10.1016/B978-0-08-097086-8.12106-3.

Mars, Kettly. "La sensualité au coeur de la vie." In *Écrits d'Haïti: Perspectives sur la littérature haïtienne contemporaine (1986–2006),* edited by Nadève Ménard, 229–33. Paris: Karthala, 2011.

——. "Présentation de *Kasalé* organisée par l'Alliance Française d'Haïti." *Journal of Haitian Studies* 11, no. 1 (Spring 2005): 158–63.

Martelly, Stéphane. *Les jeux du dissemblable: Folie, marge et littérature haïtienne contemporaine.* Montreal: Éditions nota bene, 2016.

Marty, Anne. *Haïti en littérature.* Paris: La Flèche du Temps/Maisonneuve & Larose, 2000.

——. *La littérature haïtienne dans la modernité: De la conférence à la publication.* Paris: Karthala, 2017.

McGill, Robert. *The Treacherous Imagination: Intimacy, Ethics, and Autobiographical Fiction.* Columbus: Ohio State University Press, 2013.

McKittrick, Katherine. *Demonic Grounds: Black Women and the Cartographies of Struggle.* Minneapolis: University of Minnesota Press, 2006.

——, ed. *Sylvia Wynter: On Being Human as Praxis.* Durham: Duke University Press, 2015.

McNulty, Tess. "Literary Ethics, Revisited: An Analytic Approach to the Reading Process." *New Literary History* 49, no. 3 (2018): 383–401.

Melancon, Trimiko, and Joanne Braxton. *Black Female Sexualities*. Newark: Rutgers University Press, 2018.

Ménard, Nadève. "Cléante Valcin." *Île en île*, January 11, 2021, http://ile-en-ile .org/valcin/.

———. *Écrits d'Haïti: Perspectives sur la littérature haïtienne contemporaine (1986–2006)*. Paris: Karthala, 2011.

———. "Enseigner Lucette." *Journal of Haitian Studies* 17, no. 1 (Spring 2011): 32–33.

———. "The Lasting Impact of Fleeting Encounters in Évelyne Trouillot's Fiction." *Palimpsest: A Journal on Women, Gender, and the Black International* 8, no. 1 (2019): 11–14.

———. *The Occupied Novel: The Representation of Foreigners in Haitian Novels Written during the United States Occupation, 1915–1934*. PhD diss., University of Pennsylvania, 2002.

Meretoja, Hanna. *The Ethics of Storytelling: Narrative Hermeneutics, History, and the Possible*. Oxford: Oxford University Press, 2017.

Merlet, Miriam. "The More People Dream." In *Walking on Fire: Haitian Women's Stories of Survival and Resistance*, edited by Beverly Bell, 217–21. Ithaca: Cornell University Press, 2002.

Michel, Claudine. *Aspects éducatifs et moraux du Vodou haïtien*. Port-au-Prince: Presses nationales, 1995.

———, and Patrick Bellegarde-Smith. *Haitian Vodou: Spirit, Myth, Reality*. Bloomington: Indiana University Press, 2006.

Migraine-George, Thérèse. *From Francophonie to World Literature in French: Ethics, Poetics, and Politics*. Lincoln: University of Nebraska Press, 2013.

———. "From Masisi to Activists: Same-Sex Relations and the Haitian Polity." *Journal of Haitian Studies* 20, no. 1 (2014): 8–33.

Miguel, Yolanda Martínez-San. Review of *Island Bodies: Transgressive Sexualities in the Caribbean Imagination*, by Rosamond King. *Callaloo* 38, no. 5 (2015): 1185–88.

Mika, Kasia. *Disasters, Vulnerability, and Narratives: Writing Haiti's Futures*. New York: Routledge, 2019.

Minh-ha, Trinh T. *Woman, Native, Other: Writing Postcoloniality and Feminism*. Bloomington: Indiana University Press, 1989.

Mocombe, Paul. "The Vodou Ethic and the Spirit of Communism," In *Between Two Worlds: Jean Price-Mars, Haiti, and Africa*, edited by Celucien L. Joseph, Jean-Eddy Saint Paul, and Glodel Mezilas, 91–113. Lanham, MD: Lexington Books, 2019.

Morrison, Toni. *Jazz*. New York: Knopf, 1992.

Muñoz, José Esteban. *Cruising Utopia: The Then and There of Queer Futurity*. New York: New York University Press, 2009.

Munro, Martin. "Avenging History in the Former French Colonies." *Transition* 99 (2008): 18–40.

————. *Exile and Post-1946 Haitian Literature: Alexis, Depestre, Ollivier, Laferrière, Danticat.* Liverpool: Liverpool University Press, 2007.

————. "Haiti's Worldly Literature." *Small Axe* 14, no. 3 (2010): 69–77.

————. "Kettly Mars's *Aux frontières de la soif* and the Haitian Post-Earthquake Novel." *New West Indian Guide* 88 (2014): 1–17.

————. "A New Pastoralism? La Belle amour humaine." *Journal of Haitian Studies* 20, no. 2 (Fall 2014): 20–39.

————. "Reading Rhythm and Listening to Caribbean History in Fiction by Jacques Roumain and Joseph Zobel." *Journal of Modern Literature* 31, no. 4 (Summer 2008): 131–44.

————. *Tropical Apocalypse: Haiti and the Caribbean End Times.* Charlottesville: University of Virginia Press, 2015.

————. *Writing on the Fault Line: Haitian Literature and the Earthquake of 2010.* Liverpool: Liverpool University Press, 2013.

Murray, Rolland. "The Time of Breach: Class Division and the Contemporary African American Novel." *Novel: A Forum on Fiction* 43, no. 1 (Spring 2010): 11–17.

Nash, Jennifer. *Black Feminism Reimagined: After Intersectionality.* Durham: Duke University Press, 2019.

Ndiaye, Christiane. *Relire l'histoire littéraire et le littéraire haïtiens.* Port-au-Prince: Presses Nationales d'Haïti, coll. Pensée critique, 2007.

Noel, Fania. "Unrelenting: Haitian Feminism on the Front Lines." https://tns-gssi.newschool.org/2021/02/22/unrelenting-haitian-feminism-on-the-front-lines/.

Nussbaum, Martha. "Exactly and Responsibly: A Defense of Ethical Criticism." *Philosophy and Literature* 22, no. 2 (1998): 343–65.

————. *Love's Knowledge: Essays on Philosophy and Literature.* New York: Oxford University Press, 1990.

————. *Upheavals of Thought: The Intelligence of Emotions.* Cambridge: Cambridge University Press, 2001.

N'Zengou-Tayo, Marie-José. "Fanm se Poto-Mitan: Haitian Woman, the Pillar of Society." *Feminist Review* 59 (1998): 118–42.

————. "Impact de l'Occupation américaine sur la representation des femmes dans la littérature haïtienne: Hier et aujourd'hui." In *Déjouer le silence: contrediscours sur les femmes haïtiennes,* edited by Sabine Lamour, Denyse Côté, and Darline Alexis, 55–64. Montreal: Éditions remue-ménage, 2018.

O'Callaghan, Evelyn. "Eco-criticism and Elma Napier's Literary Sense of Place." In *Beyond Windrush: Rethinking Postwar Anglophone Caribbean Literature,* edited by J. Dillon Brown and Leah Reade Rosenberg. 113–26. Jackson: University of Mississippi Press, 2015.

————. "Gardening in the Tropics." *This Ground Beneath My Feet: A Chorus of Bush in Rab Lands.* Online Exhibition Catalogue. readymag.com/u65571097/503504/gardening-in-thetropics/. Accessed on 22 November 2016.

O'Neil, Mario, and Carmen Zamorana, eds. *The Aesthetics of Ageing: Critical Approaches to Literary Representations of the Ageing Process.* Catalonia, Spain: University of Lleida, 2002.

Otto, Melanie. "Reading the Plantation Landscape." *Journal of West Indian Literature* 25, no. 1 (2017): 23–44.

Palladino, Mariangela. *Ethics and Aesthetics in Toni Morrison's Fiction.* Leiden, the Netherlands: Brill, 2018.

Paravisini-Gebert, Lizabeth. "'All Misfortune Comes from the Cut Trees': Marie Chauvet's Environmental Imagination." *Yale French Studies* 128 (2016): 74–91.

———. "Deforestation and the Yearning for Lost Landscapes in Caribbean Literature." In *Postcolonial Ecologies: Literatures of the Environment,* edited by *Elizabeth DeLoughrey and George B. Handley,* 3–26. Liverpool: Liverpool University Press, 2011.

———. "'He of the Trees': Nature, Environment, and Creole Religiosities in Caribbean Literature." In *Caribbean Literature and the Environment,* edited by Elizabeth DeLoughrey, Renée K. Gosson, and George B. Handley, 182–96. Charlottesville: University of Virginia Press, 2005.

Parisot, Yolaine. "L'écrivaine haïtienne en son miroir." In *Présences haïtiennes,* edited by Sylvie Bouffartigue, Christiane Chaulet-Achour, and Françoise Moulin-Civil, 313–24. Cergy-Pointoise, France: CRTF, 2006.

———. *Regards littéraires haïtiens. Cristallisations de la fiction-monde.* Montreal: Classiques Garnier, 2018.

Péan, Leslie. "La volupté de l'écriture de Kettly Mars." *Journal of Haitian Studies* 11, no. 1 (2005): 164–66.

Pearsall, Marilyn. *The Other Within US: Feminist Explorations of Women and Aging.* New York: Westview Press, 1997.

Perry, Imani. *Vexy Thing: On Gender and Liberation.* Durham: Duke University Press, 2018.

Posmentier, Sonya. *Cultivation and Catastrophe: The Lyric Ecology of Modern Black Literature.* Baltimore: Johns Hopkins University Press, 2017.

Poujol Oriol, Paulette. "La femme haïtienne dans la littérature: Problèmes de l'écrivain." *Journal of Haitian Studies,* vol. 3/4 (1997–98): 80–86.

Price-Mars, Jean. *Ainsi parla l'oncle.* Paris: Mémoire d'Encrier, 2009.

Puri, Shalini. *The Caribbean Postcolonial: Social Equality, Post-Nationalism, and Cultural Hybridity.* New York: Palgrave Macmillan, 2004.

Quashie, Kevin. *Black Aliveness, or A Poetics of Being.* Durham: Duke University Press, 2021.

———. *The Sovereignty of Quiet: Beyond Resistance in Black Culture.* New Brunswick, NJ: Rutgers University Press, 2012.

Racine-Toussaint, Marlène. "Préface de Paulette Poujol-Oriol." *Ces femmes sont aussi nos sœurs!: Témoignage sur la domesticité féminine en Haïti et en diaspora.* New York: Multicultural Women's Press, 1999.

Rainsford, Dominic, Andrew Hadfield, and Tim Woods, eds. *The Ethics in Literature*. New York: Palgrave Macmillan, 1999.

Reeder, Tyson. "Liberty with the Sword: Jamaican Maroons, the Haitian Revolution and American Liberty." *Journal of the Early Republic* 37, no. 1 (Spring 2017): 81–115.

Rémy, Marlène Thélusma. *Contribution de la femme haïtienne à la construction et à la survie de son pays*. Paris: Harmattan, 2008.

Rinne, Suzanne, and Joelle Vitiello. "Pref. de Ginette Adamson." *Elles écrivent des Antilles: Haïti, Guadeloupe, Martinique*. Paris: L'Harmattan, 1997.

Roberts, Neil. *Freedom as Marronage*. Chicago: University of Chicago Press, 2015.

Romain, Régine. "Ayiti: Reaching Higher Ground." *Meridians* 11, no. 1 (2011): 132–40.

Sanchez-Eppler, Karen. *Dependent States: The Child's Part in Nineteenth-Century American Culture*. Chicago: University of Chicago Press, 2005.

Sanders, Cheryl. "Womanist Ethics: Contemporary Trends and Themes." *The Annual of the Society of Christian Ethics* 14 (1994): 299–305

Sanders, Grace. *La Voix des femmes: Haitian Women's Rights, National Politics, and Black Activism in Port-au-Prince and Montreal, 1934–1986*. PhD diss., University of Michigan, 2013.

Sapp, Robert. "The Talking Dead: Narrating the Past in Yanick Lahens's *Bain de Lune*." *Journal of Haitian Studies* 23 (2017): 119–34.

Savory, Elaine. "Toward a Caribbean Ecopoetics: Derek Walcott's Language of Plants." In *Postcolonial Ecologies: Literatures of the Environment*, edited by Elizabeth DeLoughrey and George B. Handley, 80–96. Oxford: Oxford University Press, 2011.

Scott, Lindsey. "Selling Ex, Suppressing Sexuality: A Gigolo's Economy in Kettly Mars's *L'heure Hybride*." *Contemporary French and Francophone Studies*, 19, no. 5: 543–550.

Segal, Lynn. *Out of Time: The Perils and Pleasures of Ageing*. London: Verso, 2013.

Sharpe, Christina. *In the Wake: On Blackness and Being*. Durham: Duke University Press, 2018.

Sharpe, Jenny. *Ghosts of Slavery: A Literary Archaeology of Black Women's Lives*. Minneapolis: University of Minnesota Press, 2003.

Sharpe, Jenny, and Samantha Pinto. "The Sweetest Taboo: Studies of Caribbean Sexualities." *Signs: Journal of Women in Culture and Society* (Autumn 2006): 247–74.

Sheller, Mimi. *Citizenship from Below: Erotic Agency and Caribbean Freedom*. Durham: Duke University Press, 2012.

Shelton, Marie-Denise. "Haitian Women's Fiction." *Callaloo* 15, no. 3 (Summer 1992): 770–77.

———. *Image de la société dans le roman haïtien*. Paris: Harmattan, 1993.

Silvera, Makeda. "Man Royals and Sodomites: Some Thoughts on the Invisibility of Afro-Caribbean Lesbians." *Feminist Studies* 18, no. 3 (1992): 521–32.

Smith, Adam. *The Theory of Moral Sentiments*. Cambridge: Cambridge University Press, 2002.

Smith, Faith. *Sex and the Citizen: Interrogating the Caribbean*. Charlottesville: University of Virginia, 2011.

Smith, Jennie. *When the Hands Are Many: Community Organization and Social Change in Rural Haiti*. Ithaca, NY: Cornell University Press, 2001.

Smith, Matthew. *Red and Black in Haiti: Radicalism, Conflict, and Political Change, 1934–1957*. Chapel Hill: University of North Carolina Press, 2009.

Smith, Valerie. *Not Just Race, Not Just Gender*. New York: Routledge, 1998.

Song, Min. *The Children of 1965: On Writing, and Not Writing, as an Asian American*. Durham: Duke University Press, 2013.

Souffrant, Eddy. *Identity, Political Freedom, and Collective Responsibility: The Pillars and Foundations of Global Ethics*. New York: Palgrave Macmillan, 2013.

Souffrant, Kantara. "Circling Dantò's Daughter: Reflections on Lenelle Moïse's Performances of Shamelessness." *Women & Performance: A Journal of Feminist Theory* 27, no. 2 (2017): 229–34.

Sourieau, Marie-Agnès. "*La couleur de l'aube* de Yanick Lahens: Cette horrible béance obscure." *Journal of Haitian Studies* 18, no. 2 (Fall 2012): 51–63.

Sourieau, Marie-Agnès, and Kathleen M. Balutansky. *Écrire en pays assiégé: Haïti: Writing Under Siege*. New York: Rodopi, 2004.

Spear, Thomas. "Paulette Poujol Oriol's Tragicomedies." *Journal of Haitian Studies* 17, no. 1 (Spring 2011): 15–26.

Spillers, Hortense J. "Interstices: A Small Drama of Words." In *Pleasure and Danger: Exploring Female Sexuality*, edited by Carole S. Vance, 73–100. Boston: Routledge & Kegan Paul, 1984.

———. "Mama's Baby, Papa's Maybe." *Diacritics* 17 (Summer 1987): 65–81.

———. "Time and Crisis: Questions for Psychoanalysis and Race." *Journal of French and Francophone Philosophy Revue de la philosophie française et de langue française* 26, no. 2 (2018): 25–31.

Spivak, Gayatri. *An Aesthetic Education in the Era of Globalization*. Cambridge: Harvard University Press, 2013.

———. *The Spivak Reader*. New York: Routledge, 1995.

Sylvain-Bouchereau, Madeleine. *Haïti et ses femmes: Une étude d'évolution culturelle*. Port-au-Prince: Les Presses Libres, 1957.

Taylor, Keeanga-Yamahtta. *How We Get Free: Black Feminism and the Combahee River Collective*. Chicago: Haymarket Books, 2017.

"Tessa Mars, Haiti." *Africanah,* June 6, 2016, africanah.org/tessa-mars-haiti/.

Thomas, Bonnie. "Identity at the Crossroads: An Exploration of French Caribbean Gender Identity." *Caribbean Studies* 32, no. 2 (July–December 2004): 5–62.

Tiffin, Helen, and Graham Huggan, eds. *Postcolonial Ecocriticism: Literature, Animals, Environment*. London: Routledge, 2006.

Tinsley, Omise'eke Natasha. "Black Atlantic, Queer Atlantic: Queer Imaginings of the Middle Passage." *GLQ* 14, no. 2–3 (2008): 191–215.

———. *Ezili's Mirrors: Imagining Black Queer Genders.* Durham: Duke University Press, 2018.

———. *Thiefing Sugar: Eroticism Between Women in Caribbean Literature.* Durham: Duke University Press, 2010.

Travis, Mason. "Introduction to Postcolonial Ecocriticism among Settler-Colonial Nations." *Ariel: A Review of International English Literature* 44, no. 4 (October 2013): 1–11.

Trouillot, Évelyne. "Dans cette grande mouvance de lamentations n'oublions surtout pas les vrais perdants." Facebook, July 10, 2018.

———. "Respecting the Diversity of Creativity." *Words without Borders,* January 2021, wordswithoutborders.org/article/january-2021-international-black-voices-respecting-the-diversity-of-creativ.

Trouillot, Hénock. *Les origines sociales de la littérature haïtienne.* Port-au-Prince: Impr. N.A. Théodore, 1962.

Trouillot, Lyonel. "Haïti 90: l'esthétique du délabrement: Littérature haïtienne de 1960 à nos jours," *Notre Librairie* 132 (October-November 1997): 22–25.

———. *Haiti: (re)penser la cityonneté,* Port-au-Prince: Éditions HSI, 2001.

Trouillot, Michel-Rolph. *Haiti: State against Nation.* New York: Monthly Review Press, 1990

———. "The Odd and the Ordinary: Haiti, the Caribbean, and the World." *Cimarrón: New Perspectives on the Caribbean* 2, no. 3 (1990): 3–12.

Turnbull, Wally. *Hidden Meanings of Haitian Proverbs.* New York: Light Messages, 2005.

Ulysse, Gina Athena. "Introduction." *Caribbean Rasanblaj* 12, nos. 1–2 (2015). hemisphericinstitute.org/en/emisferica-121-caribbean-rasanblaj/121-introduction.

———. "Papa, Patriarchy, and Power: Snapshots of a Good Haitian Girl, Feminism, and Dyasporic Dreams." *Journal of Haitian Studies* 12, no. 1 (2006): 24–47.

———. *Why Haiti Needs New Narratives: A Post-earthquake Chronicle.* Middletown, CT: Wesleyan University Press, 2013.

———. "Why I Am Marching for Ayiti Cherie." *Ms. Magazine,* January 10, 2011, msmagazine.com/2011/01/10/why-i-am-marching-for-ayiti-cherie-beloved-haiti/.

———. "Why *Rasanblaj,* Why Now?: New Salutations to the Four Cardinal Points in Haitian Studies." *Journal of Haitian Studies* 23, no. 2 (2017): 58–80.

Valdés, Vanessa K. *Oshun's Daughters: The Search for Womanhood in the Americas.* New York: SUNY Press, 2014.

Valens, Keja. *Desire Between Women in Caribbean Literature.* New York: Palgrave MacMillan, 2013.

Vansteenkiste, Jennifer, and Mark Schuller. "The Gendered Space of Capabilities and Functionings: Lessons from Haitian Community-Based Organizations." *Journal of Human Development and Capabilities* 19, no. 2 (2018): 147–65.

Vergès, Françoise. *Un féminisme décolonial.* Paris: La Fabrique, 2018.

Verna, Chantalle, and Paulette Poujol Oriol. "The Ligue Feminine d'Action Sociale: An Interview with Paulette Poujol Oriol." *Journal of Haitian Studies* 17, no. 1 (Spring 2011): 246–57.

Vignoli, Alessia. "Des secrets sous les décombres: La (Dis)Simulation dans le roman post-sismique haïtien." *Echo des études romanes* 13, no. 2 (2017): 123–31.

"Virgile Valcin." Entry by Nadève Ménard. http://ile-en-ile.org/valcin/.

Vitiello, Joëlle. "'De l'autre côté de mes murs': Le désir de l'engagement dans l'écriture de Yanick Lahens." In *Écrire en pays assiégé—Haïti—Writing Under Siege,* edited by Marie-Agnès Sourieau and Kathleen Balutansky, 169–92. Amsterdam: Rodopi, 2004.

———. "Douceurs et violences dans l'écriture de Kettly Mars." In *Écrits d'Haïti: Perspectives sur la littérature haïtienne contemporaine (1986–2006),* edited by Nadève Ménard, 367–84. Paris: Karthala, 2011.

———. "The Human Comedy in Paulette Poujol Oriol's Novels and Short Stories." *Journal of Haitian Studies* 17, no. 1 (Spring 2011): 36–49.

———. "Représentations d'amitiés féminines dans l'écriture contemporaine." *Women in French Studies* 7 (1999): 117–32.

Walcott, Derek. "The Sea Is History." *Paris Review* 74 (Fall/Winter 1978).

Walker, Alice. *In Search of Our Mothers' Gardens: Womanist Prose.* New York: Harcourt, 1983.

Wallace, Michele. *Black Macho and the Myth of the Superwoman.* New York: Dial Press, 1979.

———. *Dark Designs on Visual Culture.* Durham: Duke University Press, 2004.

Walsh, John Patrick. "The Global Frame of Haiti in Yanick Lahens' *Failles.*" *Contemporary French and Francophone Studies* 19, no. 3 (2015): 293–302.

———. *Migration and Refuge: The Eco-Archive of Haitian Literature 1982–2017.* Liverpool: Liverpool University Press, 2019.

Warren, Karen J., ed. *Ecofeminism: Women, Nature, Culture.* Bloomington: University of Indiana Press, 1997.

Washington, Mary Helen. "The Darkened Eye Restored: Notes Toward a Literary History of Black Women." In *Reading Feminist, Reading Black: A Critical Anthology,* edited by Henry Louis Gates, 30–43. New York: Penguin, 1990.

Woodward, Kathleen. *Aging and Its Discontents: Freud and Other Fictions.* Bloomington: Indiana University Press, 1991.

———. *Figuring Age: Women, Bodies, Generations.* Bloomington: Indiana University Press, 1999.

Wright, Michelle. "Feminism." In *Keywords for African American Studies,* edited by Erica Edwards, Roderick Ferguson, and Jeff Ogbar, 86–90. New York: New York University Press, 2018.

Wyatt-Brown, Anne, and Janice Rossen, ed. *Aging and Gender in Literature.* Charlottesville: University of Virginia Press, 1993.

Zimra, Clarisse. "Haitian Literature After Duvalier: An Interview with Yanick Lahens." *Callaloo* 16.1 (Winter, 1993): 77–93.

Zylinska, Joanna. *The Ethics of Cultural Studies.* New York: Continuum, 2005.

Index

Illustrations are indicated by page numbers in italics.

Acacia, Michel, *Historicité et structuration sociale en Haïti*, 192
Accilien, Cécile, 129, 135–36, 305n8
Adichie, Chimamanda, 305n145
African American women: Black feminism as broader than, 44–45; elite Haitian women and, 18; global feminism of, 26; Haitian feminism as distinct from, 22
African diaspora: alternative models of womanhood in religions of, 93, 284; Black feminism in, 5; Black feminist ethic as lens to study texts of, 2, 6, 45; imagining "otherwise" and, 316n35; land's portrayal in, 247, 256; new articulations of cultural expression for fiction and, 9; older women's links to African ancestry, 108; Romain's photograph *Mama Ginen* as reference to, 59, 305n2; Vodou as African-derived religion, 92. *See also* slavery
African women writers, feminism of, 34–35
Agard-Jones, Vanessa, 136
agency: class division and, 25, 52, 205; of elderly women, 68, 73, 81; erotic agency, 125, 127, 132–33, 134, 162, 167, 169; in *Guillaume et Nathalie* (Lahens), 151, 153–54; of Haitian women, 23, 79, 229; in *The Infamous Rosalie* (Trouillot), 110; in *Je suis vivant* (Mars), 138; in *L'œil-totem* (Trouillot), 68, 73, 81, 90, 138; Quashie on, 50, 76
age studies, 53, 63, 64

aging and elderly women, 52–53, 59–121; ageism and universality of aging, 83; agency of, 68, 73, 81; binary representations of, 66; Black feminist ethic and, 8, 46, 62–64, 66, 120–21, 289; connection and communal bond of, 65–68, 118; disregard for, 62, 63, 66, 67; divergence from traditional view of the elderly, 65, 66, 89–90, 119; embodiment and mobility of, 65–67, 100–102, 119; ethical questions concerning, 64–65, 120; feminist response to, 77, 118; Glover's view of Caribbean womanhood and, 53; in Haitian fiction, 306n11, 306n16; interiority and, 62, 65, 90, 119–20; intersectionality with race and gender, 53, 62–64, 89, 95; as location of marginality, 53, 63, 67, 89–90, 118, 120; looking and, 64, 207; motherhood trope and, 306n19; personhood of, 63, 120, 121; *potomitan* trope and, 64; in power relations, 63; relational ethics and, 33; respect of, as cultural tradition, 61, 63, 66, 119, 306n17; Romain's photograph *Mama Ginen* and, 59–62, *60*, 86, 121; sex and intimacy of, 54, 72, 86–89, 165–67; unconventionality of, 119, 121; "watchfulness" of older women, 64, 65, 89; world-making approach to, 28. See also *Infamous Rosalie, The*/*Rosalie l'infâme*; *Kasalé*; *œil-totem, L'*
Ahmed, Sara, 73